The Wicked Cousin

Rockliffe Book 4

STELLA RILEY

Cover by Ana Grigoriu-Voicu, books-design.com

CONTENTS

	Page
PROLOGUE	1
Chapter One	6
Chapter Two	19
Chapter Three	32
Chapter Four	46
Chapter Five	58
Chapter Six	72
Chapter Seven	85
Chapter Eight	99
Chapter Nine	115
Chapter Ten	131
Chapter Eleven	147
Chapter Twelve	163
Chapter Thirteen	179
Chapter Fourteen	192
Chapter Fifteen	207
Chapter Sixteen	223

	Page
Chapter Seventeen	237
Chapter Eighteen	255
Chapter Nineteen	271
Chapter Twenty	286
Chapter Twenty-One	305
Chapter Twenty-Two	320

PROLOGUE

On a scorching August day in 1757 when he was eight years old, Sebastian Audley's life changed. And though he didn't know it, that change was to last for the next thirteen years.

It began when he couldn't find his brother. He and Theo had always shared a room. The discovery that his twin had been taken elsewhere in the house and that he had been locked in their room, sent Sebastian into a panic. No one had told him that Theo was sick … but he knew it anyway and had only one clear thought.

Theo needs me.

He shouted to be let out and screamed his brother's name till he was hoarse; he kicked the door and battered it with his fists until his hands were bruised and bloody. And through all of it, his face streamed with a ceaseless cataract of tears. Eventually, when the door remained locked, he smashed the window with a chair and climbed down the creeper clinging to the wall. Ten feet from the ground, something gave way and a gardener found him, half-conscious, scratched and bleeding on the gravel.

They put him in a different room after that and four of his five older sisters came bringing food he didn't want. They tried to calm him and to explain what to him was inexplicable, refusing to listen when he yelled and fought and insisted that he had to go to Theo.

He needs me. How can he get well if I'm not with him?

In the end, they left him alone again. And because exhaustion was taking its toll and fighting did no good, he sat on the floor and rocked back and forth in time to the fury and fear that roared and pulsed like molten lava inside his head.

1

Then, between one second and the next, it stopped ... and was replaced by a dense, deafening silence that filled his brain. And that was when he knew he'd failed. Theo was gone.

On the day of the funeral, everyone kept telling him he must say goodbye and didn't seem to understand that he couldn't. And after it, his eldest sister crushed his fingers in hers and said, 'It shouldn't have been Theodore. God should have taken you instead.'

To Sebastian, numb and crippled by the loss of half of himself, this was the first thing in days that made sense. God had made the mistake that ordinary people made all the time. He'd muddled the two of them up and let Theo catch the putrid throat instead of Sebastian. Being angry with God helped a bit. Not enough to stop the howling inside him; but enough at least to stop him actually *doing* it ... except when he was quite alone and there was no one to hear.

Then new things began to happen. When they said he wasn't to go to Eton but would continue his education at home, he hadn't really minded. He and Theo were to have gone together. Since Theo couldn't attend Eton, it seemed reasonable that he didn't either. But the other changes that followed this one added up to something different. He was no longer to mix with the village children; he wasn't to swim in the lake or take a boat out upon it; he wasn't to climb trees or leave the grounds alone or go riding without a groom. The list of things he *couldn't* do was suddenly endless. Bewildered and with the loss of Theo a raw, gaping hole in his chest, Sebastian thought he was being punished; but he didn't know *why* he was because no one explained and no one seemed angry except Blanche, which was normal. Although Mama cried a lot, she still hugged him; Papa still sometimes took him up before him on his horse; and his other sisters behaved much as they always had – except for Trixie, who

2

also cried a lot because Theo's death meant she couldn't go to London. It was all very confusing. So Sebastian worked hard at his lessons, did as he was told ... and hoped that if he was very, very good everything would come right again.

It was nearly a year before he began to realise that he wasn't being punished so much as smothered; that the invisible cage surrounding him was there to stop him following Theo into an early grave. Snatches of overheard conversation spoke of something Sebastian privately called the Audley Curse; the fact that, though Audley men sired daughters in profusion, sons were in very short supply. There were always lots of nephews and grandsons through the female line but rarely more than one direct heir. And after five daughters and the loss of Theo, Sebastian's father was determined that the seventh Viscount Wingham, like his six predecessors, would bear the proud name of Audley.

By the time he was twelve, Sebastian started to feel like a fly being kept alive in a jar; at thirteen, having learned that being good changed nothing, he began eluding surveillance at every opportunity; and at fourteen, by then slowly suffocating, he came to the bitter realisation that he was a commodity. The only male bloody Audley of his generation and the next Viscount bloody Wingham – which was apparently the only thing about him that anybody cared about.

He stopped himself going insane with the knowledge that it couldn't last forever – that his father couldn't deny him university as easily as he'd vetoed Eton. University represented freedom ... and so Sebastian started counting the days.

A month before his departure for Cambridge, his father cheerfully killed all hope. Sebastian was to go to Cambridge, yes ... but not alone. He was to be accompanied by the vicar's son who, but for Lord Wingham's generous support, would have been unable to afford a university education. Staid, trustworthy Mr Brooke, decreed the viscount, would share Sebastian's rooms and oversee their combined pecuniary affairs.

Despite knowing it wouldn't do any good, Sebastian had tried to make his father see reason and even enlisted the support of Great-Aunt Flora – the only person Father had ever been known to listen to. But neither of them dented Lord Wingham's determination to keep his precious heir alive long enough to ensure the succession. And that was when Sebastian saw that he was being condemned to three more years in the prison of his father's obsession. Brooke's hold over the purse-strings would ensure that. And the pair of them were even supposed to take the same courses – Classics, his father calmly announced.

Gripped by a mixture of blinding anger and sickening despair, Sebastian took the one decision he knew he could control and said frigidly, 'Mr Brooke can study what the hell he likes whilst serving as your jailer, sir. I, however, shall study Law.'

'Law?' His father eyed him with a sort of tolerant amusement. 'You'll soon tire of that. And what purpose can it serve?'

'A way of earning my own living and becoming financially independent of you.'

'But why? When you have wealth and a title awaiting you? It's foolish, Sebastian. Foolish and unnecessary. Also, once you are done with Cambridge we shall look about for a suitable bride for you and then --'

That had been the final straw. Rage had consumed him, his chest vibrating with it.

He said, 'No. We will not. Even if I planned to rush headlong into wedlock – which I don't – it wouldn't be to any female of your choosing. Also, the moment I have both my majority and my degree, you may be assured that I'll go to the devil my own way and by the fastest possible route.'

* * *

Sebastian Audley left university with an Honours degree in Law, a superior ability at the chessboard ... and A Plan.

The list of things he did not have was much longer.

He didn't quit Cambridge with a host of happy memories or a coterie of firm and lasting friends; he'd never drunk himself witless nor gambled away a term's allowance at cards. He hadn't participated in any of the hilarious pranks beloved of undergraduates everywhere and he hadn't visited a brothel; in fact, though he'd sooner his eyes were picked out by crows than admit it, he'd never even kissed a girl.

In short, Sebastian had spent three years acquiring a particularly fine education ... and nothing else whatsoever.

The Plan, however, was designed to change all that ... and an unexpected bequest from Great-Aunt Flora would allow him do it without the need to work for a living.

Mr Audley packed his bags, shook the dust of Cambridge from his boots and boarded the mail coach for the fleshpots of London where he intended to make up for lost time.

He succeeded spectacularly well.

As the next few years went by, his name resounded across the length and breadth of Europe, from Paris to St Petersburg. According to the scandal-sheets, the Honourable Sebastian Audley was the devil of a fellow. A man who didn't baulk at risking his neck, never refused a wager or challenge ... and who few women could resist.

The Honourable Mr Audley didn't given a damn about the gossip and rumours or what anyone said. After thirteen years in the cage he was entitled to enjoy his freedom and do what the hell he liked. So he did.

CHAPTER ONE

Serena, Lady Delahaye frowned thoughtfully at the letter in her hand and then looked across the breakfast table at her husband.

'Aunt Louisa,' she announced with a careful lack of expression, 'says that Lord Wingham has suffered an apoplexy. He is not expected to recover.'

'Ah.' Charles abandoned his own correspondence and met his wife's gaze. 'And?'

'And they've sent for Sebastian.'

Laughter crinkling his eyes, Sir Charles said, 'I imagine they've been sending for Sebastian, in solo and chorus, for years for all the good it's done them. I doubt he even bothers to open the letters. I also doubt the family has the faintest idea where he is. To the best of my knowledge, he hasn't set foot in England for the last five years.'

'Apparently he has.' Serena looked back at the letter. 'Louisa says he shows his face at Audley Court once a year, stays three or four days then vanishes again. But if Wingham dies, he'll have to come back for good, won't he? And ... well, you can guess what I'm thinking.'

'Yes. But that was all a long time ago. Gerald has grown up since then – and Sebastian may have done the same. After all, seven years of kicking over the traces ought to be long enough for anyone.'

Further down the table and from the opposite side of it, Cassandra caught the sudden interest in her younger sister's face and gave a tiny, warning shake of her head. Inevitably, Olivia ignored it and said eagerly, 'Sebastian, Mama? Wicked *Cousin* Sebastian?'

'You are being overly-dramatic, Olivia,' responded her mother, 'and inaccurate. Firstly, one would have to say that 'wicked' is probably an exaggeration. And secondly, the degree of relationship between the Audleys and ourselves is so remote that 'cousin' is barely appropriate.'

'But there is *some* kinship, isn't there?' insisted Olivia eagerly. 'And I didn't know Gerald knew Mr Audley. He's never mentioned it.'

'Doubtless your brother has numerous friends he's never mentioned. However, I would be very interested to hear what *you* know about Sebastian Audley ... and precisely how, in fact, you know anything at all.'

Cassandra busied herself buttering a slice of toast. Livy never knew when to hold her tongue – or understood that Mama could always recognise an untruth when she heard one. If her sister wasn't careful, the secret cache of scandal-sheets kept hidden beneath a loose floorboard in the old schoolroom would come to light. Mama might not be as tight-laced as some other mothers; but if she knew that Livy was reading stuff lurid enough to cause the paper to spontaneously combust, there would be hell to pay.

Olivia shrugged and reached nonchalantly for the raspberry preserve.

'From the girls at school whose older sisters made their debut when he was in London or came across him later, abroad. There were always tales about him and the wildly exciting things he does.'

Serena eyed her daughter narrowly.

'Gossip, rumour and scandal, Olivia?'

'Not *exactly*. It's just – conversation. You know what I mean, don't you, Cassie?'

Wonderful, thought Cassandra. *Now you're dragging* me *into it*. But she said obliquely, 'Girls always repeat things they've heard at home. Most of it is nonsense.' And then, before Olivia could continue worrying the subject of the unknown and apparently scandalous Mr Audley, she rose and added, 'Lord Pelham is to take me driving this morning so I should go and change my dress.'

Her father glanced across at her.

'Pelham, Cassie? Dear me.' Charles grinned. 'I don't know whether he has defective eyesight or just can't drive. Either way, you'd best get ready to hold tight to the side.'

Cassandra shook her head and left the room laughing. Papa might be correct about George Pelham having less than perfect vision. He'd once stared into her face at some length, prior to stammering out a compliment about her lovely blue eyes. Being a kind girl and aware that the poor fellow suffered from nerves, Cassie hadn't corrected him. But she hoped his mistake was the result of colour-blindness rather than galloping myopia.

Ten minutes later while Susan was lacing her into a dark green carriage dress, the door of her chamber opened on Olivia who walked in, saying, 'I don't know why you have to be so stuffy, Cassie. Aren't you the *least* bit interested in Cousin Sebastian?'

'No. Until this morning, I was barely aware of his existence.'

'Oh. Well, that explains it, I suppose. You wouldn't know that ever since you left, he's been the Beau Ideal at school.'

'The *what*?'

'Lord! There you go *again*. The particular gentleman all the girls agree is the one we'd most like to know. They must have had them in your day, too.'

They had, of course – though the silly title was new. However, to the best of her recollection no Favourite had ever reigned for more than a year … whereas Olivia was suggesting that Sebastian Audley had inexplicably held the crown for two.

Mindful of her maid's sharp ears, Cassie said, 'Since neither you nor any of the other girls can have clapped eyes on him, I don't --'

'That's not the point.' Olivia flopped inelegantly down on the bed. 'It isn't his *looks* that make him fascinating – though he's reputed to be quite handsome. It's the things he's *done*. He's fought at least three duels – maybe more. He's supposed to have caused such a huge scandal in Vienna that he was ordered out of the country – though nobody knows exactly what he did. After that, rumour said he was in St Petersburg, making love to the Empress Catherine and then --'

'Stop!' said Cassie sharply. And to her maid, 'Thank you, Susan. I can manage the rest myself.'

Susan curtsied and left the room with lagging steps. The second the door closed behind her, Cassie said, 'For heaven's sake, Livy – you've got to stop blurting out things like that! It may only be schoolgirl gossip but it's the kind that could get you in trouble.'

'I don't see why,' objected Olivia with a shrug. 'They say the Empress is very susceptible. And if Cousin Sebastian is as handsome and daring as they say, why *wouldn't* she take a fancy to him? I'm sure no one could blame her.' Olivia clasped her hands together and sighed. 'They say he never turns down a dare or says no to a wager. That makes him sound awfully brave and romantic, don't you think?'

'No. It makes him sound stupid. Or it would do if there was the smallest chance of it being true – which, of course, there isn't.'

'What do you mean – it can't be true? Why *not*?'

'Oh – use your brain, Livy,' begged Cassie. 'Supposing he's dared to put a pistol to his head ... or wagered he can't jump his horse over a seven-foot wall. Do you think he'd actually *do* it? Of course he wouldn't. Or not unless he's got some kind of death-wish.'

Olivia brushed this aside with a toss of her head.

'Those aren't proper challenges – not like duels or carriage races or travelling the length of Bond Street without touching the ground or --' She stopped, grinning. 'And only fancy Gerald being a friend of his! Did *you* know about that?'

Cassie had a sudden distant recollection of Papa raising his voice – something he very rarely did – to their older brother on the subject of wild company and unacceptable behaviour. Putting it aside for consideration later, she shrugged and said, 'No – but you must know by now that Gerald never tells us anything if he can possibly avoid it.'

'Well, next time I see him, I'm going to *make* him. You have no *idea* how envious all the girls were about me being able to claim kinship with wicked Mr Audley. Margot Claydon was absolutely *green*.'

'I daresay. But you're not at school now. So --'

'No.' The grin faded abruptly. 'And I'm not with Aunt Almeria in Lansdown Crescent either, more's the pity.'

More's the pity indeed, thought Cassie ruefully.

Being a sensible woman, Serena Delahaye did not believe in thrusting girls headlong into London society without a shred of previous experience. Consequently, at not quite eighteen years of age and just as Cassandra had done three years before, Olivia should currently have been attending small, sedate gatherings of young people under the aegis of Aunt Almeria in Bath. Sadly, before she had been there a week, Aunt's youngest daughter had fallen victim to the measles, thus enforcing Olivia's hasty return home – and an ensuing mood of black discontent.

Hoping to avoid listening to her sister's complaints for what must surely be the hundredth time, Cassie busied herself setting her hat at exactly the right angle and murmured, 'Never mind. Papa has written to Aunt Sophy so perhaps you'll be able to spend a few weeks with her instead.'

'In *Tunbridge Wells*?' came the incredulous reply. 'Are you quite mad?'

Not yet. But I'm getting there, thought Cassie, gritting her teeth. 'Go away, Livy. Lord Pelham will be here at any minute.'

'He'll wait.' Instead of quitting the room, Olivia launched herself off the bed and starting toying with a delicate ivory fan she found on her sister's dressing table. 'Is his lordship nice?'

'He's … pleasant.'

Olivia made a face.

'That sounds boring. Does he want to marry you?'

His Mama certainly likes the idea.

'The subject hasn't arisen, so I refuse to speculate. Livy – will you please leave my things alone and *go*?'

'Don't be such a cross-patch.' She exchanged the fan for a pair of ear-rings. 'By now there must be at least *one* gentleman you like.'

Perhaps. But you are the very last person I'd confide in.

Guarding her expression and watching Olivia abandon the ear-rings in favour of advancing on her wardrobe, Cassie said flippantly, 'Too many to count. Are you going?'

'In a minute.' Olivia eyed her sisters' gowns enviously. 'Can I try on your blue silk?'

'No!' snapped Cassie. 'You know perfectly well it won't fit you.'

Olivia flushed. The fact that her adolescent curves were reluctant to melt away was a sore point.

'You didn't have to say that,' she accused. And finally flounced out.

* * *

The carriage ride with Lord Pelham was neither quite as hair-raising as Papa had predicted nor any more entertaining than Cassie had expected. His lordship tried, bless him. He was mild-mannered and well-meaning. But his conversational skills were not of the highest order at the best of times and often deserted him altogether.

Sadly, he was typical of the kind of gentlemen Cassie seemed to attract. So far, there had been three offers for her hand – one of which Papa had summarily dismissed on account of some aspect of the gentleman's reputation he'd refused to explain. At the time, Cassie had rather regretted this because Lord Cheslyn had been handsome and charming and she'd been flattered by his interest. The two remaining suitors had been of the Lord Pelham variety ... and she'd refused those herself.

Just at present, she rather suspected that another such offer was brewing – if not rapidly reaching boiling point. To the best of her ability and without actually being rude, she'd been avoiding Sir Alastair Vennor for the last week in the hope of preventing a declaration. It wasn't that she disliked him. He was gentle, rather shy and by no means ill-looking. He was also, unfortunately, dull.

Mr Richard Penhaligon, on the other hand, was *not* dull. Twenty-six years old, charming and as darkly handsome as any storybook hero, he had danced with her three times and, on the last two occasions, lingered at her side for a full ten minutes afterwards.

Usually, the men she liked either didn't meet her parents' standards or treated her with affectionate brotherly teasing. But Mr Penhaligon's smile wasn't in the least fraternal; he didn't stammer or struggle to make conversation; and Cassie couldn't think of a single objection her parents could make to a gentleman whose older brother was the Earl of Keswick.

* * *

By the following evening at Moreton House, it swiftly became clear that speculation concerning the return of Sebastian Audley was already rife.

This was most obvious among the youngest debutantes as they alternately flitted about the ballroom or huddled together, giggling. Within half an hour of her arrival, Cassie had been beset by no less than five excitable, fan-fluttering girls, all of whom were convinced (thanks to Olivia's rash claims of kinship) that Mistress Delahaye *must* know when Mr Audley was likely to arrive in Town.

Sighing, Cassie said she had no idea and then dampened their hopes still further by pointing out that if Mr Audley was *indeed* returning to England to attend his father's death-bed, then the chances of his appearing in London any time soon would appear to be virtually non-existent.

Gradually, it became apparent that interest in Sebastian Audley was not confined to giddy eighteen-year-olds. Certain married ladies smiled knowingly behind their fans while their husbands scowled. Older gentlemen shook disapproving heads, while younger ones laughed and exchanged low-voiced anecdotes. Everyone, it seemed, had either an opinion or an expectation of wicked Mr Audley.

Cassie tried to ignore both the gossip and her carefully veiled disappointment that Mr Penhaligon was nowhere to be seen. It was a relief, therefore, when the Cavershams arrived. And as soon as she was sitting with Lady Elinor in a quiet corner, she said darkly, 'I could *murder* Olivia.'

Nell laughed. 'This *'my Cousin Sebastian'* nonsense?'

'That's part of it. She's never laid eyes on him, of course. He's a fourth cousin, umpteen times removed – but for no better reason than that it raised her status at school, Livy has given the impression that he's in constant communication with us.' Uncharacteristically, Cassie scowled. 'I wish she still *was* at school – or with Aunt Almeria in Bath. Or anywhere at all except in the room next to mine in Conduit Street.'

'Why? What else has she been doing?'

'She borrows my things without asking and forgets to return them. She squeezed herself into my pearl watered-taffeta and split one of the seams – oh, and last week she was fiddling with my perfumes and upset a bottle of patchouli all over the carpet. My room still reeks of it. And that,' finished Cassie a shade bitterly, 'isn't all. She'd prefer I was married before she makes her own come-out next Season – though what difference *that* makes I can't imagine. However, when she isn't making free with my belongings or obsessing about Wicked Cousin Sebastian, as she persists in calling him, she's harping on and on about my failure to find a husband. And it's driving me demented.'

'It must be the nature of sisters to be annoying. Goodness knows, Lucilla is like toothache.' And when Cassie laughed, Nell said, 'That's better. Now; humour me, please! I know *you* find the furore surrounding Mr Audley tedious – but *I* don't. He sounds intriguing and - and as if he might be *fun*.'

'That's a matter of opinion,' muttered Cassie. 'If you ask me, all those duels and love-affairs and ridiculous wagers make him sound like an idiot. What does Harry say?'

'He's never met him – though he thinks Nicholas may have done. Of course, the person we *really* need is Rock. He always knows everything about everybody. But he's still at the Priors with Adeline, so that's no help. We'll just have to interrogate Nick – if he ever deigns to put in an appearance.'

It was half an hour to midnight before Lord Nicholas Wynstanton finally sauntered in and ploughed an erratic course to Mistress Delahaye's side.

She shook her head at him and said, 'You really are hopeless, Nicholas. You never arrive at a respectable time and you never dance. I'm surprised you're still invited to balls at all.'

'No you're not,' he grinned. 'Although I don't prance about the floor with the ladies, I can be relied upon to fetch their refreshments and entertain them with witty repartee. Then again, my brother is Rockliffe. And who's going to risk offending him?'

'No one.'

'Exactly.' He subjected the room to a lazily amused glance. 'I'd lay money that everybody here is talking about the same thing.'

'And you'd win. The sole topic is the rumoured return of Mr Audley.'

He grinned.

'Well, London's been dashed dull recently. And Sebastian's just the sort of fellow to liven things up.'

'So I've gathered.'

The sour note was so unlike her that Nicholas blinked and said, 'I'm not quite sure how he *could* have ... but has he done something to upset you?'

'Aside from being a distant relative – no.'

'Well, you can't hold that against him. You know how small the polite world is and the Audleys are an old family, so they're probably related to just about everybody in some degree or other – including me, for all I know.'

'Oh – I suppose so.' Cassie drew a long breath and loosed it. 'But half the girls here are obsessed with him – yet it stands to reason that he can't possibly have done all the things Livy credits him with.'

'I wouldn't be too sure about that.'

'Since you don't know what Livy has been saying,' began Cassie. And then stopped. 'Oh. You wouldn't need to, would you? You know him.'

'I do. Not particularly well – but well enough to guess that whatever Olivia knows won't be the half – since most of it isn't fit for female ears.'

'So he's as wicked as Livy thinks he is?'

Nicholas gave a crack of laughter.

'More wild than wicked, I'd say – though there's not much he ever drew the line at. But I never heard that he deliberately set out to hurt anyone – not even in a duel.' Nicholas thought for a moment. 'He was just ... exuberant. The instant he came down from university, he started setting the town by its ears and when he'd made London too hot to hold him, he moved on to Paris and, after that, Venice – which was where I last saw him.'

'How long ago was that?'

'Three years ... maybe four. I'd met up with Dev – Lord Sarre, that is. I really must stop calling him Dev. It confuses everybody. But going back to Venice ... he and Sebastian were fairly well-acquainted. So if anyone knows what Audley's been up to these last few years, it will be Sarre.' Nicholas paused, tilting his head and said, 'Speaking of which ... have you heard from Caroline?'

'A short letter a few days ago. The Dowager Countess has finally removed to the Dower House, leaving Caroline and his lordship free to settle into Sarre Park. They'd been hoping to visit Caroline's grandfather in Halifax but snow on the Great North Road means that will have to wait until the weather improves. And meanwhile Lord Sarre is busy conducting repairs on the estate.' Cassie's brow creased a little. 'According to Caroline, he's toiling alongside his workmen – which is something I find difficult to imagine.'

'You wouldn't if you knew him better.'

'What does that mean?'

'It means,' responded Nicholas cheerfully, 'that, in Sarre's case, looks are deceiving. And if you don't believe me, ask Caroline.'

'I probably will,' replied Cassie. And then, glancing across the room, 'Oh.'

His lordship turned his head in the direction of her gaze and then, looking quizzically back at her, said softly, 'Oh indeed. Poser Penhaligon, Cassie? *Really?*'

She shot him a brief, quelling glance and smiled up at a dark-haired gentleman bowing in front of her. 'You are very late, sir. I had not thought to see you this evening.'

'I was beginning to despair of getting here myself,' he returned ruefully. And to Nicholas, 'Keswick summoned me to make up the numbers at his supper party. Always *such* a pleasure being invited just to fill an empty seat. However ... since everyone knows your lordship never dances, I've no compunction in stealing your fair companion. If,' he finished, holding out his hand, 'Mistress Delahaye will overlook my tardiness and honour me?'

Cassie stood up and felt her colour rise a little. She very carefully did *not* look at Nicholas.

'Thank you, Mr Penhaligon. I would be delighted. And Lord Nicholas will be equally happy, since I'm sure he has been positively *itching* to join his friends in the card-room.'

* * *

Having paid court to three of the ladies he was currently singling out, Richard Penhaligon left Moreton House after little more than an hour. As he sauntered round to the home of the widow he hoped might be persuaded to become his mistress, he considered the merits of the trio he'd left behind. Anna Whitcombe, very well dowered and the Season's reigning beauty; Lady Phoebe Lennox, less well-dowered but the daughter of a marquis; and Cassandra Delahaye ... distinguished only by being less tedious than the other two. However, none of this mattered in the least. What *did* matter was that he was giving the impression of a gentleman on the verge of settling down.

Once ensconced at the fireside with a glass of brandy, he contemplated the exquisite woman on the other side of the hearth and said, 'You could do much worse than me, you know.'

'I could also do much better,' replied her ladyship, twining one silver-fair ringlet about her finger. 'You can't afford me, Richard. Also, I am looking for something more ... permanent.'

'Marriage, you mean?'

'Ideally, yes. And that's not something you're willing to offer.'

'It's not a case of willingness. I --'

'Of course it is. You're waiting to see if your nephew dies before you do anything irrevocable.'

His jaw tightened. 'That's a particularly brutal way of putting it.'

'What's the point of dressing it up? Oh I'm not saying you're ill-wishing the boy. But the physicians say he won't see out the year and if they're right, you'll be your brother's heir – which will improve your options. And while you wait, you toy with this girl or that, taking care that none of them are ever *quite* sure how serious you are.' She reclined in her chair, regarding him with malicious approval. 'I'm right, aren't I?'

'To a degree – though I don't believe I'm as cold-blooded as you make me sound.'

'You think it's a criticism? It isn't. However, you can't offer me what I want, so I won't commit to you and risk missing something better. Now ... let us end this conversation. Instead, you can tell me the latest gossip.'

Mr Penhaligon scowled into his glass, took a hefty swallow and said, 'There's only one thing anyone's talking about these days. Sebastian bloody Audley.' Before silky lashes veiled the sapphire eyes, he caught a sudden gleam of interest in them and added irritably, 'Oh God. Not you, too.'

'What do you mean?'

'As far as I can tell, no one's clapped eyes on the fellow for years – yet everybody's anticipating his return as if it was the Second Coming.'

'And *is* he returning?'

'So they say.' He looked across at her, his expression suspicious. 'Why should you care? I doubt *he'll* give you what you want either. In fact, I'm surprised you've ever heard of him.'

'Scandal sheets, my sweet. Surely you know I'm addicted to them?'

'You and every other female in London, it would appear.'

Indolently stretching out her foot to admire one shapely ankle, she said, 'What's the matter, Richard? Is Mr Audley putting your nose out of joint before he's even appeared?'

'Don't be ridiculous.'

She laughed. 'You think I don't know how you like being the centre of attention? But I won't tease. Indeed ... to atone for my earlier unkindness, I'm half inclined to let you stay tonight.'

This sent a thud of surprised anticipation through his body but he said cautiously, 'Only *half* inclined?'

'That depends on you.' She relapsed into silence for a long moment before saying slowly, 'I think we might make a bargain which gives both of us something we want.'

'I'm listening.'

'It's becoming increasingly plain that a foreign title means little or nothing here in London, so I will never enter polite society without the right entrée. You could help with that. And in return, although there will be no permanent arrangement between us, you would not find me ... ungenerous.'

Mr Penhaligon's eyes travelled over every splendidly enticing curve and returned to her face. He did not, as he might have done had his brain not been clouded by the prospect of having her naked in bed, wonder why she was only now making a suggestion she might have made weeks ago. Instead, he said, 'In plain terms, I scratch your back and you'll scratch mine?'

'Exactly.' Her laugh, this time, was pure invitation. 'And in the latter case – quite literally.'

CHAPTER TWO

Having travelled via Frankfurt, Zurich and Trieste, the letter summoning Sebastian Audley home finally caught up with him in the heights of Buda.

He normally tossed such missives into a drawer, often unread … but not this one. For years, they had arrived by the handful; a packet of five, one from each of his sisters, all collected and forwarded by the eldest of them. This, by contrast, had arrived crumpled, dirty and ominously alone.

Yet still Sebastian left it unopened on the hall table, from where it radiated silent accusation.

It was from Blanche, of course – the eldest of his sisters and the only one to remain unwed. Blanche … with her pompous tendency to sermonise and her unwavering and very blatant dislike of him.

He felt oddly ambivalent. He didn't want to read the letter but knew that he'd have to; knew with bone-deep certainty that it contained something much worse than Blanche's usual rantings … something that was going to call him back. And if he was honest with himself, he knew it was time.

He had spent the last seven years doing anything he liked and everything he'd never been allowed to; and for the first five of those years, he'd enjoyed it. He'd risked life and limb in a series of spectacular, hair-raising wagers; he'd drunk, gamed, travelled and slept with numerous beautiful women. He'd played chess against masters of the game in St Petersburg, perfected his swordplay in Madrid and picked up half a dozen languages; he'd skated on the Vltava in Prague, swum the Grand Canal in Venice, scaled the walls of Dubrovnik … and half a hundred other exploits he could scarcely remember.

But during the last year, almost without him noticing it, the challenges had become less appealing and he'd started to find himself wishing that not quite *every* fellow he met was determined to devise some crazy exploit that notoriously Neck-or-

Nothing Sebastian Audley could be relied upon to try. In short, his reputation had gradually become a millstone around his neck – on top of which, an entanglement with a married lady in Lisbon had sent him running, literally, for the hills.

Buda was one of few places where he could escape and he was fond of it – even though, in late February, it was damned cold. The windows and balconies of his rented villa afforded stunning views down the hillside to the Danube and the town of Pest which lay on the far side of it. The food was good, the people friendly and the women passionate. But despite all this, Sebastian knew that he was merely marking time ... or, worse still, hiding. And the unopened letter was telling him it was time to stop.

And so, after twenty-four hours of doing his best to ignore it, Sebastian poured a glass of brandy and broke the seal.

Unusually, Blanche had come directly to the point.

Father has suffered an apoplexy. If you care anything at all for him or for our family and have any desire to see him alive, you will return immediately.

The words hit him like a punch in the stomach and he downed the brandy in one quick swallow. He thought instinctively, *No. Father's not dead. He can't be.* And then, sickeningly, *He wasn't dead when Blanche wrote. But now? How long has the letter taken to get here? Three weeks? Four? Damn. Why the hell didn't she put a date on it?*

Just for once, he decided bitterly, it would have been helpful if Blanche had supplied a grain or two of additional information – such as how severe the attack had been and what hope, if any, the doctors held out of recovery.

Father's never ailed a day in his life and he's only ... what? Sixty-seven? That isn't old. And people recover from apoplexy all the time. Don't they?

It had never been that Sebastian didn't love his father. He did. He just couldn't be what the Viscount wanted. Once every year he went home to Sussex, hoping deep inside himself that things would be different – but they never were. Father still lectured him about his duty to ensure the succession and Blanche said the sort of things she'd been saying since he was eight years old and which still hurt even though they shouldn't.

Consequently, his visits never lasted more than seventy-two hours and always ended in acrimony.

This time, however, he'd go back not hoping for anything except to find his father alive.

* * *

Travelling across a large part of Europe through bad weather and over even worse roads was unpleasant and impossible to accomplish quickly. Taking only Hobson, his valet, and leaving the Hungarian servants to pack the bulk of his belongings and close up the villa, Sebastian set out from Buda within twenty-four hours. At a different time of the year, he might have elected to begin his journey by river; but not in February, when parts of the Danube were still blocked by ice. So he hired a coach-and-four, battened down his impatience and prepared to make what speed he could.

It took five days to reach Vienna, through sleet and snow. Having accidentally made himself *persona non grata* on his last visit, Sebastian passed through the city as unobtrusively as possible and headed for Linz. Next came Munich – from whence, though he doubted his letter would arrive in advance of himself, he sent word to Blanche that he was on his way. The journey began to seem endless; the long hours of being jolted over iron-hard roads riven with pot-holes left every bone in his body bruised and aching; and as if things were not already quite bad enough, somewhere between Stuttgart and Frankfurt, Hobson caught a cold of epic proportions.

'I'm sorry,' said Sebastian, when it was obvious that his unfortunate valet was running a mild fever. 'I can leave you to recover at an inn in Cologne, with sufficient funds to follow when you feel well enough – but I have to press on.'

'Of course, sir,' managed Hobson valiantly from behind his handkerchief. 'Pray do not concern yourself. I will manage and can only apologise --'

The words were halted by a violent sneeze. Sebastian winced.

' – for the inconvenience,' finished Hobson miserably. 'And for failing in my duty.'

'You're not failing in anything. As you're well aware, I can look after myself more than adequately. But I'd prefer not to be responsible for you contracting inflammation of the lung.'

'I shall not do so, sir. I am *determined* of it.'

'Ah.' Despite himself, Sebastian felt a quiver of amusement. 'Well in that case, we don't have anything to worry about, do we?'

By the time they reached Brussels, Hobson was on the mend. Sebastian, by now more thoroughly exhausted than he'd ever been in his life, pressed on to Lille then Calais. They had been on the road for twenty-two days. On the following afternoon, they disembarked at Dover, hired two horses and set off on the last forty miles which would take Sebastian home.

* * *

Audley Court lay five miles from Rye on the East Sussex coast. The house was a neat, flint-walled manor, prettily situated but unostentatious. The only thing on Sebastian's mind as it came into view round the curve of the drive was that there was no hatchment on the door, nor any other sign of recent bereavement. He loosed a breath he hadn't known he'd been holding.

Even before he had left the saddle, the butler had the door open and was smiling at him.

'Mr Sebastian! Welcome home, sir. This is a most agreeable surprise, if you will permit me to say so.'

'Thank you, Bradshaw.' Sebastian dropped to the ground and tossed his reins to Hobson. 'I sent a note about ten days ago but clearly I've out-distanced it. The bulk of my luggage will arrive some time tomorrow – and the horses have to be returned to Dover. Meanwhile, have someone look after my valet, will you? He's ready to drop.'

'Really, sir!' expostulated Hobson. 'I assure you that I am quite well and --'

'Don't argue, Ben. Just go and let Mrs Mason give you one of her infallible cures.' Sebastian ran up the steps and, unable to wait any longer, said, 'How is my father, Bradshaw?'

'His lordship is doing well, sir. Still confined to his chamber, of course, but --'

'Sebastian!' Dark-haired and petite, his youngest sister flew across the hall and threw herself on his chest. 'You came! I knew you would. But where on earth *were* you?'

'Hungary,' he responded, catching her with a laughing gasp. 'The journey took a while.'

'It shows.' Elizabeth grinned up at him. 'You look exhausted. Actually, you look perfectly dreadful – one might almost say disreputable.'

'Thank you, Lizzie.' He let her draw him into the house, saying, 'Who else is here?'

'Just Blanche and me now – and my darling Johnny, of course. He's ridden into Rye to attend some horrid sporting event but he'll be back by dinner. Lottie and Trixie *were* here, but they went home when the doctor pronounced Papa out of danger. And Jenny couldn't come because her confinement is imminent. But --'

'Well,' said a new and frigidly disapproving voice. 'Finally.'

Releasing Elizabeth's arm, Sebastian turned slowly.

'Blanche.' He bowed slightly. 'I came as soon as I could. But you made sure I would, didn't you?'

'And how, pray, could I do that?' she shrugged. 'I merely apprised you of the situation.'

'Indeed. And so baldly as to leave me with no choice but to assume the worst.'

'Since I had no confidence in you reading the letter at *all*, there was no point in writing more. You really are your own worst enemy, Sebastian.'

'So you have said. Frequently. However ... I'm here now so you may as well tell me what your letter should have done. How bad *was* the attack?'

'Bad enough. It could all-too-easily have been life-threatening. One can never tell with these things.' Blanche avoided the question by turning away. 'You will want to see for yourself, I'm sure. But first, you had better make yourself presentable. And while you do so, I will prepare Papa for the shock of your arrival.'

Sebastian experienced a sudden, strong temptation to tell Blanche to go to hell – and might even have done so except that a hot bath was the thing he wanted most in the world.

However, before he could open his mouth, Elizabeth said crossly, 'Oh don't talk fustian, Blanche. Papa won't be shocked – he'll be delighted. And Sebastian doesn't need *you* to tell him what to do. He's quite grown up enough to decide for himself.'

Then, grasping her brother's arm and towing him away up the stairs, she said, 'How long have you been travelling?'

'Three weeks. Not bad for this time of year.'

'Heavens – no wonder you look tired.' She glanced sideways up at him. 'Don't mind Blanche. You know what she's like. Mountains out of mole-hills as usual. Papa's attack was nowhere near as bad as it might have been. His speech is a little slurred and he seems to be having difficulty gripping things with his right hand … but Dr Benson says there's a good chance that will improve. And to be honest, Papa would be recovering a lot better if Blanche would stop hovering about him as if she expects him to turn up his toes at any minute. If I was him, I'd have thrown something at her by now.'

'And missed,' he grinned. 'I never saw anyone with a worse aim than you.'

Laughing, Elizabeth opened the door of his chamber and cast a brief comprehensive glance over it. 'Good. They've lit a fire and brought your bags up. Doubtless Bradshaw has ordered hot water and food for you, so I'll see you presently.' Rising on tiptoe, she kissed his cheek and said, 'Thank you for coming, Sebastian. And please try to stay a little longer than you usually do. It will make all the difference.' Then she was gone.

* * *

Bathed, shaved and once more clad with his usual restrained elegance, Sebastian made his way to his father's rooms only to find Blanche barring his way at the turn of the stairs. He didn't know whether to be irritated or amused by her resemblance to a bull mastiff.

'Papa wishes to receive you alone,' she announced with undisguised annoyance. 'I would ask you to remember that his health is frail and that extreme care should be taken not to excite or upset him since we do not wish him to suffer a relapse. You must therefore attempt not to be contentious, Sebastian – though I'm afraid I have little faith in your self-restraint. You have never thought of anyone but yourself, so why I should imagine today would be any different, I cannot imagine.'

Her brother's dark blue eyes rested on her inimically.

'Does it never occur to you,' he asked, his tone light as the flick of a lash, 'that there are better ways of ensuring my compliance than addressing me as if I were either ten years old or an imbecile? One would almost think you *wanted* to send me to Father in a less than amiable frame of mind.'

'Don't be ridiculous. I merely know only too well how you conduct yourself.'

'No, Blanche. You don't.' Folding his arms and crossing one ankle over the other, he leaned against the wall in a negligent attitude deliberately designed to infuriate her. 'I have as much care for Father's health as you might wish and no desire to inherit his shoes for many years to come. *You*, however, must dread the day when I do.'

'Of course I dread it! How could I not? No matter how far you travel, every sordid detail of your behaviour comes back to haunt us. Scarcely a week goes by without some salacious mention of you in the scandal-sheets.'

'Really? Collect them, do you?'

She ignored this piece of provocation and stuck to her theme.

'You've shamed our family and made it a laughing-stock, Sebastian. Thanks to you, people snigger behind our backs and I doubt any decent family will permit you to court a daughter of theirs. Dear Theodore would *never* have embarrassed us all as you do. And why God chose to take him --'

She came to an abrupt stop, breathing rather hard.

'Why God took Theo instead of me?' he finished aridly and trying to ignore the pain that twisted his gut every time his twin's death was mentioned. 'There's no need to be shy, Blanche. It's no secret that you wish I'd died instead. You've been saying it since I was eight, after all.'

'And can I be *blamed* for wishing it? The prospect of you – with your frivolous, licentious ways – occupying our dear father's position? It doesn't bear thinking about.'

'And what of your own position, Blanche?'

'*My* position? What has that to do with anything? I have devoted my life to Papa and our sisters – even to you, though you'll never admit it. I could have married --'

'Could you? I always wondered. Did you choose the single state ... or did no one offer?' He waited, watching the colour rise to her face, his smile slow and not particularly pleasant. 'But you are missing the point. Since Mama's death, you have made yourself mistress of this house. You have also made your opinion of me distressingly clear. You must surely have given a modicum of thought to the consequences of those two facts when I become head of the family.'

She stared at him out of narrowed eyes.

'What is that supposed to mean?'

'It means that in the fullness of time, I will inherit the title and all that goes with it. I'll also doubtless marry.' He paused briefly. 'You have made your feelings towards me plainer than was perhaps wise and with a result that can surely not be a surprise. As my sister, it goes without saying that you will always be well provided-for and suitably housed. But not, once I am obliged to live here myself, at Audley Court.' Sebastian detached himself from the wall and sketched the merest hint of a bow. 'And now, if you will be good enough to let me pass, I will go and see Father.'

* * *

'Thought you'd never get here,' grunted Lord Wingham by way of greeting. 'Blanche been laying down the law, has she?'

'Inevitably,' agreed Sebastian, reaching out to grip his father's hand. 'How are you, sir?'

'Not about to stick my spoon in the wall just yet.'

'I'm glad to hear it.' He was also glad that, although his handshake was weak, the viscount's voice was no less robust than it had ever been. 'I came as soon as I heard but the journey took some time.'

'Where were you?'

'Buda. Hungary.'

'I know where it is,' said his lordship testily. In truth, he knew the location of every major city in Europe. Maps and the gossip-pages that his valet acquired secretly on his behalf were his only means of keeping track of his wandering son. 'Damned inconvenient place, I should think. What took you there?'

The fact that it isn't full of eager young fellows on their Grand Tour, came the instinctive thought. But he merely said, 'Nothing in particular – though the country is very beautiful.'

'And the women, no doubt?'

Sebastian smiled. 'Yes, sir. Those, too.'

Lord Wingham regarded his son and heir with mingled pride and despair. Pride in his physical appearance, immaculate posture and confident demeanour; despair of ever seeing him settle down to the business of getting a son of his own. He'd known for years that he had no one but himself to blame for how Sebastian had turned out. He'd just never admitted it to anyone but himself. His recent unexpected brush with mortality, however, had revealed this as another mistake – and one he ought to rectify before it was too late.

'Of course. Needn't have asked.' He sighed. 'Well, sit down, boy. Unless you're dashing back to bloody Buda?'

There was a wistful, questioning note in those last words which didn't escape Sebastian. Taking the chair on the far side of the hearth, he said, 'I've only just got here, Father – and through the kind of weather that only Eastern Europe can hurl at you at this time of year. I was thinking I might stay for a while.'

'In England? Or here at the Court?'

'Here, until your health improves … and in England through the spring.' He shrugged, careful to appear casual and refraining from admitting that he might stay even longer if his thrice-blasted reputation didn't prove an obstacle. 'Since, amongst other things, I need to visit my bootmaker, I thought of spending a few weeks in London.'

'Ah. Yes. Well, foreigners never could make a good boot.' The viscount paused and then, with a sly grin, 'I told Blanche not to disturb us, so it's safe to indulge. The brandy's hidden behind Shakespeare's *Histories.*'

Sebastian raised an eyebrow but rose to cross to the bookshelves.

'An illicit supply, Father?'

'No other way to do it with Blanche on the prowl. But Perkins keeps me supplied. He knows which is the good stuff, as well – though you'd have to wonder *how*, since he swears he doesn't touch it.' He fell silent until the glass was in his hand and Sebastian had resumed his seat. Then he said gruffly, 'I think I might perhaps owe you an apology, my boy.'

Noting the equivocal nature of this statement, Sebastian said merely, 'Oh?'

'I … well, I may not have gone about things the best way years ago. Keeping you caged the way I did … it was no wonder you broke free as soon as you were able. Flora warned that I'd better be prepared to reap what I'd sown but I took no notice. Convinced I knew best, you see. And look what's come of it. Years of sitting here with my heart in my mouth, expecting at any time to hear that you'd fallen off a cliff or been shot in a duel.' His lordship took a swallow of brandy and scowled over the rim of his glass. 'There. I've said it.'

Sebastian refrained from observing that, in point of fact, he *hadn't* – because he'd never expected his father to come within a hairsbreadth of such an admission and suspected that he'd only done so now because he was afraid he might die. He said slowly, 'None of the things I did were done with the intention of causing you anxiety, sir.'

'I know that. You did 'em because I'd been doing your breathing for you. Perhaps if I'd left you free to enjoy university in the normal way … if I'd talked about a Grand Tour after Cambridge rather than finding you a bride … you'd have got a lot of what came later out of your system. But I didn't, so you went to extremes.'

'That's certainly one way of putting it.'

Lord Wingham nodded.

'Not that it's an adequate excuse … but after we lost Theo, I couldn't …' He stopped, drained his glass and then said explosively, 'I was afraid, damn it!'

'I know.'

'Do you?'

'Yes. *Now* I do.'

'But not in the beginning?'

'No.' *I didn't want to take Theo's place – I just wanted him back. But nobody understood that. And nobody told me why my life was suddenly different.* 'I felt like a commodity. I also couldn't see the sense in any of it. You had nephews and, thanks to Trixie and Lottie, the first of your grandsons. They might not bear the Audley name but they're all of your blood. So with me or without me, the line was never going to end with you.'

'The name still matters to me, Sebastian. I won't pretend otherwise. And though you don't think it now, you'll feel differently when you have a son of your own.'

'*If* I do,' came the uncompromising reply. 'Given the scarcity of male offspring through the last four generations, I may never do so - and since I've yet to produce any offspring at all, we've no way of knowing.' He drew a long breath and then loosed it. 'I'll say it one more time, Father. Audley men all have the same blue eyes and the same ridiculous red hair. Both are inherited characteristics, not shared by the Audley women. It seems to me that our habit of siring females is another of the same.'

This time the silence was a long one. Finally, the viscount said, 'I won't push you. I know it doesn't do any good. But you're twenty-eight years old. I hope you've enjoyed yourself these last years and I don't begrudge that you've done so. But --'

'But you can't help hoping that I *have* now got it out of my system?'

'Yes. I'd like to see you settled before --'

'Don't say it!' Sebastian got up and reached for the decanter. 'You are *not* going to die. And since talking as if you might isn't going to make me mend my ways, you can save yourself the trouble. Furthermore, as I've just spelled out to Blanche, I'm not ready to step into your shoes – so I'm depending on you to remain healthy for a good few years yet.'

'Ah.' Lord Wingham blinked rapidly and held out his glass. 'That's ... thank you. You're a good son, Sebastian.'

'No, I'm not. I'm a reckless, loose-living wastrel.' And with a sudden dazzling smile, 'But don't they say that there's hope for us all?'

* * *

Elizabeth's husband, Jonathan, Lord Holdenby, returned from Rye in time to spend the half-hour before dinner privately with his brother-in-law. Once he'd described at some length the boxing match he'd attended and received, in return, an account of Sebastian's most recent travels, he said thoughtfully, 'Correct me if I'm wrong, but I get the impression that kicking up the dust ain't as much fun as it used to be.'

'How did you guess?'

'Well, if the absence of your name from the scandal rags is any indication, you haven't been doing very much of it recently.'

'No. It has become a trifle ... tedious. And hard work. But don't, I beg of you, tell Blanche I said so.'

'Wouldn't dream of it, dear boy.' Jonathan grinned. 'Actually, I stay out of her way whenever possible. The woman's a Gorgon.'

Sebastian laughed. 'Scared, Johnny?'

'Bloody terrified! And don't pretend you're not. She usually sends you gibbering back across the channel in a matter of hours.'

'True. But I've half-promised Father a longer stay this time.' He paused, contemplating the ruby brightness in his glass. 'And I thought I might show my face in London.'

'Brave fellow!'

'Why do you say that?'

'Because I had a note from Nick Wynstanton a few days ago saying that – if and when you turned up – I might warn you that speculation about your return is already rife.'

Sebastian looked at him aghast.

'Tell me you're joking.'

'No. According to Nick, the clubs are taking bets on whether – and when – you'll appear and the females are twittering like starlings.'

'Christ,' muttered Sebastian. 'That's all I need.'

'Well, you shouldn't be so damned colourful, should you?' returned Jonathan reasonably. 'And it can't be *all* bad. After all, there must be some old friends you'd like to catch up with.'

'Precious few. I've acquaintances spread across most of the Continent … but friends in England? Not so many.' He thought for a moment and then said, 'Truth to tell, I can only think of one. Is Eastry around?'

'Eastry?' For a moment, Jonathan looked baffled. 'Oh – you mean Sarre. I suppose you wouldn't have heard. He inherited the title about three years ago but only returned from France a few months back and immediately got himself leg-shackled, if you can believe it. Caught an heiress, then disappeared to Kent.'

'Kent? He's at Sarre Park?'

'As far as I know. Write to him … or take your chances and ride over there, why don't you?'

Sebastian nodded. 'When my backside has recovered from three weeks on the road, I might do that. Is Anubis still in the stables?'

'That four-legged fiend? Yes. And he's still the horse from hell. If he don't manage to break your neck on the way, he'll have you over to East Kent in a blink.'

CHAPTER THREE

Caroline, Lady Sarre looked with satisfaction at the changes she'd wrought in the south parlour. Due to the Dowager Countess's reluctance to remove to the Dower House coupled with Adrian's refusal to leave Sandwich Bay until she'd done so, they'd been at Sarre Park for only three weeks and it had taken Caroline all of that time to turn just one room from a chilly cavern to something more inviting. Since the rest of the house was equally unwelcoming, she could see she was going to be kept busy for quite some time.

Her one and only meeting with the Dowager had not gone well but Caroline had been polite and kept her temper. She'd continued to keep it despite the provocation of patronising remarks and disparaging glances. And she might even have gone *on* keeping it had not her ladyship surveyed Adrian as if he'd crawled out from under a stone and listed both his supposed failings and the many ways in which he was wholly unfitted to his position - which was when Caroline's patience had finally snapped.

'That's enough, ma'am. Adrian is a better son than you deserve – and I won't have him spoken of that way.'

The Dowager's colour had risen alarmingly and she said, '*You* won't have it? *You* – the child of some clod-hopping northern cloth-weaver?'

'Yes. I had wondered if Adrian was being a little harsh in insisting that you occupy a separate establishment but now I see that he was not. Indeed, given your low opinion of him, I'm sure you can't want to reside under his roof. However ... as he has said, we wish to move here at the end of next week. And if your own servants are not equal to the task of transferring your belongings to the Dower House, we'll be happy to supply you with extra help.'

'*Brava*, darling,' murmured Adrian softly and with amusement.

Caroline had nodded and turned a bright, hard smile on her mother-in-law.

'As for the 'northern cloth-weaver' you referred to – he is actually my grandfather and, thanks to him, I have an extremely substantial dowry. I won't sink myself even further in your estimation by naming the exact sum.' She'd paused to enjoy the sight of her ladyship's jaw dropping. 'Oh – and we spent the days after our wedding as guests of the Duke and Duchess of Rockliffe. So you see, ma'am ... you have completely the wrong end of every possible stick.' And with a brisk curtsy, 'Good day.'

Adrian had laughed almost the whole way back to Devereux House ... and the Dowager had quit Sarre Park within four days.

Now, three weeks later, Caroline was just considering which room to attack next when Bertrand wandered in and said, 'We have a visitor. His name is Audley and he is asking for Adrian.'

* * *

Sebastian looked with interest at Lady Sarre. Though her figure was good and her smile warm, she wasn't the sort of obvious beauty that Adrian usually favoured. And then, in the second that thought occurred to him, he realised that she was staring.

Oh God, he thought resignedly. *My damned hair, I suppose. Why do they always have to get* poetic *over it? Why can't they just call it what it is? Red.*

Had he known that words like *garnets* and *Burgundy wine* were floating through Caroline's mind, he'd probably have groaned out loud. Since he didn't, he bowed gracefully over her hand and, when she apologised for Adrian's absence, said, 'The fault is mine, Lady Sarre. I should have written – not dropped upon you unannounced. And I can call again at a more convenient time. Indeed, another day will do just as well. I hope Adrian is well?'

'Perfectly well, thank you. Do I gather that you haven't seen him for some time?'

'Three years, give or take.' His smile was sudden and spectacular. 'In Venice, as I recall. I generally live abroad, you see – as did Adrian at that time.'

'Oh.' Fleetingly, Caroline wondered how much Mr Audley knew about the various skeletons in her husband's overcrowded closet. 'Well, if you've travelled some distance to see him, I should *certainly* have Adrian summoned because I'm sure he won't want --' Her words trailed off at the sound of carriage-wheels on the gravel outside and she turned automatically towards the window. 'Dear me. This is unusual. You are our very first visitor, sir – and now it appears you are not to be the only one. I wonder -- ?' Again, she stopped, eyes flying wide and both hands pressed briefly to her mouth. 'Oh my God. *Grandfather?*'

Just for a second, Sebastian wondered if she was going to faint. Then she whirled past him saying breathlessly, 'Forgive me, Mr Audley – and please don't *think* of leaving!'

Through the open doorway, Sebastian watched with amusement as her ladyship hurled herself on a lean, grey-haired gentleman while the sandy-haired French fellow who had answered the door looked on over very un-butler-like folded arms.

'Grandpa!' she cried. 'Oh Grandpa – I can't believe it. You're here – really here!'

'Of course I'm here, you daft lass.' He wrapped her in a hard embrace. 'Did you think I'd wait forever for you and this earl of yours to get up to Halifax?'

'But the snow? The roads? You might have been stranded!'

'Very nearly *was* – and more than once.'

Lady Sarre took his cloak and handed it to the Frenchman whilst taking the opportunity to whisper something that provoked an even more un-butler-like crack of laughter.

Then, as she drew her grandfather towards the warmth of the parlour, the old man said, 'Now, Miss … where's this husband of yours? Ah.' He stopped as his eyes lit upon Sebastian. 'Well, young man. I reckon you've got a bit of explaining to do, don't you?'

A gleam of laughter lit the dark blue eyes. 'Not really, sir. No.'

'*No?*' Mr Maitland's chest expanded alarmingly. 'Running off with my grand-daughter without so much as a --'

'Grandpa – stop,' interposed Caroline hastily. 'This gentleman is a visitor.'

'So he's *not* the earl?'

'No. Bertrand is sending someone to find him. Oh!' A sudden thought seemed to strike her and, turning back, she called, 'Bertrand – have Grandfather's carriage taken round to the stables, would you? And when Adrian gets here --'

'Yes, yes.' The Frenchman flapped a dismissive hand. 'I know. But on your head be it.'

The Countess merely grinned, turned back to her guests and made the necessary introductions. Sebastian shook hands with Mr Maitland and prepared to enjoy himself. He'd grasped the situation within seconds and was looking forward to seeing how his friend was going to extricate himself from the trouble it appeared he was in.

Adrian arrived, hot-foot and agitated, some half hour later to fling open the parlour doors, saying anxiously, 'Caroline? What's wrong? Are you all right?'

Then he stopped dead, presumably absorbing the fact that his wife was not only perfectly composed and sipping tea, but also entertaining one man he recognised and another he didn't – but whose identity he could probably guess.

Managing not to laugh, Sebastian watched Lord Sarre swallow a curse. His hair was damp and windblown; he was wearing neither cravat nor vest; his shirt was filthy and he himself was sweat-stained and dirt-spattered, with grime under his fingernails. Standing ramrod straight, he nodded a brief acknowledgement at Mr Audley and then looked, with a total lack of expression, at his wife's grandfather.

Not appearing in the least discomposed, Caroline rose and smiled sunnily at him.

'Adrian. I'm sorry – did whoever Bertrand send not explain? There is no emergency. It is merely that we have guests. I believe you know Mr Audley. And this is my grandfather, Mr Maitland.' She turned affectionately to the older man. 'Grandpa, allow me to present my husband, the Earl of Sarre.'

Despite his growing hilarity, Sebastian spared a moment to feel sorry for his lordship – who was quite clearly wishing the ground would swallow him up. If there was one thing he recalled about Adrian Devereux, it was that he'd never seen him less than perfectly groomed. Right now, he looked like a farm labourer.

Mr Maitland fixed Adrian with a gimlet stare and eventually said, 'You're the earl?'

'Unlikely as it may seem – yes,' replied his lordship stiffly.

'My little Caro's husband?'

'I have that honour, sir.' This time Adrian managed a slight bow. Then, on an indrawn breath, 'You must forgive me, Mr Maitland. I would very much like to offer you my hand but am afraid it must wait until I've washed. You too, Audley.'

'Oh don't mind me.' Sebastian grinned. 'I can only apologise for intruding at such an inopportune moment.'

Hubert Maitland continued to gaze at Adrian through narrowed eyes for a moment or two. Then, on a sound resembling a snort, he advanced, hand out-stretched, saying, 'There's nowt wrong with a bit of dirt, young man – and it says a lot about you. So take my hand and tell me what you were about when my little lass sent for you?'

Adrian accepted the proffered hand and found his fingers seized in a powerful grip. He said helplessly, 'I – we are in the process of repairing the roofs of the estate cottages.'

'Ah. And not enough workmen to get the job done without you rolling up your own sleeves, my lord?'

'No. That is we have plenty of willing hands, sir. I help out from choice, not necessity.'

'And why might that be, lad?'

Adrian blinked. He didn't think that, in his entire life, anyone had ever addressed him as 'lad'. Not even Betsy, who'd known

36

him since he was six. He looked at Caroline, positively glowing with satisfaction. And that was when he realised what she'd done and why he was standing in the middle of the south parlour and meeting Hubert Maitland for the first time whilst looking as though he'd been rolling in a ditch.

His shoulders relaxed and he said simply, 'My father was an indifferent landlord and I want our people to know that I am cast in a different mould. Working alongside them seemed the quickest way to prove it. And now,' he finished pleasantly, 'if you will all excuse me, I am going to restore myself to some degree of respectability. I believe I will also have a few choice words with Bertrand.'

As the door closed behind him, Caroline tucked her hand into her grandfather's arm and said, 'There. He's not what you expected, is he?'

'He's not much like any aristocrat I ever saw, if that's what you mean.'

'Unless he's changed a great deal since we last met,' murmured Sebastian, 'I suspect he's currently remedying that.'

'Oh - undoubtedly,' agreed Caroline. And to her grandfather, 'I knew if you saw what Adrian *really* is, that you'd like him.'

'Who says I like him?' grumbled Mr Maitland. 'The fellow may not be too grand to get his hands dirty – but that don't change the fact that he ran off with you in that hole-and-corner way.'

'Actually,' she said wickedly, 'it was the other way about. I ran off with him. How else do you think I was going to catch an earl?'

The old man gave a bark of laughter.

'Minx. Good thing I know better than believe that, isn't it? But I reckon you better explain it to this young fellow over here.'

'No.' She smiled at Sebastian. 'No. I think I'll leave that particular task to Adrian.'

* * *

Once more dressed to his own satisfaction, Adrian submitted to an hour-long grilling from Mr Maitland from which he emerged mentally exhausted but triumphant. He'd admitted that, despite having inherited little save debts, he was now part-owner of a lucrative gaming-club and thus made it clear he didn't need to marry for money; but he'd successfully avoided all mention of the Evie Mortimer scandal, his acting career in Paris and the fact that when Caroline had eloped with him, she'd believed him to be a French highwayman.

At the end of their conversation, Maitland had contemplated him in silence for a time. Then he said bluntly, 'I reckon you'll do. You're not some useless fribble and you make my lass happy. Do you love her?'

'Yes.' Adrian coloured slightly. 'And count myself fortunate to have her.'

'Good.' The old man's face creased into the first real smile Adrian had seen. Then he said unexpectedly, 'One wing of this house looks ready to fall down. Been like that a while, has it?'

'Years. Indeed, I don't recall the north wing ever being habitable. But the rest of the house is in a good state of repair – unlike most of the tenants' cottages. So --'

'So you're investing in them first. Yes. I've understood that.' Mr Maitland got to his feet. 'Right, then. Let's go and take a look at it.'

'The north wing?' asked Adrian, startled and every nerve in his body recoiling from the idea. 'Sir – it's in bad shape. Bad enough to be dangerous, which is why we keep it closed off. There's every kind of rot you can imagine and ... to be honest, I haven't been there myself in over a decade.'

The old man shot him a sharp glance.

'Bad memories, are there? No. You needn't tell me. We all have 'em. We just don't need to let 'em rule us. Come and show me the damage.'

'Mr Maitland, I really don't think this is --'

'Nonsense. If I fall through the floor, you'll just have to pull me out. But if I'm going to give you the money it'll take to put matters to rights, I'll need to see how bad the problem is, won't I? Now – let's go.'

* * *

While Lord Sarre was closeted with Mr Maitland, Sebastian was given the chance to become acquainted with her ladyship – who immediately surprised him by saying, 'If you're to see anything of Adrian at all, sir, you're going to have to stay the night.'

'That is an extremely kind offer … but I don't wish to intrude.'

'You won't be. *Can* you stay?'

He hesitated and then, since she seemed to actually mean it, said, 'Yes.'

'Excellent.' She rose to pull the bell. 'Adrian will be pleased. And by the time my grandfather has finished with him, I think he'll have deserved the chance to sit down with an old friend over a glass of wine.'

Sebastian eyed her thoughtfully.

'You're very understanding. Adrian is fortunate.'

'So am I. And I hope Grandpa is beginning to realise it. We'd intended to travel to Halifax as soon as the roads were fit but he has beaten us to it. Goodness knows how he managed to get here … but he's a very determined gentleman.'

A tap at the door was followed by the housekeeper.

'My lady?'

'Mr Audley will be staying the night, Betsy. So you'll need to prepare another bedchamber – and have someone locate his bag.'

'I've already done so, my lady. Mr Maitland will occupy the Willow Suite and this gentleman, the blue room. Fires have been lit and their things are waiting for them. Will dinner in an hour suit, do you think?'

'Perfectly. Oh … are the gentlemen still locking horns in the library?'

'No. They are not.' Mrs Holt's face expressed severe disapproval. 'They've gone tramping through all the mildew and filth of the north wing – and his lordship only just having cleaned himself up from this morning.'

'Oh dear,' said Caroline, trying not to laugh. 'That is unfortunate. Still, I'm sure they must have had a good reason.'

'If they're both to come out treading mouse-droppings on my clean floors and with their hair full of cobwebs, I would certainly hope so.'

'Well, that's odd,' remarked Caroline, when the door closed behind the housekeeper. 'But if they're invading a part of the house that is quite unusable, it at least means that Adrian isn't still under interrogation. I know it was naughty of me to make sure he turned up in all his dirt – but if the first thing Grandpa had seen was one of his outrageous vests, he might never have recovered.'

Sebastian grinned. 'He still wears them, then?'

'Oh yes. The collection is vast.' She paused. 'Are the two of you close friends?'

'In that we don't meet very often, perhaps not. In other ways, I'd like to think so. Adrian was rattling about Europe due to his family's fear of some scandal or other; *I* was doing it because I was being stifled with over-protectiveness. That created a bond of sorts … and somehow it never mattered how rarely we met.' He made a slight careless gesture with one hand. 'My wandering lifestyle results in a myriad of acquaintances but very few real friends. I count Adrian one of them.'

'I see.' Caroline rather thought she did see and felt a little sorry for him. Knowing better than to show it, however, she said, 'Yet somehow you lost touch?'

He nodded. 'It was after I returned from Russia --'

'*Russia?*'

'Yes. I play chess, you see.'

'Chess? No. I don't see at all.'

'Russians take the game very seriously,' he explained. 'Some of the best players in the world are to be found there. I wanted to … test my skill.'

'And did you win?'

'Sometimes. And when I didn't win, I learned.' His smile was fleeting and a little self-deprecating. 'But after Russia, it was as though Adrian had vanished. Until three days ago, I didn't know he'd inherited the title – let alone returned to England and married.'

'Well, the last two events are relatively recent,' said Caroline, rising to pour two glasses of sherry. 'As for where Adrian disappeared to ... I suggest you ask him. He may even tell you.'

* * *

Dinner passed pleasantly despite a good deal of talk about rising damp and sagging roof timbers but no explanation of the sudden interest in either. And when the meal was over, Mr Maitland elected to join Caroline for tea in the parlour, thus leaving Adrian and Sebastian to take their port in private.

'It seems a little late to be saying it,' remarked Adrian, sliding the decanter in Sebastian's direction, 'but welcome to Sarre Park. It's good to see you.'

'And you – though I should apologise for arriving at such an awkward moment.'

'Don't. Your presence didn't make it any more awkward than it would have been anyway. You can't fail to have realised that Caroline and I eloped. Naturally, Mr Maitland wasn't going to be thrilled about that; and equally naturally, he was bound to wonder if I was only after the money.'

Sebastian's brows rose. 'Money?'

'Yes. The man has vast quantities of it and has settled a hefty sum on Caroline. Given what he'd already seen of the state of this house before he laid eyes on me, he couldn't be blamed for suspecting my motives,' replied his lordship dryly. 'But enough of that. How was Russia?'

'Uncomfortable. The nobility spy on each other and *everyone* spies on the foreigners. I don't think I took a step without feeling eyes on my back.'

'And the chess?'

Sebastian's face lit up.

'Extraordinary! There was one fellow in particular – Dimitri Makarovsky. I played him three times and didn't even come *close* to winning. The man's a genius. But in the end, when he was sure

I was worth his time, he taught me a brilliant stratagem involving the Queen's rook which ...' He stopped, laughing. 'I'm sorry. The technicalities are wasted on you, aren't they?'

'Completely.'

'And yet you count cards as naturally as breathing.'

'No accounting for it, is there?' Adrian took a sip of port and sat back, contemplating his glass. 'Actually, that particular ability is a nuisance now I've assumed the title and turned respectable. One doesn't want to fleece one's friends, even by accident.'

'I suppose not.' Sebastian hesitated and then said, 'Was it difficult – re-entering society after so long?'

'Less so than I'd expected.'

'The past didn't come back to haunt you?'

'No – or only by the man largely responsible for it.' Adrian's tone gathered a note of grim amusement. 'It's a long story and I'll tell you about it some time. But it was the things I *had* done that could have created the biggest problems if they'd become generally known. Fortunately, they didn't.'

'Your lady wife hinted at something of the kind when I told her you'd disappeared.'

This time Adrian laughed.

'I didn't disappear. You just didn't look in the right place.'

'Which was?'

'On stage at the *Comédie Française* – and no. I'm not joking. Ask anyone in Paris about an actor called *L'Inconnu*.'

Sebastian blinked. 'Good God!'

'Exactly. And that's not all – though it will do for now.' Adrian reached for the decanter and re-filled both glasses. 'Why did you ask about my resurrection? Are you contemplating something similar?'

'Perhaps. I came back because my father is ill but he's no longer in danger so I thought ... I was considering spending some time in London. The trouble is that I'll have every Tom, Dick and Harry hurling challenges at me.' He gave an irritable shrug. 'Truth to tell, I've had my fill of all that – or grown out of it, more like.'

'Then you'll simply refuse.'

'There's nothing simple about it. They don't give up. And it's damned tiresome.' Sebastian gave a sudden, short laugh. 'From what you say, you've managed to keep all your misdeeds quiet. *Mine* — both the real and the imaginary — have been trumpeted across the length and breadth of Europe to the point where there's no escaping them.'

'Yes. I see.' Adrian fell silent for a moment. 'You could say your father's ill-health has made you realise it's time to settle down.'

'Who'll believe that? After the idiotic things I've probably said --'

'Such as what?'

'Lord — *I* don't know. I spent the first six months after Cambridge making up for twenty-one years of sobriety. I was drunk often enough to have bruited my supposed woes to half of London.'

'Then you'll have to wait until the furore dies down — as it will do, eventually.'

'I'd thought that myself — until my brother-in-law told me he'd had a note from Nicholas Wynstanton saying that the clubs are already taking bets on my possible re-appearance,' said Sebastian bitterly. 'Can you believe that? I've spent the last four months lurking quietly in Buda and only been back in England just over a week, for God's sake!'

'Ah. That doesn't sound good.'

'*Good*? It's bloody appalling!' Then, seeing laughter tugging at Adrian's mouth, 'All right — *have* your revenge for earlier. I know I sound ridiculous. But devil take it, Adrian — if Nick's right, I'm doomed. I've promised my father I'll remain in England through the spring but I can't spend the whole time at Audley Court without going insane.'

'In which case, you'll *have* to brave London.' The ghost of an idea stirred and his lordship took a moment to let it crystallise. Then he said slowly, 'What you said about bets being laid in the clubs … you might make use of that.'

'How?' asked Sebastian dubiously.

'Since accepting wagers is principally what you're famous for, you could let it be known that you've already entered into a private one. Something that takes precedence – and which means the wilder challenges can't be accepted.' He paused, thinking rapidly. 'You have Aristide record it in the private betting-book at Sinclairs so the exact nature of the wager won't become common knowledge.' A faint smile dawned. 'Yes. That might work. Considering your reputation, it's as near perfect a solution as you're likely to find.'

'I haven't followed any of this,' objected Sebastian. 'What wager? And Aristide – Sinclairs – private betting-books? What are you talking about?'

'Sinclairs is a fashionable gaming-club and Aristide Delacroix is the Frenchman who runs it. In addition to the usual public betting-book, he keeps a private one for wagers between small groups of gentlemen or individuals.'

'I know I've been away from London a while – but is a handshake no longer enough?'

'Of course. But some men like to have things recorded.'

'Each to their own, I suppose. However ... this notion of yours. I don't suppose I need to ask with *whom* I've made this fictitious wager. So I imagine you must have some idea of what it's to be about.'

'I have,' agreed Adrian, amusement lurking behind his eyes. 'And it won't be fictitious. If Aristide is to record it, the bet will be real enough – make no mistake about that.'

'Point taken.' Sebastian leaned back and folded his arms. 'So?'

Entirely without haste, Lord Sarre stood up and looked down upon his friend. Then, very slowly and with a great deal of enjoyment, he said, 'Mr Audley ... I am wagering that, within eight weeks of your arrival in London, you cannot make yourself sufficiently acceptable in society that a respectable parent will permit you to pay your addresses to his daughter ... in person and in private.'

It was a long moment before Sebastian could make his lungs work. Finally, he groaned, 'Hell, Adrian. That is truly evil.'

'Take it or leave it.'

'But you're basically challenging me to get married!'

'No. Think about it. There's nothing to stop you losing. Equally, there's nothing to stop you winning ... but choosing to propose to a girl you know would never, in a million years, accept you.' Adrian grinned. 'And meanwhile, you have eight weeks in which to refuse all other wagers whilst allowing your reputation to die a natural death. Well?'

'You have a very devious mind,' complained Sebastian. 'What are the stakes?'

'Something more interesting than money. I've an interest in horse-breeding and have acquired a particularly fine mare. I've also seen that magnificent black you rode here. It occurs to me that their combined offspring might be something out of the ordinary.'

'Ah. And then?'

'Whoever wins the wager gets the first foal. What do you think?'

'I must be mildly insane.' Mr Audley held out his hand and, when his lordship grasped it, said, 'All right. I agree. But if something goes disastrously wrong and I end up at the altar, don't be surprised if I shoot you.'

'You're not a complete idiot, Sebastian. If you end up at the altar, it will be because you want to.'

CHAPTER FOUR

Thanks to letters from Lady Sarre, the person in London best-placed to predict the arrival of Mr Audley was Cassandra Delahaye. She was not, of course, in a position to profit from her knowledge by placing a wager at either White's or Sinclairs; but she did eventually impart a little of what she knew to Lady Elinor.

'He doesn't seem at all as we'd expected. He plays chess, for heaven's sake! That doesn't sound much like either a dare-devil or a rake, does it?'

'Well, I suppose he can't be risking his neck or – or raking – quite *all* the time,' replied her ladyship dubiously. 'But I must admit it doesn't sound very promising. What else does Caroline say?'

'The house is full of noise and dust, thanks to the army of workmen renovating --'

'Not that. What else has she said about Mr Audley?'

Cassie rolled her eyes and sighed.

'He sits with his father who's recovering from an apoplexy and he rides over to Sarre Park from time to time. Aside from that, not a great deal, other than that she likes him and that he has red hair – though apparently 'red' doesn't quite describe it.'

'But he *is* coming to London?'

'Some time in the next week, I believe – possibly with Lord Sarre,' said Cassie. 'But you are *not* to go round telling everyone, Nell. And I'll know if you do – because people will assume that you had it from me and ask endless questions. Also, I haven't even told Mama. So --'

'Or Olivia?' suggested Nell, wickedly. And then, 'All right – all right. Not a word shall pass my lips. I won't even tell Harry – although I daresay he'd be glad of a little privileged information. Happy now?'

'Moderately.'

'Good. Are you attending Lady Vennor's rout on Thursday?'

'Yes. Unfortunately.'

'Unfortunately?'

Cassie nodded. 'Unless I'm very careful, Sir Alastair will ask me if he can speak to Papa. And when I say no he'll look hurt and confused ... and I'll feel as though I've kicked a puppy.'

Lady Elinor gave a peal of laughter.

'Oh dear. And I suppose his Mama is encouraging him?'

'Of course she is.' A mulish, slightly bitter twist touched the normally soft mouth. 'Sweet, well-bred, eminently-suitable Cassandra Delahaye? I'm exactly the kind of daughter-in-law all the mothers want. As to what their sons want ... it's debatable.'

Her laughter fading, Nell frowned slightly.

'And what do *you* want, Cassie?'

'Not Alastair Vennor or George Pelham, that's for sure.'

'What about Richard Penhaligon?'

Cassie looked sideways at her. 'What about him?'

'Well, he's very good-looking and has been seeking you out recently. So I wondered if perhaps ...' Nell stopped, appearing to change her mind. 'Actually, I didn't wonder *anything* until, for no reason I could see at the time, Nicholas told me he doesn't like him.'

'Why?'

'He didn't say. He was just vague in that annoying way men have.'

'No. Why would what Nicholas thinks of Mr Penhaligon have anything to do with me?'

'Because he wouldn't want you hurt. You know how fond of you he is.'

'Oh yes. He treats me more like a sister than my own brother does.'

Nell shot her friend a sharp glance, wondering if there had been a hint of acidity in those words. Then, deciding that it was unlikely, said, '*Do* you like Mr Penhaligon?'

'I like him better than the other gentlemen I've mentioned,' said Cassie carefully, 'and I enjoy dancing with him. But so do half a dozen other girls I could name. As for what Nicholas may or may not think … he's entitled to his opinion but should leave me to form my own.'

'In other words, I shouldn't have said anything,' sighed Nell. 'Very well. Let's talk of something else. It's the Cavendish assembly on Thursday – swiftly followed by Lord and Lady Amberley's ball next week. Have you decided what you will wear?'

'The blue silk and silver tissue Olivia is dying to try squeezing herself into for Cavendish House,' responded Cassie, with the glimmer of a smile. 'As for the Amberley ball, I've a final fitting for a new gown tomorrow but have begun to wish I'd been more adventurous.'

'Adventurous? Why? You always look elegant.'

'No, Nell. I always look the *same*. If you're free, come with me to Phanie's and you'll see exactly what I mean.'

* * *

Lady Vennor's rout was no different to any other. The rooms were hot, stuffy, over-crowded and heavy with far too many warring scents. Cassie soon abandoned the hopeless task of preventing her gown from becoming crushed; she spoke to all the same people she'd spoken to last night and the night before; and she made sure that Lady Vennor's son never had an opportunity to speak to her privately. The whole evening, she decided grimly, was both tedious and hard work and she wished Mama hadn't insisted they attend.

Twenty minutes later, Richard Penhaligon fought his way to her side and everything changed. Greeting her with no more than a smile, he said, 'This is appalling, isn't it? Why do you suppose hostesses do it?'

'If it isn't too crowded to move, it isn't a success,' she replied, quelling the impulse to beam up at him. 'And people accept the invitation rather than risk anyone thinking they didn't get one. But I didn't expect to see you here tonight, sir. Most of the younger gentlemen avoid functions like this.'

'True,' he laughed. 'And usually I'd have been one of them. But Lady Vennor is a relative-by-marriage … so here I am, dutiful as ever. And finding *you* here means that virtue has been rewarded and the evening won't be entirely dull.'

Since, as compliments went, this sounded a touch half-hearted, Cassie wasn't sure how to answer him. Then, in the seconds she hesitated, Mr Penhaligon said, 'There must be *somewhere* where one can converse without shouting. I'm tired of dodging elbows – and I should think you must be, too.'

'Yes.' This time she couldn't help beaming or hoping that he had something particular he wished to say to her. 'It's impossible to get inside the refreshment room ... but perhaps the gallery?'

He nodded and offered his arm. 'We can but hope.'

The gallery was indeed less packed, with space to breathe and even to move a little.

'Ah – that's better.' He smiled at her again. 'I haven't been in this house for a while but if memory serves, there is a rather fine Rubens at the far end. Would you like to see it?'

'I'd love to.' Hope grew. It was easy to talk about anything one liked whilst appearing to study a painting. 'Do you know much about art?'

'Only what appeals to me and what doesn't.' Warm, appreciative dark eyes met hers, causing her pulse to beat a little faster. 'Here it is. The ruins about the Palatine Hill in Rome. What do you think?'

It wasn't hard to admire the painting. But Cassie wondered why Mr Penhaligon continued drawing her attention to certain features of it even though his gaze, when it strayed to her, was saying something completely different; and why, once he had apparently run out of observations, he said, 'I heard, by the way, that Sheridan has a new play in rehearsal at Drury Lane. Another comedy of manners, I believe – and even better than *The Rivals*, if the rumours are true.'

'Oh? I haven't seen *The Rivals*. But Papa took us all to see *The Duenna* last year and I enjoyed that very much.'

'The comic opera? Yes. A departure for Sheridan, to be sure ... but a successful one.'

Cassie agreed and then waited.

Surely, she thought, *he's going to talk about something other than paintings and plays?*

He was. He moved on to books – at which point Cassie started to wonder why he'd sought her out at all. It occurred to her that Mr Penhaligon had a tendency to blow hot and cold – a notion which raised another question entirely.

That of whether or not he was doing it deliberately.

* * *

The following morning at Maison Phanie, Mistress Delahaye stared critically at her reflection in a large mirror and, without turning her head, said, 'You see?'

'Yes,' agreed Nell, sounding baffled. 'It's lovely.'

'Of course it's lovely. Everything Madame *makes* is lovely. That's not the point.'

Her ladyship continued to survey the gown; misty-green and lilac shot silk, over an exquisitely embroidered underskirt. It clung to the edge of Cassie's shoulders and reduced her waist to a mere wisp. Try as she would, Nell couldn't see anything wrong with it.

'I'm sorry, Cassie. You're going to have to explain.'

'It – it's so *safe*. And at Amberley House? I'll blend into the wall-hangings.'

Nell gave a splutter of laughter.

'Don't be so ridiculous. Of course you won't. Whatever is the matter with you?'

Richard Penhaligon, thought Cassie edgily, *who looks at me as if I mean something and then embarks on a conversation he could have had with my mother.*

'I want … just for once I'd like to be flamboyant. I want scarlet or jade or --'

'No, Mademoiselle,' said a firm but slightly amused voice from the doorway. 'Forgive me – but you do not. Those colours are not for you and neither would I permit them.' Madame Phanie walked towards Cassie, lips pursed thoughtfully. 'However … if what you desire is a hint of drama, of theatre … this is easily arranged.'

Cassie stared at her. 'It is?'

'Indeed. I shall show you. But first we will try a different style of corset.' Madame's dark eyes twinkled. 'If we are to create drama, Mademoiselle, it begins not with the gown but with what lies beneath.'

* * *

Three days later and having warned no one but his servants in Cork Street, the Earl of Sarre arrived in London with Mr Audley in tow.

'I shan't stay more than a few days,' Adrian told his guest, 'but I took a year's lease on this house so you may as well have the use of it.'

'That's generous of you.'

'Not really. I don't expect to be here much but have been keeping the house open with a skeleton staff, so you're more than welcome to it.' He continued flipping through a small stack of invitation cards. 'Ah. Good. This one will do.' And looking up with a grin, 'Formal dress this evening, Mr Audley. We'll dine in one of the private salons at Sinclairs and record the wager … after which, we're off to a ball.'

Sebastian groaned. 'Must we?'

'Unless you want the whole of London knowing you've arrived and going into a ferment of excitement about when you'll first appear --'

'You're exaggerating again.'

'Am I? In that case, we'll stroll through the main floor at Sinclairs and --'

'Stop.' Sebastian let his head drop back and contemplated the ceiling. 'Fine. You win. We'll attend the damned ball – to which, I'd remind you, I haven't been invited.'

'Since every hostess in London would be battering down our door if they knew you were here,' remarked Adrian, smothering a laugh, 'I don't think that will be a problem.'

'Excellent. It's a relief to know that at least *one* thing won't be.'

'However, since we'll be entering Sinclairs discreetly the back way, I suppose I ought to tell you that Aristide Delacroix and I own the place jointly.'

Sebastian sat up. 'You what?'

'I'm part owner of an extremely successful gaming club.'

'That's what I thought you said.' There was a long pause and then, 'How many people know that?'

'Outside myself, Aristide and now you? Five. And I'd like to keep it that way.'

'I think I've gathered that much.' Mr Audley started to laugh. 'Card-counting, acting, an elopement and now this? You *have* been a busy fellow, haven't you?'

* * *

Monsieur Delacroix greeted Lord Sarre imperturbably, raised one brow at mention of the private betting-book and shook Mr Audley's hand. He said, 'Go on up. It's quiet yet – though, as is becoming usual, Lord Nicholas is already here, tonight with Mr Fox. But --'

'Nicholas dines here regularly?' asked Adrian, surprised.

'Nearly every evening. He haunts the place.' Adding, with a small smile and a shrug, 'The reason is not hard to guess.'

'Ah. Madeleine?'

'Madeleine,' agreed Aristide. 'Of course, Nicholas is going the wrong way about it – but he hasn't realised that yet. Meanwhile, Madeleine will show you to one of the smaller dining-rooms and when you have eaten, I will bring up the book.'

'Who is Madeleine?' asked Sebastian as they made their way upstairs.

'Aristide's sister. Both he and I have suspected for a while that Nick is *épris* in that direction but it appears he's now given up being subtle – though it's hard to know what he expects to come of it.' Adrian glanced at the other man. 'When you've seen Madeleine, you'll understand. Just remember that looks aren't everything and that she can carve out your liver at ten paces with a single sentence.'

52

'Dear me. If that's the kind of lady taking his fancy these days, Nicholas must have changed a lot since I last met him.'

'He hasn't changed at all. However ... since both he and Charles Fox are almost certainly bound for the same ball as ourselves, it won't matter if we meet them. In fact, it may help.'

'And where exactly *are* we going?'

'Cavendish House,' replied Adrian with satisfaction. 'Everyone who is anyone will be there so it gives you the advantage of making your second debut under the eyes of the entire Polite World. Ah ... and here is Madeleine.' He made a low bow. '*Bonsoir*, Mademoiselle Delacroix.'

The clear green gaze rested on him inimically.

'Good evening, Lord Sarre.' Madeleine dropped the merest suggestion of a curtsy. 'I was not aware that we were to expect you this evening.'

'And *I* wasn't aware that prior notice was a requirement,' he returned sweetly. 'However, allow me to present Mr Audley.'

Sebastian, whose lungs had briefly ceased functioning, dragged in a breath and outdid his lordship with a flawlessly elegant bow of his own.

'Mademoiselle ... a pleasure.'

'Mr Audley.' Her expression said she'd heard of him but she merely accorded him a cool nod and, turning back to Adrian, said, 'You are joining Lord Nicholas and Mr Fox?'

'Later, perhaps. For now, Mr Audley and I would prefer to dine privately.'

'As you wish.' She turned, opened a nearby door and gestured them inside. 'I shall send a footman with information about Gaspard's specialities for the day – but alternatives are always available. As for our wine-cellar, you need only ask.' And she was gone.

'Bloody hell,' muttered Sebastian weakly. 'What is Nick *thinking*?'

'I've no idea. But it had better not be a *carte blanche*. She'll kill him.'

The promised footman arrived and began to describe in exhaustive detail the gastronomic delights currently on offer. Adrian silenced him part-way through the recital, ordered a bottle of Chambertin and waved the fellow away with an instruction to have Gaspard send up whatever he considered most suitable.

'Sinclairs offers the best food in Town,' he told Sebastian. 'Whatever we get, you won't be disappointed.'

'And what of the gaming tables?'

'Scrupulously honest. Downstairs caters for all tastes and pockets … up here, it's solely cards – mostly basset – and the play is deep. Often, extraordinarily so.'

'The warning is appreciated.' Sebastian smiled wryly. 'Staking thousands on the turn of a card was the very *first* thing I learned not to do.'

'That's going to disappoint a few people. Indeed, it would appear that you're quite the dull fellow these days.'

Wicked laughter flared suddenly in the blue eyes.

'Not entirely. I still retain at least one of my vices.'

Adrian grinned back and said, 'Retain it, by all means – but you'll have to also *restrain* it for the next eight weeks. Think you can?'

'If you want the truth, I've been pretty much restraining it since Lisbon --'

He stopped as the door opened upon a pair of footmen bearing an array of silver-covered dishes which they proceeded to arrange with geometric precision. When they had accomplished this to their satisfaction and left the gentlemen to serve themselves, Sebastian looked at the copious amounts of food and said, 'Are we expecting company?'

'No.' Adrian took a portion of salmon and crab terrine and pushed the dish across the table. 'Equally, there's no law that says we have to eat it all. However … you were saying something about Lisbon.'

'Ah. Yes. That.' Sebastian took a bite of the terrine and groaned appreciatively. 'God. I haven't tasted anything that good since I was last in France. Why can't the English cook?'

'I don't know. It's a mystery. Like Lisbon.'

Mr Audley took his time buttering a tiny, sweet white roll. Finally he said flatly and with a hint of bitterness, 'She was married. After those first months of freedom and being called out, I stopped getting entangled with married women. And even in the days when I *did*, I took care not to leave a cuckoo in someone else's nest and only ever dallied with ladies who'd already produced an heir or two. That wasn't true in Lisbon. She hadn't 'done her duty', as the saying goes – and I shouldn't have gone near her. But she was incredibly beautiful. More than that, she knew just how to tease and tempt and turn me inside out until I scarcely knew what I was doing.' He stopped and then said, 'That's no excuse. It happened only fifteen months ago and I was no callow youth to be bowled over by a clever, seductive female. Yet somehow, with her, I broke my own cardinal rule; and by the time I started to come to my senses, she'd begun talking about leaving her husband and divorce and how we could be married one day.'

'I imagine that broke the spell fairly fast,' observed Adrian.

'Yes. I explained that divorce was out of the question and that even had it not been, I wouldn't be party to it. So she smiled and said it didn't matter because we could live in Italy where no one would care if we were married or not. But I knew she wouldn't let it lie, so I ended the affair; and when she continued dogging my footsteps, I left Portugal for Spain – only to learn that she was *still* trying to track me down. So I fled further afield. First to Prague ... and then to Buda.' He reached for his glass, but simply stared into it. 'I expect you think I'm an idiot.'

'No. You're neither the first nor the last man to make a fool of himself that way.' Adrian helped himself to some venison. 'You may not believe it ... but that part of your life will resolve itself when you least expect it.'

'Are we talking about love – or marriage?'

'It's not unknown for the two to go hand in hand, you know.'

'Perhaps not – but it's rare. I've seen how it is between you and your lady; and my youngest sister and her husband are equally besotted with each other. But how many other couples are so fortunate?'

'I could name you at least four – one of them being Rockliffe and his duchess.'

'You mean that, in addition to the necessary lineage and looks,' said Sebastian cynically, 'his Grace also managed to find love?'

'I don't think lineage and looks had very much to do with it.'

Mr Audley toyed with lamb cutlets in Madeira sauce for a few moments before saying, 'I don't know how love – *that* kind of love – feels. I've never experienced it. And how does one ever know when it's real?'

Adrian smiled a little. 'You expect it to arrive with a fanfare of trumpets?'

'You mean it doesn't?' Sebastian applied himself once more to his plate. 'Damn.'

By the time Monsieur Delacroix joined them they had done reasonable justice to the dishes in front of them and were broaching a second bottle of wine. Once assured that his guests had eaten their fill, Aristide summoned a footman to clear the table and, when this had been done, sat down and opened the betting-book.

'Very well, gentlemen. Which of you has proposed this wager?'

'I did,' said Adrian. And proceeded to dictate the conditions.

At the end, Aristide looked with some amusement at Sebastian. He said, 'Are these terms acceptable to you Mr Audley?'

'They are.'

'And you accept the wager?'

'I do,' replied Sebastian solemnly.

'Then all it requires now is for both of you to sign.'

Lord Sarre's signature was level and precise; Mr Audley scrawled his with a flourish.

Aristide sanded the page and closed the book.

'This,' he told them, 'is kept under lock and key in my office. Only those who, like yourselves have recorded an entry in these pages, ever see it.'

'Good,' said Sebastian, rising from his chair and stretching. 'Because if fathers everywhere find out that I've committed myself to merely *appearing* respectable, I'll be doomed before I start.'

CHAPTER FIVE

Examining her reflection prior to leaving for Cavendish House, Cassie had to admit that Madame Phanie had been right about the corset. She had resisted the temptation to wear the new mauve-green watered silk which Madame had enhanced in all the right places with the addition of narrow violet ribbon … but she hadn't been able to resist the corset. It made the neckline of the blue and silver gown look significantly lower than it had before and Cassie felt positively daring.

For the first hour of the ball, she enjoyed herself immensely. Had she not taken the precaution of saving two dances, her card would have been full. She danced with Lord Milton and Mr Cardew and trod a minuet with Harry Caversham. It needed only one thing to make the evening perfect; and surely Mr Penhaligon was bound to arrive eventually?

By the end of the second hour, when she was starting to regret those two saved dances, the carrying tones of Dolly Cavendish's major-domo brought the entire room to a standstill.

'Lord Nicholas Wynstanton,' he intoned. 'Mr Charles Fox; the Earl of Sarre; Mr Sebastian Audley.'

The buzz of conversation stopped as if cut with a knife. Even the orchestra faltered, then resumed, raggedly and *pianissimo*. For at least five seconds no one spoke while everyone craned their necks to see the newcomers; then voices began murmuring and swelled quickly to a *crescendo*.

Cassie caught a glimpse of an outrageous blue-powdered wig that could only belong to Mr Fox; and then a small hand closed firmly about her wrist and Nell said, 'If Nicholas knew about this, the only thing that will save him from a horrible death is an immediate introduction. Come on.'

'No.' Cassie resisted the imperious tug. 'I don't care whether I meet Mr Audley or not. And you won't get near him, anyway. Look.'

Nell looked.

Chattering excitedly, a swarm of the youngest debutantes were closing in on their prey.

'God,' her ladyship muttered. 'Did *we* ever behave like that?'

'No. And I don't intend to start now. Also, it's not as though he's going to vanish in a puff of smoke, is it? Considering the company he's just walked in with, we're bound to meet him sooner or later.'

Fortunately, since Nell looked poised to argue, Lord March arrived to claim her hand for the minuet. Consulting her own card, Cassie saw that this was one of the dances she'd kept in reserve. Suddenly annoyed with herself, she thought, *Saving dances for a man who may not come? What on earth was I thinking? As for the situation with Sir Alastair – I can't go on hiding from him. It's ludicrous.*

Half-hidden by a potted fern, Sir Alastair was watching her with his usual expression of mild anxiety. Cassie drew a bracing breath and sent him a bright smile. His jaw dropped and he turned to see if there was someone behind him. Then, realising the smile really *had* been meant for him, he approached with caution and said, 'If you are not f-fully engaged, may I b-beg the honour of a dance, Mistress Delahaye?'

'Of course.' She pretended to consult her card, 'The supper dance, perhaps?'

For an instant, he looked so completely overwhelmed that she was afraid he might choke. But finally he managed to say, 'Thank you. I – I would be d-delighted.'

She inclined her head, murmured a polite reply and moved away. Across the room, she saw that the crowd of young ladies surrounding Mr Audley remained unabated and that Nicholas and Mr Fox, together with Lords Sarre and March, were clearly deriving a good deal of amusement from it. Cassie might have been amused too, except that her mind was occupied with finding somewhere quiet where she could compose a kind but definite refusal for Sir Alastair. There would be no peace in the ladies' retiring-room or in any of the various withdrawing rooms either. But the library … yes, that might do.

The room was deserted and lit only by the fire burning in the hearth and one branch of candles. Gratefully, Cassie closed the door, crossed the thick carpet towards the windows, on the far side of the room and was just trying to calculate how long she had before she'd need to return to the ballroom when she heard the sound of the door-handle turning. For a second, she froze. Being caught alone here was going to make her look either odd or, worse still, as though she had a clandestine assignation. So when the door opened a few inches, she shot into the shadowy corner behind a large wing chair and, heedless of her gown, dropped into a crouch behind it.

The intruder closed the door with a snap, took three impatient strides into the room and said in a furious undertone, 'Hell's teeth! If I'd known it would be this bad I'd have stayed in sodding Sussex – Blanche or no Blanche.'

Cassie sank still lower behind the chair, trying to breathe silently and thinking, *Go. Please go. I can't be found here.*

But he didn't go. Instead, he must have noticed the decanter on the table because she heard the chink of glass followed by the sound of liquid sloshing into a tumbler. Then, presumably before he'd got the drink to his lips, came the chatter of feminine voices and one, more strident than the rest, saying, 'In here. It's the only place left.'

Cassie shuddered. She knew that voice only too well. Then, to her horror, the door opened again.

Even more horrified than Cassie, Sebastian halted with the glass half-way to his lips.

Four of them, for God's sake. Three simpering little misses and a slightly older ferret-faced female in pink. If there's a worse nightmare than this, I can't imagine it.

'Naughty man!' said Miss Ferret archly. 'Stealing away from the ball-room instead of dancing? But we have found you out!'

'Yes, yes. We have,' giggled the Greek Chorus. 'Indeed we have.'

Sebastian set down the glass. He didn't attempt to smile. It was as much as he could manage just to be civil. He said, 'So I see. Why?'

There was a short baffled silence.

Ha! thought Cassie appreciatively. *Get out of that one, Cecy.*

'Well, we … we wished to welcome you back to London. Not, as you'll be aware, having had the opportunity earlier.'

Oh. Cassie's nerves twitched. *It's Cousin Sebastian. Of* course *it is. Who else would be attracting silly girls like flies?*

'Which is rather the point, is it not?' It struck Sebastian that this was the perfect moment to start playing the Soul of Propriety. 'I appreciate your good wishes, ladies. But since we have not been introduced --'

'Oh – a fig for that,' interrupted Miss Ferret forcefully. 'We can introduce ourselves well enough. I'm Cec --'

'Please stop.' He held up a restraining hand. 'Although I will be happy to meet all of you under the proper circumstances, you ought not to be here now and should return to the ballroom forthwith.'

The Chorus made little bleating sounds. The Ferret narrowed her undistinguished eyes and said, 'Well – I never thought you'd be so stuffy. Not with *your* reputation.'

Cassie clapped her hands over her mouth to stifle a gasp. No matter what one knew or thought, a lady never *ever* referred to a gentleman's reputation to his face.

Sebastian folded his arms and said nothing. He didn't need to because the sudden icy silence spoke volumes.

One of the acolytes said nervously, 'P-Perhaps we should go, Cecy? If my Mama hears about this …'

'Mine too,' whispered the second, while the third merely nodded.

All three dropped awkward curtsies and started backing away. The Ferret, on the other hand, stood her ground and said rudely, 'I don't see why you're being so pompous --'

'I think,' cut in Sebastian, walking to the door and opening it, 'that you have said quite enough and should leave before you make a worse impression than you already have – though I must say that is scarcely possible. Well?'

The Chorus crept out. The Ferret flounced after them with an audible sniff.

Sebastian shut the door with a snap, turned the key in the lock and leant his forehead against the oak panels. Then, on a long extremely irritable breath, he muttered, 'This is unendurable.'

Having heard the click of the lock, Cassie realised that she now had no choice but to reveal her involuntary and hitherto unsuspected presence. She just prayed that Mr Audley would find the situation as awkward and embarrassing as she did and therefore not ask too many questions. Struggling to her feet, she attempted to shake out her skirts and was just opening her mouth on an apology, when Sebastian swung round to trap her in a furious gaze.

'Christ!' he said. 'Not *another* one!'

'No. I'm sorry. I didn't think anyone else would --'

'How many *more* of you are there?'

'More what?'

'Don't be obtuse. It's not what – it's who. More of *you*.'

Cassie lost some of her inclination to be conciliatory.

'That's a big and quite mistaken assumption,' she began. Then, when he stormed over to the windows and started dragging back the curtains, 'What are you doing?'

'What does it look like? I'm checking there aren't any other over-excited schoolgirls lying in wait.'

The injustice of this took her breath away.

'I am *not* a schoolgirl – excited or otherwise. Neither, since I can't read minds, was I lying in wait.'

'No? How else would you explain it?'

'I don't have to explain *anything* to you. You're being ridiculous.'

'*I'm* being ridiculous?' Having reached the last window, Sebastian spun to face her. 'Weren't you listening just now?'

'I could hardly help it, could I?'

'So you'll admit that I have some excuse for finding somewhere to hide.' He regarded her over sardonically folded arms. 'Do *you*?'

She blinked. 'Do I what?'

'Have a good excuse for lurking behind a chair, eavesdropping.'

If he'd been within reach, Cassie thought she might actually have hit him.

'I *wasn't* eavesdropping! I --'

'What else would you call it?'

'I came in here for a few moments of privacy. I didn't --'

'Privacy? If you wanted that, why come to a ball?'

'Will you please stop interrupting!' she snapped coldly. 'I needed a few moments to myself. I did *not*, of course, expect to be joined by you and your – your entourage of female admirers. As for why I was hiding behind the chair ... if you will stop and *think* for a moment, you might be able to work out why I didn't want to be seen.'

'You didn't want to be seen but you'd risk being caught sitting on the floor?' he asked mockingly. 'Really?'

'I thought,' said Cassie with the strained patience of one addressing an imbecile, 'that you would go. I did not expect Cecily Garfield and her friends to follow you and I did not expect you to lock the door. I did not want to be found here by anyone at *all* because lurking in empty rooms at a ball leaves one open to misinterpretation. Is that plain enough for you – or are you determined to continue enjoying your tantrum?'

Sebastian's spurt of temper began to lose ground to his sense of humour.

'I suppose,' he conceded slowly, 'that you may have a point.'

'You *suppose*?'

'Well, be fair. After being pursued here by a quartet of peahens – not to mention the avalanche of feathers and fans I was subjected to in the ballroom – I merely made a natural assumption. However, I'm willing to admit that I may have been mistaken about you.'

'How magnanimous of you,' said Cassie witheringly.

Quite unexpectedly, he laughed, the sound of it genuine and annoyingly infectious.

'That's me. Magnanimity personified.'

Cassie refused to be charmed by the warmth in his voice. Mr Audley, she told herself, was arrogant and conceited. So she absolutely did *not* wish that there was just a little more light in the room so she could see the precise shade of the hair that had made such an impression on Caroline – but which, in the shadowy gloom, merely looked dark.

She suddenly realised that Mr Audley was conducting an appraisal of his own; a lazy, very thorough and blatantly *masculine* appraisal, a faint smile touching his mouth. Cassie felt her colour rise and sought for some suitably quelling remark so that she'd stop wondering what he was thinking.

In fact, Sebastian was unashamedly regretting the poor light – less because it prevented him seeing her face as clearly as he might have wished than because, in it, the silvery stuff overlaying her gown shimmered with a strange, almost otherworldly effect. Had he been of a superstitious turn of mind, he reflected whimsically, he might have taken her for a ghost.

However, realising that he'd been staring, he said, 'It seems I owe you an apology.'

'You owe me at least three,' retorted Cassie without stopping to think.

His brows rose but this time he managed not to laugh, appreciating the fact that she had no missish qualms about hitting back.

'Well, that was straight from the shoulder, wasn't it? But I daresay I deserved it.' He appeared to consider the matter. 'Yes. I recall using some rather strong language earlier when I thought I was alone. And I clearly did you an injustice in likening you to those other ladies.' He strolled towards her. 'I suppose you know who I am?'

'Mr Audley ... there is no one in this house and, by now, probably half of London who *doesn't* know who you are.'

'I hope you're mistaken about that.'

'I'm not.' Cassie made another attempt to make her gown look less creased, prior to returning to the ballroom. 'My younger sister and her school friends have been following your exploits for --'

She stopped abruptly as the handle of the door rattled and her appalled gaze flew to meet Sebastian's. He muttered, 'Hell. Not again, *surely*!'

Whoever was outside tried the handle a second time and then, realising that the door was locked, knocked upon it. Drawing a breath of sheer frustration, Sebastian bore down on Cassie and said rapidly, 'I'm sorry, sweetheart, but it's back behind the chair for you.'

'No! I can't!' she protested, resisting the pressure of his hands and thinking crossly, *Sweetheart? Not yours, certainly.* 'I promised the next dance to --'

'That's immaterial right now. You can't want us to be found together any more than I do – and the person outside that door knows there's someone in here. So the choice is simple. Either *you* hide or *I* will.'

Recognising the threat, Cassie mumbled something incomprehensible and subsided on to the carpet. Sebastian tucked a fold of her skirt out of sight and murmured, 'Don't worry. I won't let them find you.'

Then he strolled over to unlock the door ... and, in the sudden flood of light from the corridor, found himself looking into the face of a stunningly lovely woman. Eyes blue as a summer sky, a gleaming mass of white-blond hair and the kind of body designed to inspire male fantasies ... all of them belonging to Miranda Silvarez, the woman he'd said goodbye to fifteen months ago in Lisbon.

Shock paralysed his lungs and turned his mind dark and there was an unpleasant lurching sensation in his chest. He tried to speak but no words came out. He didn't even manage to resist when she pushed him backwards so that she could step into the room.

'I'd ask why you're skulking here in the dark behind a locked the door,' she said, her voice husky with amusement, 'except that the answer is clear enough. The young girls are already besotted … and hunting in packs, it would appear.'

Sebastian shook his head, trying to clear it. 'Miranda.'

'Well – obviously. Why so shocked, my darling?' She smiled, slid her hands around his neck and pulled his face down to hers. 'Didn't you know I was in London?'

'I – no.' Swallowing, he said, 'Forgive me. I believe I am … more than a little shocked.'

'So it would seem. But you're happy to see me, aren't you?'

He wanted to say he wasn't. He wanted to say he'd hoped never to see her again. He wanted to end this before it started. But because, thanks to him, a girl was trapped on the other side of the room, he realised that being honest right now wasn't an option. He was going to have to lie and pretend … and deal with the unpleasant consequences of that later.

'How could I not be?' He managed to free himself from her embrace and forced his brain to work. 'I can't believe that you're here – and as lovely as ever. It's an occasion for champagne, don't you think? So let's go and find some.'

She dimpled at him and, reaching behind her, pushed the door closed. Then she leaned into him and stretched up to nuzzle his jaw.

'Not just yet. Not until you've kissed me. I've missed you, Sebastian – very, very much. And I've something vastly important to tell you.'

'You have?' *God, she's like a limpet,* he thought with revulsion. *Or do I mean an octopus? Either way, her hands are everywhere. How the hell can I get her out of here?*

'Yes.' Her palms were sliding up his chest beneath his coat. 'James is dead.'

For a moment, the sense of it didn't reach him. When it did, he felt sick.

Miranda waited and when he didn't speak, she gave him a slight shake.

'Don't you understand, my love? My husband is dead – and has been for nearly a year. I'm a widow. I'm *free.*'

He'd thought earlier that he was living through his worst nightmare but he'd been spectacularly wrong. He was caught in it here and now. Also, unless he was very much mistaken, Miranda didn't just want his body in her bed; she wanted the same thing she'd wanted in Lisbon. His name. And now, with her husband's death and her undeniable beauty, she believed she would have it. Unfortunately, because it was clear she wouldn't take dismissal lightly ... because there was no knowing what she might say ... but mostly because of the girl hiding in the shadows ... he couldn't blurt out that it would be a cold day in hell before he resumed any kind of relationship with her; that in fact he'd traversed virtually the whole of eastern Europe to escape her.

He said, 'Then we should talk about that – but not here and not right now. *Now*, I have an overwhelming urge to make all the men out there envy me for having the most beautiful woman in London on my arm. Shall we?'

'Not,' said Miranda seductively, 'until you've kissed me.'

God. Do I have to? he thought. And then, *Damn it to hell.*

The ensuing silence told Cassie that Mr Audley must be complying – and the length of it suggested the kind of kiss she couldn't begin to imagine. She was tempted to peer round the edge of the chair but had the sense not to risk it. And finally the lady said a trifle breathlessly, 'Well ... I'm glad you haven't lost any of your skill.'

'It's a relief to me, too. So let's seek out the champagne and perhaps you will also allow me a dance?'

'Of course – though it must be after supper, since I promised that set to Lord Burford and one doesn't snub a marquis. If only I had known earlier that you would be here ...'

Her voice faded away as the door opened and then closed again.

As soon as she was sure they had gone, Cassie prepared to make her escape before any further catastrophe could overtake her. Out in the corridor and once more vigorously shaking out her petticoats, she considered what she'd overheard. Clearly, that woman had once been Mr Audley's mistress and, equally clearly, she expected their liaison to resume. What Mr Audley wanted was less obvious. Indeed, Cassie had a vague suspicion that he wasn't entirely comfortable.

A small smile touched her mouth and she thought, *He really isn't having a good evening, is he? First Cecy Garfield – and now this. But I suppose rakes with a reputation for being irresistible have to expect such complications. And that hint of unease was doubtless embarrassment because he knew I could hear every word.*

Sebastian saw her re-enter the ballroom and be immediately surrounded by three gentlemen. The impression he'd gained in the half-light of the library hadn't been mistaken. She was a trim little thing with hair the colour of cognac and big dark eyes. Not a beauty, perhaps ... but not the simpering sort either. It was a pity that after tonight's debacle, she wouldn't want to know him. He watched her send the first man away with what he guessed was a graceful apology and the good-looking dark-haired fellow with an equally graceful refusal – which appeared to come as a shock to him. Then, turning, she gave her hand to the gentleman who had been hovering nervously behind her.

'Taking stock of the possibilities, Sebastian?' Adrian materialised at his side and, apparently not expecting a reply, added, 'Where did you disappear to? Nick and Charles Fox were hoping you'd join them for a hand of cards.'

Sebastian wished he had done. As things had turned out, he'd have been a damned sight safer in the card-room than he'd been in the library.

'I thought they'd already had enough fun at my expense without bringing money into it.' Still watching the gavotte currently in progress, he gave a small huff of amusement. 'Who's the fellow in puce satin? The one who looks in imminent danger of tripping over his own feet.'

'I've no idea. But poor Cassie has my sympathy.'

Sebastian glanced at him. 'You know her?'

'Cassandra Delahaye. She's a friend of Caroline's.'

'Delahaye? *Gerry* Delahaye's sister?'

'I don't know Mr Delahaye – but it sounds likely. As for Cassie – she's that rare creature, a thoroughly nice girl with no artifice. Indeed, she's probably the only young lady in London that everyone of both sexes actually *likes*.'

'Is she betrothed?'

'Surprisingly enough, no.' Adrian shot his friend a suddenly acute glance and added flatly, 'Don't even think of it, Sebastian. Yes – Charles Delahaye is exactly the kind of father referred to in our wager. But if you trifle with Cassie's affections, Caroline will fillet and bread you. And I'll be happy to watch.'

Ruefully, Mr Audley reflected that Mistress Delahaye was unlikely to allow him within ten feet of her but he said merely, 'Does that mean you won't introduce me?'

'Not unless you promise to maintain a respectable distance.' Adrian paused and then, relenting, said, 'I imagine you've found this evening less than enjoyable and it's already served its purpose. Do you want to leave?'

Sebastian's mouth tightened.

'I can't. I've promised to dance the first set after supper.' He gave a short, hard laugh. 'Do you remember me asking if your past had come back to haunt you?'

'Yes. Why?'

'Because mine just has. It's over there dancing with the Marquis of Burford.'

* * *

A little later and silently thanking God that the dance was over, Cassie sat in the supper room waiting for Sir Alastair to come to the point. She hadn't rehearsed what she was going to say but comforted herself with the thought that, if one could deal adequately with one's wicked cousin, one could manage a very anxious baronet.

Eventually, having fortified himself with a glass of claret and two lobster patties, Sir Alastair said, 'Mistress Delahaye ... you m-may perhaps be aware that I have c-conceived a great – a very great admiration for you. May I have your l-leave to seek an interview with your father?'

Just for an instant, he looked so relieved merely to have got the words out that Cassie felt sorry for him. But it was her cue to put him out of his misery and so, as gently and kindly as she could, she did so ... and watched his expression change to one of resignation. Somehow, the fact that he'd expected a refusal but still forced himself to ask made it all worse.

Laying an impulsive hand on his cuff, she said, 'I'm sorry, sir – truly. But I am quite sure you will find a lady much better suited to you than me and I shall look forward to wishing you happy. And now, if you will excuse me, I see Lord Barclay coming to claim his dance.'

In truth, rather than dance the quadrille Cassie suddenly realised that she'd prefer to go home. It had been oddly satisfying to see the disbelief in Mr Penhaligon's face when she'd told him her card was full; but though it was a relief to have resolved the situation with Sir Alastair, it would be a while before she stopped feeling guilty about it. As for the interlude in the library ... it had been the most peculiar, alarming and exhilarating half-hour of her life and she still didn't know what to make of it.

But she smiled at Lord Barclay and allowed him to lead her to their place in the set. It was only when they joined the three waiting couples that Cassie found herself facing a silver-fair beauty she'd never seen before; and beside her, the tall, perfectly-proportioned form of the Honourable Sebastian Audley.

Set beneath level dark brows, eyes the exact shade of the last moments of twilight filled with mingled amusement and apology met hers for an instant as he bowed. But Cassie was barely aware of it, her vision suddenly dazzled by what the blaze of light in the ballroom did to his hair. It was thick and glossy and lightly curling. It was also, as Caroline had said, the colour of Burgundy wine and garnets ... and, more than that, of rich, dark fire; as living and beautiful and dangerous.

For a handful of heartbeats, Cassie's mind went utterly blank. Until this moment, she'd thought Richard Penhaligon good-looking but he was a candle to the sun of this man. Olivia had dismissed Mr Audley's looks as being less important than his various exploits but to Cassie, those antics sounded like the kind of thing he ought to have grown out of at university. His looks, however ... height, bearing and beautifully-sculpted features ... were little short of devastating. And with the utmost reluctance, she saw what she had been unconsciously determined *not* to see. She saw what all the fuss was about.

The music began, forcing her to concentrate on steps she could normally have done in her sleep. And when the dance required her to place her hands in those of Mr Audley, something she didn't recognise but instinctively knew she didn't want stirred behind her blue and silver bodice.

Quite deliberately, she turned her gaze back to the lady at his side.

The woman from the library, of course ... and I got the idea he wasn't entirely pleased to see her? How foolish. She's exactly the type who would *appeal to a man like him.* Then, with a faint sigh, *Actually there probably isn't a gentleman in this room she* doesn't *appeal to. But the real question is whether she really is what I think she is... and, if so, what she's doing in Dolly Cavendish's ballroom.'*

CHAPTER SIX

On the following morning at breakfast, Serena Delahaye surveyed her elder daughter thoughtfully and said, 'Did something untoward happen last night, Cassie?'

'No.' Cassie looked up from the egg she had been absentmindedly cutting into tiny pieces and thought, *No. I just got trapped in the library with Sebastian Audley and the woman he probably slept with last night.* Then banishing the hugely improper notion, 'That is ... not untoward exactly. Sir Alastair asked for my permission to speak to Papa and I refused. But that has been brewing for some time.'

Sir Charles looked up from his newspaper.

'You saved me from an interview with Alastair Vennor? My dear ... feel free to go out and buy something frivolous.'

'Don't be flippant, Charles,' his wife admonished him. 'Sir Alastair is a perfectly nice, respectable man. He just suffers from nerves – for which I believe his mother is largely to blame.'

'Not largely - completely. She terrified her husband into an early grave, then set to work on her son.' Charles grinned at Cassie. 'Aside from Sir Alastair's own defects, you really wouldn't want to acquire Cornelia Vennor as a mother-in-law.'

'But you can't go on turning *every* gentleman down,' objected Olivia. 'Sooner or later, you've got to marry someone.'

'And I expect I will,' replied her sister tranquilly. 'Just not Sir Alastair.'

'Who, then? This is your second season, after all. And --'

'That will do, Olivia.' Serena spoke quietly but her tone was firm. 'Cassie's marriage prospects are not your concern and I would prefer that you didn't make them so. And now, since you appear to have finished eating, I suggest you attend to your music.'

'Oh *Mama*! Must I? I'm never going to be any good at it and --'

'You certainly won't be if you don't practice. And the piece lying on the harpsichord must be gathering dust by now. Off you go, my dear. I shall join you in a little while to see how you're getting on.'

With unconcealed reluctance, Olivia left the room. As soon as the door closed behind her, Serena turned back to Cassie and said, 'Sebastian Audley was at Cavendish House last night. Did you meet him?'

Knowing how bad she was at lying and reluctant, in any case, to do so, Cassie sought a way around the truth. 'He danced the quadrille in the same set as Lord Barclay and me and he bowed, of course – but we weren't introduced.'

Charles abandoned his newspaper and raised enquiring brows at his wife.

'Audley is in Town? Why did you not mention it earlier?'

'Because Olivia takes far too much interest in him,' replied Serena. 'And judging by what I saw last night, so do too many of the other very young ladies – a lot of whom made complete exhibitions of themselves.'

'Mobbed, was he? Well, he must be used to that. It was exactly the same when he was in London before. But since Wingham's supposedly making a good recovery, I'm surprised Sebastian came back ... and even more surprised he's chosen to re-enter society. Perhaps he's decided it's time to settle down.'

'And find a wife?' asked Serena. 'His reputation is likely to get in the way of that.'

'Not in all quarters. He's Wingham's heir and doesn't need to marry for money. That will help – as will the fact that though the Audleys may not have come over with the Conqueror, they weren't very far behind him.' Charles rose and pushed back his chair. 'As for his notoriety ... worse sinners than Sebastian have put their past behind them. And I doubt he'd have done half the things he has if his father hadn't been such an ass.' He strolled towards the door, pausing to pat Cassie's shoulder as he passed. 'Marriage is a life-sentence, my dear, so you're quite right not to

take a man you don't truly want. And when one you *do* want
comes along, you'll know.' Upon which note, he walked out.

Cassie looked at her mother.

'What did Papa mean about Lord Wingham?'

'Exactly the question I would have asked myself but for the
sudden switch to admittedly excellent paternal advice. However,
all I recall is that the viscount apparently kept his son on too tight
a leash which, in your father's opinion, was largely responsible for
Sebastian's wild behaviour.' Serena spread expressive hands and
sent her daughter a mischievous smile. 'My own opinion, for
what it's worth, is that any gentleman with hair of that particular
shade would be likely to live up to it.'

* * *

In Cork Street and also at breakfast, Lord Sarre tossed half a
dozen gilt-edged invitation cards across the table to Mr Audley.

'Certain hostesses appear to have been burning the midnight
oil.'

Flicking through them, Sebastian said, 'My God. So soon?
But how did they even know where to send them?'

'Did you tell Charles Fox you were staying with me?'

'Yes.' And then, catching Adrian's look, 'Oh.'

'Oh,' agreed his lordship, his attention largely fixed on the
brief note in his hand. 'That's unfortunate. I was hoping to go
home the day after tomorrow but Rockliffe asks that I remain
until the end of the week. He's bringing his household back to
London – probably due to the Duchess's approaching confinement
but also because the House has scheduled a debate on the Road
Improvement Bill.'

'He has an interest in that?'

'Yes – and knows that I do, too.' Adrian surveyed his guest
meditatively. 'We were unable to talk about last evening's
unexpected complication with Nick and Charles Fox accompanying
us home and insisting on making a night of it. But if you want to
do so now, I'm at your disposal.'

'Thank you.' Sebastian toyed abstractedly with his coffee cup
and finally said slowly, 'I'm under orders to call on Miranda today

– though I'd have done so anyway to make it clear to her that there is no longer anything between us and never will be. Indeed, I'd have done it last night if I hadn't suspected she might make a scene. But the fact that I didn't isn't likely to make today any easier.'

'Did you not make matters clear to her in Lisbon?'

'I thought so – along with a sapphire bracelet.' He paused briefly. 'But it's worse now. Her husband is dead.'

'Ah. That *is* a problem.' Adrian leaned back in his chair. 'Who is she exactly?'

'Now? Lady Silvarez. Originally? I've no idea. She never spoke about what took her to Portugal in the first place or how she came to be married to Silvarez. At any rate, by the time I came along he was spending most of his time on his estate in Madeira. I never actually met the man – which is probably why I allowed myself to pretend he didn't exist. At the time, she had me so bewitched I scarcely questioned it. Later I wondered if she'd somehow tricked him into marriage and he'd only realised it when it was too late. In any event, I doubt if I was her first lover – and I'd lay money that there have been numerous others since I left.'

'Yet despite all this time apart, she still thinks you'll marry her?'

'That is my suspicion. The only thing I *don't* understand is why, if she's been widowed a year, she hasn't already married someone else. You've seen her. She wouldn't have found it very difficult. And the possibility that she's been waiting for me to reappear is just too ludicrous to contemplate.'

'Is it? You don't believe she's in love with you?'

'I don't believe she's capable of loving anyone – though I *am* starting to wonder if I've become an obsession with her. After all, if she's driven by ambition, she could do a hell of a lot better than me.'

'From what I saw last night,' grinned Adrian, 'there are a good many young ladies who would disagree with that.'

'Oh – for God's sake!' groaned Sebastian. 'Don't you think I've suffered enough? It was ghastly enough having to *deal* with those bloody girls without Nicholas and Charles passing a jolly hour twitting me about them.'

His lordship laughed. 'You're the latest novelty. It won't last.'

'I certainly hope not – or I may be tempted to slit my wrists. And only think! I've still got to run the gamut of the young bucks with their dares and wagers.'

'You can begin on that at Sinclairs this evening.'

'Lovely. I can't wait.' Sebastian stood up. 'This morning however, I intend to visit my tailor and my bootmaker. Then I'll present myself in Half Moon Street and attempt to convince Miranda once and for all that we have no future together; not as lovers and *certainly* not as husband and wife.' He gave a wry grin. 'She'll probably throw things at my head. But so long as she takes no for an answer and stops trying to dig her hooks into me, it will be worth a few bruises.'

'And I,' responded Adrian, also rising, 'am off to see how Caroline's mother and sisters have settled into their new home in Twickenham. I left my man of business to find them a house and take care of all the details – but Caroline will want a personal report.' He grinned suddenly. 'With a bit of luck, the three of them will have got over their compulsion to curtsy every time they speak to me ... and I hope to God they've run out of plum cake.'

* * *

At a little after three o'clock, Sebastian handed his card to Lady Silvarez's servant. The man bowed and said, 'Her ladyship is expecting you, sir. This way, if you please.'

Of course she's expecting me. It wouldn't cross her mind that I might not come. She thinks she has only to crook her finger and I'll come running, he thought edgily. *And I have done, damn it.*

He was shown into a small, pleasantly-furnished parlour and the door closed softly behind him. For a moment or two, Miranda merely smiled at him from the sofa where she was reclining in a pose of graceful invitation and looking seductive enough to tempt any man with a pulse. Though formally gowned in an afternoon dress of pale blue tiffany styled to display her magnificent bosom to advantage, her mane of silver-gilt hair was loosely and suggestively tied in a narrow ribbon – a small fact which spoke volumes. Extending a lazy, beckoning hand and in a tone of complete satisfaction, she said, 'Sebastian.'

Ignoring her hand, he stood his ground and bowed. 'Good afternoon, Miranda.'

Her brows rose a little. Then, when he still did not move, she stood up and on a tiny gurgle of laughter, said, 'You are very punctilious today. I know last night was a shock – but you must surely have got over it by now. And if you're lurking by the door because you are afraid we might be interrupted, you need not. Andrews is aware that I'm not at home to other visitors. So stop trying to intimidate me with that stern expression and come and kiss me.'

She waited, confident that he would obey. That humiliating certainty added a touch of anger to Sebastian's other feelings and he said coolly, 'Please don't address me as if I were a lapdog or a child, Miranda. I am neither.'

'Oh – trust me, my sweet. I *know* you are not.' Her gaze slid over his body, lingering in places where no lady should be looking before returning at length to his face. 'But you are also clearly not in the best of humours.'

That, he thought grimly, was fast becoming an understatement. He'd hoped to keep this exchange cordial for as long as possible but she was already setting his teeth on edge. Unclenching his jaw, he said, 'If I have given that impression, I can only beg your pardon. But the simple fact is that I believe we need to clarify a few things.'

'Of course we do – and we will. But there's no hurry.' Since he'd refused to come to her, she strolled towards him, once more offering her hand. Still utterly sure of herself, she tossed back the torrent of pale gold curls and said huskily, 'We have all the time in the world, do we not?'

No. We don't.

Tempting as it was to say it, he realised he couldn't be quite so blunt – or not until he'd established that her expectations really were what he thought they were. Summoning something he hoped resembled a smile, he said, 'Humour me, if you please.'

Her expression narrowed, making it quite clear that she *didn't* please. But she turned away, sank into a chair and said, 'Very well. By all means let us get it over with. What was it you wanted to say?'

'You said your husband died nearly a year ago. What happened?'

'He was set upon in the street. A robbery gone wrong, the authorities said – though the culprits were never caught. His body was found in the Tagus a few days later.'

From her tone, she might have been talking about an overset milk jug. This, coupled with the fact that Silvarez must have met his death only a short time after Sebastian himself had quit Lisbon, bred a suspicion that chilled him to the bone. He tried to tell himself he was letting his imagination run away with him and shoved the question to the back of his mind.

He said slowly, 'And then you returned to England?'

'Yes. There was nothing for me in Lisbon and I'd had enough of the place.'

He wondered how financially comfortable Silvarez had left her. He also wondered how she'd managed to inveigle her way far enough into polite society that she'd received an invitation to Cavendish House. He knew how the world of the English aristocracy worked; it closed its ranks against anyone who didn't have the right connections – and he was fairly sure that Miranda Silvarez didn't.

He tried a gentle probe. 'Of course. I imagine you have family here.'

'Some distant relatives. No one of any consequence, if that's what you mean.' came the slightly impatient reply. 'What is all this about, Sebastian? You're behaving very oddly.'

'Then perhaps I should come to the point. To my certain recollection, we said goodbye to each other in Lisbon ... but your behaviour last night suggested that you think otherwise.'

'Of course I think otherwise! And your memory is at fault. Our parting was never meant to be final. You left because James was returning from Madeira. Once he went away again, I expected you to come back. Perhaps you'd like to explain why you didn't.'

Blinking, Sebastian thought, *I didn't because I never intended to. And as for the rest, that's not how I remember it at all.*

It was true that Silvarez had sent word that he was travelling to Lisbon and also true that he himself had used that as an excuse to leave. But he'd never said he'd return; indeed, he distinctly recalled telling Miranda that their affair was over.

Who is she lying to? he wondered. *Me – or herself?*

'I don't believe,' he said carefully, 'that I made you any such promise.'

'You didn't need to. We both knew we were destined to be together – even though at the time, it wasn't possible. But James's death has changed that.'

And there it was ... announced as though there was no possibility of argument.

'Has it? In what way?'

'Oh don't be so obtuse. What on earth is the matter with you?' She was still smiling but there was a hard glint in her eyes. 'Back in Lisbon, we talked of divorce but you said it wasn't possible. *Now* I'm a widow so there are no longer any obstacles between us and nothing to prevent us marrying.'

Nothing except that I'd sooner have my fingernails torn out, he thought grimly. *However, I suppose I'd better not say it in quite those words.*

As it happened, Miranda didn't give him chance to say anything at all. Tucking a hand through his arm, she said, 'When James died, I tried to find you so I could let you know. I discovered you'd gone to Madrid – but after that, it was as if you'd vanished into thin air. Then I realised that you would return to England eventually so I came here to wait until you did. And now we're reunited at last.'

Sebastian was starting to feel faintly queasy. Could she seriously believe this rubbish about fate and the two of them having some unspoken but implicit understanding? One thing was plain, however. Whether she believed it or not, it was time to put the reality of the situation beyond any possible doubt.

Withdrawing his arm from her hold, he said, 'I don't wish to upset you, Miranda and I certainly don't want to be rude, but I think it best to speak plainly. Quite simply, I believe I made it clear that our affair ended when I left Lisbon and that there was never any intention of resuming it. I'm sorry if you see it differently. But for my part, that is how it was – and still is.'

She shook her head and said emphatically, 'I don't believe that. I'll *never* believe it. You haven't forgotten how it was between us. You can't have done.'

'What I may or may not remember isn't the point; though if I'm honest, I find it difficult to accept that you've wasted months waiting for me when you must have had other, much better offers.'

'Is that what troubles you? The possibility that I've had other lovers?'

'Not at all. My concern is --'

'Foolish Sebastian.' She laughed but the sound was slightly off-key. 'I haven't sought other offers – and there *certainly* couldn't be better ones. As for waiting for you ... how can you possibly imagine that I wouldn't? You know that I love you – just as you love me.'

For several incredulous seconds, words failed him. Then he said curtly, 'Next you will be saying that I actually told you that.'

'Of course you did. Often.'

'No, Miranda. I've never in my entire life said those words to *any* woman and I most assuredly did *not* say them to you. Oh – I don't deny that I was completely besotted with you. Idiotically so, in fact. But love? No.'

This time there was a very real spark of anger in both eyes and voice.

'You've changed your tune since last night. Why *is* that, I wonder?'

'Last night, as you very well know, I was taken by surprise. Also, we were in what amounted to a public place.'

'Not so public that you couldn't kiss me in a way that told me *exactly* how you feel about me – but which you are now trying to worm your way out of.'

'You aren't listening.' Sebastian could feel his patience growing thin. 'You are an extraordinarily beautiful woman and we had a very enjoyable affair which lasted longer than most. But it ran its course and ended over a year ago. It can't be rekindled and I haven't the remotest desire to try. As for the death of your husband ... that is immaterial as far as you and I are concerned. There was never any question of marriage between us – neither in Lisbon, nor now. How much clearer must I make it? I will not marry you. And though I'm sorry if that isn't --'

'There is someone else?' she demanded sharply. 'Some other woman?'

'No.' He sighed. 'I'm not contemplating marriage at all. This is about you and me – no one else. I'm simply asking you to understand what I've said and accept that it isn't going to change. There is nothing between us any more, Miranda. It was over – *permanently* over – a long time ago.'

'I see.' The thick, silky lashes veiled her eyes and there was a long silence during which he allowed himself to hope that she might give in gracefully. Then she looked up at him with a cold, hard smile and, in an ominously soft voice, said, 'It would be unwise to make an enemy of me, you know.'

Given his suspicions about the death of Silvarez, Sebastian recognised that this was probably true. She'd always had a ruthless streak and, due to her incredible looks, believed that to want was to have. He'd known her supreme self-confidence meant she wouldn't take rejection well. In truth, he doubted if she'd ever before encountered it. But he couldn't let her go on thinking he could be tempted back into her bed or that there was the remotest chance of him offering her his name.

'Enmity, Miranda? That was never – could never - be my intention. But I had to put an end to these misconceptions of yours. *Not* to do so would be inexcusable.' He decided a placating lie couldn't hurt. 'And with the past behind us, I'd hoped we might be friends.'

'*Friends*? If that is what you hoped, you are going about it very badly. I never took you for a stupid man, Sebastian ... but really, I'm starting to wonder.' She came to her feet and took a few steps away before pivoting to face him. 'So I deserve your honesty, do I?'

Her tone had acquired a cutting edge and the expression on her face worried him.

'Yes. Of course.'

'I didn't deserve it last night though, did I? Why *was* that? I'd assumed you were hiding behind a locked door to escape from foolish little girls ... but perhaps I was mistaken. Did I stumble on a tryst? Was there a lady concealed somewhere in that room?'

Sebastian's throat tightened but he gave a careless laugh and said, 'Concealed where? Under the table? Behind the curtains? That's an absurd notion – particularly since I'd been in London less than twenty-four hours. Even *I* can't move that quickly.'

'Perhaps ... perhaps not. But you were certainly very eager to get me out of the library, weren't you?' She stared at him and, with a sinking feeling, he watched her put it together. 'Ah. That's what the kiss was about, wasn't it? Getting me away from the library and back to the ballroom? But why? If there *wasn't* some silly little chit listening to every word ...' She paused and gave a harsh laugh. 'Oh you poor, pathetic man. Terrified I'd claim you'd compromised me and you'd have to marry me anyway, were you?'

Recognising that the gloves were now off with a vengeance, Sebastian shrugged.

'On present showing, that's not something that can be discounted.'

'I will *never* be that desperate!' she spat back. 'However ... you say I deserve honesty. So let's talk about what *you* deserve, shall we? Has it escaped your notice that I was prepared to forgive the insulting way you quit Lisbon with scarcely a word, fleeing as if the hounds of hell were after you? And then, nothing. Not even a note. But though you *didn't* deserve it, I decided to forgive you; to be generous – and you've flung it back in my face. And don't - don't say *that* wasn't your intention either. Your intentions don't matter a jot.' She looked at him over folded arms, venom in both eyes and voice. 'I offered you a second chance, Sebastian. Do you know how often I've done that? How many men I've considered worthy of it? None. Not one, ever ... until you. You should be on your knees in gratitude. I gave you what dukes have *begged* for. You – a man with no title of his own and heir only to a paltry viscount. What *can* I have been thinking?'

He hadn't meant to say anything. He'd meant to let her rant until all the bile was gone. Instead, he said dispassionately, 'Probably that the dukes wouldn't offer you marriage but the paltry future viscount might.'

She slapped his face so hard that his ears rang.

'Do you think there was a man in that ballroom last night who wouldn't give a *fortune* for what you have refused?'

'Not very many.' He managed an encouraging smile. 'Perhaps you should make a list and ask those at the top of it to submit bids.'

For a long, scorching moment Miranda stared at him, wild with temper. Then she said slowly, 'You will regret this.'

'No. I don't believe I will.'

'And that,' she replied, stalking past him to open the door, 'is the *second* big mistake you've made this afternoon. Now get out.'

* * *

Almost before the front door shut behind Mr Audley, Lady Silvarez was scrawling a furious summons to Mr Penhaligon. And when, some hours later, he obeyed it, she said, 'Are you still finding Sebastian Audley an inconvenience?'

He shrugged, unsure where this was coming from.

'An irritation, certainly. Why?'

'He has insulted me.' Both eyes and tone were razor-edged. 'I want him to pay for it.'

'Oh no, Miranda! If you think I'm challenging him to a duel --'

'Don't be a fool. I don't want him dead. I want him *destroyed*. And though I have an idea about how to achieve that, it will take time to arrange – meanwhile, I want you to make his life difficult and damage his social standing. It shouldn't be hard. The man's never been able to resist a challenge.'

CHAPTER SEVEN

It didn't take Olivia long to find out that Wicked Cousin Sebastian had finally appeared in society and, trapping her sister away from Mama's keen ears, she demanded details. Cassie maintained the same fiction she'd given their mother and with as little additional information as she was allowed to get away with.

Yes, she had seen Mr Audley. No, they had not been introduced. And yes, he was quite handsome; tall and elegant with blue eyes and red hair. Olivia had found the last of these disappointing. Cassie refused to wax lyrical over what precise *shade* of red because Livy frequently jumped to undesirable conclusions. Privately, however, she thought, *You wouldn't be disappointed if you'd seen it.*

The excuse of not having been introduced to Mr Audley lasted for four days. During them, though he had been present at a couple of social events, they had not been the ones attended by Cassie. He had been seen in the park, astride a powerful chestnut and rumour also spoke of a sleek town-carriage – causing a furore of speculation among the younger ladies about which of them would be the first to ride in it. But the gossip among the gentlemen which did *not* reach the ladies was of the sudden rash of would-be wagers inside the elegant surroundings of Sinclairs.

Although Sebastian had expected it he still found he had to work quite hard at appearing relaxed. Fortunately, the first few were easy to dismiss.

'Swim the length of the Serpentine,' said Algernon Dudley.

'I've already done that.'

'At the fashionable hour?'

'Of course. Otherwise, what would be the point?'

Mr Dudley thought about it and then said hopefully, 'Naked?'

'Ah.' Idly shuffling a pack of cards, Sebastian smiled slowly. 'You are suggesting a race?'

Lord Nicholas Wynstanton gave a crack of laughter.

'*A race?*' Mr Dudley narrowly avoided choking. 'No. Not at all.'

'What a pity. If you had, I might have been tempted.'

This time everyone laughed.

'Hold up a coach on Hounslow Heath,' offered Ludovic Sterne lazily.

'I've done that, too.' Sebastian glanced round and added, 'Lord Maybury will confirm, I believe.'

'Stole my grandfather's watch and returned it next day with a note of apology,' grinned his lordship. 'Didn't recognise him at the time – but then I *was* pretty foxed.'

'*I'll* give you a race,' called out Viscount Carling. 'To Brighton – on horseback.'

Sebastian sighed. 'I've done that at least three times.'

'Not with a doxy riding pillion, you haven't.'

'Actually ... I have. Against Gerry Delahaye, as I recall. Sorry.'

More laughter, followed by a brief pause as numerous gentlemen strove to think up something Mr Audley *hadn't* done.

'A carriage race?' said someone without much hope.

'Ask me again when I've acquired a racing vehicle – and if the terms are sufficiently interesting, I'll consider it.'

Another silence. Then, Richard Penhaligon said slowly, 'Letty Laroux is the newest face at the Theatre Royal and currently open to offers, I believe. Take her to a *ton* ball and pass her off as a foreign countess.'

Well, thought Sebastian. *At last.*

'I did once take a courtesan to a *levée* at Versailles,' he confessed, 'but that isn't quite the same thing as abusing a gentleman's hospitality under his own roof, is it?' He let a long pause develop and then shrugged. 'My apologies, sir. I can't do it. It would result in my losing a private wager to which I'm already committed.'

A murmur of renewed interest rippled around the room.

'What wager?' asked Mr Penhaligon, his tone openly disbelieving. 'And with whom?'

'With me,' said Lord Sarre simply. 'As to the nature of the wager – that is between Mr Audley, myself and Monsieur Delacroix's private betting-book.' Then, to Sebastian, 'That's a shame. For a moment there, I thought I'd won.'

* * *

It was at Amberley House that Lady Elinor Caversham finally caught sight of distinctive red hair and immediately pounced on her brother to bludgeon him into presenting Mr Audley to both herself and Mistress Delahaye.

Lord Nicholas made the required introduction and added, 'Satisfied now, Nell? Not that it matters. I'm for the card room.'

'This is a ball, Nick,' remarked Sebastian, amused. 'It's usual to dance at least once – if only for the look of the thing.'

'Not me. And Cassie wouldn't dance with me if I paid her.'

Cassie, who had been trying not to stare at Mr Audley's extraordinary hair or notice the elegance and exquisite fit of his gold-laced, black brocade coat, smiled and said, 'That would depend on how *much* you paid me. But you really ought to make the attempt, you know. It isn't that difficult.'

'Not to you, perhaps – but to me all the dances seem the same.'

He began to move away but paused when Nell said, 'Wait. Did you know that Rock and Adeline are expected in Town tomorrow?'

'Yes. Sarre told me.' He slanted a grin at Sebastian. 'Do you know my brother?'

'I was introduced to him once. But it was a long time ago.'

'Well, nothing escapes him. Ever. You might want to bear that in mind.'

And he wandered off.

His sister eyed Mr Audley speculatively and said, 'I'm glad to have finally met you, sir, because I'm hoping you'll tell me about your travels. Somebody said that you've been to Russia. Is it true?'

'Yes. I spent some time there a couple of years ago, mostly in St Petersburg.'

'And Venice ... and Naples ... and Vienna?'

'All of those and a good many others.'

'I'd like to hear about them. If I arrange a small informal gathering, may I count on you accepting an invitation?'

He bowed. 'I would be honoured. Thank you.'

'Good. That's settled, then. Oh – and Cassie? You haven't already given the supper-dance away, have you?'

'No. Why?'

'Well, I promised to dance it with Harry – but if he leads *you* out instead, I can trap Lord Sarre and we'll be able to make up a little party over supper.'

She floated away, leaving Sebastian looking at Cassie – or rather trying *not* to look at the *décolletage* of her shot-silk gown which had been trimmed in a way calculated to engage a man's attention and was, in any case, already just low enough to be interesting. Fixing his gaze resolutely on her face he realised that the eyes he'd expected to be brown were in fact a changeable storm-cloud grey and fringed with thick lashes a few shades darker than those cognac-coloured curls. Quite lovely, he thought. And wondered why he was surprised.

'Lady Elinor is very ... spirited,' he remarked.

'Bossy is the word you were looking for. Fortunately, her charm makes up for it.'

There was a tiny, awkward pause. Then very quietly, Sebastian said, 'I can't apologise sufficiently for what happened a few days ago. You were put in an intolerable position and it was entirely my fault.'

'Not *entirely*, perhaps,' replied Cassie judiciously. 'You weren't to know that Cecily Garfield and her hand-maidens would follow you. Or that ... that other lady. And you made it possible for me to escape undetected.'

'That was the very least I could do.' He hesitated, wanting to tell her that nothing she'd heard between himself and 'that other lady' was as it seemed, but knowing he shouldn't. He was also thanking God that Miranda didn't seem to be present this evening – and that he'd seen nothing of her at all since that unpleasant interview in Half Moon Street. Now, since he had been left in the company of Mistress Delahaye and also, as he'd remarked to Nicholas, because this was a ball, he said, 'Will you dance with me? Not now, if you are already engaged – but later perhaps?'

With some surprise, Cassie detected a faint note of uncertainty and then realised that, after what she'd overheard at Cavendish House, he probably expected her to refuse. For perhaps five seconds, she considered it. There were still three spaces on her card, this being one of them – and she could see Mr Penhaligon heading in her direction, which offered an interesting choice. As yet, she wasn't sure what she thought of Mr Audley – though having seen his current mistress, it would be stupid to begin admiring anything about him other than his extraordinary looks. However, she wasn't blind to the *cachet* of being one of the first ladies with whom he took to the floor. And it was time Mr Penhaligon learned that blowing hot and cold – if that *was* what he was doing – was not a fool-proof way of holding the attention of quite *every* lady. Consequently, she inclined her head and said, 'As it happens, I'm not engaged for this dance. Thank you.'

Sebastian might have been surprised had he not caught the direction of that quick glance and recognised the dark-haired fellow as the man who'd offered him an unsavoury wager.

Ah. Either she doesn't like him at all or she likes him very much indeed and wants to pique his interest, he thought, smiling and offering his arm. *Fortunately, I don't mind helping out.*

It was a minuet and they took their places behind Lady Elinor and Lord March. Sinking into a deep curtsy, Cassie said casually, 'Did you play chess in Russia?'

It caught him mid-bow. 'Yes. How did -- ?'

But it was too late. The dance had begun and she was stepping gracefully away in a shifting swirl of lilac and misty green.

Anything resembling proper conversation would now be impossible until the dance was over, so Sebastian confined himself to random observations and occasionally successful attempts to make her laugh. And by the time the music ended, he had already worked out the answer to the question he'd been prevented from asking. So as he led Cassie from the floor, he said, 'You correspond with Lady Sarre, don't you? That's how you know I play chess.'

'She mentioned it, yes. She says you take it seriously.'

'Which, considering all the *other* things people say of me, you find hard to believe?'

'I find it ... unexpected,' she temporised. 'Is it true?'

'Yes. I started playing as a substitute for other amusements and then grew fascinated with the complexities of the game. I've pitted my skill against many of the most respected players in Europe ... but my eventual aim was always Russia where chess is regarded with almost religious fervour.' He stopped and smiled ruefully. 'Forgive me. That was more than you really wanted to know, wasn't it?'

'Not at all. Why would you think so?'

'It's the usual reaction.' He paused. 'Am I right in thinking that Gerald Delahaye is your brother?'

'Yes.'

'Is he well?'

'Perfectly. But he prefers to spend most of his time at Minsterley Vale these days, overseeing the estate. In case you were wondering.'

He hadn't been ... but he knew what she was implying. Fortunately, Cassie removed any need to reply by saying, 'Did Gerald ever mention that there is a degree of kinship between your family and ours?'

'No. *Is* there?'

'It would seem so – though it's very remote. But the fact that it exists at *all*,' she continued, blithely, 'allows my younger sister to score points over her school friends by referring to you as her Wicked Cousin Sebastian.' Mr Audley winced. Cassie smiled and added, 'Apparently they've all been following your exploits for the last two years, which accounts for the ... over-enthusiasm ... of the younger ladies.'

This time he actually groaned, leaving her unable to suppress a tiny gurgle of laughter and the simultaneous realisation that he was dangerously easy to like.

Surveying her out of slightly narrowed eyes whilst preparing to relinquish her hand to the myopic-looking gentleman hovering a few feet away, Sebastian murmured, 'You are a very alarming young lady, Mistress Delahaye.'

She shook her head decisively but not without a hint of regret.

'You won't find anyone to agree with you about that.'

'No? But then our acquaintance began under rather unusual circumstances, didn't it?'

'That is certainly one way of describing it.' A nasty suspicion occurred to her and she said baldly, 'Please assure me you haven't told anyone about that?'

'Of course not. What do you take me for?' And when she merely raised her eyebrows, 'Ah. A question best not answered perhaps?'

'*Definitely* not,' agreed Cassie, demurely. And turning, gave her hand to Lord Pelham.

When, after the dance, his lordship escorted her towards a group of friends which included Lady Elinor, she found Mr Penhaligon lying in wait.

'Dare I hope,' he said with his usual charming smile, 'that you are not going to blight my evening by once more telling me that your card is full?'

'Far be it from me to blight anyone's evening,' replied Cassie, in a tone calculated to tell him she didn't consider that remark worth taking seriously. 'But I do have just one dance free. The next one, as it happens.'

'Then may I claim it?'

'By all means,' she began. And then, eyes widening as she looked across the room, 'Good heavens! Rockliffe's here.'

'Is that so surprising?'

'He wasn't expected until tomorrow. But of course he'll have made a special effort for Lord and Lady Amberley.'

They took their places in the set and Cassie realised that it was a gavotte, which meant that conversation would be even more limited than it had been with Mr Audley. This, she decided, was no bad thing if Mr Penhaligon was going to chat about the décor of Lord Amberley's ballroom.

But it seemed that he wasn't. During the opening bars of the music, he said, 'I met the infamous Mr Audley briefly the other evening and got the impression that he's no longer in the market for unbridled audacity. If so, it will disappoint a good many people.'

'Only those who enjoy watching someone else hazard his neck,' returned Cassie prosaically. 'And such folk will soon find a new source of entertainment.'

'Ah. Do I gather you find the gentleman amusing?'

Since she knew he must have watched her laughing at some of Mr Audley's remarks, Cassie considered this question unnecessarily disingenuous. She said lightly, 'As yet, I scarcely know him ... but he seems pleasant and rather more interesting than I'd have expected.' And suspected, from the tightening of Mr Penhaligon's expression, that her words had hit a spot she hadn't intended but which she decided not to correct.

Mr Audley, she noticed with approval, was dancing with Harry Caversham's cousin, Henrietta – now in her third season and all-too-frequently left languishing amongst the chaperones.

Well done, thought Cassie. *That was kind.*

Mr Penhaligon complimented her on her gown and asked if he would see her at the Bedford House masquerade. He was handsome and suave; he dressed beautifully and danced gracefully ... and his brother was an earl. A week ago she'd wondered if she could fall in love with him. Now, the fact that she suspected him of playing games had told her that she couldn't. And that was nothing at *all* to do with a gentleman who teased and laughed at himself and whose smile had an unfortunate tendency to make her nerve-ends tingle.

The next dance was the one before supper. Harry strolled over and said, 'Presenting myself for duty, ma'am.'

'But Lord Sarre apparently has not. Luckily, Nell has found a replacement. Look.'

'Oh God,' groaned Harry in mock despair. 'Sebastian Audley. I might have known. And she's virtually hauling him into the set.'

'One would hope,' said a lazily smooth voice from behind them, 'that the gentleman is wise enough not to put up a fight.'

'Rock!' Harry grasped the duke's hand. 'Nick said you weren't arriving until tomorrow.'

'That was the original plan. But it seemed churlish of Dominic and Rosalind to hold their ball while I was still in the country. I was sufficiently affronted to advance our departure by a day.' Rockliffe turned to Cassie and bowed over her fingers. 'That is an extremely fetching gown, Cassandra. I am at a loss to understand why you are not … besieged.'

'Papa beats them off with a stick, your Grace,' she laughed. 'How is the duchess?'

'The duchess,' he drawled in a pained tone, 'is the most maddening female in the entire universe and appears hell-bent on driving me into an early grave. In other words …' He paused, flicking open the inevitable snuff-box, '… she is flourishing.'

'I am so glad. I know she won't be appearing in society just now – but may Mama and I call? I should so like to see her.'

'And she would be delighted to receive you, I am sure.' Rockliffe glanced at Harry, 'I suppose Nicholas is in the card-room?'

'With Sarre and some others. You'll join our table for supper, of course?'

'I shall be charmed.' His Grace bowed to Cassie, humour glinting in his eyes. 'Meanwhile, I will leave you to join this set while I seek a word with Adrian.'

By the time everyone sat down to supper, Lady Elinor's 'little party' had grown large enough to fill two adjacent tables … and Sebastian unexpectedly found himself part of it. Aside from Nicholas, Adrian, Harry and Lady Elinor, the group also contained Philip Vernon and Jack Ingram with their wives, Cassandra Delahaye and her parents, the Duke of Rockliffe and later, after touring the room on her husband's arm, the Marchioness of Amberley. Some of these people, Sebastian began to realise, were related to each other. But it wasn't kinship that created the feeling of family. It was the fact that all of them clearly knew each other well and had an easy rapport that Sebastian couldn't help but envy.

No one stood on ceremony and there was a great deal of laughter and good-natured raillery. Sebastian even became the focus of some of the latter himself when, the ladies having formed their own little circle, Nicholas described the way half the gentlemen at Sinclair's had been cudgelling their brains to find a challenge Sebastian *hadn't* already accomplished.

Toying absently with his wine-glass, Rockliffe said, 'I have been remiss, Audley. How is Lord Wingham's health?'

'Continuing to improve. All in all, he has made an excellent recovery – and he'll be pleased to hear that your Grace was kind enough to ask after him.'

'I'm sure your own recent ... restraint ... will do him even *more* good. You will forgive me for asking, I am sure – but may we count on it lasting?' The Duke smiled and added gently, 'Don't misunderstand me. I found your earlier antics as entertaining as anyone else. But to everything there is a season, you know.'

'Yes, your Grace. I *do* know. At present, however, my reputation for hell-raising is proving a slight handicap.'

'You don't seem to have had much difficulty rejecting all comers, so far,' remarked Sarre. 'Rather disappointing, really.'

'Yes,' grinned Sebastian. 'It must be.'

'Correct me if I'm wrong,' said Nicholas, his tone unaccustomedly grim, 'but you'd have refused Poser Penhaligon's challenge anyway, wouldn't you – even *without* this mysterious wager you've made with Adrian?'

'Naturally. *What* did you call him?'

'A poser – and he is. Half of what he does is done purely for effect.'

'Well,' remarked Rockliffe, 'we all have our small affectations, you know.'

'Not *all* of us. And at least yours are amusing.'

'Why thank you, Nicholas. You relieve my mind.' His Grace let the laughter subside and then said, 'Do I gather you do not care for Mr Penhaligon?'

'I can't stand the fellow. And everybody knows he's waiting for dead men's shoes.'

'Is he?' asked Sebastian. 'Whose?'

'Those of his thirteen-year-old nephew ... only child of his elder brother, the Earl of Keswick,' replied Rockliffe. 'Complications at the boy's birth had two unfortunate consequences. Lady Keswick is unable to have more children and the boy himself was damaged in a way which means he is unlikely to reach adulthood.'

'So if the lad dies,' continued Nicholas, 'Penhaligon becomes Keswick's heir – and it's my impression that he's counting the days.'

'Unlike yourself, of course.'

'Me? God, no! I'm depending on you and Adeline producing an heir of your own – otherwise you'll just have to outlive me.'

'I shall do my poor best,' returned Rockliffe sweetly, 'on both counts.'

This provoked more laughter. Then, turning an enigmatic gaze on Mr Audley and returning to the original topic, Charles Delahaye asked mildly, 'May one ask what exactly was the wager that Mr Penhaligon suggested?'

'A foolish prank,' shrugged Sebastian, 'and too tedious to be worth discussing.'

Sir Charles looked thoughtful but refrained from enquiring further.

'Fair enough,' said Harry. 'Tell us about the secret wager instead. Is it in the book?'

'It is,' replied Lord Sarre. 'And don't imagine you can persuade Aristide to give you any clues. You can't.'

'We know that,' remarked Philip Vernon. 'The man's a pillar of discretion.'

'And his sister is a citadel,' laughed Harry. 'Still hunting for the key, Nick?'

Lord Nicholas coloured faintly.

'No such thing! I merely find it convenient to dine at Sinclairs occasionally.'

Hiding a smile, Adrian turned the conversation in a new direction. 'Aristide's bought a house. The object is to reduce Madeleine's involvement in the club or at the very least, to stop her living above it. Inevitably, she's fighting him tooth and nail.'

'If that's the case, he might as well give up now,' said Harry.

The ladies, meanwhile, had discovered that Althea Ingram was in an interesting condition and after surrounding her with congratulations and good wishes, were making plans to pay a collective call on the Duchess of Rockliffe. Under cover of all this, Lady Elinor leaned close to Cassie and whispered, 'He doesn't seem wicked to me. What do you think?'

There was no need to ask who 'he' was. On the other hand, reflected Cassie, Nell didn't know about the beautiful, smug-looking mistress.

'It's too early to tell. Are you really going to hold a supper party?'

'Of course.' Her ladyship's dark eyes sparkled with laughter. 'And unless Harry objects, I'm considering inviting Monsieur Delacroix and his sister. He owns the gaming club where all the gentlemen go these days. It's as respectable as White's, apparently and --'

'All *which* gentlemen?'

'Harry, Nick, Lord Sarre, Rock when he's in Town – *all* of them,' returned Nell impatiently. 'Harry says Nick is fascinated by *Mademoiselle* Delacroix which is something I wouldn't mind seeing. Of course, she and her brother might not come but --' She broke off as, around them, everyone started rising and preparing to return to the ballroom. 'I'm promised to Lord Sarre for the quadrille. I made him exchange it for the supper-dance so I could trap Mr Audley.'

Cassie had to laugh. 'Nell, you're incorrigible!'

'Nonsense. I just arrange matters so that the things I want to happen *will*. What's wrong with that?' And over her shoulder, 'You should try it some time.'

* * *

On the following day, Cassie received flowers from two gentlemen. Both were equally surprising.

First came an unostentatious posy of violets tied up with silvery-green ribbon – a neat tribute, she realised, to the gown she had worn the previous evening; and on the accompanying card were the words, *In appreciation of your company, Y.W.C.S.* It took Cassie less than a minute to work this out … but most of the morning to stop giggling every time she thought about it afterwards.

The second bouquet, two dozen pink and white roses, was delivered later in the day and in person by Mr Penhaligon. Glimpsing him in the doorway and half-tempted to doubt the evidence of her own eyes, Cassie was glad she was sitting down. Across the room, Olivia – who had been permitted to join the company because it consisted mostly of young people – stared at him in slack-jawed admiration.

As it turned out, Mr Penhaligon's actual call was much less momentous than the fact he'd paid it. He laid the roses in Cassie's hands with a graceful compliment, thanked Lady Delahaye for receiving him and awarded the other visitors with brief, amicable greetings. Then, precisely fifteen minutes after he had arrived, he bowed over Lady Delahaye's hand, invited Cassie to drive with him the following afternoon … and left.

Later, when everyone had gone, Olivia sailed into her sister's bedchamber and said dreamily, 'I think Mr Penhaligon is the best-looking gentleman I've ever seen. Is he courting you?'

'I doubt it.'

'But he brought you flowers and is to take you driving,' argued Olivia. 'And --'

'Stop.' Holding up a hand to stem the flow, Cassie said, 'Although those things *can* be an indication of courtship, one can't assume that they *are*. Firstly, not all gentlemen are looking for a

97

bride – and those who *do* intend to marry, take time making their choice.' She hesitated and then said, 'Look at it this way. When you go to buy a new hat, how many will you try on before you decide?'

'Lots. Half a dozen, at least.'

'Exactly. And that's what the gentlemen are doing. They're shopping.'

'*Shopping?*'

'Yes,' said Cassie firmly. 'One or two of them may be hoping they'll find love. But the majority are looking for the biggest dowry or the best family connections or the most biddable disposition or the prettiest face.'

'It doesn't sound very romantic,' grumbled Olivia.

'Usually it isn't – though I believe it can be.' She smiled suddenly. 'Fortunately, the gentlemen aren't the only ones who can pick and choose. You don't have to accept the first one who asks.'

'So I've noticed.'

'Quite. And it would be nice if you tried to understand why.'

CHAPTER EIGHT

While the Road Improvement Bill was passing its final reading in the House, Mr Audley disappointed his many female admirers by giving his new carriage its first airing with beautiful Anna Whitcombe sitting beside him. Truth to tell, her looks aside, he found the young lady tedious and would have much preferred the more invigorating company of Cassandra Delahaye. But he'd danced with her at the Amberley ball and sent flowers ... so here he was on a sunny April afternoon, being bored half to death by Mistress Whitcombe.

Having speculated at length on Mr Penhaligon's reasons for calling on the Delahaye household the previous afternoon, she now had her teeth into the forthcoming masquerade ball at Bedford House. Sebastian was just smothering a yawn when a familiar voice said, 'A sedate drive in the park, Mr Audley? How *respectable* of you!'

And he looked down into Miranda Silvarez's gentian gaze.

The gentleman on whose arm she was strolling allowed her to draw him to a halt – which meant that Sebastian had to pull up his team if he was not to appear rude. Inwardly groaning, he said, 'Is it? I can't imagine what makes your ladyship think so.'

'Really?' She drawled the word and followed it with an overtly sensual purr of amusement. 'I seem to recall that in Lisbon your amusements were very much more ... physical.'

'Lisbon?' Sebastian kept the rising temper out of his voice. 'It is some considerable time since I was last there – but perhaps your memory is better than my own.' He turned his gaze to her companion and said, 'Lord Harding, isn't it? I believe we met at Sinclairs one evening. And I imagine you know Mistress Whitcombe?'

'Yes, indeed.' His lordship bowed. 'Always a pleasure.'

Anna inclined her head but before she could speak, Miranda said, 'I, however, do *not* know her. Perhaps you would care to introduce us, Mr Audley?'

It was the last thing Mr Audley wanted to do – and the situation was getting worse by the minute. The carriage approaching from the opposite direction was driven by Richard Penhaligon; and sitting beside him beneath a cream lace parasol, was Cassandra Delahaye. Having formed a poor opinion of Mr Penhaligon, Sebastian thought Cassandra deserved better. More importantly, having danced the quadrille in the same set, she couldn't fail to recognise Miranda as the lady who'd pursued him to the library of Cavendish House and was therefore probably having her misconceptions reinforced.

He said curtly, 'Mistress Whitcombe – Lady Silvarez. And now I believe I must drive on before we bring the traffic to a standstill.'

Before he could put his horses in motion, however, Miranda struck again.

'A pleasure, Mistress Whitcombe. I do *so* respect your courage – out driving with a gentleman like Mr Audley and you so *very* much the type of beauty he most admires.'

This, since both ladies were almost equally fair-haired and blue-eyed, was so blatant that even a complete idiot couldn't misunderstand it. And though Anna Whitcombe's intellect was not of the highest order, she could detect a rival at twenty paces. She said icily, 'Indeed? I fear I must take your ladyship's word for that.'

In a minute or less, Penhaligon's carriage would be alongside his own and Sebastian could see himself being left with no alternative but to introduce Miranda to Cassandra. It didn't bear thinking about. He said swiftly, 'I'd get her ladyship to safety if I were you, Harding – before you both get squashed.' And wasted no time in urging his horses forward.

Thanking God there was a carriage waiting behind him, he drove on merely tipping his hat and saying briefly as he went by, 'Good afternoon, Mistress Delahaye – Penhaligon.' And then the nasty moment was behind him.

Anna Whitcombe, on the other hand, wasn't. Sebastian sighed.

* * *

After due consultation with her husband, Lady Elinor Caversham sent out invitations for a supper party to a select group of friends – and two people she'd never met at all.

Lord Sarre, preparing to depart for Kent, sent her ladyship his regrets then walked round to Sinclairs to take his leave of Aristide. Half-way along the corridor leading to the private office, Madeleine's raised voice informed him that – as so frequently happened – he was about to walk in on an argument.

'No,' snapped Madeleine. '*You* may do whatever you wish – but do not expect me to accompany you because I won't.'

'Why? You'll be acquainted with most of the other guests.'

'I'm acquainted with the *gentlemen*. I have never laid eyes on the ladies. And I very much doubt if any of *them* have the slightest wish to associate with someone as far below their social standing as myself.' *Or you either*, her tone suggested. 'Indeed, I cannot imagine why Lady Elinor sent us a card. It is quite ridiculous.'

'No, Madeleine. It's not. And it isn't an attempt to belittle us, either.'

'Since, like me, you've never met her, how do you know?'

Aristide opened his mouth to reply and then, catching sight of Lord Sarre leaning against the door-jamb, said instead, '*You* tell her. She might even listen.'

'Unlikely,' said Adrian before Madeleine could add vitriolic words to the glare that was impaling him. 'But if you think Harry Caversham would be party to anything spiteful, you're doing him an injustice.'

Knowing this was true but unwilling to say so, she shrugged irritably and said, 'There's no guarantee his wife isn't a different matter. Men are often stupid about such things.'

'Harry isn't.'

'Perhaps and perhaps not. But I will not go. And that is an end of it.'

'So you say,' sighed Aristide. 'But you still haven't said *why* you won't.

'The answer to that is pretty clear, I should think,' remarked Adrian with a provocative smile. 'It's because Nell Caversham's brother is likely to be one of the party.'

'Nonsense!' Madeleine narrowly avoided stamping her foot. 'Lord Nicholas has nothing to do with it.'

'Doesn't he?'

'No! Why should he?'

'You're the only one who can answer that,' said Adrian calmly.

'There's nothing to answer. Moreover, none of this has *anything* to do with you and I refuse to discuss it further.' Upon which note, she stalked from the room in an affronted swirl of jade green taffeta.

Aristide and Adrian looked at each other. Finally, Aristide said, 'It *is* Nicholas, of course. But it might have gone better if you hadn't said so.'

Adrian laughed. 'You think so?'

'No. Probably not. I still haven't persuaded her to so much as set foot in the house – even though it is furnished, staffed and ready for occupation. Tired as I am of the arguments, I will give her another few days to reconsider. After that, I'll have everything she owns packed up and moved to Duke Street whether she likes it or not.'

'What is it she's objecting to? Or rather, what does she *say* she's objecting to?'

'She says it's a pointless extravagance when the fact that we run a gaming establishment means we will never be socially acceptable. That translates as *I won't give people the chance to snigger behind their hands.*' He shrugged. 'She may be right. But I would like her to have a life outside the club and the chance to make friends – perhaps even to marry one day. Leaving the matter of Sinclairs aside, her birth is genteel enough. Our father was a gentleman; weak and a wastrel, of course – but presumably Mama only saw the gentleman part when she ran off with him.'

This was the first time Aristide had ever mentioned his father. Adrian said, 'Is he dead?'

'I wouldn't know. He abandoned us when I was sixteen and we never saw him again. But even through the worst times when it was a struggle to put food on the table, Mama insisted on maintaining standards. I think Madeleine sometimes forgets that … or fails to recognise she now has a chance of the life Mama would have wanted for her.'

'And this invitation from Nell Caversham could herald the start of that?'

'Perhaps. But though I can probably force her to move into the house, I can scarcely drag her kicking and screaming to a private party, can I?' Aristide turned away to pour brandy. 'It would help if I knew what is going on in her head with regard to Lord Nicholas – but of course she simply denies that *anything* is.'

'A fact which tells its own story, don't you think?' Adrian accepted the glass and took a sip. 'Call her a coward, then. Or say Nick hasn't been invited.'

'Hasn't he?'

'On the contrary, I think he most assuredly *has*. His attempts to engage Madeleine's attention haven't gone unnoticed, you know.'

'Wonderful. That makes it all *so* much better,' grumbled Aristide. Then, 'Will you be there?'

'No. I'm leaving for home first thing tomorrow morning. And before you ask – no, I can't put it off. I've already stayed longer than I intended and aside from the fact that I miss Caroline, I want to see what her grandfather is doing to our house.'

* * *

On the point of stepping into his carriage the following morning, Adrian said cheerfully, 'Six weeks left, Sebastian. Think you can do it?'

'Six and a half,' corrected Mr Audley. 'And yes. Possibly. But in the meantime, the wager is serving its turn. I've been able to dodge two further challenges in the last three days – one to scale Westminster Abbey on the outside and the other to smuggle an opera dancer into Sinclairs.' He shook his head. 'The idiot who came up with *that* one actually suggested recording it in Aristide's book, for God's sake. I sometimes wonder about certain gentlemen's mental capacity.'

'Only sometimes?' Adrian held out his hand. 'I daresay I'll be kept abreast of your doings through Caroline's correspondence with Cassie. And speaking of that lady – don't forget what I said.'

'Trifle with Mistress Delahaye and Caroline will pursue me with a hatchet,' recited Mr Audley dutifully. 'Yes. I know. Just take yourself back to Kent, will you? Absence from your lady is plainly making you tetchy.'

After Lord Sarre had taken to the road, Sebastian sat down with a pot of coffee and evaluated his progress. He'd avoided having to do anything stupid; he'd charmed and surprised his various hostesses with his impeccable manners; and he had begun paying scrupulously equal attention to several ladies. This even-handedness, he had quickly realised, was of paramount importance if he didn't want to find himself in deep water. The whole thing was as big a balancing act as travelling the length of Bond Street via the rooftops – a feat he'd accomplished three months after leaving Cambridge.

Although he was mindful of Adrian's strictures, Sebastian rather regretfully suspected that they were unnecessary – partly because Cassandra Delahaye knew something about him he wished she didn't and partly because she had too much intelligence. And in addition to that, the fact that he and her brother had once spent three hilarious months setting society by the ears was hardly likely to endear him to her Papa. In fact, of all the fathers in London, Sir Charles Delahaye was the one most likely to show him the door.

As soon as that thought occurred to him, Sebastian wished it hadn't. It was one thing to kill his reputation as a dare-devil but quite another to eradicate his basic inability not to enjoy challenging himself. *Would* Sir Charles show him the door? On balance, he suspected probably not. One didn't order one's butler to deny a caller without a damned good reason. And Sir Charles was nothing if not courteous. Not that he was particularly friendly, either – having so far shown no signs of wanting any closer acquaintance with Sebastian, distant cousin or not.

He's waiting to see if I keep up the good behaviour, thought Sebastian with a slight grimace. *And after the larks his son and I indulged in – most of which Gerry will have laid at my door – who can blame him?*

But though the temptation to call in Conduit Street lingered, he resisted it. A week went by and during it, the novelty of his return to London society began to wear off. The number of young ladies competing for his attention at every assembly he attended gradually lessened and, aside from one unpleasant encounter, he found he could enjoy a hand of cards without some young blood proposing a lunatic wager.

It had been a few days after Sarre left for Kent and Sebastian had called in at the Cocoa Tree but failed to find any of his friends. Instead, he'd found two mildly inebriated fellows – one of whom had wagered that he couldn't seduce Cecily Garfield.

His expression one of frigid disgust, Sebastian said, 'And you are?'

'Viscount Norville. Ned, to m'friends.'

'Of whom I am not one. The answer is no. Now get out of my way.'

'Don't be hasty, Audley. Girl's shrew-faced and virtually on the shelf. She'd probably be grateful. Reckon even *I* could do it. And ain't you supposed to be game for anything?'

'What I am,' snapped Sebastian cuttingly, 'is a gentleman. Now *move*.'

It was as he strode from the room that he caught sight of Richard Penhaligon watching closely from a nearby table ... and, as he passed him, could not resist saying, 'Friends of yours, Penhaligon? Or trained poodles?' And walked on without waiting for a reply.

However, with the exception of that one occasion, it seemed that the Beau Monde was beginning to accept that the twenty-eight year-old Sebastian Audley who had returned was not the twenty-two year-old who had left. It was all eminently

respectable and … dull. The only outlets for his energy that
wouldn't get him into trouble were fencing at Angelo's or a gallop
in the park at some ungodly hour of the morning while there was
no one to witness it. Sebastian found that he was starting to grit
his teeth.

It was at the end of his second wild morning ride when he
was cantering sedately toward the gates, that he realised he no
longer had the park to himself. Two riders, still some distance
away; a lady and presumably her groom – though the fellow had
dismounted and appeared to be checking his girth. Frowning,
Sebastian continued onwards at an easy pace. Then, even as he
watched, something shot between the hooves of the lady's
mount, causing it to half-rear before taking off at a gallop, its rider
clinging desperately to the reins and seemingly unable to control
the sudden flight.

Sebastian spurred Ajax forward to career across the turf in
the hope of cutting the runaway off before the inevitable
happened. From the tail of his eye, he saw that the idiot groom
had still to get back in the saddle – meanwhile the lady's horse
had bolted off the track and into the trees. Given the danger of
low branches and potholes, it would be a miracle if the woman
managed to keep her seat. Ducking and swerving at breakneck
speed as he followed her, Sebastian recognised that he'd be lucky
to keep his own.

His hat whirled away behind him and twigs slapped him in the
face. But finally, after a hair-raising minute or two, he came up
beside the fleeing horse and gripping Ajax between his knees,
managed to get close enough to reach over and grab the lady's
bridle. Then, using all his strength, he hauled her mare to a
standstill.

Still clutching the reins in a death-grip and her breath coming
in a series of shallow gasps, the girl let her head fall forward for a
moment. Then, straightening her spine, she turned … and
Sebastian found himself looking into a pair of frightened, storm-
cloud eyes. His heart, already beating forty to the dozen, lurched

up into his throat and, despite the wild ride, he turned suddenly icy cold. Cassandra.

'Th-thank you,' whispered Cassie. And aware that Mr Audley looked furious, 'I'm sorry. It – it was a squirrel, I think.'

'I'll speak to you in a minute.' Releasing her bridle, Sebastian wheeled round on the ashen-faced groom who was just catching up with them and snapped, 'What the devil were you playing at back there?'

'I – it was the girth, m'lord. It seemed to be coming loose so -_'

'And *had* it become loose?'

'Y-Yes, sir.'

'I see. Did you saddle the horse yourself?'

The man nodded miserably.

There was a long, ominous silence. Finally, Sebastian said softly, 'And Mistress Delahaye's mare? You saddled that, too?'

'Yes.' The groom had no more colour to lose. He said, 'I'm sorry, m'lord.'

'You'd have been a damned sight sorrier if the lady's girth hadn't been secure when her horse took fright.' Sebastian's tone was arctic. 'You do *know* your job, I take it?'

'Yes, sir. Such a thing's never happened before, I swear.' He looked at Cassie, hoping to find some sympathy there. 'I'm sorry, Miss – really I am.'

She opened her mouth but before she could get a word out, Sebastian said flatly, 'Don't. Do not even *think* of excusing this. Anything could have happened – and this fellow was failing completely in his duty by not being in a position to help the instant you found yourself in difficulty.' And once more addressing the groom, 'Go. I'll escort Mistress Delahaye home myself.'

Watching the man ride disconsolately away, Cassie struggled to think of something she could say that wouldn't bring Mr Audley's wrath down on her. Mr Audley, unfortunately, didn't give her the chance. Having indicated that they should start making their way back and in a voice rough with what might have been temper, he said, 'I'll accept that your mare was startled and you yourself taken by surprise. But you ought, at the very least, to have been capable of keeping her out of the trees. You realise that, if you'd come off, you might have broken every bone in your body?'

Cassie was still shaking. She hoped he couldn't see it but felt resentful that he wasn't being a bit more sympathetic. 'Yes.'

'If your horse takes fright, the first rule is to keep control of the direction. What were you *thinking*?'

'Not falling off,' she mumbled.

Sebastian's heart-beat began to slow. 'Aside from that.'

'Nothing. I don't ride very well.'

'That's an understatement.' He shoved a hand through his hair, most of which had come loose. 'For God's sake, Cassandra - you could have been killed!'

'I kn-know.'

The last of his terror-inspired anger melted away.

'Why were you riding at such an hour and with only a groom, anyway?'

'Because of Olivia. She wants to ride in the park but Mama doesn't trust her to behave unless I'm with her – hence the need to practise.'

'Olivia? This is the sister who calls me her wicked cousin?'

'Yes.' She summoned a hesitant smile. 'I haven't thanked you for the flowers.'

'Ah. You worked that out, then.'

'The initials? Yes. Of course.' She paused, then added, 'And thank you for rescuing me just now. I'm not sure what would have happened if you hadn't been there.'

'Neither am I – which accounts for any lapses in gentlemanly behaviour. My apologies for that. However, I would like to be assured that you will tell Sir Charles what happened this morning.'

'Is that really necessary?'

'Yes. It is. The squirrel making your horse bolt was bad luck and bad timing – but lack of care whilst saddling up is inexcusable.'

'Very well,' said Cassie reluctantly. 'I'll mention it to Mama and she can decide --'

Sebastian's hand came down hard on her bridle again and his eyes trapped hers. He said implacably, 'You will not merely 'mention it' as if it's of no account, Cassandra. You will tell the whole story. I shall call in Conduit Street this afternoon and, if you haven't done so, *I* will.' Glad of the excuse to do what he'd wanted to do anyway, he released her bridle and added wryly, 'Don't worry. I shan't expect you to paint me as a hero.'

She wanted to tell him he had no business using her given name — and she would have done so had he not used it in its entirety which, to her secret regret, no one else ever did. She had also become acutely aware of how splendid Mr Audley looked on horse-back. So she contented herself with saying crossly, 'If you're going to continue snarling, there's little chance of my doing that.'

A glint of amusement returned to the blue eyes.

'I don't snarl. And you give as good as you get, darling.'

That really was a step too far even if it did produce an odd little quiver in the pit of her stomach. She lifted her chin, the picture of maidenly affront.

'I'm not your darling, Mr Audley. You may address me as Mistress Delahaye.'

'Yes, ma'am,' he agreed meekly before spoiling it by adding, 'And you may address me in any way you please.'

'Don't tempt me,' muttered Cassie, watching the laughter in his eyes tugging at his mouth. 'Very well. I'll tell Papa — so there's no need for you to call.'

'Of course there is. If I don't pay a formal call, how else am I to offer to ride with you and your sister?'

For a second, words failed her. Then she said flatly, 'No. Absolutely not. No. Don't you dare do any such thing!'

As soon as the words were out of her mouth, she recognised her mistake.

'Oh dear.' Sebastian grinned. 'You really shouldn't have said that.'

* * *

Sebastian arrived in Conduit Street at the appropriate hour but, instead of being shown to the drawing room, found himself being conducted to Sir Charles' private study. He didn't know whether this was a good sign or a bad one. But as the door closed behind him, Charles rose from behind his desk and advanced, hand outstretched.

'Mr Audley,' he said pleasantly. 'Cassie has told me what occurred this morning and it seems that I am in your debt.'

Accepting the proffered hand, Sebastian shook his head slightly.

'Not at all. I'm glad I was able to help. But I hope Mistress Delahaye made it clear that my main concern – and the reason I wanted you to know of the incident – was the groom's carelessness?'

'She did. She also, with the utmost reluctance, admitted that you saved her from injury – or worse.' Charles' eyes twinkled a little. 'Gave her a scold, did you?'

'That may be how she regarded it. But the truth is that, between an unpleasant few minutes thinking she was going to come to grief followed by the discovery of how very much worse it could have been if the groom had saddled her horse as badly as he'd done his own, I ... temporarily forgot my manners.'

'Most understandable.' Charles waved his guest to a seat and went to pour wine. 'At any rate, you certainly seem to have made an impression.'

'And the groom?'

'Will remain under close supervision until I decide otherwise.' He handed Sebastian a glass, took the chair facing him and said, 'I take it that Lord Wingham's health is no longer a cause for concern?'

'I believe not. His valet sends me regular bulletins – though in a week or two, I'll probably go down to Sussex to see for myself.'

Sir Charles' brows rose slightly but he refrained from asking why Sebastian was in communication with his father's valet rather than his father himself. Instead, he said mildly, 'Do I gather that, but for today's debacle, you hadn't intended to call on Serena and me?'

Sebastian swallowed, suddenly uncomfortable.

'I … hadn't decided. In truth, I wasn't sure I'd be welcome.'

'Because of the scrapes you and Gerald indulged in seven years ago.'

It wasn't a question but Sebastian answered it anyway. 'Yes.'

'All of them being your fault, of course?'

'Not quite all. But I'm aware we must have caused you some embarrassment.'

Unexpectedly, Sir Charles laughed.

'Nothing I wasn't prepared for. And thanks to his association with you, Gerald sowed all his wild oats with remarkable speed and efficiency.'

'That sounds almost like approval, sir,' said Sebastian cautiously.

'Oh – I wouldn't go that far. But at least my son grew up a good deal quicker than you seem to have done. No.' This as Sebastian would have spoken. 'You needn't explain. I'm aware that you had your reasons – perhaps even some cause. Losing your twin brother must have been hard enough without the other consequences his death led to. However … may I ask if this visit to London marks the turning of a new leaf?'

'The leaf turned some time ago,' came the candid reply. 'Just … less publicly.'

'Good.' Charles finished his wine and stood up. 'We had best repair to the drawing room. I believe we have a number of callers today – most of whom I imagine you know. Ah. I almost forgot. Cassie says you offered to ride with herself and Olivia. She further insisted that I should on no account give you permission to do so.'

Mr Audley also rose and, smothering a laugh, said, 'Of course she did. It is something to do with her sister – though after this morning she's also a little annoyed with me.'

'Oh she's certainly annoyed with you – which, for Cassie, is very unusual,' agreed Charles calmly, leading the way from the room. 'As for Olivia … well, I'm sure you'll rise to the challenge. Ride with them by all means, if you wish.'

Seeing her father lead Mr Audley across the room to bow over Mama's hand and receive a much warmer smile than might previously have been expected, Cassie promptly forgot what she had been saying. Laughing softly, Isabel Vernon said, 'Dear me, Cassie. First, driving in the park with a gentleman who claims he *never* drives females; and now wicked Mr Audley paying a courtesy call. Whatever next?'

'He isn't wicked – just infuriating,' returned Cassie. Then, 'What do you mean – Mr Penhaligon doesn't drive females?'

'He doesn't – or very rarely. And he doesn't pay morning calls either. It's an affectation which I suspect he thinks makes him seem more interesting than he actually is. But the fact he chose to make an exception in your case is --'

'Cassie!' Olivia erupted at her sister's side, eyes wide with excitement. 'It's him, isn't it? It's Cousin Sebastian. He's gorgeous, isn't he? Almost … yes, *almost* as handsome as Mr Penhaligon.'

Fortunately, before Cassie could blurt out something she'd doubtless regret, Isabel Vernon said, 'Do you think so, Olivia? But of course, you won't have met Rockliffe or his brother yet, I suppose. And though I have a preference for dark-haired gentlemen myself, even *I* have to admit that Mr Audley's looks are extraordinary.'

'Yes. I suppose so. Cassie – will you introduce me? Please? I promise I won't --'

'Olivia.' Beckoning her younger daughter, Lady Delahaye spoke with quiet authority. 'Please re-join the other young ladies and the conversation you abandoned with Mistress Galloway. And Cassie, my love … perhaps you would get Mr Audley a cup of tea and introduce him to anyone he isn't already acquainted with?'

Olivia made a sulky withdrawal, Isabel Vernon turned away to answer a remark addressed to her by Lily Brassington … and

Cassie found herself meeting teasing blue eyes in an otherwise solemn face.

Reaching for the teapot, she said quietly, 'Please tell me you didn't ask Papa if you could ride with Livy and me.'

'I did not.'

She gave a sigh of relief and continued pouring the tea. 'Thank you.'

'I didn't ask because Sir Charles raised the subject himself and gave his blessing.'

Her hand jerked and the tea missed the cup.

'I'm so sorry,' he said, innocently. 'That was entirely my fault.' And when she glanced up from reaching for a clean cup, 'The tea, I mean. You can scarcely blame me for the other thing since it was something *you* said that piqued your father's sense of humour.'

'In other words, if I hadn't said anything, you wouldn't have raised the subject?' She shook her head. 'You don't really expect me to believe that, do you?'

'No – but it was worth a try.' He watched her add milk to the tea and, taking a small step back, said, 'Please don't give in to temptation. I'm wearing a new coat.'

Cassie gave an involuntary choke of laughter.

'You are absurd. I don't throw tea over Mama's guests.'

'Excellent.' Sebastian accepted the cup and said, 'Is the thought of riding in the park with me so *very* dreadful?'

'It isn't you that concerns me.'

'At *all*? Now that's a truly lowering thought – and I such a hell of a fellow.'

This time she managed not to laugh but failed to disguise the fact that she wanted to. As severely as she was able, she said, 'Mr Audley – will you please stop teasing or flirting or whatever it is you're doing. The problem, as you very well know, is my sister.'

'One of those over there, I presume?' An almost imperceptible movement of his head indicated the corner where four very young ladies sat whispering to each other in between sending soulful glances in his direction. 'What is the worst she can do?'

'Interrogate you about every exploit of yours that ever appeared in the scandal sheets? She has them all, you know. Embarrass us both by telling her friends – and therefore the whole of London – that Wicked Cousin Sebastian is showing interest in her almost-on-the-shelf sister? With Livy, nothing is impossible.' Cassie paused, then added aridly, 'I take it you remember Cecy Garfield and her hand-maidens at Cavendish House?'

He shuddered slightly. 'Vividly.'

'Well, Livy and her friends are worse because they're younger. And right now – in case you haven't noticed – they're heaving admiring sighs and hatching ways in which to bring themselves to your attention.'

'Heaving admiring sighs?' Sebastian looked interested. 'Are they really?'

'Yes. And stop pretending you like the idea. You don't.'

'All right. I don't.'

It occurred to Sebastian that, in only a handful of meetings, he had come to like Cassandra Delahaye much more than was probably wise – as his reaction to the morning's near-catastrophe should have told him. He also thought that she was either exaggerating her sister's annoying qualities or, having recently seen him in the company of a female she almost certainly believed was his mistress, was using Olivia as an excuse. He had offered to ride with her in order to, if not improve her horsemanship, then at least to increase her confidence and because he enjoyed her company. The younger sister was of little if any consequence as far as he was concerned. But everything else pointed to the wisdom of not allowing his acquaintance with Cassandra to deepen.

Shrugging slightly, he said, 'Very well. The choice must be yours, of course. And since you have apparently already made it, there's nothing further to say. Dare I assume I'll have the pleasure of seeing you at Lady Elinor's supper party tomorrow evening?'

CHAPTER NINE

On the evening of the Cavershams' party, Aristide made a last-ditch attempt to persuade his sister to accompany him by saying flatly, 'If this childish behaviour of yours really *is* nothing to do with Nicholas Wynstanton, you'd better prove it. My impression – and probably his, too – is that you haven't got the nerve to spend more than two minutes in the same room as him. Well?'

Madeleine stared at him in mute exasperation. Then she snapped, 'All right. All *right*! If it will stop everyone jumping to stupid conclusions, I'll come. Just don't expect me to make a habit of it.'

'I gave up expecting you to be reasonable some time ago,' he replied. 'But you *will* move into the damned house. I want to employ an assistant and your current rooms will be the most convenient place for him to work.'

Her response was the one he had learned to expect. Impaling him on a fulminating stare, she swept from the room. She still hadn't spoken a word when their carriage drew up in Mount Street.

At the same time that Aristide was berating his sister, Cassie Delahaye was doing the same thing to herself but without much success. The instant Mr Audley had given way on the previous afternoon, some perverse part of her had immediately wished he hadn't. Equally annoying was her inability, despite having Susan lay out all of her other evening gowns for inspection, to resist the lure of the lilac and green shot-silk that had inspired him to send her violets. Luckily, the violets themselves were now past their best. If they hadn't been, Cassie had the awful suspicion that she'd probably be pinning a couple of them to her bodice. And worst of all was the single, common thread running through all these things ... which ought to frighten her silly but somehow didn't.

In Mount Street, whilst waiting for their guests to arrive, Harry Caversham shook a reproving head at his wife and said, 'You're a conniving minx, Nell. I hope you've thought what you're going to do if it turns into a disaster.'

'It won't be a disaster. It will be a perfectly pleasant evening with friends.'

'That's not what I meant. I didn't think Aristide would persuade Madeleine to come so I let you talk me into keeping quiet about it. But now she *is* coming ... and Nick has no idea. I realise he may be pleased and that, even if he's not, he'll behave. But I wouldn't like to speak for Madeleine. She's got more prickles than a hedgehog.'

'Oh – stuff!' said Nell airily. 'You worry too much.'

An hour later, all but two of their guests were assembled and chatting happily over glasses of wine in the drawing room. Jack and Althea Ingram had arrived with the Marquis and Marchioness of Amberley; Philip and Isabel Vernon had brought Mr Audley; Lady Delahaye set Cassie and Harry's cousin, Henrietta down in Mount Street *en route* for her own dinner engagement at Cavendish House; and Lord Nicholas, handsome in pearl grey silk, sauntered in around the time Nell was considering sending Harry off to fetch him – possibly at gunpoint.

Cassie, who had been avoiding any possibility of a *tête à tête* with Mr Audley, sidled over to Nell and said, 'Well, Nicholas is here – but where are the gentleman from the gaming club and his sister?'

'She wasn't going to come – then she changed her mind around the time when any sane female would have been half-way through dressing. So they'll be late.'

'Does Nicholas know?'

'Of course not. I want to see his face when she --' Nell broke off, her eyes brightening as she heard sounds betokening further arrivals. 'That must be them now. Where's Harry?' And she rustled off in search of her husband.

In the space of ten seconds, Cassie suddenly foresaw what was about to happen. Nell would produce her surprise guests with a dramatic flourish, bringing the whole room to a standstill … and the unknown Frenchwoman, who hadn't wanted to come, was going to be embarrassed.

Grabbing Henrietta Leighton's hand, she said rapidly, 'In about two minutes' time, everyone's going to stop talking and stare. They mustn't. Get help. Isabel - Mr Audley – oh, anyone quick-thinking! I need to warn Nicholas.'

Although she blinked in astonishment, Mistress Leighton didn't waste time asking questions. And Cassie, gaining Lord Nicholas's side, said urgently, 'Nell's planned a surprise. She means well but it may not turn out that way.'

'What?' He looked back, half laughing and half baffled. 'Explain, please.'

'I can't. There's no time. Just turn away from the door and keep talking to me.' Then, fiercely, as he opened his mouth to speak, 'This isn't about you, Nick – so just do as I say!'

He frowned slightly but did as she asked. Beyond his shoulder, Cassie saw Nell and Harry enter the room with a fair-haired gentleman and a stunning, willowy redhead. Exactly as she'd feared, about half the guests fell silent; the rest, fortunately, continued talking with unabated determination.

'Can I look now?' whispered Nicholas; while at exactly the same moment, Lady Elinor said triumphantly, 'Lord Amberley … I believe you're acquainted with Monsieur and Mademoiselle Delacroix?'

Cassie relaxed. One could always rely on Amberley to banish awkwardness and both Philip Vernon and Mr Ingram were already moving towards them. From further cross the room, Mr Audley tossed a cheerful grin in Aristide's direction and accorded Madeleine a bow of acknowledgement, then went on with what he had been saying to Isabel.

Nicely played, thought Cassie.

Nicholas, meanwhile, simply froze, before very slowly turning around. He ignored his sister, allowed his eyes to connect briefly first with those of Lord Harry and then Aristide … and finally they settled on Madeleine.

A faint and not very convincing smile on her lips, Madeleine kept her chin at a defiant angle and her gaze on the marquis. Smiling easily, Amberley bowed over her hand, murmured some conventional pleasantry and then, drawing his wife forward in the curve of his arm, said, 'Rosalind – I'd like you to meet Mademoiselle Delacroix and her brother. Either Nell or Harry must have worked some kind of miracle in order to persuade them to join us this evening.'

'Oh?' Rosalind held out her hand, encountered cold, stiff fingers and closed her own around them before they could be withdrawn. 'It's a pleasure, Mademoiselle – though I don't believe my husband's talk of miracles. Nell's usual technique is one of simply bludgeoning us all into submission.'

The cold hand grew a little less rigid and Madeleine said, 'In that case, she has a great deal in common with my brother.'

Rosalind laughed. 'Is that true, Monsieur?'

'No. It is defamation of the worst kind.' Knowing of Lady Amberley's disability, Aristide captured her fingers and bowed over them. 'And for myself ... I am delighted to have the privilege of meeting so lovely a lady.'

'Steady, Aristide,' warned Amberley, deliberately dissolving any lingering tension, 'I'm a fair shot, you know.'

Through the ripple of male laughter, Nicholas strolled towards the newcomers. He shook hands with Aristide and then, bowing to Madeleine, said, 'This is an unexpected pleasure, Mademoiselle. Allow me to say how lovely you look this evening.'

She curtsied and, with a complete absence of expression, said, 'Thank you, my lord. You are most kind.'

Silence loomed on the horizon again and, sensing it, Isabel took measures of her own. She rapped Sebastian's wrist with her fan and said clearly, 'That's quite enough of that, Mr Audley. Philip may not shoot quite as well as Lord Amberley but I am assured that he has a very punishing Left – whatever that may be.'

Philip grinned. Sebastian, who had in fact been reciting chess terminology, gravely remarked that, in *that* case, he would behave … which left Isabel free to ask for an introduction to the newcomers.

Nell, meanwhile, bore down on Cassie.

'You told him, didn't you?'

'No. I merely made sure that not quite *everybody* stopped talking and turned to stare.'

'They wouldn't have.'

'Yes, Nell. They would. Not for very long, I admit – but long enough to make Mademoiselle uncomfortable. I assumed you wouldn't want that.'

'No, of course not. But I *did* hope Nicholas might have had some reaction.'

'He did. He just had the wit not to show it.' *And will almost certainly have something to say to Harry later, unless I miss my guess,* she thought, as Nell stalked away – apparently once more in relentless hostess-mode.

Cassie took the opportunity to look at her fellow guests. With the exception of Mr Audley who was conversing with Harry's cousin Henrietta, the other gentlemen were gathered loosely about Monsieur Delacroix, allowing the ladies to draw his sister into their own circle. Lightly-built and only a little above medium height, Aristide Delacroix was blond, blue-eyed and impeccably dressed; he was also quite good-looking, thought Cassie – and might have appeared more so had he not been in the same room as Nicholas Wynstanton and Sebastian Audley. As for Madeleine Delacroix … it was no mystery why Nicholas might want to capture her attention. She was stunning. Pale red hair, alabaster skin, eyes the colour of water running over moss and the slender, lissom body of a dancer. Some girls, reflected Cassie ruefully, were born with a whole battery of unfair advantages.

Mr Audley and Henrietta walked over to join her.

Henrietta said, 'Beautiful, isn't she?'

'Very,' agreed Cassie. And with a sideways glance at Sebastian, 'I suppose you've met the lady before?'

'Just once.'

'And?'

'And as you have both said, she's uncommonly lovely.'

Cassie sensed something he wasn't saying but couldn't think of a way to ask what it was. So instead, she said cautiously, 'Nell thinks that Nicholas has formed a *tendre* for her.'

'Yes. A common theory ... but one I've never heard Nicholas say anything to support.'

'You're suggesting we all mind our own business.' Henrietta smiled up at him, prior to moving away to join the cluster of ladies gathered around Madeleine, admiring the elegance of her bronze-green taffeta. 'And you're right. We should.'

Left temporarily alone with Sebastian and addressing the silver embroidered vest beneath the beautifully cut dark blue coat, Cassie said abruptly, 'If I was rude yesterday, I apologise. I know you only meant to be helpful.'

'That was certainly one of my motives – though not necessarily the only one.'

'Oh.' Her eyes flew to meet his but before she could say anything further, Nell was claiming everyone's attention.

'I thought,' she announced, 'that we might have a little dancing before supper – if Althea wouldn't mind playing, that is.'

Mistress Ingram blushed. 'No, really Nell – I'm sure one of the other ladies --'

'Well, I can't speak for Mademoiselle Delacroix - but none of the rest of us play nearly as well as you do, Thea. So will you? Just a gavotte and perhaps a quadrille? And it doesn't matter that one of the gentlemen must be left without a partner because Nicholas won't dance anyway.'

Minutes later Althea was seated at the harpsichord with Nicholas lounging at her side, ostensibly to turn the pages while everyone else found partners. Much to Cassie's surprise, Monsieur Delacroix bowed to her and said gravely, 'It's a breach of etiquette, since we have not yet been introduced – but I believe your father is Sir Charles Delahaye?'

'He is indeed.' Cassie smiled, curtsied and extended her hand. 'Since Nell has decided we shall not be formal this evening, I think your sister later. Meanwhile, I'm very happy to meet *you*, sir.'

Aristide's serious expression melted into a startlingly warm
smile.

'Ah. Yes. From the little Lord Sarre has told me, I thought
that I would like you.'

This was neither socially correct nor even predictable. Cassie
blushed.

The opening gavotte was followed by a quadrille which Cassie
danced with Harry – and after which Nell begged for a minuet
before supper.

'Only if someone else plays,' said Mr Ingram pleasantly. 'I'd
like to dance with my wife.'

'Oh – of course. That's only fair.' Nell glanced hopefully at
the other ladies. 'Cassie?'

'Absolutely not! When someone is listening, all my fingers
turn into thumbs.'

'Oh. Isabel, then? Henrietta? Anyone?'

'Why,' asked Sebastian, 'does it have to be one of the ladies?'

And handing Althea from the bench, he sat down himself and
launched upon a brief and lively jig. Several jaws dropped, then
toes began to tap; and taking Henrietta Leighton completely by
surprise, Philip Vernon twirled her expertly the entire length of
the room, laughing all the way.

The tune ended as quickly as it had begun and in a scattering
of appreciative applause.

'Where on earth did you learn to do that?' asked Lord Harry.

'Don't be too impressed. I play by ear and that's one of the
few tunes I mastered. As for where – Cambridge. It passed the
time when there was nobody to take me on at chess.'

Music and chess? thought Cassie. *That's not how young men
usually spend their time at university.* And then, *It sounds rather
lonely.*

'Well – vexing as it is – you can't play now,' Nell was saying
firmly. 'That would leave a lady without a partner.'

121

'I'll do it,' volunteered the Marchioness of Amberley. And seeming not to notice the mild shock her words had produced, added, 'I don't play as well as either Althea or Mr Audley, of course … but I can manage a minuet.'

Along with the rest, Madeleine watched the Marquis guide his wife to the harpsichord; she watched her ladyship sit down and run silent, searching hands over the keys without looking down at them; and the truth suddenly dawned.

Oh my God, thought Madeleine. *She's blind. That lovely, kind woman is blind – and not once in the last hour did I guess it.* Then, bitterly, *And I thought coming here to face Nicholas Wynstanton made* me *brave. What a fool I am.*

'There are conditions, by the way,' remarked Rosalind, picking out a series of chords.

'Name them,' invited Harry. 'No one's in any position to argue.'

'The married couples dance together; the remaining gentlemen choose a lady they haven't partnered before; and, since I clearly don't need a page-turner, Nicholas – go and join in. Dominic won't mind sitting this one out.'

For the first time that Nicholas could remember, he half-wanted to join in the dancing and had even briefly considered it. The last time he'd danced had been at the Pantheon with Caroline Maitland, as she'd been then. But Caroline had laughed the whole time and it had been fun. The only lady he wanted to dance with tonight wouldn't laugh. She'd think his mistakes were a deliberate ploy to make her look foolish. So he groaned and said, 'You don't know what you're asking, Rosalind – though nearly every lady here could tell you – and I don't want to spoil anyone's evening.'

'Don't be silly. You're among friends, are you not?'

'That's just the trouble. There's not an ounce of Christian charity among 'em.'

'True enough,' grinned Philip Vernon. 'Come on, Nick. We won't laugh … much.'

While this had been going on, Sebastian decided he'd been good long enough and had earned the right to have what he wanted. Since the moment Cassandra had walked in wearing that ethereal green and amethyst gown, one thought had been hammering through his brain. *If I'd sent more violets, would she have worn them?*

Offering her a mischievous grin, along with his hand, he murmured, 'If Nick's as bad as you said, he won't do it. Mademoiselle Delacroix doesn't strike me as someone who has truck with anything less than perfection.'

Cassie drew a long breath and made the ultimate sacrifice.

'So if they won't let Nicholas say no, *I'd* better dance with him.'

The twilight eyes rested on her thoughtfully.

'That would clearly be the kind thing to do. Unfortunately, I'm not feeling quite that charitable.' And he tucked her hand through his arm and held it there, causing something inside Cassie to dissolve into mindless joy.

Madeleine watched Lord Nicholas trying to elude his friends' teasing but suspected that, male pride being what it was, he'd end up doing what they wanted. It was also clear that she was going to be the one partnering him – a prospect that put her nerves in a tangle. But recalling Aristide's words about proving her indifference, she caught then held Nicholas's glance ... and waited.

Nicholas didn't know whether to trust that look or not. What he *did* know was that he wasn't going to escape ridicule, no matter what he did. So he summoned a smile and said, 'All right. I give in. Since you're all determined to see me make an ass of myself, on your own heads be it. Mademoiselle Madeleine ... will you help me indulge them?'

She smiled back, albeit coolly. 'Certainly, my lord. But perhaps we may surprise them?'

'No chance of that, I'm afraid.' Taking her hand, he led her to join the others and while Rosalind played some bars of introduction, said quietly, 'I apologise in advance for the fact that the best I can promise is not to tread on your toes. If you felt inclined to be helpful, the odd indication of Right, Left, Forward or Back wouldn't go amiss.'

The green eyes widened but she gave a single, tiny nod. And then the dance began.

Madeleine hadn't expected to enjoy it. She stayed away from Nicholas Wynstanton because he destroyed her peace of mind when she didn't. Moreover, though she rarely had the opportunity to dance, she did it well and therefore appreciated a partner of equal ability. For both reasons, treading a measure with Lord Nicholas could only be torture. And yet, it wasn't. After bumping into him when he turned right instead of left and having to catch him when he stepped forward instead of back, she took him at his word and started issuing directions. Things went better after that; and though he somehow managed to trip Lord Harry and elbow Philip Vernon under the jaw, it was fairly clear that these mishaps weren't accidental. Sitting beside his wife, Lord Amberley was responsible for a number of missed notes by whispering a running commentary which made her giggle.

When the dance ended and Madeleine made the mistake of looking up into his lordship's face, she discovered that it was brimming with laughter. Just for a second, he was so irresistibly attractive that her brain stopped functioning.

Bowing over her hand, he said, 'Well ... that wasn't so bad, was it? What do you think?'

Without warning, answering laughter welled up inside her and it required every ounce of control she had to repress it. She said, 'I think I'd prefer not to comment.'

'That,' remarked Sebastian Audley, 'is undoubtedly wise. Have you met Mistress Delahaye yet? No? Cassandra – Mademoiselle Delacroix.'

Cassie shot him a brief sideways glance, then offered her hand to Madeleine saying with a smile, 'I've been waiting all evening for an introduction – mostly for the chance to compliment you on your gown. It's beautiful.'

'As is yours,' came the polite reply. 'Maison Phanie, of course.'

Nipping this conversation in the bud, Nicholas said, 'Nell is herding everyone in to supper. If you want to talk fashion, you can do it over food. The one thing I'll say for Nell is that she keeps a good table.'

The second they moved away, Cassie paused beside Sebastian and over the odd, melting sensation that had still not gone away, said, 'I've never given you leave to use my name.'

'Give it to me now.'

'Why?'

'Because it's a lovely name and it suits you. And you might appreciate there being at least one person who doesn't shorten it.' He waited and when she said nothing, asked curiously, 'Why do you let them?'

'It's not a question of 'letting'. Everyone just does it. It's a habit.'

'Break it. God knows, anyone who was ever crass enough to call me either Seb or Bastian learned their mistake in short order.' He grinned suddenly. 'Now ... who do you want to sit with? The Amberley-Ingram-Vernons or the group currently gathering about Harry, Aristide and Mistress Leighton?' *Or better yet*, he added silently, *just me?*

Having managed to separate herself and Nicholas from the others on the pretext of going back for her fan, Madeleine paused just outside the supper room and looked him in the eye. Then, stiffening her spine, she said, 'I hope that we have now laid to rest any misconceptions you may have had regarding my attitude towards you, my lord.'

Nicholas blinked. 'I'm sorry?'

'I am referring to my reasons for generally preferring to avoid your company.'

He shook his head. 'I'm afraid you're going to have to spell it out.'

'Very well. You have given every indication of wishing to pursue me. I have attempted to make it plain that I would rather you didn't. This is not due to personal dislike or, indeed, any personal feelings at all. I would say the same to any gentleman who appeared to entertain the hopes I suspect that you do.'

'Ah.' Much of his lordship's pleasure in the last half hour evaporated. 'Well, that's certainly put me in my place, hasn't it?'

'That wasn't my intention. I only wanted to make the position clear.'

'Then let's finish the job, shall we?' Nicholas told himself that the tight feeling inside him was annoyance. 'Precisely what *are* these hopes you think I have?'

'Given the great gulf between our stations in life, I can only think of one thing.' The effort to keep both face and voice utterly dispassionate was beginning to strain her resources and she'd hoped to avoid saying what she'd have to say next. 'If you are looking for a mistress, Lord Nicholas, you should look elsewhere.'

The feeling that actually hadn't had anything at all to do with annoyance suddenly became a gust of blazing anger. Grasping her wrist, Nicholas yanked her out of sight of the other guests and immediately released her. Then, in a tone of dangerous softness reminiscent of his brother, he said, 'What the hell do you think I am, Madam? Aristide is a friend of mine and you are his sister. Even if I was in the habit of seducing respectable females – which I'm not – those two facts render you untouchable.'

Pale with shock, she absorbed the muscle beating in his jaw and eyes filled with temper. Feeling as if she had strayed into quicksand, she said, 'Then what *do* you want with me?'

'Now? Nothing. Previously? I had the idea that I would enjoy getting to know you better.' His smile was hard and the sudden fury had been replaced with frigid courtesy. 'My mistake, it seems. And now, allow me to relieve you of my unwelcome company and escort you to join the others.'

The buffet supper was a feast for the eyes as well as the palate and contained numerous unfamiliar delicacies that Madeleine would have liked to sample in order to describe them to the Gallic genius who ruled Sinclairs' kitchen. As it was, she could barely force anything past the inexplicable obstruction in her throat. While everyone ate, drank, talked and migrated from group to group, she became aware that Lord Nicholas neither came within ten feet of her nor even glanced in her direction. She tried to tell herself she'd done what was necessary and that he'd get over it; but somewhere deep down inside, she felt ashamed.

In due course, she was drawn into a circle composed solely of the married ladies. At first, the conversation was all about fashion or the latest gossip. But after a while, Lady Elinor said, 'I probably shouldn't ask and if you'd rather not talk about it you need only say … but I wondered if you'd tell us about Sinclairs, Mademoiselle. It's very provoking when one's husband spends his evenings in a place one can never go oneself.'

'Yes. I can imagine.' Madeleine summoned a smile and briefly described Sinclairs – being sure to include the fact that, aside from members of staff, no females ever entered the premises.

By the time she stopped speaking, Nell's eyes had gathered an expression that both Isabel Vernon and Althea Ingram knew spelled trouble. She said, 'The club is closed during the day, isn't it?'

'At present, yes. Why do you ask?'

'I thought … I wondered if some of us might have a private tour one afternoon.'

'Stop it, Nell,' said Isabel.

'Why?'

'You're asking Mademoiselle to break a house rule,' contributed Rosalind. 'And if *I* were her, I might suppose you'd invited me here this evening with that very thing in mind.'

'But I didn't!' Nell looked at Madeleine, her gaze slightly stricken. 'Truly, the idea only just occurred to me.'

'Of course,' murmured Madeleine.

'Don't let her off too lightly,' advised Isabel. 'The rest of us are quite accustomed to these wild starts.'

'I only asked,' grumbled Nell. 'What's so terrible about that? Don't tell me the *rest* of you aren't curious because I won't believe it. And if Mademoiselle says no, then that's the end of the matter.' She smiled invitingly at Madeleine. 'Well?'

Not unlike others before her, Madeleine felt as if she'd fallen into the path of a tidal wave. But these ladies had welcomed her in a way she'd never expected so she said slowly, 'I would have to consult with my brother, of course ... but I cannot see that it would pose much difficulty. And perhaps you would all care to call me Madeleine?'

Having no idea what his wife was plotting, Harry Caversham poured his brother-in-law a glass of port and said quietly, 'What's wrong, Nick? Annoyed I didn't warn you?'

'Should I not be?'

'Perhaps. But I've a suspicion it's more than that.'

'Indigestion,' said his lordship negligently. 'Something seems to have disagreed with me. Is there any chance of a quiet hand of cards, do you think?'

'Not tonight. Nell was adamant that the party shouldn't split in two.'

Nicholas looked at him. 'She has more torture planned?'

Harry grinned ruefully. 'I wouldn't be surprised.'

'Hell.'

When she was sure everyone had eaten and drunk their fill, Nell re-assembled her troops in the drawing-room and said, 'Who'd like to suggest a game?'

Nicholas wasn't the only guest who groaned and Jack Ingram said, 'Parlour games, Nell? Aren't we all a little old for that?'

'Speak for yourself,' retorted Philip.

'In fact, he was speaking for me as well,' remarked Lord Amberley. And when Philip opened his mouth to reply, 'Don't. Do not point out that I am the oldest person present. If games are to be the order of the day, I suspect I shall feel the weight of my years without being reminded of them.'

Since the Marquis of Amberley was thirty-seven years old and one of the handsomest men in London, his wife wasn't the only one who laughed. Lady Elinor, however, sensing an undesirable distraction, said, 'How about Charades?'

Cassie and Isabel nodded, Nicholas dropped his head in his hands and, pleasantly but with finality, Amberley said, 'No.'

'Dominic – it doesn't matter,' murmured Rosalind.

'It does.'

'Of course it does,' echoed Nell. 'I'm sorry. I didn't think.'

'Blind Man's Buff,' said Sebastian, looking with raised brows at the marquis who grinned and gave an almost imperceptible nod.

'*Yes!*' Rosalind sat up, laughing. 'None of you will stand a chance!'

'That,' remarked her husband, 'is unfortunately true. Her instincts are frightening.'

'Blind Man's Buff it is, then,' declared Harry. 'The ladies can find a blindfold while we gentlemen move the chairs. Rules? Are there any?'

'Stay in the circle,' said Nell, twisting a silk scarf into a narrow strip. 'Keep moving until the Blind Man counts to twenty, then stand still – though ducking is allowed.'

'A slightly different round, to begin,' suggested Amberley. 'I'll wager five guineas that Rosalind can identify everybody here. Any takers?'

'Only if you put a time limit on it,' said Philip. 'Otherwise I'm not wagering a groat.'

'Thirteen people to identify,' mused Harry. 'A minute each, do you think?'

'Too generous. All of us inside … seven minutes?'

'Done,' said Rosalind happily, as her husband guided her to the centre of the circle and started gently turning her. 'Place your bets, gentlemen – and get ready to pay up.'

When she stopped counting and everyone was still, Rosalind crossed to the first person she found and said, 'Jack. The only gentleman wearing hair powder.'

Mr Ingram laughed and sat down.

After that, everyone else was named with remarkable speed and efficiency.

'Bergamot scent … Cassie.'

'Philip ... too much braid on your cuffs as usual.'

'Your gown rustles delightfully, Madeleine.'

'Ah. Dominic. You may kiss me.'

'Isabel ... lemon soap.'

'Mm. Tricky. But ... yes. Mr Audley, I think.'

And so it went on, each sitting down in their turn, until Rosalind said, 'That's all thirteen. How long?'

'Six minutes fifteen seconds.' Mr Ingram put his pocket-watch away, tossed a coin to Lord Amberley and submitted to being blind-folded. 'I should have known better.'

Jack made three incorrect guesses before eventually identifying Aristide; Aristide named Henrietta on his first attempt; and Rosalind astounded everyone further by dropping into a crouch a split second before she could be touched.

From his position on the far side of the circle, Sebastian watched Cassandra trying to emulate the marchioness's tactics and lose several hairpins when she ducked too late and Philip's hand collided with her upswept curls, several of which came down to bounce against her neck. Managing to grab her, Philip proceeded to identify her as Althea Ingram.

Sebastian found this mistake incomprehensible. He was fairly sure *he* could recognise Cassandra at ten paces. If that thought was mildly alarming, the one that followed it – though no more than a logical progression – set alarm bells ringing. The storm-cloud eyes sparkled, the petal-smooth skin was flushed with laughter ... and Sebastian wanted to kiss her. Indeed, had circumstances permitted it, he realised he probably *would* have kissed her. And then, because he wasn't in the habit of deceiving himself, he acknowledged that there was no 'probably' about it. All of which added up to one simple fact. For a sensible man who was very definitely *not* looking for a bride, it was time to give this particular lady a very wide berth indeed.

The trouble was, as Sebastian knew only too well, he'd never been particularly sensible ... and he had a fatally low resistance to temptation.

130

CHAPTER TEN

On the following afternoon, Mr Penhaligon received a summons from Lady Silvarez which he had the disappointing feeling was not going to lead to the bedroom.

Coming directly to the point, she said, 'I thought we had an agreement. I asked you to provide me with an *entrée* to polite society and all you've done so far is to smuggle me in to the Cavendish ball which has achieved precisely nothing. I also asked you to disrupt Sebastian Audley's life but again, all you've done is to propose a wager and send your pets to do the same – neither of which succeeded. I don't think you're even *trying*.'

'The things you want aren't that easily accomplished,' he shrugged, hiding the fact that Norville's failure was a sore point and Audley's subsequent reaction, downright infuriating. 'Also, you didn't use Cavendish House to its best advantage.'

'What do you mean?'

'Attracting the gentlemen won't win you invitations. The way to do that is through the ladies.' He paused, letting her digest this. 'However, I do have two suitable events in mind. One is the Bedford House masquerade tomorrow evening. Such affairs are always less formal and this particular one is a full-blown costume ball. If you wish to go, I'll take you.'

She smiled. 'Excellent. And the other thing?'

'Sheridan's new play opens at the Theatre Royal on the eighth of May. My brother keeps a box at Drury Lane which he never uses so I'll make up a party of two or perhaps three couples. They, in turn, will have acquaintances who may visit during the interval – and if you're wise, you'll pay more attention to the ladies than to their husbands. For the rest, the theatre is an excellent place for being seen and I imagine on *that* night everyone who is anyone will be there.' Lifting one eyebrow, he said, 'Does this earn me a reward?'

'It might. Yes. Perhaps.' Reaching out, she brushed his lips with one fingertip until he drew it into his mouth and gently nipped it with his teeth. Then, sitting back again and favouring him with a much warmer smile than before, she said, 'We can return to that later. First, tell me what – if anything – you are doing about Mr Audley.'

'I've been considering the options.'

Quite aside from the Norville fiasco, Mr Penhaligon would enjoy throwing a few obstacles in Mr Audley's way. He was irritated by Sebastian's popularity with the ladies and the ease with which he'd been accepted by men like Rockliffe. It also irked him that, amongst the females to whom Sebastian was currently paying attention, were some of his own personal conquests – in particular, Anna Whitcombe. Admittedly, he didn't want to marry the girl himself. But until Sebastian had burst upon the scene, he'd known that – should he choose to cast his handkerchief – Anna would have been quick to pick it up. However twice recently whilst dancing with her, he'd seen her gaze combing the ballroom; and he had the annoying suspicion that he knew exactly who she was looking for.

'Audley seems bent on re-establishing his respectability. Take this private wager with Lord Sarre, for example. I don't know the precise terms but --'

'Can't you find out?'

He stared at her as if he thought her completely demented.

'Break into Delacroix's office and have my membership of Sinclairs revoked? No. I can't. And the terms are immaterial. Whatever they are, they preclude Audley indulging in his usual shenanigans. And for the rest, he's living an apparently blameless life.' Richard paused and started ticking things off on his fingers. 'He doesn't drink to excess. He plays cards but only at Sinclairs and generally with the same group of men. If he has a mistress or visits brothels, I've been unable to discover it. His dealings with married ladies are of the utmost decorum and he's never alone with the *un*married ones even for a minute. Also, as if all that wasn't enough – aside from Sarre, who's no longer in Town – his

friends are Nicholas Wynstanton and Harry Caversham. One is
the Duke of Rockliffe's brother and the other, his brother-in-law.'

Miranda waved this aside.

'What difference does that make? *Your* brother is an earl.'

'This isn't a question of rank,' said Richard edgily, 'this is
bloody Rockliffe. He is not someone any sane man would want as
an enemy.'

'Oh.' Although she still didn't appear convinced, Miranda
returned to the main point at issue. 'Well, there must be
something you can use against Audley. A man like him doesn't
just change overnight.'

'If you have suggestions, please share them. The only
alternative *I* can see is to set a deliberate trap – but every
possibility I've considered has flaws. However, if and when I think
of something fool-proof, I'll let you know.'

There was a long silence. Finally, Miranda looked at him and
said, 'Then perhaps we should work on the problem together.
Later.'

* * *

Mr Penhaligon was not the only one making plans which
included *The School For Scandal*. Nell Caversham also intended to
assemble a party – making use of Rockliffe's box since, with
Adeline's confinement due any day, he wouldn't be using it
himself. But like everyone else, her most immediate priority was
the Bedford House masquerade.

'Harry and I are going as Charles the First and Henrietta
Maria,' she told Cassie. 'How about you? I promise I won't tell
anyone.'

'A medieval lady,' replied Cassie. 'I got the idea from a
tapestry. You know the kind of thing; a pointy head-dress with a
veil and a gown with trailing sleeves.'

'That sounds pretty. Elegant, too, I should think.'

'Yes.'

Nell's brows rose. 'You don't sound very sure.'

For one very good reason, this was an understatement but
Cassie wasn't about to share that reason with Nell; so she

shrugged, made a vague remark about finishing touches ... and changed the subject.

The truth was that as soon as Cassie had tried on the undeniably lovely gown of blood-red silk, she'd discovered a serious and completely unforeseen complication. The wide, boat-shaped neckline clung to the edges of her shoulders and the sleeves fell away from her elbows to the floor in graceful folds, just as they should; but the gown was designed to follow her body in one long, sinuous line, to and beyond the gold-embroidered belt worn low on her hips. The problem, therefore, was not with the gown itself but with what could – or more pertinently could *not* – be worn beneath it.

Ignoring her maid's shock and trying to sound blasé, Cassie said, 'Oh dear. Medieval ladies can't have worn corsets, can they?'

'So it seems, Miss. But modern ladies *do*.'

'Yes. And it's completely ruining the effect.' For a long moment, she stared at her reflection in the glass before coming to a decision. 'So ... let's try it without, shall we?'

'No, Miss Cassie – indeed we will not. The very idea!'

'Quite. But we have to start somewhere – so unlace me, if you please.'

* * *

On the following evening Cassie once more stood before her mirror, viewing herself from every possible angle until she was satisfied that the red gown flowed faultlessly from shoulder to toe. Behind her, Susan continued her catalogue of scandalised objections, finishing with, 'Her ladyship will dismiss me for letting you go out like that, Miss!'

'Since we are agreed that one can't tell by looking,' returned Cassie, disguising her own inner qualms, 'Mama won't know what I'm *not* wearing unless you tell her. And you aren't going to, are you?'

Silence. That was an improvement.

She turned sideways and peered over her shoulder to where the gown dipped to a deep V between her shoulder-blades and was fastened by cross-lacing to well-below her hips. Personally, Cassie thought it looked wonderful; sleek, just a tiny bit seductive and, best of all, totally unlike her usual self. She put on the small gold mask and picked up the tall, conical head-dress with its floating gold veil. 'I can't wear this in the carriage so I'll need to take some hair pins.' And catching her maid's expression in the mirror, 'Stop sulking, Susan – and don't worry. Everything will be fine.'

Downstairs, Good Queen Bess and Francis Drake awaited her. Having approved the gown in theory but only previously having seen it laid out on Cassie's bed, Lady Delahaye gave her daughter a long, thoughtful look and then said, 'You will need to avoid dark corners and lonely antechambers, my dear. What do you think, Charles?'

'That it's a good thing I shall be with you this evening.'

Relieved, Cassie said, 'I told Rockliffe that you beat my admirers off with a stick.'

'And tonight I'm wearing a sword. You might remind them of that.'

* * *

Bedford House was full of noise and light and colour. In the first ten minutes, Cassie counted three Henry the Eighths, four pirates and five Cleopatras. She danced with a gypsy and then one of the pirates. The Romany gazed at her with blatant admiration and flirted outrageously; the lopsided cloth parrot attached to the pirate's shoulder which kept threatening to drop its beak down her neckline had her in fits of laughter. At the end of the dance, she found herself unexpectedly beset by some half-dozen gentlemen, all vying for her hand until they were ousted by a dashing Cavalier, complete with blond love-locks and she looked up into Harry Caversham's astounded gaze.

'Cassie?' he said weakly. 'God. I didn't realise.'

'That it was me?' she asked, delighted. 'Really?'

'Really. You look ... different.'

'*Everyone* looks different. That's the whole point, isn't it?'

'Yes. But that's not what I meant.' He placed her fingers on his arm and led her into the *allemande*. 'Just be careful, will you? Some of the fellows here tonight aren't quite … well, respectable.'

'I'm not worried,' she replied blithely. 'Papa is armed.'

It was during the course of the *allemande* that Cassie caught sight of a dazzling fair-haired Greek goddess with sapphires on her wrist and at her throat. She wore a white pleated sheath which left one shoulder bare and was fastened on the other with a gold brooch. Gold ribbons drew the gown in below her breasts, emphasising their perfection … and when she moved, a slit in the skirt revealed a calf, bare except for the lacing of her gold sandals. The silver-gilt hair and the provocative ensemble left Cassie in little doubt as to the lady's identity and put the words, *I'll bet she's not wearing a corset either*, into her head.

Banishing them, she smiled at Lord Harry and asked where Nell was.

'No idea,' came the wholly unconcerned reply. 'The last time I saw her, she was dancing with March – so I daresay we'll trip over her sooner or later.'

It was a further hour before Mr Audley strolled in and caused a mild furore.

His costume was that of a Russian nobleman of the previous century. The extremely full sleeves of his black silk shirt were gathered into deep, braided cuffs and, over it, a high-collared tunic, heavily embroidered with bronze and green thread reached almost to his knees where loose-fitting breeches disappeared into soft leather boots. Slung about his hips was a broad, enamelled belt, through which was thrust a long, jewelled-handled knife; and beneath a fur-edged hat, the famous Audley hair flowed untrammelled about his shoulders. He looked handsome, a little wild and very, very dangerous. Of the three ladies who glimpsed him first, two forgot to close their mouths and the third found she needed to sit down.

'You are being very naughty, Mr Audley,' said a voice near his elbow. 'One is supposed to be masked.'

He smiled lazily down at Elinor Caversham.

'There seemed little point. Since I find both wigs and hair powder equally abhorrent, no one is likely to be in any doubt of my identity, are they?'

'I suppose not.' She eyed him appreciatively. 'That is a very striking costume. Russian fashions?'

'Yes – though not for some decades.'

'I never did get the chance to ask you about your travels, did I?'

'No. You were too busy embarrassing your brother and Mademoiselle Delacroix.'

The dark eyes widened. 'I wasn't doing any such thing!'

'Perhaps not. But it's what would have happened if Mistress Delahaye hadn't taken a hand.'

Nell opened her mouth, closed it again and then said, 'Mr Audley ... are you scolding me?'

'Should I not?'

'No. Harry and Cassie have already done it.' She paused again and added unexpectedly, 'You like Cassie, don't you?'

Sebastian knew better than to answer questions like that.

'Doesn't everyone? Or at least, that's what Lord Sarre says.'

'And he's right – though that doesn't answer my question.' She sent a searching glance around as much of the room as was possible. 'I haven't found her yet – though I know she's here somewhere because I saw her father a little earlier.'

'Do you know how she'll be dressed?'

'Yes, but I promised not to tell.' Her smile brimmed with mischief. 'So – having taken me to task – are you going to make up for it by asking me to dance?'

'*Would* it make up for it?'

'It might. And it would also enable you to escape the ladies hovering a little way to your left, waiting to pounce ... assuming, that is, you *want* to escape them.'

Sebastian risked a brief glance in the direction she'd mentioned, then immediately turned back and bowed low over her hand.

'Dare I hope your ladyship will honour me?' he begged.

And, 'I thought you'd never ask,' laughed Nell.

As their dance drew to a close, Charles Fox materialised beside them. Tonight, his elaborate wig was powdered in lilac and since, as ever, his entire ensemble was utterly *outré*, he had eschewed costume in favour of a mask edged with brilliants, a heliotrope domino and a painted fan.

Smiling languidly at Sebastian, he said, 'Forgive me, sir … but I can't help but observe that you really do look quite alarmingly barbarous. Is the knife … real?'

'Real and exceedingly sharp.'

Mr Fox gave a gently theatrical shudder. 'Then I shall remove myself from its orbit. Lady Elinor … this must be my dance, surely?'

Nell grinned over her shoulder at Mr Audley and let herself be led away.

As he watched them go, Sebastian caught a glimpse of Miranda Silvarez – some distance away and dancing with the youthful Earl of Mar. Pivoting on his heel, Sebastian crossed to the far side of the ballroom and offered his hand to Anne Boleyn.

It was during the ensuing gavotte that he first caught sight of a filmy gold veil drifting from a tall, pointed head-dress. The lady wearing it had her back to him so the next thing he became aware of was a torrent of glossy curls, tumbling past white skin made visible by the plunging line of her dress and the provocative cross-lacing which drew the eye inexorably down towards her buttocks. And along the way, he could not help but notice the sinuous line of back, waist and hips … smooth, undulating and wickedly enticing.

Sebastian felt a single sharp pulse of pure lust. Inevitably, though hopefully without Mistress Boleyn noticing it, he tried to keep that golden pennant in sight, only to lose it as the dance took him in the wrong direction; and when he was once more facing the right way, he couldn't find it again. Impatience threatened to choke him until he spotted the lady – further away this time but no longer with her back to him. He had time to notice a small, gold mask and to absorb the fact that, unlike that tantalising back view, the front of her gown was quite modestly cut ... and then she spun away again, the teasing veil floating playfully behind her.

Clever lady, he thought. Then, *Who are you?* And finally, against every possible ounce of sense, his mouth dry and something shifting oddly inside his chest, *Why do I feel I should know?*

Charming as his current partner was, the dance began to seem interminable. Finally, however, the music drew to a close and he was able to extricate himself with as much grace as haste would allow – only to find his path blocked by Aphrodite. At least, Sebastian *supposed* it was Aphrodite. A goddess sprung from Classical mythology ... except that, as so often happened in those stories, *this* goddess was actually a harpy in disguise.

'Well, Sebastian.' The ripe mouth smiled but, through the mask, Miranda's eyes were hard. 'I think you at least owe me a dance, do you not?'

She could not know that she had chosen a bad time – or that, even if she hadn't, his response wouldn't have been much different. As it was, leaving aside his desire to find the lady in the red gown before she vanished, Sebastian wanted to stay as far from Miranda Silvarez as was humanly possible.

Touching the sapphire bracelet on her wrist with one light finger, he said, 'Do I owe you anything, Miranda? I thought that this settled any account between us.'

'Accounts? Dear me. You sound like a tradesman. And is one dance too much to ask?'

He wanted to say that it was. But in the hope of getting away from her without conjuring up a storm, he said, 'Later perhaps. But tell me something. Why me? What is so special about me?'

'Unless you have turned suddenly modest, that is a very stupid question.'

'It might be – except that we both know I can't offer what you want.'

'And you know what that is, do you?'

'Yes. And you could get it easily from the right man.' He looked about them. 'Take Lord Morpeth, for example. He's wealthy and old enough not to bother you long – thus leaving you rich, free and with an English title. Worth some consideration, don't you think? And now, I'm afraid you must excuse me.'

Miranda watched him go, struggling to control her temper. She decided that it would be useful to see to which lady Mr Audley paid particular attention in order to throw an obstacle in his path.

Sebastian scoured the ballroom until he finally spotted the golden veil at the centre of a trio of noisy fellows near the doors to the terrace. Then, even as he watched, the group surged outside, taking the red-clad lady with them. Frowning, Sebastian started pushing his way across the room. She might be happy, confident and perfectly capable of dealing with her enthusiastic admirers – in which case he'd simply watch for a time before asking her to dance with him. Equally, she might be tired of being jostled and prefer to be escorted back to the comparative safety of the ballroom. Either way, he intended to find out.

A brief glance along the lamp-lit terrace told him that other guests were also taking the air at the far end of it. Meanwhile, a few yards from the open doors, three young and not entirely sober fellows were arguing with each other; a highwayman, a wizard and a jester, complete with bells. Sebastian's eyes moved past them to the lady in red and the mouth-watering sight of that beautiful, lissom back. Since, however, the wizard and the Fool appeared to be indulging in a tug-of-war with its owner, he didn't stop to admire it. Striding forward, he said crisply, 'That will do, gentlemen. Give the lady a little space – and a good deal more respect.'

Taken by surprise, the pair clinging possessively to her hands, promptly let go … enabling her to unpin the ridiculous head-dress which had been knocked askew in the struggle. Then she turned around … and the ground shifted beneath Sebastian's feet when he found that the wide grey eyes behind the gold mask belonged to Cassandra Delahaye.

Cassandra? he thought, his mind unable to encompass the enormity of it. *That siren's body belongs to Cassandra? And I never noticed?* It didn't seem possible. Except that here she was, standing in front of him looking somewhat ruffled and rather relieved.

She said, 'Oh - Mr Audley. I am so sorry. This is our dance, isn't it?'

'It is indeed,' he replied, supporting the lie because it was sensible and what he wanted to do wasn't. 'I'm sure these … gentlemen … will excuse you.'

'Now wait a minute!' Merlin protested. 'Get to the back of the queue. We're ahead of you in the lists.'

'I doubt if the lady agrees with you – and I certainly do not.' Shock was being replaced by temper but Sebastian kept his tone level. 'There are plenty of other young ladies inside. Go and find them.'

'Not like this one – and we found her first,' said the Fool, his tone sullen and his voice mildly slurred. 'So bugger off, why don't you?'

Stalking forward, Sebastian snapped, 'Watch your mouth.'

'Why? No dashed business of yours, is it?'

'If you're wise, you'll leave before it becomes so.'

'Careful, Ben,' cautioned the highwayman. 'Fellow's got a damned nasty-looking knife.'

In his present mood, Sebastian reflected that his knife was the least of their worries.

'Hah!' scoffed the Fool. And grabbed Cassie's arm again.

She promptly abandoned ladylike behaviour and, unable to pull her left hand free, dropped her headgear in order to deal him a stinging slap with her right which set all the bells jingling. He let her go quickly enough then but was still stupid enough to round on her with a muffled curse instead of beating a retreat.

Having given them fair warning, Sebastian decided he'd had enough. Taking the Fool by the scruff of the neck, he hauled him away from Cassie, then released him in order to deliver a crashing blow to the jaw which sent him backwards over the low parapet to land in an ungainly and unconscious heap in the shrubbery four feet below.

In response to startled glances from further along the terrace, Sebastian made an easy gesture and called pleasantly, 'Nothing to worry about. Just a degree of over-indulgence, I fear.' Then, adjusting his sleeve and turning cold eyes on the pair left staring at him open-mouthed, 'Anyone else? No? Good. Then I suggest you remove both your idiot friend and yourselves before you annoy me further.'

Finally, they heeded the warning and shuffled away. Sebastian looked at Cassie and said, 'Well?'

'Well what?' she asked, still reeling from the visceral thrill of seeing a gentleman defend her with his fists. 'I didn't mean to come out here with them, if that's what you mean.'

'I believe I was aware of that.' Arms folded, he regarded her out of hooded eyes. The hair which cascaded down her back was drawn severely away from her face, revealing temptingly shadowed hollows at the base of her throat and the pure lines of both cheek and jaw. As for the supple blood-red gown … it clung in all the right places, making him want to trace those lovely, slender curves with his fingers. Clearing his throat, he said abruptly, 'You can't be out here alone with me. We should go back to the ballroom.'

And without thinking, Cassie said, 'But we're not *completely* alone, are we? And would a few more minutes really matter?'

This was more temptation than he'd either expected or was ready for. Telling himself that, even though he wasn't masked, *she* was, he gave way to it but retained enough sense to say, 'A few minutes, then. But a little closer to the other guests, I think. And there is a bench, if you wish to sit.'

She nodded, turned … and recoiled slightly as she stepped on her hat. Automatically, Sebastian placed a steadying hand against her back – and immediately snatched it back as if scalded.

'*Jesus!*' he breathed.

Stooping to retrieve the hat, Cassie glanced round enquiringly.

'I'm sorry. What did you say?'

'Nothing.' He dragged some air into his lungs, tried to summon some finesse ... and failed. 'Are you wearing anything at *all* under that torment of a dress?'

Her colour rose slowly while she struggled to think of what to say. In the end, she settled for, 'That is – *isn't* a question a gentleman should ask.'

'I know that. *Are* you?'

'Am I what?'

'Completely naked under that bloody dress. Or no. Don't tell me. I'm not sure I could stand the answer.'

'In which case, why did you ask? And what exactly is *wrong* with my gown?'

'Nothing – or everything, depending on your point of view.' Tossing down the fur-edged hat, he dragged a hand through his hair and tried to get a grip on his unruly tongue. 'Have you *any* idea of the risks you've been running this evening?'

'What risks? Even just now, nothing would have happened.' She stopped, then said resignedly, 'All right. So I'm not wearing a corset. Though how on earth --'

'Why not?'

'Because it spoils the line of the gown,' she replied impatiently and smoothed the silk down over ribs, waist and hips to demonstrate her point.

Sebastian shut his eyes.

By now thoroughly baffled, Cassie said, 'What is the matter with you? And how do you know what I'm not wearing? I made quite sure it wasn't at all obvious.'

'Oh God.' The blue eyes opened again. 'You really don't know, do you?'

'Know *what,* for heaven's sake? You're beginning to sound demented.'

He ignored this.

'My sweet, witless innocent ... like myself, every man who's touched you tonight knows what you're *not* wearing. And that's because we gentlemen are accustomed to encountering whalebone and buckram rather than warm, soft delicious curves. Is that clear enough for you?'

This time Cassie turned absolutely scarlet and promptly lost her head. She said tartly, 'I'm sure you are perfectly accustomed to d-delicious curves. That woman from the library – with whom I saw you conversing just the other day in the park and whose relationship with you isn't hard to guess – is here tonight. And I doubt very much if *she* is wearing a corset either!'

There was a brief appalled silence while she regretted her outburst and Sebastian tried once again to keep his tongue in check. Then, failing, he said, 'You may be right about the corset ... but you're completely wrong about the other thing.'

'Meaning what?'

'Meaning that no, the lady is not my mistress and hasn't been for some considerable time. Upon which infelicitous note, I think I should escort you back inside – before I say something else I shouldn't.'

* * *

Lady Silvarez moved away from the place, just inside the windows and half-hidden by the gentle drift of the curtains, where she'd managed to witness quite a lot of this scene; this highly informative and utterly *infuriating* scene. Then she went to find Mr Penhaligon in order to tell him that Sebastian Audley had just knocked a young man into the shrubbery, prior to spending ten minutes alone with a young lady whose name she didn't know.

Not having encountered Cassie that evening, Richard didn't know either – but that hardly mattered. Within half an hour, he'd spread the word that Mr Audley wasn't perhaps quite such a dull fellow these days after all ... and started speculation about who he'd punched and why and, most interesting of all, the identity of the lady in red.

* * *

Later that night, Sebastian sat beside an empty hearth, an untouched glass of brandy in his hand, trying to make some sense out of the jumbled thoughts and emotions that were seething inside him. He stared vacantly at the partly-played game on the chessboard which normally occupied the last hour before bed; a small ritual which tonight had lost its usual meaning. Instead, four words hammered over and over inside his head.

What am I doing?

The wager between himself and Adrian had never been more than a means to an end so winning it didn't matter. What hadn't ever occurred to him was that, whilst the game was in play, he might find himself forming an attachment. And yet that was what seemed to be happening.

At Nell Caversham's party, he'd wanted to kiss Cassandra Delahaye. That had been harmless enough. After all, there were lots of girls one might want to kiss from time to time and, so long as one didn't act on it, it meant nothing. Tonight, however, he'd glimpsed what he'd thought was an unknown lady across a ballroom and been flooded with something he could only describe as recognition, along with a species of indefinable knowledge ... to which both his mind and his body had responded in a way he'd never experienced before. The subsequent discovery that that stranger was Cassandra had sent him reeling and thrown him completely off-balance; and that, of course, had been directly responsible for him punching that young idiot when he needn't have done so. If he was honest, the whole episode scared the hell out of him and effectively stopped him asking himself the question hovering at the edges of his brain.

Abruptly, he stood up and drained the glass in one swallow.

April was nearly over. He'd been in London for four weeks and had always intended to make a brief visit to Sussex at some point to see how his father did. This, he decided, would be as good a time as any. A few days away would enable him to put things in perspective and return to town in a less muddled state of mind.

Yes. In the morning, he'd cancel his forthcoming engagements and ask Hobson to pack for a brief stay at Audley Court. Five days should do it. Two spent largely in travel and three at the Court. He could also pay Adrian a visit ... which might help more than anything else he could think of.

CHAPTER ELEVEN

While Mr Audley was driving to Sussex, Aristide finally persuaded his sister to accompany him to the house in Duke Street. Madeleine had been oddly subdued of late and though he'd so far refrained from commenting on it, Aristide suspected he knew why. But it was only sensible, while she was being less difficult than usual, to take advantage of it.

The house wasn't as large as Madeleine had feared and was furnished with the sort of spare elegance that spoke of her brother's influence. Standing in the drawing-room and looking around with a critical eye, she said, 'Was it like this when you bought it?'

'No. There was too much furniture and a great many ugly ornaments.'

He waited and when she said nothing further told her that he had engaged a housekeeper, a butler, two housemaids and a footman. He did not trouble to mention that both the butler and the footman possessed additional skills; he rather supposed that when Madeleine saw the muscles on them, she'd draw her own conclusions.

At length, since she still remained silent, he said, 'Come and see the bedchambers.'

There were four, all of them light and of good proportions. There was also a room suitably equipped to serve as an office.

'I thought,' suggested Aristide mildly, 'that you might wish to attend to some of your paperwork here rather than at the club.'

Madeleine ran her fingers over the gleaming surface of a lovely little rosewood desk and eventually said, 'Very well. Since you're determined on it, I'll live here.'

He heaved a silent sigh of relief. 'Thank you. Do you like it?'

'It's well enough, I suppose. Do you intend to live here as well?'

'Eventually, perhaps. But for now I'll *appear* to do so in order to spare you the necessity of a female companion.'

The green eyes impaled him on a withering stare.

'Continue to spare me that, Aristide. It's one battle you will *never* win.'

He nodded and wandered away to look through the window.

'Do you want to tell me what happened between you and Nicholas Wynstanton?'

Her nerves snarled but she said, 'There's nothing to tell. Why do you think there is?'

'He's changed his habits since that evening at the Cavershams. Though he still meets friends and plays in the main salon, he no longer dines upstairs.' He turned and eyed her with an air of calm enquiry. 'I thought you might know why.'

'I don't.'

'No?'

'No.' She swung away towards the fireplace. 'Lord Nicholas's habits are nothing to do with me – or you either, if it comes to that. So can we please drop the subject?'

'As you wish.' He thought for a moment. 'What answer have you given Lady Elinor about her request to see the club?'

'None – since you and I have yet to discuss it properly. Do you have any objection?'

'Not unless she and the other ladies have some idea about not telling their husbands what they're up to and expect me to do the same. For the rest, I don't see any harm in a private visit – though I don't understand their desire for it.'

'That's because you're a man and can go anywhere you want to. Ladies like these, can't. Sinclairs is the forbidden zone where their husbands are regular visitors. Of *course* they're curious.'

'Do you know who will be accompanying Lady Elinor?'

'Not definitely. But my guess would be Mistress Ingram, Lady Isabel and the Marchioness of Amberley.'

'Very well. Arrange it. Any afternoon between two and four … and though I'll be present myself, I'd prefer they also brought a gentleman with them. If there are other details, I leave them to you.'

'Good.' She strolled back into one of the bedrooms. 'You may also leave me here to look around on my own. And before you say it – yes, when I am ready to return to Sinclairs, I promise to take the damned footman with me.'

She waited until she heard the front door close behind him and even stood at the window to watch him walk up the street. Then, when she was quite sure she was alone, Madeleine skimmed down the curve of the stairs to the drawing-room and whirled round in a rare moment of pleasure she hadn't expected to feel. The house promised something she hadn't known since she was ten years old. A proper home.

That thought was almost enough to make her forget the heavy, lingering darkness caused by the knowledge that Nicholas Wynstanton had not forgiven her and probably never would. Almost … but not quite.

Resolutely telling herself she'd only got what she'd asked for, Madeleine retraced her steps to the room that would be her private office and wrote a note to Elinor Caversham.

As for moving into the house, she would do it tomorrow.

* * *

Lady Elinor received Mademoiselle's note and began her own arrangements, only to find them hitting an unexpected snag. However, since she was confident that this was merely temporary, she replied to Madeleine suggesting a day at the end of the week. Then she summoned her carriage and went off to ask Cassie to take a drive with her.

As it happened, Mistress Delahaye had spent an uncomfortable morning. Immediately after breakfast, Sir Charles had drawn her to one side and said quietly, 'I am wondering, Cassie, if you spent any time with Mr Audley at Bedford House the other evening – aside, of course, from when he escorted you in search of your mother and myself. I am also wondering if you know anything about an alleged brawl on the terrace.'

Her brain started to whirl. She didn't know why Papa was asking but could see, all too clearly, the ramifications that the truth would create. She'd have to admit allowing herself to be drawn – however unwillingly – out of the ballroom by three gentlemen with whom she wasn't acquainted but who she'd known weren't sober. Then there was the inescapable fact that it had been she, not Sebastian, who had wanted to stay outside after she'd watched him knock a fellow over the parapet. And finally there were the things that Sebastian had said to her and the equally unacceptable things she'd said to him. None of it bore thinking about.

Cowardice won.

'No, Papa. I didn't even dance with Mr Audley.' That, at least, was true. 'And I don't know anything about a – a fight. It sounds a bit unlikely though, doesn't it?'

'One would hope so.' Charles continued to regard her thoughtfully for a moment but finally said, 'Very well, my dear. There has been some talk which includes mention of a lady in a red gown. I realise that you were one of numerous ladies wearing red that evening ... but you will understand why I felt it necessary to ask.'

'Yes, Papa,' she agreed weakly. 'Of course.'

It was only then that she realised what she should have thought of in the first place. Papa might put the same questions to Mr Audley; and Cassie had the lowering feeling that Mr Audley would tell the truth.

She was grateful when Nell bore her off in the carriage and even more grateful to her when she revealed something reassuring.

Having told her friend all about the planned expedition to Sinclairs and suggested that she might like to join it, Nell said, 'Monsieur Delacroix's only stipulation is that we take a gentleman with us. And though all the husbands are happy for us to go, we ladies have agreed that we don't want it to be one of them who escorts us. My first thought was Nicholas – but he virtually bit my head off when I mentioned it. So I decided upon Mr Audley, only it turns out he's gone out of town for a few days which means I can't ask him.'

Thank goodness, thought Cassie. *Papa won't be able to ask him anything either. And with luck, by the time he returns whatever talk there has been will be forgotten.*

'Well?' demanded Nell. 'Do you want to come to Sinclairs or not? It's probably the only chance you'll get. And though you may not be very curious about the place *now*, that will change when you find yourself married to a gentleman who spends half his evenings there.'

'I don't think Mama would permit it.'

'Then don't tell her. No one else will because everyone's sworn to secrecy.'

Having told one lie today, Cassie wasn't sure she was ready for further deceit. On the other hand, joining the Sinclairs party might enable her to get to Mr Audley before Papa did. Temporising, she said, 'When will you go?'

'I've sent Madeleine a note suggesting Friday – though that may change if Mr Audley hasn't returned.' Nell grinned encouragingly. 'It will be an adventure, Cassie. So throw caution to the winds and come.'

'I'll think about it,' she said. And to herself, *As for throwing caution to the winds ... given the way I'm starting to feel about Sebastian Audley, I suspect I've already done that.*

* * *

Sebastian found his father back on his feet and filled with a new determination. As soon as the moment of welcome was behind them, he said, 'You need to learn the workings of the estate and its responsibilities, my boy. Should have started this long ago – so we've a lot of time to make up, beginning tomorrow morning.'

And that was that. Sebastian spent three very long days with scarcely a minute to himself. He rode about the estate with Hapgood, the land steward, meeting tenants who scarcely remembered the boy who had gone off to Cambridge a decade ago. He spent hours locked in the library with Hapgood and his father, poring over holdings, acreages, rents and a score of other things, all of which left his brain feeling as if it had been pummelled. And in the evening, after a dinner during which Blanche glowered silently at him across the table, he sat beside his father's hearth and was tested on the day's lessons.

He resisted none of it because he understood. It was another consequence of Lord Wingham having recently come face to face with his own mortality; but it was also a part of Sebastian's education that should have been taking place during the years he'd spent playing. He also realised that when his father died, he'd have to shoulder his new responsibilities immediately. It was a sobering thought and one he tried not to dwell on; but he put aside any idea of visiting Adrian and applied himself to the best of his ability.

In the only hour he took for himself, he sat in the family graveyard with Theodore. Even when paying the most fleeting of visits to Audley Court, he never failed to come here. In childhood, he'd come to cry and to shout at God for taking Theo away. Then, as the years passed, he'd remember times gone by; the days when he'd got Theo into trouble but always done his best to get him out of it again – or, if he couldn't, to at least take the blame. Gradually, those memories had made it easier to smile.

Today, however, he did something he rarely did. He sat on the grass beside Theo's tomb and talked. Not to the eight year-old child who'd died; but to the brother, only minutes older than himself, as if the years had kept pace with them both.

'It should be you, you know. By now, you'd know all this stuff Father and Hapgood are trying to cram into my head. You'd know all the tenants by name and which has a new child or has lost a grandfather ... and they'd smile and wave when you ride by. And the prettiest girls in the neighbourhood would be trying to catch your eye ... unless you're already married, with a beautiful wife who adores you. It should be you, Theo. Instead of which, they're stuck with me – the idiot who wasted years on things which, when it comes right down to it, never mattered a jot.'

He fell silent for a moment, pulling a single small weed from beside the headstone and turning it between his fingers.

'Here's the thing. There's a girl ... a lady. You'd like her. I was going to say that I do, too – but the truth is that it's gone way beyond that. Twice inside a week she turned me into a gibbering idiot; once by scaring the hell out of me when she nearly got herself killed and then by going to a masquerade ball in a gown that ...' He stopped , breathing a little fast. 'God. I can't even *think* about that without ... well, you know. But it isn't just lust, Theo. She makes me want the things that are meant to go with it; things I've never wanted before. Love, I suppose – though I know damn all about it. All I *do* know is that I've got this all-encompassing sense that she's mine but nobody knows it, not even her. How stupid is that?'

Tossing the weed aside, he draped his arm across the small, marble tomb.

'Every now and again, I catch myself thinking of marriage. There. That's shocked you, hasn't it? It shocks me, too. I hadn't expected it and I certainly wasn't *looking* for it ... yet now it's inescapable, even though there's no certainty that she'd have me.' He gave a brief laugh. 'She's ripped up at me a couple of times which I gather isn't like her, so that might be a good sign, I suppose. But even if she *would* have me, financially I'm not in a position to marry anyone. And if I ask Father for help, he might use the purse-strings to force me to live here at the Court ... and I can't do it. Part of the year, yes. But permanently? I can't. I just can't live in the same house as Blanche. So the only answer is to stay away from Cassandra ... except that I'm not sure I can do that either.' Sighing, he leaned his cheek against his arm. 'If you've any suggestions, brother, now would be a good time to make them.'

* * *

Having promised Lord Wingham that he'd return in four weeks' time, Sebastian arrived back in Cork Street to a small pile of invitations, among which were no less than three missives from Elinor Caversham – each one littered with more exclamation marks than the one before it. Grinning, Sebastian scribbled a brief reply and despatched it to Mount Street. Then he sauntered round to Sinclairs for a belated dinner.

As he crossed the main floor, he gradually became aware that he appeared to be the focus of a number of odd looks; some curious, some mildly disapproving and others clearly amused. It wasn't until later, when Philip Vernon joined him for a glass of port that he understood the cause.

'What's all this about you knocking seven bells out of two or three young pups at Bedford House?'

Sebastian gave a startled laugh. 'What? I did no such thing.'

'Well, it's what everyone is saying. And there's also talk of a mysterious lady in red who is supposedly at the heart of the matter. Depending on who you talk to, she either cast herself upon your chest in gratitude for your heroics or, having despatched your rivals, you damned near ravished her yourself.' Philip shrugged. 'Nick and I have been doing our best to squash it but it's tricky because saying too much makes everything worse. You know what people are like.'

Sebastian knew *exactly* what people were like. He said a shade grimly, 'Is anyone putting a name to the lady?'

'By now, they've put a dozen. Fortunately.' A pause, and then, 'Is there any truth in it?'

'Very little. Three fellows fresh out of university and unable to judge their capacity for wine were importuning a lady and one of them was manhandling her. Since he didn't heed a polite warning, I ... repeated it more forcefully. His friends picked him up and took him away and the lady thanked me and returned to the ball.'

'That's it?'

'Yes. Do you know where the rumours originated?'

'No. It could have been anyone. And it's been passed on so often now that you'll never find out how it started.' Philip grinned. 'Isabel says Nell's detailed you for escort duty tomorrow. You know that not a word of it is to pass our lips?'

'Her ladyship's note did mention it once or thrice. What I
don't understand is why, since I wasn't here, she didn't ask
Nicholas instead.'

'She did – but he refused point blank. And he spends less
time here these days.'

'Ah.'

'Quite. That's exactly what the rest of us are thinking,'
agreed Philip obscurely. 'Probably for the best though, wouldn't
you say?'

'Almost certainly, I should think.'

* * *

Mr Audley collected his charges from Mount Street the
following afternoon and discovered that there had been a belated
addition to the party. Lady Elinor's notes had told him to expect
only married ladies; herself, Isabel Vernon, Althea Ingram and
Lady Amberley. But there amongst them, looking wary and a little
strained, was Cassandra; and Sebastian, wondering how much of
the recent gossip had reached her ears, felt a knot of worry
tighten in his chest.

Inevitably, he had no opportunity to ask her. Monsieur and
Mademoiselle Delacroix greeted their guests in the foyer of
Sinclairs and the tour began with the main gaming floor. Once
they had admired the comfort and restrained elegance of the
décor and seen the private card rooms, Aristide explained the
extremely simple rules of Hazard, produced some gaming chips
and asked who would like to play. Unsurprisingly, everyone did –
including, with Madeleine's help, the Marchioness of Amberley.
In no time at all, even shy Althea Ingram was laughing with the
rest and clapping her hands when she won. Consequently, it was
quite some time before Aristide could tempt the ladies away from
the tables to the exclusive rooms upstairs where, in one of them,
Madeleine had made preparations for a lavish tea to be served.

'This is lovely,' said Nell, eyeing the array of tiny cakes and
pastries with enthusiasm. 'But you shouldn't have gone to so
much trouble. It's enough – more than enough – that you let us
come here at all.'

'It was no trouble. Gaspard, our chef, enjoys making fancies but there isn't much call for them.' Madeleine smiled. 'I was to say that if anyone wished to visit the kitchens, he would be honoured to welcome you.'

'And that,' interposed Aristide gravely, 'is not a thing he offers often. Or ever, in fact. To tell the truth, he barely tolerates *me*.'

This provoked some laughter and a number of questions about the day-to-day running of an establishment such as this and the number of staff required.

Finding herself seated next to Sebastian, Isabel Vernon said thoughtfully, 'It isn't at all what I expected. I imagined red velvet and gold cherubs, not blue brocade and mahogany. I suppose, having met Monsieur Delacroix, I ought to have known better.' She glanced sideways at him. 'I'm assuming that you are a member, Mr Audley?'

'Yes. In fact, I dined here last night – as your husband may have told you.'

'He mentioned it, yes.' She hesitated and then said quietly, 'Don't pay too much heed to the current gossip. As far as I can ascertain, the tale about the fight that apparently no one actually *saw* is circulating mostly among the gentlemen and will die down now you are back to refute it.'

'And the ladies?' he asked dryly.

'Well, that's a different matter, of course.' Mischievous amusement lit Isabel's soft brown eyes. 'The few who have heard it are madly jealous of the lady whose honour you defended – particularly if the incident ended in an embrace.'

Sebastian gave a short, sardonic laugh. 'The truth would be a disappointment, then.'

'Of course. Isn't it always?'

Cassie, meanwhile, perched on the edge of a chair with a selection of tiny cakes she wasn't sure she could swallow and attempted to converse with Althea whilst wondering how to achieve a private word with Mr Audley. Nell had monopolised him for quite ten minutes and now he was on the other side of the room, chatting with Monsieur Delacroix. So far, she'd barely exchanged two words with him. Everyone else, of course, was having a thoroughly delightful time.

As if divining her thoughts, Sebastian suddenly looked across at her, held her gaze for a long moment and gave an almost imperceptible nod. Then he turned back to the Frenchman, laughed at something that had been said and made a seemingly joking reply. Feeling marginally reassured, Cassie ate a cake and then, almost without noticing, polished off the other two.

Sebastian, meanwhile, said quietly, 'I need a few minutes private conversation with Mistress Delahaye. I'm telling you so you'll prevent anyone looking for us.'

Monsieur Delacroix looked steadily back at him.

'*Just* conversation?'

'Yes.' He hesitated and then added, 'Help me out, Aristide. Do you think I'd ask if it wasn't important?'

'No. I suppose not. Very well. When the ladies have enjoyed sufficient tea and cake, Madeleine and I will conduct them along the upper gallery for its view over the main floor and from there, down to charm Gaspard. Lag behind, then re-join us in the kitchen.'

'Thank you.'

'Unnecessary. But you might return the favour by trying to find out what Madeleine has said to offend Lord Nicholas. If it helps, you can tell him that I believe she is sorry for it.'

A little while later, Aristide gave his arm to the Marchioness of Amberley and his sister began shepherding the other ladies towards the gallery. Hoping she was doing the right thing, Cassie paused to replace her gloves, managing to drop one in the process. Mr Audley strolled forwards and smoothly retrieved it, murmuring, 'Good. Slowly, now. There will be servants coming to clear this room, so we'll make use of one of the smaller ones across the corridor. Aristide will occupy your friends for a little while.'

She nodded ... and a minute later, they were alone with the door closed behind them. Cassie let out a breath of relief and said, 'I need to talk to you.'

'I gathered that. What's wrong?'

'Papa asked if you and I had – had spent time together at Bedford House and if I knew anything about a brawl. I thought telling the truth might end with having to admit other things so I ... lied.' She swallowed and looked him in the eye. 'As soon as I'd done it, I realised that Papa might ask you the same questions and that, if he did, you might ... well, you probably would ...'

'*Not* lie?'

'Yes,' she agreed miserably. 'I wouldn't want you to think I make a habit of it – lying, I mean --'

'I don't think it.'

'You don't? Oh.' Cassie hesitated briefly. 'Is there *much* talk?'

'Some. You haven't heard any of it?'

She shook her head. 'Is it bad?'

'It's stupid and wholly inaccurate. But so far as I am aware, your name isn't featuring in it and you may rely on me to keep it that way. In truth, there'd *be* no talk if I'd sent the young fools on their way without using my fists.'

'Equally,' returned Cassie, fair-mindedly, 'if I hadn't been too polite to tell them to just go away and let me alone, neither of us would have been on the terrace at *all*.'

'True. But that still doesn't excuse subjecting a lady to uncivilised behaviour.'

'I didn't mind. Actually, I thought you were splendid.' Her colour rose a little. 'I suppose I oughtn't to have said that. But really, the only time I ever saw anything like it before was when Gerald hit Danny Colebrook for pulling my hair. And I was only ten then, so it wasn't nearly as exciting.'

Sebastian grinned. 'So I'm splendid and exciting, am I? No, no. You don't have to answer that. I suspect I'd prefer you to leave it as it stands. And now we should probably follow the others.'

'In a moment. Can you tell me what people are saying? No one else will, you see.'

'I overcame three fellows single-handedly and then claimed a kiss,' he said flippantly. And when, against all expectation, Cassie started to giggle, 'Yes – utter nonsense. But not that funny, I wouldn't have thought.'

'Yes, it is,' she gurgled. 'It's the best bit. No one is *ever* going to think it was me now.'

'Why not?'

'The k-kiss.' She dissolved afresh. 'The idea of you – or any gentleman, really – being overtaken by p-passion for *me* ...' She shook her head. 'I'm sorry. It's just too ridiculous.'

It didn't seem at all ridiculous to Sebastian and he was faintly annoyed that she thought it was. He said, 'I'm afraid you'll have to explain.'

'I already have.'

'Not in a way that makes any sense to me. Try again.'

Her expression suggested that she couldn't understand why he was missing such an obvious point. But she said slowly, 'I'm seen as a model of impeccable behaviour and perfect propriety – so everyone treats me as such. No one is ever going to suspect me of letting a gentleman take liberties. And even if by some miracle they *did* suspect it – who do they suppose is likely to want to?'

There was a long and very ominous silence. Then, 'Me,' said Sebastian simply.

Cassie's jaw dropped. '*What?*'

'I'd like to kiss you,' he repeated calmly. 'Shall I?'

She still couldn't believe he'd said it.

'Why? What I just told you ... it wasn't meant as a challenge.'

'I didn't take it as one. You're assuming that because no gentleman ever *has* kissed you, none of them has ever *wanted* to or even thought of it – but you're wrong. I've done both.'

Cassie's breath leaked away. He had narrowed the distance between them and his voice had grown low and mellow, while his eyes lingered on her mouth. It made it difficult to say she didn't believe him. It made it difficult to say anything at all.

Sebastian waited and then, closing the final space between them but still not touching her, said again, 'I want to kiss you. But I won't without your permission. May I have it?'

She didn't dare let herself think. If she did that, she'd move away from him and say no; and she didn't want to say no. She wanted to know what a kiss was like. More particularly, she wanted to know what Sebastian Audley's kiss would be like and this was probably the only chance she'd ever get. So she nodded and whispered, 'Yes.'

He smiled at her, slid one arm around her waist and lifted a hand to the nape of her neck, his thumb gently stroking her jaw. 'Thank you.'

Cassie's pulse was already racing and her eyes fluttered shut.

Sebastian bent his head and brushed her lips with his own. He felt a tiny tremor run through her and reminded himself to be careful ... to remember that she probably had very little idea of what to expect. He placed a butterfly kiss at the corner of her mouth, followed by others across her cheek and drew her a little closer. Then he returned to tease her lips with the tip of his tongue. She gasped in surprise and, taking advantage of it, he settled in to kiss her properly. She tasted of sunshine and strawberries and something else he already dimly suspected was addictive. Everything in him shouted for more but he didn't take it. Instead, he tempted and offered and asked until she was utterly pliant in his arms and her hands were around his neck, holding him to her. And then, despite telling himself it was time to stop, he allowed the kiss to deepen just a little further before very, very reluctantly drawing his mouth from hers.

The door opened and Aristide's head appeared around it. 'Damn it, Sebastian!' he hissed. 'Conversation, you said.'

Hurled without warning from languorous delight into panic, Cassie snatched her hands from Mr Audley's hair and pushed herself away from him. Sebastian's colour rose a little but he smiled reassuringly at her and, without looking at Monsieur

Delacroix, said, 'And I meant it. But there's no harm done, I believe … and that will doubtless continue to be the case.'

'I won't speak of this, if that's what you mean – but that's for the lady's sake, not yours,' snapped Aristide. 'Mistress Delahaye … allow me to escort you to the other ladies. They are drinking wine and charming my chef into giving up his secrets.'

She was still breathing too fast and staring at Sebastian out of wide, dilated eyes with absolutely no idea what to say. Realising it, he murmured, 'If it helps at all, I can apologise. But don't ask me to say I regret it. I don't.'

* * *

Later, when she was alone and able to think rationally again, Cassie decided that she didn't regret it either. That the kiss itself had been a revelation was undeniable. But better even than that had been the unexpected joy of being held in Sebastian's arms; of touching his shoulders and hair; of knowing, on some indefinable level, that this handsome, charming – if sometimes infuriating – man actually wanted her, even if only for a moment.

There was a price, of course. And in a little while, when the euphoria had faded, she would pay it. She could and *must* continue pretending to everyone, including Mr Audley himself that her feelings for him were purely platonic. There was no choice about that. But Cassie could no longer deceive herself. When Sebastian Audley was in the room, no one else existed … and when he looked at her, the world shrank to the compass of his gaze. The kiss had merely sealed her fate.

* * *

A few streets away, Sebastian moved the Black King's rook forward to threaten the White Queen's bishop. Then he spun the board round … and realised what he'd done.

Christ. A bloody stupid beginner's mistake. Haven't I made enough of those today?

He'd told her he didn't regret the kiss and that was true – though he could have done without Aristide walking in when he had. But on other levels, kissing Cassandra had made everything both better and worse. Better because he'd wanted it so badly;

161

worse because it confirmed and intensified everything he'd told Theo he felt and because Cassandra's response told him that she was far from indifferent to him. Also, although it was going to make it hellish difficult not to look for an opportunity to kiss her again, it was clear that, for her sake, he mustn't.

He knew he attracted women easily. He also knew that with that ability came equal responsibility. Until he knew what he wanted to do about this feeling he'd neither sought nor expected but which was filling up his entire being ... or, more to the point, until he knew what was *possible* ... he had no business encouraging Cassandra to form an attachment.

If he hurt her that way, Lady Sarre might as well come after him with a hatchet because nothing she could do to him would be worse than the torments he'd be inflicting on himself.

CHAPTER TWELVE

The day after the Sinclairs expedition, several ladies received identical notes of urgent appeal from the Duchess of Rockliffe. Another, slightly different one, lay beside Lord Amberley's plate at breakfast and made him laugh.

'What is it?' asked Rosalind.

'Adeline is calling out the militia – or, in real terms, us,' he replied. 'She says Rock is in dire need of an evening with his friends and that *she* is even more desperate for it than he is. Consequently, she asks that you and some other ladies will spend this evening with her in St James Square, while I mobilise the gentlemen. She feels that Rock will fall in line easily enough if he knows she has company but if he still proves recalcitrant, she suggests forcible abduction.'

When his Grace of Rockliffe realised that his house was filling up with the wives of his friends and that the friends themselves were refusing to take no for an answer, he reluctantly bowed to the inevitable. The ladies, including his heavily pregnant duchess, waved him off with a good deal of cheerful chatter ... and Lord Amberley took him to join the rest of his hurriedly assembled party for dinner at Sinclairs.

Left alone with the ladies, Adeline gave a sigh of relief and said, 'Do *all* men turn into mother hens at times like this?'

'Well, Dominic did,' admitted Rosalind judicially, 'though I suppose he had more cause than most. And it wasn't all bad. *No one is better at massaging feet.*'

'My feet have not been an issue.' Adeline stretched one out and peered down at it. 'My back, however, is another matter and I suppose you're right about husbands having their uses.' She smiled across at Althea Ingram. 'You've all this to look forward to, Thea.'

Turning a little pink, Althea said, 'I shan't mind. The baby will make it worth it.'

'It will,' agreed Serena Delahaye, 'eventually. But before that you'll likely find yourself cursing Jack to Hades and back and vowing never to go through it again. Trust me.'

Although she kept a smile on her face, Isabel Vernon did not join in the chorus of laughter. She and Philip had been married for over three years without any sign of a child and though she never spoke of it, she was starting to despair.

On the other side of the room, Nell was conducting a low-voiced interrogation.

'Oh – for heaven's sake! You and Mr Audley were gone ages yesterday, so don't tell me you weren't doing anything. You must have been.'

'We talked a little,' said Cassie, knowing her colour had risen and hoping Nell hadn't noticed. 'I asked how his father did and whether he'd visited Lord Sarre and --'

'You're lying,' accused Nell. And then, her eyes suddenly widening, 'He kissed you. Didn't he?'

'Of course he didn't. Why on earth would you think that?'

'It's written all over your face, you goose. So stop prevaricating and tell me the truth. Did he kiss you or not?'

Cassie sighed and gave up. 'Yes.'

'I knew it! Was it nice? Did you like it?'

The words 'nice' and 'like' didn't begin to describe it. Cassie had tossed and turned half the previous night, re-living those moments in Mr Audley's arms. She said disjointedly, 'It … I … yes. But you mustn't tell anyone, Nell – not even Harry. It isn't likely to happen again, after all.'

'Of course I'm not going to tell anyone. And why *shouldn't* it happen again? He likes you. I know he does because, when I asked him, he dodged the question exactly the way men always do.'

'Oh God.' Resisting the temptation to drop her head in her hands, Cassie stared at her maddeningly well-meaning friend. 'Don't *ever* do anything like that again, Nell. The truth, since you're set on having it, is that he kissed me because of something I said and because he had the opportunity. It didn't mean anything – so please stop trying to make it into something it wasn't.'

* * *

At Sinclairs, eight gentlemen enjoyed a leisurely meal along with several bottles of wine. In addition to Rockliffe, Amberley and the other husbands, the party was augmented by Mr Audley and Lord Nicholas. Everyone noticed that his lordship did not so much as glance in Madeleine Delacroix's direction when she made her usual brief, business-like appearance. Inevitably, however, the only person tactless enough to comment on it was Philip Vernon who, as soon as they had quit the dining room for one of the private card rooms, said, 'Lost interest in that direction, Nick – or just abandoned hope?'

'Neither. I merely got tired of the questions and innuendos.' Nicholas's tone barely escaped being clipped. 'I imagine Sebastian is feeling pretty much the same by now.'

'That is one way of putting it,' agreed Sebastian, breaking the seal on a pack of cards. 'Fortunately, I think my own notoriety was cast in the shade just this afternoon.'

Lord Amberley looked up from pouring wine. 'By what?'

'I believe,' drawled his Grace of Rockliffe, 'that Lord Anson's wife pushed his mistress into the Serpentine.'

Lord Harry gave a choke of laughter. '*Did* she?'

'So I hear.'

'For a fellow who, to the best of my knowledge, scarcely leaves his wife's side these days,' remarked Charles Delahaye, 'it's a mystery how you manage to remain so well-informed.'

'Yes. It must be.' Rockliffe's gaze rose from contemplation of his snuff box to encompass Mr Audley. 'On the other hand, even I cannot know quite *everything*.'

'God! If Rock hasn't guessed the lady's name yet, no one will,' laughed Philip.

Sebastian shrugged and continued shuffling the cards.

'What can I say? She was masked.'

'I am always a great admirer of discretion,' remarked Rockliffe. 'Upon which happy note, perhaps we may now play cards? And since you have all been kind enough to answer my wife's summons, I feel sure you will also accord me the first bank.'

By the time Rockliffe lost the bank to Mr Ingram, nearly all of the gentlemen were substantially out of pocket and the game broke up for a time. Seizing the opportunity when Nicholas sauntered out to stretch his legs and call for more wine, Sebastian followed him to say bluntly, 'It's not my business and I'm asking no questions. But Aristide thinks you might wish to know that his sister is repenting whatever it was she said to you.'

Nicholas looked back at him for a long moment. Then he said, 'In which case, it is up to her to tell me so, isn't it?'

'Yes. But you'll need to give her the chance.'

'I'm here, aren't I? If she wants to speak to me, she'll find a way. She's done it before, after all – and had no trouble at all saying precisely what she means. Now ... where's the damned footman?'

Knowing better than to say any more, Sebastian let Nicholas go and turned back towards the card room only to find his way blocked by Charles Delahaye.

'Sebastian ... a word, if I may.'

A small chill made its way down Sebastian's back.

'Of course.'

'I don't know whether to thank you for sparing my daughter annoyance or reprimand you for not being more discreet about it,' said Charles very quietly. 'And please do not pretend you don't know what I mean. Like most people who rarely lie, Cassie does it badly.'

'Ah.' He managed a baffled frown. 'Since as far as I know she had nothing to hide, I'm not sure why --'

'No. Neither am I. She's a sensible girl and she knows how to conduct herself. Equally, I do you the credit to assume that, aside from depositing young Mr Woolridge amongst the rhododendrons, no other impropriety occurred.'

No. I got round to that yesterday, thought Sebastian somewhat wildly.

'The reason I assume that,' continued Sir Charles inexorably, 'is because if there was any truth in the rest of this ridiculous rumour – regardless of whether or not Cassie's name was attached to it – I would expect you to have called on me by now.'

'Yes, sir. Naturally, I would have done so.'

'Good. I'm glad we understand one another.' Sir Charles held out his hand. 'You're a fool, Sebastian – though not a complete one. But next time, don't use your fists.'

Further along the corridor, Nicholas finally found a footman and ordered wine. Then, almost against his will, he hesitated for a moment, before spinning on his heel, taking the stairs to Aristide's office and striding in without knocking.

Looking up, Madeleine promptly dropped the sheaf of bills she was holding.

'Lord Nicholas,' she said weakly. 'Is – is there some problem?'

'Not as far as I'm concerned,' he replied curtly. 'But I've been led to believe that you wished to speak with me.'

Her nerves snarled into a knot and she stared at him. 'By whom?'

'Your brother, via Sebastian Audley. Well?'

She swallowed, half-unable to equate this chilly, intimidating stranger with the laughing, easy-tempered man she used to watch from the shadows of the gallery. Then, summoning her courage, she said, 'I believe I may ... owe you an apology.' She waited for a moment and when he said nothing, ploughed on. 'Although I didn't intend to insult you, it appears that I have done so.'

'You insulted me most thoroughly, madam.'

'There were things I didn't quite understand.'

'Clearly.' Nicholas folded his arms. 'If you want to apologise, perhaps you might simply do it? I'm sure you've no more wish to prolong this conversation than I have.'

Colour flooded the porcelain skin and a familiar spark appeared in her eyes. For the first time ever, he watched her control her temper and found it curiously satisfying.

'Very well. I apologise. I'm sorry. What I said to you ... I didn't mean it the way it sounded.' The words came out in a jerky rush. 'There. Will that do?'

'Well, it's hardly the most graceful apology I've ever heard,' remarked Nicholas, 'but I suppose it's better than nothing. Apology accepted.'

And with his usual careless bow, he turned and walked out – leaving Madeleine wrestling with a temptation to throw something.

* * *

With the return of Mr Audley to town and the Lady Anson scandal, the Bedford House rumour slowly died down. Lady Silvarez, however, was still determined to learn the identity of the woman in the red gown and becoming increasingly frustrated by her failure to do so.

Recalling what she'd overheard, she had expected it to be easy.

That woman from the library – with whom I saw you conversing just the other day in the park and whose relationship with you isn't hard to guess – is here tonight.

What *that* meant was that the female with Sebastian at the Bedford masquerade had also been concealed somewhere in the library of Cavendish House – and that Sebastian had known it. The knowledge made Miranda incandescent with rage. Whoever the woman was, something had been going on between them for weeks and was probably responsible for Sebastian's rejection of herself – which wasn't something she intended to either forgive or ignore. As for the rest, to the best of her recollection only two ladies were likely to have taken note of her speaking to Sebastian in the park; one was Anna Whitcombe who had been sitting beside him ... and the other was the girl Richard himself had been driving. It had to be one of them.

Omitting the things she didn't want Mr Penhaligon to know, she'd laid her theory before him and promptly had it squashed.

'Anna Whitcombe was dressed as a fairy queen,' he'd said. 'I danced with her and her wings were a bloody nuisance.'

168

'And the other girl?'

'Cassie Delahaye?' He'd stared at her and begun to laugh. 'I didn't see her at Bedford House ... but I can assure you that there is no way on this *earth* that she'd have been on the terrace, wearing a red dress but no corset and being fought over by Cyril Woolridge and his friends. It just isn't possible. In fact, it's the funniest idea I've heard in a while.'

Several times since that conversation, Miranda had cross-questioned him about the possible alternatives, always to no avail. And now it seemed Mr Penhaligon was consumed with enthusiasm for a new idea.

'The rumour lasted longer than one might expect and got bigger all the time. I don't know why we didn't think of this before. There's no need to actually *put* Audley into an awkward situation. It's enough merely to drop the odd hint of reputed scandal in a receptive ear or two and let gossip do its work. No matter how unlikely the tale, one can always count on someone embroidering it.'

Miranda nodded vaguely and continued staring into her wine.

'That's a good idea. But first, find out who that woman was.'

Richard was beginning to be exasperated by this particular obsession.

'Why? It doesn't matter. In fact, having virtually the whole of society puzzling over her identity was largely what kept the talk alive. Now – thanks to the Anson comedy – nobody is interested.'

'*I* am. I want to know her name.'

'Want away, then,' he retorted. 'You've consistently refused to tell me just what Audley did that merits this revenge quest of yours. Fine. But though I'm willing to participate in it up to a point, I draw the line at ruining any reputation other than his.'

'What makes you think *I'd* do so?'

'Why else would you want this lady's name? I don't suppose you're going to invite her to take tea with you.'

Fast losing patience with what she saw as Richard's idiotic scruples, Miranda wanted to scream and throw something – to tell him not to be so damned feeble. Instead, because unleashing her temper wouldn't get her what she wanted, she hid it behind a seductive smile and said, 'I'm just curious, that's all. Tell me you'll try.'

Tired of the entire subject and refusing, for once, to be charmed, he surveyed her over folded arms. 'And supposing that, by some miracle, I find out what no one else has been able to discover – what then?'

I'll clear the bitch from my path, was her instinctive thought. She shrugged carelessly. 'I don't know. Nothing probably.'

'Well, include this in your calculations. If the lady in red is unmarried, coupling her name with Audley's in respect of a juicy bit of gossip can only have one result. Some angry male relation is going to hold a pistol to Audley's head and demand that he does the honourable thing. I understand that you want to make the man miserable … but I suspect that the very *last* thing you want is to see him leg-shackled.' Mr Penhaligon drained his glass and stood up. 'Think about it.'

* * *

Having been given Rockliffe's permission to make use of his box at the Theatre Royal, Lady Elinor sent out invitations to the Ingrams and the Vernons … and because she was convinced that a bit of match-making couldn't hurt, to Cassie and Mr Audley. Then, when the first evenings of May turned unexpectedly balmy, she invited the same people to join Harry and herself for supper at Vauxhall before the weather broke again.

The party travelled by boat, arriving just as it was growing dark and the myriad of coloured lanterns began glowing in the trees. Sebastian glanced at Cassie … and found himself unable to look away. Her hair was piled high on her head and an amber domino covered her pale yellow gown. But it was the look of pure pleasure lighting her face that held his gaze and made something tighten in his chest.

God, he thought sourly. *How do I keep my distance when this whole place is just one great invitation to dalliance? I ought to have pleaded a previous engagement.*

Cassie, meanwhile, had decided that the best way to avoid embarrassment over The Kiss was to pretend it hadn't happened. Unfortunately, it only needed one look at Mr Audley – sinfully handsome in a black domino thrown carelessly over a coat of silver-laced dark grey silk – for her to realise that this was easier said than done. She stiffened her spine and made some inane comment about the grottos.

The party settled into one of the private booths where Harry had bespoken supper.

Cassie said, 'This is a lovely idea, Nell. I haven't been here for ages and nearly didn't manage to persuade Papa to let me come tonight. He loathes Vauxhall - says it's teeming with unseemly persons. Truthfully, I think the only thing that swayed him was that Jack and Isabel would be with us.'

Lady Elinor looked offended. 'Not me?'

'No,' laughed Cassie. 'Nor Harry nor Philip, either. Far too flighty, all three of you.'

'I object to that,' said Philip. 'I'm a model of respectability. Ask anyone.'

'Except Sir Charles, apparently.' Harry picked up a small printed leaflet from the table, then looked up, his eyes dancing. 'This says Tenducci's singing here tonight.'

'The celebrated castrato?' asked Isabel eagerly. 'I've never heard him. He's said to be quite extraordinary.'

'He's that, all right.' Philip grinned at Harry. 'Did you see that piece in *The Whisperer*? The piece about him having – you know.'

'Well, he had to explain those two children somehow, didn't he? After having been divorced on the grounds of --'

'That's enough,' interposed Mr Ingram quietly.

'You read *The Whisperer* as well, do you Jack?' asked Harry innocently.

'No. I don't. But I know the sort of thing they print and can be fairly sure it isn't a suitable topic of conversation in mixed company.'

'The most entertaining things never are,' complained Nell. 'I don't see why men should have all the fun.'

'If it's any consolation,' offered Sebastian, 'I'm feeling equally left out.'

'Tell you later,' promised Harry. 'And Jack's right. *The Whisperer* is a wickedly witty scandal sheet which doesn't hold back from printing names. Come to think of it, I'm surprised you haven't come across it since you've --'

'Oh look!' cut in Cassie, brightly. 'A fellow on stilts! How on earth do you suppose they get up there to begin with?'

Harry looked mildly startled but took the interruption in good part. Sebastian turned a long, thoughtful look on Cassie and, as soon as the opportunity presented itself, said softly, 'Don't tell me. *The Whisperer* features in your sister's extensive collection?'

'It *is* my sister's collection,' she replied. 'With all mentions of you marked up in red. That's why I had to stop Harry. *He* might have seen some of those pieces – but I doubt if Isabel or Jack or Thea ever has.'

'Ah. That bad, were they?'

'I don't know because I haven't read them. But I doubt they were worse than some of the things sharing the page with them. If Mama only knew what Livy reads she'd have a fit.'

Over glasses of wine, the conversation turned to *The School for Scandal* and an amicable wrangle about whether or not it could possibly outshine *The Rivals*. Then, in her usual fashion, Lady Elinor insisted on a dance before supper and the entire party decamped for the Rotunda to make a set up for the quadrille.

Supper was a cheerful, laughing affair that Sebastian was beginning to recognise as typical of a Caversham gathering. No one gave more than a nod to formality; and everyone interrupting each other with teasing remarks regularly sent the talk shooting off in a new direction – which was why Sebastian wasn't sure how the topic suddenly became the Earl and Countess of Sarre.

'There was something very odd about that,' remarked Nell. 'Rock put it about that they married at the Priors but I have my doubts. One *might* suspect they'd eloped – except why would they need to? Also, before that evening at the Pantheon, Caroline and Lord Sarre were barely acquainted ... then, in no time at all, they were married.' She looked enquiringly at Cassie. 'You know her better than me. What do you think?'

'All I know is that Caroline is blissfully happy,' responded Cassie, shrugging. 'So how it came about doesn't really matter, does it?'

'The girl was an heiress, wasn't she?' asked Philip. 'That might have had something to do with it.'

'Adrian did not marry for money.' His tone pleasant but very firm, Sebastian looked up from his wine-glass. 'And he is as ... blissfully happy ... as his lady.'

'A love-match?' Harry raised his own glass. 'Here's to it, then.'

Elbows resting reprehensibly on the table, Nell leaned her chin in her palms and said dreamily, 'In that case, I like my own theory best.'

'And what is that?' asked Isabel, smiling.

'I think Lord Sarre fell hopelessly in love and proposed — but Caroline rejected him.'

'Why on earth would she do that?' objected Philip. 'Sarre isn't exactly a gargoyle — and an earl, to boot.'

'She thought he only wanted her for her money,' pronounced Nell. 'Naturally, Lord Sarre was distraught.'

'Naturally,' agreed Cassie, laughing. 'So what did he do?'

'He abducted her.'

This triumphant declaration was greeted with a chorus of groans into which Nell said defensively, 'Well, he could have. Only think how romantic!'

'Abduction isn't romantic, Nell,' said Jack. 'It's about force. No man who truly cared for a lady would contemplate it ... and Sarre is a gentleman.'

'But isn't that what makes the difference?' mused Cassie. 'I should imagine that being abducted by the *right* gentleman might be very romantic.'

'Twaddle,' said Harry. 'Jack's right. Sarre isn't such a loose screw.'

'Lord and Lady Sarre aside,' said Isabel thoughtfully, 'I agree with Cassie. I wouldn't have minded being abducted by Philip.'

'Nor I by Jack,' confessed Althea shyly.

'That makes three of us, then,' grinned Nell. 'So what do you say to that, Harry?'

He laughed, stood up and pulled her to her feet with him.

'I say I'll abduct you as far as the Azalea Walk, my lady. Romantic enough for you?'

She dimpled at him. 'It will do ... for now.'

Since Isabel and Althea expressed a desire to listen to Signor Tenducci, Mr Ingram volunteered to accompany them. Meanwhile, the rest of the party decided to pass the hour before the fireworks were due to begin by strolling about the gardens. Reminding himself to be sensible, Sebastian left Philip to take Cassie's arm while he himself was drawn into conversation with Harry and Nell. Then her ladyship announced that she and Cassie would enjoy a gossip while the gentlemen talked amongst themselves, 'Probably,' she added naughtily, 'about things unsuitable for female ears.'

Having a fair idea what Nell wanted to gossip about, Cassie wasn't surprised when her ladyship murmured mischievously, 'I can guess who *you'd* like to be abducted by.'

'Stop it, Nell. Your imagination is running away with you again.'

'And yours isn't?' She glanced over her shoulder, aware that the gentlemen had paused to greet one of Philip's acquaintances. 'You might at least admit that he's desperately good-looking. That hair of his is extraordinary! *Such* a good thing he doesn't like powder. Think what we'd all be missing.'

Cassie couldn't help laughing. 'You really are outrageous, you know. It's a good job Harry can't hear you rhapsodising about another man's hair.'

'Harry is a darling and knows perfectly well he has nothing to fear. Just because one is happily married doesn't mean one goes blind. Also --'

'Dear me – Lady Elinor, is it not?' The musical voice interrupted Nell's words and pulled her attention to its owner; a silver-fair beauty in blue, accompanied by Algernon Dudley. 'How pleasant to see you again.'

Cassie encountered gleaming blue eyes and the air evaporated in her lungs.

Nell's brows rose and she said coolly, 'Forgive me. If we have met before, I'm afraid I don't recall it.'

'Hardly surprising. Bedford House was *such* a crush, was it not?' Waving her fan in the direction of her escort, 'I'm Miranda Silvarez. And you know Mr Dudley, of course.'

Barely – but as much as I want to, thought Nell, dropping the merest suggestion of a curtsy while, scarlet with embarrassment, Mr Dudley stared mutely at his feet. Finally, seeing no help for it, Nell said frostily, 'My friend, Mistress Delahaye.'

The fan fluttered again and Miranda conducted a brisk head-to-toe appraisal. Then, with an inclination of her head which narrowly avoided being dismissive, her eyes returned to Nell and she said, 'Perhaps your ladyship's party would care to join Mr Dudley and myself for a glass of wine in our booth?'

And that was when, without realising it and engulfed by a wave of crippling jealousy, Cassie made a fatal mistake. Not bothering to hide her expression or dignify the invitation with a reply, she said baldly, 'The concert will have finished, Nell. We should find the others. I'm sure this lady will excuse us.'

Still several paces away, Sebastian suddenly became aware of Miranda's presence. With a brief muffled curse, he said, 'Harry – for God's sake get Nell and Cassandra away from that woman. They don't know her – she's scraping an acquaintance. Hell! *I* don't know. Just *do* something, will you?'

Harry blinked. 'If you're so worried, why can't *you* -- ?'

'Because she's my ex-mistress and that's exactly what she wants!'

It was Harry's turn to curse but he had the sense to do it on the move.

Meanwhile, Miranda's sharp gaze had focussed solely on Cassie. She said slowly, 'Have we met before?'

'No.'

The blue eyes drifted past her, locked briefly with the furious ones of Mr Audley and returned to Cassie. 'Are you sure?'

'Perfectly.' Cassie met stare with stare. 'My memory is excellent.'

'Nell, my love ... Philip wants to find Isabel.' Smoothly offering one arm to his wife and the other to Cassie in order to draw them back the way they had come, he said, 'Shall we?' And nodding coolly to the other couple, 'Dudley ... Madam. You'll forgive us, I'm sure.'

As soon as they were they were out of earshot, Nell muttered, 'Who *was* that? I don't believe I ever met her before in my life.'

'Dudley probably pointed you out as Rock's sister,' replied Harry, more than half of his mind on the prospect of asking Sebastian for an explanation. 'Trying her hand, I imagine.'

Nell peered round him at Cassie. 'You behaved very oddly. *Had* you met her?'

'No. And I guessed you hadn't either so I ... I didn't mind being slightly rude.'

Waiting for them beside Sebastian and with no idea what had taken place, Philip said, 'Barclay says that Hawtrey's stables are coming up for auction next week. Might be worth a look, don't you think?'

Sending a brief level glance in Mr Audley's direction, Harry agreed that it might.

Sebastian waited for a suitable opportunity and then, searching Cassie's face, said quietly, 'I'm sorry.'

'It wasn't your fault.'

'In essence, I'm fairly sure it was.'

So was Cassie and the thought brought that hot tide of feeling back. Setting her gaze on the path ahead so he could no longer read her expression, she said, 'What did she want?'

'Probably to make mischief. She ... isn't accustomed to rejection.'

'Oh.' The tide receded a little. 'No. I imagine not.'

Sebastian hesitated, crushing back the impulse to say something he knew he shouldn't.

Fortunately, at that moment, Jack appeared with Isabel and Althea, while overhead, the first fireworks burst in the sky. Startled and laughing, Cassie turned her face to the heavens, the light of a dozen sparkling colours dancing in her eyes; and seized by an even more unsuitable impulse, Sebastian shoved his hands in his pockets to stop himself yielding to it.

* * *

At home in Half Moon Street, Miranda relieved her feelings by smashing a smug-looking china shepherdess in the hearth.

That's her? was her first incredulous thought. *That dull, ordinary creature? But of course it is. The Delahaye girl Richard said was too prim-and-proper to go out without her corset and have men scrapping over her. So I was right all along. She recognised me – first in the park, then again tonight. And how else could that happen if she didn't already know who I was? The supercilious little bitch was in the library that night, listening to every damned word I said. And bloody Sebastian knew it and let her.*

At this point, the shepherd nearly followed his mate.

Since the day Sebastian had said he wanted nothing more to do with her, Miranda had swung between extremes. She wanted him and hated him with equal ferocity. A part of her didn't believe he'd meant his rejection and that he'd come crawling back; another part hungered to destroy his life by wreaking the worst kind of revenge; and somewhere inside all of that was just one, very clear fact. Sebastian Audley was hers. And if she couldn't have him, no other woman would either.

Has he completely lost his wits? If he prefers her to me, it's either that or ... or he's in love with her. Is he? Could it possibly be that? She gave an unsteady laugh. *God. How perfect. There are a dozen ways I could wreck that for him.* Her eyes narrowed. *And I don't even need Richard to do it. The theatre, yes ... introductions, yes ... but nothing else. Even this notion of using rumour ... I can do that myself. In fact, I'll make a much better job of it than*

Richard would by dropping a few hints into drunken ears over the card table. Indeed, if everything goes according to plan, Richard will soon become completely expendable. She laughed again as a whole new idea occurred to her. *Or then again – maybe not. Oh yes. If it could be done, that would be perfect. But first things first.*

And crossing to her writing desk, she drew a clean sheet of paper in front of her and picked up her pen.

CHAPTER THIRTEEN

Madeleine stared at the expensive paper inscribed in a hand she didn't recognise, that awaited her at the breakfast table and touched it hesitantly with one finger.

'You could open it,' suggested her brother.

Although he still mainly resided at Sinclairs, Aristide had formed a habit of spending a couple of random nights a week at the house so it didn't appear that Madeleine lived there alone but for the servants.

Slowly, she broke the seal and even more slowly, digested its contents. Then she said, 'It's from Lady Isabel, inviting me for tea this afternoon.'

Aristide lowered his newspaper. 'Will you go?'

'I don't know. It's kind of her – but several orders are being delivered today and I had intended to look into the wine bill from Teague's. I'm fairly sure they have been over-charging. And --'

'Excuses, Madeleine. All of those things can easily be attended to by someone else – preferably by an assistant, were you to take my advice and engage one. If you haven't the courage to go to Great Jermyn Street, at least summon up enough nerve to admit it.'

'That isn't fair!'

'No?' He folded the paper, placed it neatly beside his empty plate and stood up. 'In that case, I beg your pardon.' He headed for the door but paused a few steps from it to turn and say, 'Since Lord Nicholas is once more dining with us from time to time, I assume that you and he have reconciled your differences.'

'You might say so.'

He sighed. 'Have you or haven't you?'

'Oh for heaven's sake!' She surged to her feet. 'Yes. I apologised – and he made me wish I hadn't. Satisfied now?'

'As much,' replied Aristide with a wry smile, 'as I can possibly hope for.' And was gone.

Madeleine drew a long breath and slid back into her chair, to stare mutinously at Isabel's polite invitation. Then, muttering French curses beneath her breath, she went upstairs to write a note of acceptance.

* * *

While Madeleine was taking tea with half a dozen ladies in Great Jermyn Street, Lord Harry ran Mr Audley to earth at Angelo's Fencing Academy.

Passing the smaller salon, he caught sight of Richard Penhaligon apparently trouncing Alastair Vennor. This, Harry knew, wasn't very difficult since Sir Alastair was blessed with no more than moderate ability. If he'd been feeling charitable, Harry would have supposed that Vennor was the only available opponent; but as he didn't like Penhaligon very much, he concluded that the fellow enjoyed having an inflated sense of his own skill.

Mr Audley was in the main salon. His opponent was the Duke of Rockliffe.

Hell's teeth, thought Harry. And catching sight of Amberley leaning against the wall further down the room, pocket watch open in his hand, *Didn't you warn him?*

Both men were barefoot and clad only in shirt and breeches. The fight eddied and flowed across the floor in a sequence of swift, complex moves punctuated by brief pauses. Harry remained in the doorway and watched. Rockliffe didn't appear to be making any allowances, yet Sebastian was managing to hold his own. This, since there were very few men who could stand against the Duke for more than a handful of minutes and everyone knew that Angelo would have been happy to engage his Grace as an instructor, was quite an achievement. Harry was impressed.

Rockliffe made a sudden lunge followed by a driving attack which sent Sebastian back down the room before he managed to halt it. Then, moving quickly to one side, he dropped the point of his foil to the floor and held up a hand.

'Enough,' he said, his breath coming hard and fast. 'I yield.'

Rockliffe lowered his own blade and, catching the towel tossed to him by the Marquis, said, 'How long?'

'Eleven minutes,' replied Amberley, snapping the watch shut and throwing a second towel to Sebastian. 'A very respectable showing.'

'Respectable?' Sebastian managed an uneven laugh. 'I nearly killed myself for merely *respectable*?'

'Be fair, Dominic,' said Harry, strolling into the room. 'He did damned well. *I've* never managed to keep hold of my foil for more than *five* minutes.'

'That is because you are predictable, my dear,' drawled his Grace, draping the towel around his neck and advancing on Sebastian, hand outstretched. 'Well done, Mr Audley. Those were the most enjoyable eleven minutes I've had for some time.'

'Glad to have been of service,' said Sebastian. 'I'll volunteer again some time when I've got over today.'

The Duke merely smiled and glancing at Lord Harry and the Marquis said, 'White's, don't you think? When Mr Audley and I have made ourselves presentable, naturally.'

An hour later when the four gentlemen had settled into a quiet corner with a tray of coffee, Amberley said, 'So what brought you to Angelo's today, Harry? It's not one of your more regular haunts, is it?'

His lordship hesitated briefly. 'I wanted a word with Sebastian. Privately.'

'You can speak of it here,' sighed Sebastian. 'Indeed, if that kind of thing is to occur again, you may as well – or I'll do it myself, if you like.'

Harry nodded. 'That might be best. And you can trust Rock and Dominic.'

'I know.' Setting aside his coffee and keeping his eyes fixed on his hands, Sebastian said, 'A woman with whom I once had an affair in Lisbon is now a widow and in London. She had convinced herself that I would marry her and was less than philosophical when I made it plain that I wouldn't. Last night, she must have caught sight of me at Vauxhall and decided to cause me embarrassment. But she didn't approach me directly. Instead, she accosted Lady Elinor and Mistress Delahaye and introduced herself to them.'

'Ah.' Rockliffe toyed thoughtfully with an emerald-studded snuff-box. 'Exactly the kind of thing one may expect at Vauxhall. But I digress. So ... what happened next?'

'Nothing.' It was Harry who spoke. 'Sebastian alerted me to the problem and I got the girls away without mishap.' He looked across at Mr Audley. 'You said confronting her yourself wasn't a good idea.'

'And it wouldn't have been. She might not have made a scene ... but she has a talent for unpleasant innuendo.'

'Well, I suppose you can't be blamed for the incident. Everybody's got at least one skeleton that won't lie quiet.'

'Speak for yourself,' retorted Amberley. And to Sebastian, 'Why do I suspect that you are concerned by something more than a woman of dubious morality trying to force her acquaintance on Nell and Cassie?'

Sebastian took his time about answering but finally said, 'The Bedford House rumour travelled faster and lasted longer than seemed normal. It occurred to me that someone was stirring the pot.' He reached into his pocket and tossed a copy of *The Whisperer* on the table. 'This suggests I was right.'

Harry's brows rose and he picked it up. He said, 'This is today's edition.'

'I know. Someone left it on my doorstep this morning.'

We at The Whisperer *are delighted to welcome back the Honourable and Notoriously Entertaining Mr Sebastian Audley who has been absent from our pages far too long. A week ago, Mr Audley came to our notice at Bedford House ... but that is now Old News. More recently, is word of a brief disappearance from the Beau Monde, during which the Gentleman is reputed to have indulged in prolonged debauch in a certain Nunnery where he undertook a Marathon involving no less than a dozen fair Cyprians. Can it be that Mr Audley has not, as was thought, renounced his former ways? See the next Edition!*

'Good Lord, Sebastian!' Grinning, Harry tossed the sheet back on the table. 'You're clearly a hell of a fellow.'

'I would be – if I hadn't been in Sussex visiting my father,' came the calm reply. 'But what interests me is that publications such as this don't generally make up stories out of thin air and risk being sued – which means someone supplied this farrago in such a way as to make it seem credible. And the only name which springs to mind is that of Miranda Silvarez.' He paused. 'I'm not telling you this out of self-preservation. My concern, after last night, is that she may involve others.'

'That point is well taken,' remarked Rockliffe. 'However ... I would advise you not to ignore this. An official letter to *The Whisperer* pointing out their error ought to be sufficient to deter them from repeating it. If you have no man-of-law of your own, I would be happy to set the task before mine.'

A hint of colour stole along Sebastian's cheekbones.

'That is uncommonly good of you.'

'Not at all. Mr Osborne is rarely over-burdened with work. And mention of my name is not without its effect, I find.'

'Talking of names,' mused Amberley. 'Silvarez isn't one I know. Is she received?'

'I don't believe so, though she somehow managed to get into Dolly Cavendish's ball as well as Bedford House.'

'In which case – society being what it is – someone is helping her.'

'That,' said his Grace, rising from his chair, 'is an extremely good point. But this is where I shall leave you in order to return to my increasingly fractious lady. Dominic tells me that these last days can be trying ... but really, that in no way describes them.'

* * *

That evening, Mr Audley arrived at Lady Crewe's assembly in time to see Mistress Delahaye treading a gavotte with Mr Penhaligon. She was wearing pink silk and silver lace and appeared to be enjoying herself. Since it was too late for Sebastian to offer his hand to another lady and he really didn't want to hover on the edge of the floor watching Cassandra smile at Penhaligon, he wandered out to the terrace and leaned against the balustrade.

The rules of the Polite World that everyone obeyed were beginning to irritate him beyond bearing. He met Cassandra at this party or that and could dance with her – but not too often; he could take her driving in the park, so long as it was in an open carriage; and if he met her at any other time, she had to have a maid or groom or footman with her. How the bloody hell was anyone to get to know anyone else under restrictions like those? And yet matches were made on no more than that every day.

All right, he thought. *Time to admit it. I'm fathoms deep in love with a girl most of whose knowledge of me comes from gossip, rumour and the well-known catalogue of my various misdeeds. In addition, we've had a few snatched conversations and two occasions of privacy when I wasn't exactly on my best behaviour. And now, to top it all, there's this lurid trash in* The Whisperer. *If I have any intention of courting her – and God knows I want to – I'd better start putting some of that right.*

The orchestra was bringing the gavotte to an end. He re-entered the ballroom in time to see Penhaligon escorting Cassandra to the edge of the floor. Sebastian stalked purposefully in their direction and arrived at exactly the same moment as a youthful exquisite in apricot satin.

'Mistress Delahaye,' the young man began, 'may I hope --'

'Unfortunately not,' cut in Sebastian cheerfully. 'Cassandra ... my dance, I think?'

Her eyes widened and then filled with unexpected laughter. Meanwhile, the other fellow blustered, 'I say, sir – you are most importunate. And --'

'A pirate. Yes, I know. But I'm sure you'll weather the disappointment.' And so saying, he led Cassandra on to the floor, leaving the apricot-clad gallant gibbering in their wake.

'That was atrocious of you,' she reproved, still struggling not to laugh.

'Not as atrocious as that coat. If you ask me, gentlemen who dress that badly ought to be turned away at the door.'

'You're very severe.'

'No. I'm just preventing him clashing with your gown – which, by the way, is extremely fetching.' His mouth curled in a sudden dazzling and rather wicked smile. 'It's not obligatory, of course ... but if you wished to tell me that I also look particularly dashing this evening, I wouldn't mind.'

Cassie rather suspected that he didn't need to be told how he looked. Against the dark blue of his coat, his hair glowed like fire. And that smile was positively dangerous. She said carefully, 'I'll admit that you have excellent taste.'

'That is perfectly true. And not only in clothes.'

There was a possible double-meaning in that which brought colour to her cheeks but luckily the music began, sparing her the need to reply.

At the end of the first figure, all levity stripped from both eyes and voice, Sebastian said, 'It would be pleasant to hold a conversation that isn't structured around the moves of a dance, don't you think? Will you ride with me tomorrow – early and without your sister?'

His abrupt switch from flirtation to gravity made Cassie's pulse trip. 'Why?'

'Purely so we may talk in more than half-sentences.' The movement of the minuet parted, then re-united them. 'Unlike now. And you need not fear a repetition of what happened at Sinclairs – however much I might wish it. You will naturally bring a groom and though I'd prefer he remained out of earshot, you will never be out of his sight.' The twilight gaze trapped hers with sudden intensity. 'So will you? Please?'

She knew she should refuse – not only because his request was improper but because every meeting tightened the invisible thread that bound her to him. But telling herself that she was only inviting disappointment and heartache didn't do any good at all when he looked at her like that. So she said, 'Very well. What time ... and where?'

* * *

Attended by her groom, Cassie turned into Hyde Park through the Duke Gate promptly at eight the following morning and found Mr Audley cantering up towards her.

'Good morning, Mistress Delahaye,' he said for the benefit of her groom. 'This is a charming surprise. I was about to return home – but perhaps you will permit me to ride with you for a time?'

'Certainly, sir. That would be most pleasant.' She gestured for the groom to fall back to a discreet distance and drew her mare alongside Sebastian's powerful chestnut.

He said quietly, 'Thank you for coming. I thought you might change your mind.'

'I changed it at least five times,' she replied truthfully. 'Then I realised that I couldn't just leave you waiting in vain – so here I am.'

And here am I ... and now that I have the chance, I don't know where to start, thought Sebastian. 'I wouldn't have blamed you for not coming. Virtually nothing you know about me resounds to my credit, does it?'

'Oh I don't know. As we agreed last evening, you dress very well.'

It surprised her that he didn't laugh. Instead, his mouth twisted a little and he said, 'Not the most useful recommendation, perhaps – but at least it has the merit of coming from personal observation. Nearly everything else you or anyone else knows of me is allied to my adventurous past, courtesy of the scandal sheets.'

Cassie eyed him curiously, sure now that he'd asked for this meeting in order to tell her something in particular. 'What do you want to say to me?'

Sebastian opened his mouth on a cautious beginning. Instead, what came out, was, 'Did you know I had a twin brother?'

Whatever she might have expected, this wasn't it.

'No.' And realising exactly what he'd said, '*Had*?'

'Yes. Theodore. He died of the putrid throat when we were eight.' He glanced sideways at her, his eyes hooded. 'Some people call it the Boulogne throat. Did you know that? I've often wondered what they call it in France. The Dover throat, perhaps? Harwich? Or, my personal favourite, the Gravesend throat. A little dark ... but beautifully apt.'

He stopped abruptly, unsure where any of that had come from and aware that a raw note had crept into his voice. Resolutely banishing it, he said, 'After five daughters, the birth of Theo and me was the miracle my father was almost past praying for. So when Theo fell ill ... more especially, when they knew what ailed him ... they wouldn't let me near him in case I caught it too.'

There was a pause, as if she wasn't sure what to say. Then she said softly, 'I'm sorry. For a little boy, that must have been terribly hard.'

Hard? No. There isn't a word that describes how it was. We were always together, Theo and I. Always. He wouldn't have understood why I didn't come when he needed me. He wouldn't have known they kept me away. I shouted as loudly as I could but I didn't know if he could hear me. And I never saw him again so I could tell him.

'Sebastian.'

Dimly, he heard Cassie speak his name and realised that she had brought her mare close enough to touch his arm. Blinking, he said, 'Forgive me. I – my mind wandered for a moment.'

She'd known that and, despite having only his rigid profile and the grip of his hands on the reins to guide her, had a fairly accurate picture of what he'd been thinking.

'You don't need to apologise.' She removed her hand. 'I understand.'

He looked at her then and even managed something resembling a smile.

'Yes. I see that you do. But I imagine you're wondering why I told you.'

'No. I was wondering whether your brother was older or younger ... and whether the two of you looked alike. But perhaps you'd rather not talk about him?'

Sebastian hesitated, not sure what the truth was. He *didn't* talk about Theo, not to anyone – though he'd thought about him every day for the last twenty years, usually late at night over the chessboard. But he'd spoken of him now ... and she'd asked.

He said slowly, 'Theo was older by a few minutes; and yes, we looked almost exactly alike. The same blue eyes and awful Audley red hair – which we thought God should have visited upon our sisters, not us. But in other ways, we were different. Theo was gentler than me ... less impatient and sweeter-natured. He was ... easy to love.'

And so are you, thought Cassie, a faint line of confusion marking her brow. *Why do you think you aren't?* But she couldn't ask that, so she said softly, 'You still miss him.'

'Yes. But there's more to it than that.' The darkness in his eyes faded a little but his jaw remained tight. 'After Theo died, I was suddenly of paramount importance. My father was terrified he'd lose his sole remaining heir so he took every possible measure to ensure it didn't happen. I was educated at home and denied any activity that could threaten either my health or my safety. I won't bore you with the list of things I wasn't allowed to do – suffice it to say that it was extensive and that it continued even when I went to Cambridge. I didn't have the same university experience that your brother or Nicholas and the rest of them had. I had my studies ... and chess.' He paused and, with a hard smile, added, 'For thirteen years I lived in a securely padded cage. So when the lock finally sprang open, I set out to make up for lost time. And as everyone is only-too-aware, I succeeded.'

Wanting nothing more than to put her arms around him, Cassie found it a struggle to keep her voice level. She said, 'Given the circumstances you describe, any young man might have done the same. But I'm glad you told me.' She thought for a moment. 'Why did you?'

This brought Sebastian to the edge of the cliff. Did he explain that, financially, he wasn't as eligible as people supposed ... or did he simply ask if she'd allow him to approach Sir Charles? The third alternative, of course, was give way to cowardice and waste everything he'd said so far by failing to come to the point at all.

Whichever course he chose, he didn't want to do it from the back of a horse so he said, 'Do you think we might dismount? There's a bench just over there and your groom could watch the horses for a little while.'

At some instinctive level, Cassie recognised that he was hovering on the brink of something vital, so she nodded and let him help her from the saddle.

Sebastian led both horses to the groom, tossing the fellow a guinea and muttered, 'Give us a moment, would you?'

The groom, a fatherly sort of man who had known Cassie since she was six, grinned.

'Blind and deaf, sir – as long as there's no harm to my young lady.'

'There won't be.'

Cassie took Sebastian's arm and strolled with him towards the bench. Tension radiated from him, yet he retained her hand to toy idly with her fingers, making her wish they weren't both wearing gloves.

Sebastian fixed his gaze on their joined hands, considering how best to begin and wishing he'd prepared a speech. Then, for the second time in the last half hour, the words that escaped his mouth weren't at all the ones he'd meant to say.

'I love you.'

He heard her indrawn breath and the fingers in his became suddenly rigid.

'Wh-what did you say?' she whispered.

He looked into her face, meeting stunned grey eyes and hoping his own reflected the very real emotion hidden behind words that seemed thoroughly inadequate.

'I love you. I know it's sudden – and God knows I hadn't meant to blurt it out that way. But the truth, though I hope I haven't been too blatant about it, is that this has been growing and building since the night we met. I ... I just *love* you. And I am hoping you will give me leave to ask your father if he'll permit me to court you.' Realising she was about to say something and not ready to hear a refusal, he said, 'No – please don't give me your answer yet. Obviously, you'll want time to consider. And in any case, I ought to tell you that, even if you give *your* permission, by the time I've laid my circumstances before him, Sir Charles is unlikely to give his.'

During this rapid torrent of words, Cassie had started breathing again, though her heart still threatened to fill her entire chest and her head was spinning from the enormity of being offered what she hadn't dare hope for. Her immediate instinct was to say, *Yes – oh yes. Please.* But because it seemed too good to be true, a niggling little voice in her head said, *And perhaps it is. Perhaps he falls in and out of love all the time.*

It was so very easy to become infatuated with Sebastian Audley. His smile alone was enough to bring any girl to his hand without further effort; and when one added charm, intelligence and humour, the man became well-nigh irresistible. Certainly, *she* hadn't resisted. She'd slid effortlessly into love with him almost without knowing it. And just now, he'd added something surprisingly powerful to the mix. He'd revealed the private pain he still felt about his twin and thus shown himself capable of a depth of feeling that she might not otherwise have guessed at.

She had been silent for so long that Sebastian was beginning to fear what she might eventually say. As lightly as he was able he said, 'Lost for words, Cassandra?'

'Yes. You ... you've rather taken my breath away.' She stared down on her hand, still enfolded in his. 'You want to court me. Have I understood that correctly?'

He nodded. 'It seemed the most I could reasonably hope for just yet – and I thought I could get around to the rest later. Meanwhile, I'd be allowed to call on you and let you get to know me without resorting to stratagems such as this.'

'*I* could get to know *you*?' She glanced up. 'Don't you also need to get to know *me*?'

'No. Oh – there are a thousand things I'd like to discover *about* you but I already know everything that matters.' His smile was a little crooked. 'I don't think you do. But given time, I may manage to convince you that I'm not quite as black as I'm painted.'

The humility bound up in his uncertainty all but undid her. He'd said he loved her – *her*, Cassandra Delahaye. How could he doubt his reception? With a tremulous smile, she said, 'I believe I already know that. But for now ... yes. You may speak to Papa.'

'You're sure?' Sebastian's fingers tightened on hers as joy, relief and triumph flooded every nerve and sinew. And when she nodded, 'Thank you.' Then, on a shaky laugh, 'He may say no, of course.'

'He won't.'

'I'm glad you think so. Unfortunately, I'm not quite that confident.'

CHAPTER FOURTEEN

Mr Audley wrote a formal request for an interview with Sir Charles Delahaye on the following morning. He knew that the tone of his letter couldn't fail to tell Sir Charles exactly what was in the wind – but, given the importance of doing this correctly, that was unavoidable. Knowing that they would see each other next evening at the theatre, he and Cassandra had agreed that she would say nothing to her father unless asked directly ... so Sebastian despatched his note, set up the chessboard for a completely new game and settled down to wait.

A response came when he was considering his fourth move. Sir Charles would be pleased to receive Mr Audley the following day at eleven in the morning. Mr Audley discovered that he felt slightly sick.

Having taken more than usual care with his appearance, he presented himself in Conduit Street on the stroke of eleven and was shown to the same room as before. Sir Charles rose from his desk with a pleasant greeting and an extended hand. If he knew why Sebastian was there, nothing in his demeanour showed it.

Waving his visitor to a chair, he said, 'Well, Sebastian. What may I do for you?'

Sebastian cleared his throat and resisted the impulse to tug at his cravat.

'I imagine you must have guessed, sir. I would like your permission to – to court your daughter.' And then, in case he hadn't been clear, 'Mistress Cassandra, that is.'

Charles hid a smile. 'Yes. I rather gathered that's who you meant.'

Sebastian kept his mouth shut and cursed himself for an idiot.

'Why are you asking for leave to court her rather than to pay your addresses?'

'We have only been acquainted for a matter of weeks. I thought you might consider a proposal of marriage ... premature.'

'I see. And does Cassie know about this?'

'Yes. If she wasn't prepared to consider me, I didn't want to waste your time. So I thought it best to ask her.'

'You appear,' remarked Sir Charles mildly, 'to have done a great deal of thinking.'

'I needed to give myself the best chance,' admitted Sebastian wryly. 'I know that, strictly speaking, this isn't the proper way of going about things but --'

'You may stop apologising, Sebastian. I am not objecting. I'm just surprised – though perhaps I shouldn't be. Cassie usually spares me the need for the conversation you and I are about to have.' Charles looked directly into slightly baffled blue eyes and added, 'Your wits don't appear to be fully functional this morning. I'm saying that you are the first gentleman she's ever sent to me. And that means I have to take you seriously.'

That sounded promising. Sebastian said cautiously, 'Thank you, sir. I realise you'll have questions – mostly about my circumstances. And naturally --'

This time Sir Charles lifted one hand to stem the flow.

'We'll come to your circumstances presently. For now, I only want to know why.'

'Why?' echoed Sebastian blankly.

'Why do you want to marry Cassie?' asked Charles with patient amusement.

There was a brief pause while Sebastian tried to get a better grip on his faculties.

'I'm sorry. It didn't occur to me that you wouldn't realise there's only one thing that could have brought me here.' And spreading helplessly expressive hands, 'I love her.'

'I see. And how does Cassie feel?'

Sebastian felt himself flush. 'You will have to ask her, sir. I wasn't brave enough. All I'm sure of is that she likes me well enough to allow me to approach you.'

'So I see.' Charles rose to pull the bell. 'And that being so, there is clearly some point in discussing other details – which will require coffee.' The footman arrived and left again. 'We can dispense with the things I already know. I am acquainted with your father, though it is some years since we met. I'm aware that the Audley name is an ancient and distinguished one and that you are heir to a well-maintained and prosperous estate; that all but one of your sisters are married and that, upon the demise of your father, you will be a relatively wealthy man.' Steepling his fingers, he surveyed Sebastian over the top of them. 'On the other side of the coin, I also know as much as I would wish to about your various excesses. By and large, I'm inclined to make allowances – though it is my opinion that you went too far and for too long – but I'm aware that most of the blame for that lies at Lord Wingham's door. You told me you'd turned over a new leaf. What I want to hear *now* is your categorical assurance of it lasting.'

'You have it. My 'excesses' palled quite some time ago and I returned to England in the hope of living them down – which I believe I'm now doing.'

'And the wager with Lord Sarre?'

For the first time since he'd walked into the room, Sebastian smiled.

'That was Adrian's idea – and it was designed to provide me with an easy way of refusing the worst challenges.'

The footman tapped at the door, entered and placed his tray upon a table. Charles waited until the door closed again and said sardonically, 'Easier than saying no?'

'Yes. The younger men don't give up, you see. As to the wager itself ... since it's served its turn, I'm perfectly content for Adrian to win it.'

Charles poured coffee for them both.

'So I need not worry about unfortunate developments?'

'No,' began Sebastian. Then, suppressing a groan, 'Yes. A couple of days ago, something unpleasant appeared in one of the scandal sheets.'

'*How* unpleasant?'

'Very. It was a tissue of lies and if I had to prove that, I could. Fortunately, his Grace of Rockliffe has kindly undertaken to have the publication informed of its mistake in a way that should prevent anything of the kind happening again.'

Sir Charles gave a small snort that might have been amusement but said merely, 'If Rock is prepared to stand behind you, I'd say you have little to worry about. However ... let us now move along to your financial circumstances – unless you'd rather I had that particular conversation with your father?'

'No, sir – I wouldn't. Neither would it tell you what you need to know.'

'It wouldn't?'

'No.' This was the part Sebastian had been looking forward to least. Drawing a long breath, he said, 'Throughout my years at university, Father controlled my life by means of the purse-strings. Since I was determined to prevent that continuing, I studied Law because it offered a means of earning my own living – though as things turned out it was never necessary because my Great-Aunt left me a moderate legacy. It provides me with sufficient income to live comfortably, though not extravagantly. I don't gamble beyond my means; I don't have debts; and I don't live off my expectations. But ...'

He stopped and Charles said gently, 'Yes?'

'But as things stand, I can't afford to lease a house in town or support Cassandra in the way I – or you – would wish.'

This time the silence was a long one.

'Let us be quite clear about this,' said Charles at length, his tone noticeably cooler. 'Are you saying that Lord Wingham does not make you an allowance? That he does not, in fact, support you in any way and has never done so since you left Cambridge?'

'That's about the size of it, yes – but it was my choice. I wanted my independence and didn't know how else to ensure it. *Now* it's been going for so long, I doubt if Father actually remembers I don't cost him a penny.'

Sir Charles stood up.

'If you hope to marry my daughter, I suggest you remind him.'

'Sir, it isn't that simple,' said Sebastian tightly.

'Isn't it?'

'No. Oh – Father would be delighted to see me married and even more delighted if my bride was Cassandra, I'm sure. But the

London house was disposed of after my youngest sister was married; and knowing that I would spend part of each year in Town, Father might choose not to replace it if that meant he could keep me chained to Audley Court.'

'I see.' Sighing, Charles resumed his seat. 'You're concerned that having constrained you in that way once, he may try to do it again.'

'Yes. It isn't that I don't want to spend sufficient time at the Court to learn everything I'll need to know – but I can't give my whole life to it yet. And I certainly wouldn't allow my wife to be subjected to it.' Sebastian paused, raking a hand through his hair and then regretting it. 'I may be doing Father an injustice, of course. He's finally admitted he made mistakes and perhaps he's also learned from them. But I can't assume that. And it would be wrong of me to hide the possibility.'

'Dear me. You certainly come imbued with complications, don't you?'

'Yes,' came the bitter reply. 'This is where you're supposed to show me the door.'

'That is certainly one course of action. It's possible, however, that Cassie may have something to say about that.'

Sebastian allowed himself a small flicker of hope. 'Perhaps.'

'I suggest, therefore, that you leave the matter of Lord Wingham to me. I shall write to him, explaining that I will permit you to ask for my daughter's hand when he fulfils two conditions. First, that he provides you with an allowance suitable for a married man; and second, that he uses the money he has saved these last seven years to purchase a house in a good part of town, the choice of which he leaves to you. What do you think?'

That Cassandra's father might offer to help had never occurred to Sebastian. He said unevenly, 'Sir ... if you are willing to do that ... well, it's more than I'd ever expected. To be truthful, I didn't think I stood a chance. And with most fathers, I don't believe I would have.'

Charles stood up again and held out his hand, smiling a little.

'You're not out of the woods yet, Sebastian. I'll write to your father once I've ascertained Cassie's feelings – though I see no need to explain your pecuniary difficulties to her at this stage. And since my wife will want to judge your merits for herself, you'd better dine with us this evening. For the rest, don't be *too* grateful. I'm not going to pretend that besting Lord Wingham won't have its enjoyable side.'

* * *

After a long conversation with her husband, Serena Delahaye had an even lengthier one with Cassie. Then, satisfied that Mr Audley appeared to be behaving with propriety and also that, although she hadn't actually said so, Cassie was clearly head over heels in love with the man, she took the precaution of arranging for Olivia to spend the evening with a party of other young girls under the aegis of Lady Barclay. It would be a great deal easier, Serena decided, to evaluate what exactly was going on between Cassie and Mr Audley without Olivia goggling at him across the table and asking endless unsuitable questions; and aside from all that, Olivia's constant pleas to be allowed to attend Mr Sheridan's new play the following evening were becoming decidedly tedious.

Olivia was at first delighted and then, catching sight of Cassie's embroidered aquamarine silk, deeply suspicious. She said, 'You're dressed very fine.'

'This?' Cassie eyed her reflection consideringly. 'I've worn it before.'

'Maybe so – but not for dinner at home.'

'As usual, you're making too much of it.' She sat down to allow Susan to finish pinning up her hair. 'And you're looking very nice yourself. That shade of pink suits you. I expect Margot will be quite jealous.'

Invoking the rivalry between Livy and her best friend never failed.

'Hah!' grinned Olivia, preparing to sweep from the room. 'That is the plan.'

Once Olivia was *en route* to her party, Cassie felt it safe to go downstairs. Sitting still once she got there, however, proved to be impossible. She prowled restlessly around the drawing room until her mother said, 'Does Mr Audley *know* he has this effect?'

'No. At least, I don't think so.' Cassie gazed back despairingly. 'Mama ... why is it suddenly so difficult to be sensible?'

'I suspect you know the answer to that.' And tilting her head, 'I also suspect that he has arrived ... with unprecedented punctuality, too.'

Sebastian entered the room with her father and Cassie felt the now-familiar tightening in her chest. Tonight, he wore the bronze brocade she'd seen once before and, as usual, he looked impossibly handsome. But it was the expression in his eyes when he greeted her that melted something low in her body and made her aware that *not* being sensible was suddenly eminently desirable.

Lady Delahaye welcomed him with her usual calm smile; Sir Charles poured sherry; and Sebastian found himself sitting no more than a foot away from Cassandra on a satin-and-gilt sofa while his host and hostess encouraged him to describe his travels. Gradually, he became aware that she was leaning towards him, hanging on every word. After talking at some length about Bohemia and Hungary, he slanted a smile at her saying, 'And as you're aware – despite rumours to the contrary – I went to St Petersburg to play chess.'

'Chess?' Charles's eyes brightened. 'You played chess in Russia?'

'Oh dear,' murmured Serena. 'This would seem a good moment to go in to dinner – otherwise we may all starve. You may give me your arm, Mr Audley.'

He rose, bowed and said, 'Would suggesting you use my given name be premature?'

'I don't know, sir,' she retorted pleasantly. 'Would it?'

And watching as laughter flared enticingly in those extraordinarily blue eyes thought, *Oh Cassie. You never had a chance, did you?*

Precisely as Serena had expected, mention of chess and Russia dictated the course of much of the conversation during dinner. At some point over turbot in cream, Charles said, 'You learned the Makarovsky stratagem from the man who invented it?'

Sebastian nodded. 'Obviously, you play yourself – and seriously, if you've heard of him.'

'I'm a member of Parsloe's Chess Club – as is Jack Ingram – though whether either of us are up to your standards is debatable.'

'I had no idea there *was* a chess club in London.'

'It's relatively new and is limited to a hundred members. I'll propose you, if you wish. Meanwhile, we can arrange a game. Tomorrow evening, perhaps?'

'Tomorrow evening,' interposed Serena, 'is the opening night of Mr Sheridan's new play so we will be spending it at Drury Lane. We are sharing the Cavendish box and I imagine that, like Cassie, Mr Audley is similarly engaged with Nell Caversham's party.' She raised enquiring brows at Sebastian. 'Am I right?'

'Her ladyship was kind enough to invite me,' he agreed.

'So … chess will have to wait.' She rose and beckoned Cassie. 'Time to leave the gentlemen to their port, I think.'

'Perhaps,' said Charles, 'we might either forgo the port for this evening – or take it in the drawing-room. What do you say, Sebastian?'

'Whatever suits you and her ladyship best, sir.' Dragging his eyes away from Cassie, he added, 'For myself, I'm happy to drink tea with the ladies.'

'Yes. I thought you might be. Take him away, Cassie – and ring for the tea-tray. Your Mama and I will be with you directly.'

Serena frowned. 'Now, Charles --'

'Five minutes, Rena. He can't get up to much in that time – even supposing Cassie would let him.' He waved them away. 'Off with you.'

The second they were outside the door, Sebastian removed Cassie's hand from his arm and linked his fingers with hers. 'Five minutes? Your father has forgotten a few things.'

'What do you --?'

The question died unspoken as he whisked her into the drawing-room, drew her down on the sofa they'd occupied earlier and raised her hand to his lips. Then smiling into her eyes, he turned her palm upwards and pressed a warm, slow kiss in the centre of it. Cassie gave a tiny startled gasp.

'You have lovely hands,' he murmured turning the one he held captive again in order to salute her knuckles. 'Have you ever imagined the things you might do with them?'

She hadn't – not really. But the suggestive note in his voice had her imagining sliding them over bare skin. *His* skin. His tongue slid just a little way between each of her fingers, causing heat to blossom in surprising places. She said unevenly, 'You – you ought not to be doing that.'

He flicked a sultry glance up beneath his lashes. 'You don't like it?'

'I – well, yes.'

'Good. So do I.' Uncurling her hand, he took the tip of her index finger into his mouth and lightly bit it before stroking it with his tongue. 'Mm. Strawberries, again.'

'Wh-what?'

'Strawberries.' He lifted his head, his eyes resting on her parted lips with an intensity as potent as a kiss. 'Your mouth tastes of strawberries too. I remember it distinctly. But I suppose you'll forbid me to sample that just now?'

Not sure that her voice would work properly, Cassie managed to nod.

He sighed. 'You're right, of course. But it's a tremendous pity. And if you're going to look at me like that, you can't blame me for trying.'

* * *

The Cavendish box being next to Rockliffe's, both parties migrated to and fro before the play began. The upper gallery was filling up fast and the pit was already heaving with people. A small hiatus was caused when Lord Nicholas strolled in, thus causing an argument with his sister because he hadn't been invited.

Cassie and Sebastian meanwhile, had taken possession of adjacent chairs and were ostensibly studying the playbill. In fact, Sebastian was flirting so outrageously that she was in fits of laughter.

'Stop it – now, before Nell asks what is so funny.'

He grinned at her. 'Be grateful. If I said what I'm *really* thinking you'd be blushing like a peony and that would be a lot harder to explain.'

She shook her head reprovingly. 'You are being deliberately wicked.'

'I know,' he agreed. And then, differently, 'But you like me, don't you? Just a little bit?'

The note of appeal in his voice was reflected in his eyes. Something inside Cassie's silver-grey bodice splintered into a hundred pieces. She thought, *Oh Sebastian. How can you not know?* But said softly, 'Yes. Just ... a little bit.' And knew from the sudden change in his expression that he had understood.

Having dealt with her annoying brother by informing him that he was welcome to stay if he didn't mind standing, Lady Elinor sat beside Cassie and looked round to see who was settling into the other boxes.

'I don't believe there's a seat to be had,' she remarked. And then, 'Good heavens, Cassie – it's that woman from Vauxhall.'

'Where?' demanded Sebastian quickly.

'In Lord Keswick's box. Don't look now – she's actually *bowing* to me, the encroaching creature! To the right, third box from the stage. With Mr Penhaligon and some others.'

At which point, with perfect timing, the curtain rose on *The School for Scandal*.

In the wake of his recent brush with *The Whisperer*, Sebastian saw the irony in sitting down to watch a comedy based largely around the use of rumour and innuendo to destroy reputations.

He was also acutely aware that, while Lady Sneerwell was hatching her plots onstage, her real-life counterpart was probably storing up tips for future use. Overall, however, he decided that Miranda's presence wasn't so surprising; all the world and his wife were crammed into the Theatre Royal tonight. He did, however, wonder how well she knew Richard Penhaligon and whether the question merited further investigation.

During the intervals, visitors came and went. Discussion revolved around the excellence of the play, Mr Sheridan's recent purchase of the theatre from David Garrick and, inevitably, speculations on poor Mr Garrick's health – he not having been seen on-stage for some considerable time. Mr Audley paid his respects to Dolly Cavendish, exchanged polite courtesies with Sir Charles and Lady Delahaye and offered Mr Ingram a game of chess. Then he settled down to concentrate on the performance only to be distracted this time by Cassie's glowing face and delicious gurgles of laughter. His mind wandered again and he found himself silently praying that his father would see reason.

By the fourth act when Charles Surface was selling his family portraits to a man he hadn't realised was his uncle, the entire theatre was rocking with laughter; and the moment when the screen collapsed, revealing that Lady Teazle had been eavesdropping from behind it halted the performance for several minutes until the actors could make themselves heard again.

The final Act closed in a storm of applause which prevented Mrs Abington from speaking the epilogue for quite five minutes and the cast took countless curtain calls amidst much cheering and stamping.

When the curtain closed for the last time, Cassie said, 'That was wonderful. I don't ever remember laughing so much.'

'Me neither,' replied Philip Vernon. 'Everyone said that this couldn't possibly rival *The Rivals* but in my opinion Sheridan has outdone himself. What do you think, Audley?'

'That it will be interesting to see what the critics make of it,' replied Sebastian. And turning to Nell, 'Lady Elinor – it was a splendid evening. Thank you for inviting me.'

202

Nobly refraining from remarking that he had appeared to spend quite half the play watching Cassie, Nell merely said that she was happy he had been able to join them and led the exodus from the box to the crush outside it. Once again, the Cavendish and Caversham parties merged and everyone made their way slowly down to the equally crowded foyer.

Outside on the street, people continued to chat whilst waiting for their carriages. Dolly Cavendish invited Nell's party to join her own for a light supper. Jack Ingram thanked her but refused, saying that Althea was tired; a nod from Isabel had Philip smiling an acceptance; and, hearing Cassie say that she would go if her parents did, Sebastian was just about to take up the invitation on his own behalf when there was a sudden disturbance.

A woman dragging a very small child of indeterminate sex pushed through the remaining crowd, shouting and waving an accusing fist.

Amidst a fast and furious torrent of foreign words that only one person understood was a word that *everyone* understood.

Sebastian's name.

Little by little, the previously laughing and chattering crowd fell silent while the woman continued to rant in her own tongue.

'What's she saying?' asked Nicholas.

'No idea,' shrugged Philip. 'I don't even know what language she's speaking.'

Sebastian did but had the sense to realise that this was no time to admit he spoke Portuguese and be forced to translate.

'*You! Finally I find you, Sebastian! And see – here is the child you abandoned!*'

So he stood like a stone, the blood draining slowly from his skin. And when, eventually, the female stopped speaking in order to shove the child towards him, he felt eyes piercing his back like knives as the people around him started to wonder.

He looked down into the huge, frightened eyes of the child and then back at the woman. Finally, in a level voice pitched to carry, he said, 'Who are you?'

Her reply was another torrent of words; but this time a handful of them were in English. Among them were *wife, child* and *starve* ... just sufficient to cause most of those standing nearest to Sebastian to distance themselves, muttering with shock and disgust. Cassie, by contrast, took an involuntary step towards him and would have taken another had she not been restrained by her mother.

'No.' Serena kept a firm hold on her daughter's wrist. 'You can't help.'

'But --'

'No! You'll make it worse for him.'

Taking one brief glance at Cassie's distressed face and determined to keep her out of this horror, Sebastian took a step away from her and towards the strange woman. Very briefly, he glanced round. A few yards away, Miranda was watching the drama unfold out of eyes avid with enjoyment which told him who he had to thank for this scene; and Richard Penhaligon was staring at her with an expression that meant he clearly knew it too.

Turning back to the woman and shaking his head, Sebastian said clearly, 'You are mistaken. I do not know you.'

Another barrage of Portuguese followed, subtly laced with the words *promise* and *marry*. Whoever she was, thought Sebastian feeling extremely sick, she had been well-rehearsed.

He tried again. 'I think you are saying that some man has abandoned you. If that is so, I am sorry. But that man was not me.'

By way of answer, the woman dragged the shawl away from the child's unkempt head. Brilliant red hair glowed in the light of the theatre's torches and the mutter which had been growing behind him became a collective gasp.

Someone said, 'For shame, Audley! It would cost little enough to provide for the brat.'

Several voices agreed with this.

'And if the child was mine,' said Sebastian coldly but with little hope of being attended to, 'I would have done so. As it stands, I have never seen this woman before in my life.'

Cassie looked about her at faces grown suddenly hostile and thought, *How can anyone believe this? And why aren't our friends helping? They must know it isn't true – that it could never be true.* Engulfed in anguish, she watched Sebastian facing his accusers, looking so terribly alone; and swinging round on her father, she said, '*Do* something!'

'That won't wash!' a new voice was saying. 'Where else did the child get that hair?'

His expression grim, Charles Delahaye moved to Sebastian's side and said, 'Whatever the truth of the matter, you need to get mother and child out of the street.'

'And take them where? Home with me? I think not.'

Harry Caversham emerged at Sebastian's other side.

'Give her some money and she'll go away.'

'She won't. She's already been paid for this performance – and me handing her money, merely reinforces the illusion.' He dropped his voice and said, 'You recall what I told you the other day? Look over your left shoulder.'

Harry looked. 'Hell!' he breathed. Then, 'All right. We can sort this out later. But for now, something needs to be done.'

'Certainly it does. So if the woman and her child have nowhere to go, *I* will take them.'

The firm, cool tones of Isabel Vernon effectively silenced the contemptuous rumbling of those who stayed to see the entertainment through to its conclusion.

'No, Isabel – really!' expostulated Philip. 'We can't possibly --'

'Yes, we can – and fortunately, here is our carriage.' She walked to the woman and, smiling, laid a gentle hand on the child's head. Then, pantomiming in time with her words, 'Come and I will give you food and a bed. You will be safe. Yes?'

'*Sim*,' agreed the woman. 'Yes. *Obrigado*.'

'Good.' Isabel turned quietly to her husband and said, 'I'll take her home. You can follow – and Mr Audley had better come with you.'

'But --'

'No, Phil.' It was Harry who spoke, his tone extremely grim. 'Sebastian wouldn't leave a by-blow to starve any more than you or I would. There's mischief at work here. Let me send Nell on with Dolly, then you and I and Sebastian can take my carriage.'

'You're coming too?' asked Philip.

'Yes. And I only wish Rock was here as well.'

CHAPTER FIFTEEN

By the time the gentlemen arrived in Great Jermyn Street –
Lord Nicholas having elected to tag along with the others – Isabel
had installed her unexpected guest in a bedchamber with food,
water for washing and such things as could be found for the child.

'Her name is Luiza and she's Portuguese,' said Isabel when
what Harry called the Council of War had assembled in the library
and refreshments had been brought. 'That is all I've managed to
find out since she either can't or won't speak English. But I'm
hoping you can help with that, Mr Audley.'

Sebastian nodded wearily. His brain was still reeling and he
felt ill. All he could see ahead was imminent disaster because,
unless he could prove that the child wasn't his and the whole
scenario specifically created to make him look like the worst kind
of libertine, no one was going to believe there was smoke without
fire. Rumour would do Miranda's work for her and he felt as if
he'd strayed back inside *The School for* sodding *Scandal*.

He said, 'Yes. I have a basic grasp of Portuguese. Does she
know I'm here?'

'Not yet. First, I'd like your assurance that the child upstairs is
not yours; and I also think Philip and I should be told whatever it is
Harry already knows.'

'The child isn't mine. I've never seen that woman before. I
believe the whole charade to be the work of a woman called
Miranda Silvarez – but I can't prove it.' He glanced round the
circle of faces and said simply, 'I'm sorry. And grateful, Isabel. If
you hadn't stepped in, I'm not sure ...' He stopped, making a small
helpless gesture.

'What we know so far is this,' said Harry, sparing Sebastian
the need to think. 'On the heels of all the talk about Bedford
House, there was a piece of filth in *The Whisperer* the other day –
apparently coming from nowhere. Between those two things, the
Silvarez woman tried to foist herself on Nell and Cassie at Vauxhall

– and she was at the theatre tonight with Richard Penhaligon. All of it adds up to what Sebastian has already told myself, Amberley and Rock. She's out to do him harm.'

'Why?' asked Nicholas, baffled. 'I mean – I never thought much of Penhaligon. But what have you done to this female?'

Sebastian looked up, a crooked smile curling his mouth. 'I said no.'

Nicholas didn't pretend to misunderstand. 'Ah. That would do it, I suppose.'

Philip shifted uncomfortably in his chair. He said, 'If this is going where I think it is, I'm not sure Isabel needs to hear it.'

'Don't be foolish, Philip,' said his wife crisply. 'I'm not prone to the vapours and there are things to be decided.' She turned to Sebastian. 'I imagine you will want to question Luiza. My own suspicion is that the child isn't even hers. Aside from the dissimilarity of colouring – a brown-eyed, black-haired mother and a blue-eyed, red-haired child – I haven't seen her show an *ounce* of maternal feeling. The poor little thing can't be more than two years old and is too terrified even to cry.' Isabel paused to conquer the disgust in her voice. 'But if I'm right about that and *you* are right about this being a plot, how was it arranged?'

'Miranda was married to a Portuguese count and lived for some time in Lisbon which is where I met her,' said Sebastian tiredly. 'She wouldn't have had much trouble finding Luiza – indeed, she may even have brought her to England when she returned herself. As to the child ... I don't know. An orphanage, perhaps? But I suppose I must begin by speaking to the woman. Perhaps with only Isabel present?'

'Certainly.' Isabel rose with a purposeful air. 'I'll have a maid summon her. Meanwhile, you may take Harry and Nicholas to your study, Philip – assuming they don't wish to leave?'

'And miss the next instalment?' demanded Nicholas. 'Hardly!'

Left briefly alone with Isabel, Sebastian said, 'It is uncommonly good of you to help in this way – especially since Philip isn't happy about it. Why you are doing it?'

'I don't think you deserve this and I'm *sure* that unfortunate child doesn't. As for Philip, he occasionally falls victim to attacks of old-maidish prudery which luckily never last very long.' She eyed him shrewdly. 'I'm going to say something which is none of my business, Mr Audley. If, aside from the obvious, you are worrying about what Cassie Delahaye may be thinking – don't. She is nobody's fool.'

'I know.' The scene outside the theatre had left him incapable of dissembling. 'I know she's not. But if this mess can't be cleared up, I can't go near her. I won't risk her being smeared with the mud that will be thrown at me.' He sounded utterly sick. 'And even if I was stupid enough to call in Conduit Street, Charles would have me kicked down the steps.'

'Do you really think so?'

'It's what he ought to do. We all know how the world works. I can shout my innocence on every street corner – but who is going to believe me?'

A tap at the door heralded the maid Isabel had sent to bring Luiza downstairs. She said breathlessly, 'My lady, I'm ever so sorry but she's gone!'

'Gone?' Isabel stood up. 'That's ridiculous. She can't have gone. Are you sure?'

'Yes, my lady. That poor little mite's huddled up in a corner and no sign of the mother.'

'Perhaps she left the room and got lost. Have you searched the house?'

'Mr Porson's got the footmen doing it now.'

Isabel spared a glance to where Sebastian had dropped his head in his hands. Then, turning back to the maid, 'Very well, Mary. Send Porson to me when he knows the situation – and go to his lordship's study and ask him to re-join me here.'

The maid curtsied gratefully and sped off.

'That,' remarked Sebastian, sitting up, 'is all I need. We'll never find her now. But at least we know the child isn't hers – so I suppose that's something.'

Philip walked in followed by Harry and Nicholas.

'Isabel? What's happening? Where is the child's mother?'

'Gone,' said Isabel bitterly. 'At least, it seems so. I'm just waiting for Porson to confirm it. Meanwhile, I'm furious with myself. I might have guessed she wouldn't wait to be questioned – particularly if she knew Sebastian can speak her native tongue.'

'And the child?' asked Harry.

'Oh she's left that for *me* to deal with,' Sebastian informed him sardonically. And then stopped as the butler came in.

'My lady, I regret to say that the young person has indeed left the premises – we believe, through the garden door. She has also taken the silver cutlery and cream jug from her supper tray. Meanwhile, I have sent Mary to remain with the child until such time as your ladyship decides what must be done.'

'Excellent, Porson. Thank you.' The butler withdrew and Isabel looked back at the assembled gentlemen. 'Do any of you have a suggestion about what we *are* going to do?'

'Yes.' Sebastian stood up. 'If you will keep the child tonight, I'll do my best to make other arrangements tomorrow – though I've no idea how or what. But this is my mess and I won't see you burdened with it longer than necessary.'

There was a brief airless silence. Then Philip said, 'Sit down, Sebastian. You can't solve this on your own. So sit down and let's think it through. But first, you'll take a brandy. You look as if you need it.'

'Thank you, no. I --'

Nicholas stopped any further protests by the simple expedient of shoving Mr Audley into the nearest chair while Philip poured brandy for everyone, including Isabel.

'Now,' said Harry. 'Putting the child's future aside for a moment, what are you thinking of doing with regard to the Silvarez woman?'

'Christ,' muttered Sebastian. 'I don't know. There's not much I *can* do. I've no proof, so confronting her isn't going to achieve much. She's hardly likely to admit it – not even to me privately, let alone to anyone else. And the fact that Luiza has vanished doesn't help. It will look as if I'm being forced to make the provision I've previously refused.'

'What about Penhaligon?' asked Nicholas. 'He knows Silvarez so he may know what she's up to. He may even have had a hand in it, for God's sake. If frightening him a bit – or even a lot – might produce some information, I'll be happy to help.'

'That isn't a bad idea,' said Philip slowly. 'He may know something. And he's taken to practising at Angelo's most days so it won't be hard to track him down.' An idea struck him. 'If we could pair him up with Rock, we'd have the information in no time.'

'I'd rather go and sit on him,' grunted Nicholas.

'We know,' grinned Harry. 'But we don't need Rock. At least, we do in *other* respects and one of us can see to that tomorrow. But we don't need him to face Penhaligon over the foils. Sebastian will do just as well.' And when the other men stared at him, he added simply, 'He held Rock for eleven minutes. Saw it myself.'

'I agree that Penhaligon is involved in this,' said Sebastian slowly. 'A few weeks ago, a couple of fellows who trot at his heels tried taunting me into a particularly vile wager while Penhaligon sat in a corner and watched. But I don't see how fencing with him at Angelo's will help. I can't scare a confession out of him using a weapon he knows can't possibly hurt him. He'll laugh.'

'He won't. I've seen him fence. You can wipe the floor with him and make him look a complete idiot before witnesses. Then, if he's *still* reluctant to talk, Nicholas can sit on him.'

'Thank you.' Nicholas raised his glass in gratitude.

'Fighting talk is all very well,' remarked Isabel, 'and I'm sure I wish you all well with it. But the scandal that is bound to result from this evening still has to be dealt with. And equally important is the future of that child upstairs. I hope that by tomorrow I can coax some words out of her – enough at least to determine if she's English. But --'

'Stop.' Sebastian suddenly sat up, a new light in his face. '*She*? The child is a *girl*?'

'Yes. Didn't I say?'

'No. And I didn't ask. I just assumed ...' He stopped and then, dropping back in his chair, gave way to weak laughter. 'A girl. Thank you, God. Miranda's made a mistake.'

Philip frowned. 'I don't understand. What are you talking about?'

'Colouring,' said Sebastian succinctly. 'Red hair and blue eyes.'

'What of it?'

'For some incomprehensible reason, only Audley males inherit that colouring. I have five sisters and numerous aunts ... all of whom have dark hair and grey eyes. Anyone who knows my family knows that. Anyone at all.' He smiled for the first time since the woman Luiza had first appeared outside the theatre. 'If the child is a girl, none of those people are going to believe she's mine.'

*　*　*

After a largely sleepless night, Sebastian arrived at the breakfast table to find a curt note from Sir Charles Delahaye summoning him to Conduit Street at his earliest convenience. Sebastian grimaced, drank two cups of coffee and went back upstairs to allow Hobson to make him presentable.

Yet again, he was shown directly to the study where Charles awaited him with an expression that did not bode well. He said, 'What in hell happened last night, Sebastian? And I'll have it with neither omissions nor beating about the bush, if you please.'

Since he hadn't been offered a chair, Sebastian remained on his feet and strove to look more composed than he felt. He said, 'Plainly, then ... my former mistress returned from Lisbon and re-applied for the position. I declined. She is now intent on disrupting my life and last night was her latest stratagem. The Portuguese female she presumably paid to make the scene outside the theatre disappeared from Philip Vernon's house, leaving the child behind – which means it wasn't hers. More pertinently as far as I am concerned, the child is a girl. I'm presuming you'll understand the significance of that.'

'A girl?' The implacable stance relaxed a trifle. 'Yes. I see. Well, that's fortunate.'

'Isn't it?'

'Don't try to be clever. And don't think to see Cassie this morning either. Until your name has been washed clean of the gutter, you will not come within a dozen *yards* of her.'

'You think I would?' asked Sebastian coldly.

'I've no idea what you'd do. Quite aside from that vulgar scene outside the theatre, I've since had Cassie ranting at me more or less non-stop.'

'Ranting? Cassandra? I can't imagine --'

'Neither could I before last night. Throughout the ride home and for a further hour after we got here, Serena and I were subjected to a diatribe on your innocence and the utter impossibility of anyone with half a brain believing otherwise. Inextricably mixed up in all that were accusations of malicious tinkering by a female who I suppose must be the former mistress you just referred to. Bedford House came into it somewhere – as did an incident in Dolly Cavendish's library, which frankly appalled me.'

Sebastian winced inwardly. *Oh love … I wish you hadn't mentioned that.*

'Needless to say, I'm currently wondering what *else* has been going on between the pair of you behind my back. Well?'

'Nothing.' *Well, nothing so very terrible, at any rate.*

'Sure about that, are you? Because somewhere along the line, you appear to have transformed my daughter into a person I don't recognise. When, despite her protestations on your behalf, Serena and I still insisted that she was to stay away from you until further notice, the battle moved to new ground.' Surveying Sebastian over sardonically folded arms, Charles said, 'You could call what happened next a hurling down of several gauntlets. Serena and I are to understand in absolutely no uncertain terms that Cassie loves you *à corps perdu* as the saying goes; that you are completely honourable and let no one *dare* say a word to the contrary; and that if you ask her to marry you, she will do it even

STELLA RILEY

if it means a trip to Gretna Green. There was a great deal more, all of it in the same vein and accompanied by a great deal of gesticulation and far too many exclamation marks. And throughout it all, there were floods of tears – *not*, as you might suppose, of unhappiness or fear or worry – but of sheer uncontainable fury.' He paused. 'You, Mr Audley, have turned my lovely girl into a damned Valkyrie.'

In addition to the mingled joy, relief and incredulity came a mental image of Cassandra, shield in hand and her hair flowing loose beneath a winged helmet. In one sense, it was funny. In another, since it made his groin tighten, it wasn't. He said raggedly, 'I'm sorry, sir. I'm having trouble taking that in.'

'*You* are having trouble? How do you think *I* feel?' Quite suddenly and against all expectation, Sir Charles smiled, albeit a trifle sourly. 'She's always been the perfect daughter; biddable, gentle and demure, as if there wasn't an ounce of real passion in her. Even when I first spoke to her about *you*, she merely sat with her hands folded in her lap and said she'd be happy to receive you – which did nothing to dispel my fears that she was destined to become the perfect, dutiful wife ... or to put it another way, a doormat. Ugly as last night was, it has at least removed *that* particular worry. So you'd better clear your name and be quick about it, Sebastian. Otherwise, Serena says we may need to start hiding the best china.'

This, Sebastian decided, was even more bizarre than the notion of Cassandra in an uncontrollable temper. Shaking his head to try and clear it, he said, 'I'm meeting Nicholas, Harry and Philip at Angelo's in an hour. Since Miranda attended the theatre with Richard Penhaligon last night, we're hoping to shake some information out of him. I don't know how successful that will be ... but you're welcome to join us if you wish.'

'One of you intends to fence with him?'

'Yes. Me.'

* * *

By the time Mr Audley and Sir Charles arrived at the fencing academy, Lord Harry had arranged for sole use of the smaller

214

salon but there was as yet no sign of their quarry. Then Nicholas strolled in with Philip saying, 'No chance of getting Rock here, I'm afraid. Adeline's pains have started. Amberley is there, lending Rock his support – though personally I'd have thought Adeline more in need of it. All the proud father has to do is while away a few hours with a couple of glasses of claret and a few rubbers of piquet.'

'How little you know,' murmured Charles with faintly disquieting sympathy.

All four younger gentlemen eyed him uneasily but forbore to ask what he meant.

It having been decided that the occasion should appear as normal as possible, they each stripped down to shirt and breeches and took a foil from the rack. And since – for reasons which annoyed him – Philip had been elected to face Sebastian, Harry and Nicholas took on each other.

Sebastian said, 'Don't look so peevish, Philip. We'll dance about a bit until after Penhaligon gets here, then you can make some excuse and quit the field.'

'I'm not peevish – I'm bloody insulted. *Nobody* is worse than Nick. He charges about as if he was trying to stop a herd of elephants.'

'And I'd have to show more skill than I want to in order to stay out of his way.' Sebastian flexed his foil and checked that the button was securely in place. 'We have a plan. Let's stick to it.'

Mr Penhaligon sauntered in some ten minutes later, stopped dead when he spied Mr Audley and would have sauntered straight out again had not Sir Charles made it impossible for him to do so by engaging him in conversation. Meanwhile, the room rang with the clash and slither of steel, a few amicable insults and quite a lot of laughter. Mr Penhaligon watched from the side-lines and relaxed.

After five minutes, Philip pretended to twist his ankle.

'Ah – damn!' he grunted, limping artistically to a bench. 'My apologies, Audley. I damaged my ankle a few weeks ago and it's still weak. Maybe one of the others will give you a bout.'

Nicholas and Harry paused in their endeavours and Harry said, 'Sorry, Sebastian. Nick has just tossed me one insult too many – so I intend to have my revenge. Ask Penhaligon. He'll give you a match, I'm sure.'

'No – really,' said Richard hastily. 'I hadn't meant to practise today. I just looked in to – to pass the time of day.'

'Pass half an hour with us, then,' invited Harry. 'See if you can cheer Audley up a bit. The poor fellow's been having a lousy time of it recently.'

'Thank you for reminding me,' muttered Sebastian moodily. 'It's up to you, Penhaligon. I'd be just as happy with a bottle for company.'

'You had enough of that last night,' said Nicholas, taking a sneaky swipe at Harry who barely managed to deflect it. 'Time to work up a sweat, my boy.'

Combined with the affable, unthreatening presence of Sir Charles Delahaye, the suggestion that Mr Audley was suffering the after-effects of the night before, served to convince Mr Penhaligon that he was in no danger. Smiling and beginning to shed his coat, he said, 'Half an hour, then. And I thank you gentlemen for inviting me to join you.'

'Pleasure,' grunted Harry, engaging Nicholas's blade without warning.

And, 'Ha! That the best you can do?' retorted his lordship.

When Mr Penhaligon was facing him over their raised blades, Sebastian merely waited for him to begin … and when he did so, deflected the oncoming thrust with a seemingly idle parry. Richard frowned a little and tried a different move, followed by a feint. Sebastian defeated the first with a flick of the wrist and ignored the second. He still didn't bother to attack. Richard's frown deepened.

After five more minutes of the same, coupled with Sebastian's expression of sulky boredom, Mr Penhaligon stepped back and dropped the point of his foil to the floor. He said, 'If you don't want to do this, you need only say.'

'God,' muttered Sebastian. 'You want me to exert myself?'

'It might make the bout a little more interesting.'

'If you say so.' With a long-suffering sigh, Sebastian raised his blade. '*En garde.*'

And then it began. Mr Penhaligon suddenly found himself facing a swift, relentless attack that drove him across the room before he could recover himself and left him too busy to notice that Nicholas and Harry had stopped fencing to watch.

After a few minutes, Nicholas said, 'If this were in earnest, it'd be a slaughter.'

'Told you,' returned Harry. And to Charles, 'Did he mention Sebastian held his own against Rock for eleven minutes?'

'No. He didn't – and if he had, I might not have believed him. As for Mr Penhaligon, I think he's just beginning to realise what he's tangling with.'

In fact, Richard was starting to sweat. Without appearing to do anything very much at all, Sebastian was making him work extremely hard just to keep hold of his foil and was pushing him around the floor like the merest beginner. Nothing he tried to halt this process did the slightest bit of good. He couldn't get past Sebastian's guard and hadn't managed to touch him even once. Sebastian, on the other hand – had the bout been real – would have left him bleeding in several places and killed him twice. Almost playfully, the tip of Sebastian's foil came to rest on the base of his throat, over his heart and once, at his groin, before withdrawing again. The whole thing was becoming an embarrassment and it wasn't made any better by the desultory bits of helpful advice being offered by Harry and Nicholas. Mr Penhaligon's shoulder was on fire and he had cramp in his sword-hand; in addition, he was out of breath and out of temper.

Needless to say, losing his *sangfroid* didn't do anything to mend matters. His play became wilder and more erratic ... while Sebastian continued to press him, looking infuriatingly unruffled and wearing a faint, mocking smile. Then, without any warning whatsoever, Sebastian delivered two tricky moves in quick succession and said, 'How deeply are you involved with Miranda Silvarez?'

Shock nearly made Richard drop his foil. 'What?'

'You were with her last night at Drury Lane. And you know as well as I do that she planned that nasty little surprise. Did you help her?'

'No!' This time, Richard leapt out of range, lowered the foil and said breathlessly, 'Enough. I don't know where you got this damned ridiculous idea - but you've had your fun and I'm leaving.'

'Not yet.' Sebastian gestured to the closed door and the fact that Philip Vernon was now leaning against it. 'Not just yet.'

'If this is about last night, that was no fault of mine.'

'And we're supposed to take your word for that, are we?' asked Nicholas.

'Yes.' Mr Penhaligon stared round at the other faces and noted a distinct lack of friendliness in any of them. 'You've jumped to conclusions based on the fact that I invited Lady Silvarez to the theatre? You're deranged – all of you.'

'I don't think so,' said Sebastian. 'One of your lapdogs offered me a wager involving a lady's virginity recently. His idea – or did you put him up to it?'

Some of the colour drained from Richard's face. 'I don't know what you mean.'

'You do. But don't worry. I haven't divulged the name of the intended victim. Yet. As for Miranda, we know someone has been helping her get a toehold in society and believe that person is you. Well?'

'So? What of it?'

'In Miranda's case, it suggests the existence of a relationship between the two of you,' observed Sebastian dispassionately. 'What is she bribing you with? The same present I refused and which started this hell-hath-no-fury campaign of hers?'

Mr Penhaligon's jaw dropped and he swallowed hard.

'Didn't she tell you about that?' continued Sebastian. 'She was my mistress for a time in Lisbon until she set her sights on a wedding ring. The moment I arrived in London, she made it plain that I was supposed to fall, first into her bed and then down on one knee. As we've seen, she doesn't like being thwarted. But right now, we'd like to know about your part in her revenge quest. Specifically, the Bedford House rumour, the wholly false accusations in *The Whisperer* and last night's farce outside the theatre.'

A bead of sweat made its way down Mr Penhaligon's cheek. He said, 'All right. She asked me to help her get some invitations and I did. *She* saw what happened at Bedford House and I ... well, I just mentioned it to a few people. But I had nothing to do with the scandal-sheet thing and the first I knew of last night was when it happened. Satisfied?'

'Not especially.'

There was a long, unpleasant silence into which Nicholas eventually said derisively, 'If you ask me, he's feeble-witted. But the question is whether or not we believe him?'

'Difficult,' murmured Sir Charles. 'I wonder if Keswick knows in what puddles his brother is playing?'

'Unlikely,' remarked Sebastian. And fixing Mr Penhaligon with a hard stare, 'I want Miranda stopped. And since you've been her partner in crime, you may prefer to be the one to stop her – because if it's left to me, you won't enjoy the results any more than she will.'

'What are you talking about?' Richard wiped the sweat from his face and summoned a flicker of bravado. 'If you're threatening to challenge me --'

'I'm not. I'm actually threatening to do much worse than that. Since *The Whisperer's* interest in me brought a letter from the Duke of Rockliffe's man-of-law down on it, I suspect the editor will be quite eager to be helpful. A piece written by myself, to the effect that Mr Richard Penhaligon has been foisting a trollop by the name of Miranda Silvarez on polite society; and that the pair of them have been conspiring to ruin the Honourable Sebastian Audley's good name in various ways – most recently by paying a female to publicly accuse him of abandoning both her and his alleged child.' Sebastian paused, smiling grimly. 'I'll also prove my innocence by mentioning that the said child is a girl ... and that no

Audley female offspring in the past three generations or more has *ever* had red hair. That particular curse is reserved for the men.'

Through the course of this, Mr Penhaligon had gone steadily whiter.

'Damn it, I've told you I had no part in last night!'

'So you did. There's no justice in the world, is there?'

Richard looked around again, desperate to leave and knowing there was only one way these men would let him. 'What do you want?'

'I want you to make the situation clear to Miranda. There are to be no more attacks on me – of any kind at all. Is that clear enough?'

'What if she won't listen?'

'It's up to you to *make* her listen. If she doesn't desist, I'll infect the pair of you with social leprosy. That thought should be sufficient incentive for you to convince her.'

* * *

While the gentlemen were frightening Mr Penhaligon into compliance, prior to heading off in their various directions to begin undoing the harm of the previous night, Cassie stared mutinously through the window of her bedchamber. Before leaving for an undisclosed destination, her father had told her mother why the child was definitely *not* Sebastian's and Mama had, in turn, passed the information on to Cassie. But although she was glad of it, she hadn't needed proof; and she found it did little to dispel the seething emotions that had consumed her since that moment outside the theatre; fury on Sebastian's behalf, worry about what he must be feeling and frustration that she wasn't being allowed to offer him comfort. All she could do, Cassie decided, was to pour her heart out to an understanding ear.

Being long, passionate and angry, the letter to Caroline was also slightly garbled, covering as it did everything between the moment when Cassie had first fallen in love with Mr Audley and the public disaster of last night. Scribbling a final paragraph, she wrote, *I love him so much, Caro and I wish I'd told him instead of*

being afraid to trust that a man like him could want a girl like me.
As for that evil witch – I could kill *her. Literally. I only wish*
someone would give me the chance.

* * *

At around the time Cassie was sealing her letter, Mr
Penhaligon was telling the evil witch that the game was over –
and why. Miranda listened with increasingly deepening colour
and dangerously narrowed eyes. And when his recital drew to a
close, she said scathingly, 'You pathetic excuse for a man. If you
can't actually stand up for yourself, couldn't you at least have
managed a credible lie?'

For a moment, he stared at her completely beyond speech.
Thanks to her, he had experienced what he devoutly hoped would
be the worst hour of his life. Four men had watched him being
pushed around at sword-point like a complete fool; he'd been
laughed at, mocked and called a lack-wit; and finally he'd been
threatened with social ruin. All of it was the fault of this woman –
and none of it inclined him towards tact.

'No,' he snapped, 'I couldn't. Haven't you understood
anything I've said? They know what you've been up to. They
knew it before they planned to lie in wait for me this morning.
And as if the four gentlemen Audley had with him were not
enough to worry about, it appears that Rockliffe is interesting
himself in the matter. As I've tried to tell you before, that man has
more influence than God.'

'Don't be so ridiculous. Have you no backbone at all? If
you'd kept your nerve, it was just Audley's word against yours.
And as far as I'm concerned, it still is.' Her teeth gleamed in a
feral smile. 'He'll be on his knees at my feet and weeping tears of
blood before I'm done with him.'

'Is that before or after he pillories us both in the scandal-
sheets? Because – make no mistake about it, Miranda – that's
what he'll do. And I'm damned if I'll be tarred with the same
brush as you.'

'You think you're one whit better than me?' she spat. 'You're not. You're just a puking coward. And Audley's bluffing about *The Whisperer*. He won't do it.'

'He will. *Jesus!* What does it take to make you see sense?' Richard paused, breathing hard. 'Can't you understand that you don't have a choice? His friends will be going around right now, dropping a few words here and there about why that child isn't a little Audley bastard. One mention of your name alongside that and there's not a door that won't be slammed in your face. If you want to hang on to the fringes of society, you'll stop trying to wreak vengeance on Audley purely because you're obsessed with him and he didn't want you. Christ! If I'd had any idea where all this was going to lead, I wouldn't have come within a mile of you myself! You've got more venom in you than a bloody viper.'

Silence touched the edges of the room while she looked back at him in a way he couldn't interpret. Finally, almost mildly, she said, 'Have you quite finished?'

'No. I want your word that you'll leave Audley alone.'

Again Miranda took her time about answering. Then, very slowly, she smiled.

'Very well.'

Mistrusting that smile, Mr Penhaligon frowned. Suddenly, it seemed too easy.

'You promise?'

'Yes. Since you assure me there's no help for it, I can't do anything else, can I?' The smile still lingered. 'No more attacks on Sebastian Audley. I promise.'

CHAPTER SIXTEEN

After leaving the fencing academy, Nicholas and Harry spent an hour at White's, sharing the newest *on-dit* with anyone they thought likely to pass it on.

Audley leaving his by-blow to starve in the gutter? Nothing of the kind.

Not even his child. How do I know? The brat's a girl, for the Lord's sake! Has anyone ever seen an Audley female with hair that colour? Only got to think of Lizzie Holdenby and Audley's other sisters – brunettes, the lot of them.

As to the mother – if she is the mother – bats in her belfry. No other explanation.

'That should do it,' said Nicholas, as they left the club. 'I even forced myself to speak to that lisping toad Ansford. He's the biggest gossip I know.'

'He thertainly ith,' agreed Harry evilly. 'I got to March – who will pass it on to Charles Fox and from there, one hopes, the world. Let's hope Philip and Sir Charles are having equal success with their wives' callers. The men will come round fast enough because the mere thought of being caught in a trap like this is enough to make us *all* shudder. But it's the ladies who need to be convinced – and that may take a little longer.'

'True.' Nicholas paused on the steps of the club. 'I think I'll go back to St James' Square to see how things are progressing. Did you know, by the way, that the club is running a book on whether Adeline will have a boy or a girl?'

'Yes. I put my money on a son and heir. You?'

'My luck has been so bad recently, I didn't want to tempt Fate by betting at *all*. No, I'm going because I didn't see Rock earlier but might manage to get a word with him now.'

'Meanwhile, I'll be taking Nell driving in the park. I wouldn't be at all surprised if everyone we meet doesn't want to stop for a chat.'

'No arguing with that. I just hope Sebastian appreciates all the trouble we're going to.'

At Wynstanton House, Nicholas found that the situation had changed little in the last four hours. The Marquis of Amberley was still ensconced in the library with coffee and a book ... but of his Grace of Rockliffe, there was no sign.

'Where is he?' asked Nicholas, tossing down his hat. 'He can't *still* be with Adeline!'

'He is.' Amberley stood up and stretched. 'The physician and the midwife have been trying to throw him out but he's refusing to leave Adeline's side until *she* tells him to go.'

'What if she doesn't? He surely can't want to be there when ... well, at the crucial moment.' Nicholas looked a trifle queasy at the notion. 'Nor Adeline either, I'd have thought.'

'Only time will tell. Coffee?'

'No thank you. I've just swallowed half a pot of the stuff at White's, setting the gossip-mill in motion.' He grinned. 'It's a pity you weren't at Angelo's. Watching Sebastian scare the hell out of that fellow Penhaligon was even funnier than Sheridan's play.'

'Am I to gather that it had the desired effect?'

'Yes,' said Nicholas. And sat down to supply details.

He had just reached the point where Sebastian had threatened Penhaligon with *The Whisperer* when the door opened and Rockliffe walked in. Nicholas stopped speaking and stared. Without either coat or cravat, the Duke was in his shirt-sleeves, much of his hair was escaping its ribbon and his expression was of something which, on another man, might have been mildly distraught.

He said, 'They've sent me away. Adeline says the swearing and screaming phase is imminent and she'd rather I didn't witness it. I don't see the logic in that, Dominic. Do you?'

'Yes.' Amberley shoved his friend into the nearest chair and placed a glass of brandy at his elbow. 'It means it won't be very much longer. Everything is all right, isn't it?'

'I've no idea. Sir Humphrey says she's doing well but it didn't look that way to me – and it's been over twelve hours now.' He held out his hand and stared at it. 'I think she may have broken a bone or two.' Then, seeming to become aware of his brother's presence, 'Nicholas. To what do I owe the honour? I doubt you're here to support me in my hour of need.'

'Not exactly – though I would if I thought I'd be of any use. But no. I wanted to talk to you about this near-disaster surrounding Sebastian – though it can wait. You won't want to be bothered with that now.'

'Tell him anyway,' advised Amberley. 'He needs to focus on something other than what's going on upstairs.'

So Nicholas began again at the beginning and, though he could see he didn't have his brother's full attention, thought he had enough of it to make the exercise worthwhile. Eventually, Rockliffe said, 'It would appear that it is now merely a question of waiting for the tale to get around. One thing puzzles me, however. Why was Charles involved?'

'No idea.' Nicholas frowned a little. 'He and Sebastian arrived at Angelo's together – which is a bit odd now I come to think of it.'

Another long silence fell, during which his Grace took to pacing the carpet. Lord Amberley said, 'That's not going to make it happen any quicker, you know. And don't even *think* about going back upstairs. If they've any sense, they'll have barred the door. God knows, Rosalind banned me from the room the instant the doctor arrived. So sit down and drink your brandy. You look like hell.'

'Thank you.'

'Don't mention it.'

A further ten minutes passed while Amberley and Nicholas chatted in a desultory fashion. Then Rockliffe said, 'There is one possibility which might account for Charles lending a hand.'

'Oh?' asked Nicholas. 'What?'

The Duke took his time and finally said, 'No. I may be mistaken. But whether I am or not, I believe I will leave you to --' He stopped and erupted from his chair as, from the hall, came the sound of hurried footsteps.

The butler appeared, his normal gravity somewhat impaired.

He said, 'Sir Humphrey invites you to go up, your Grace.'

His Grace strode from the room and was last seen taking the stairs two at a time. The butler bowed and followed rather more sedately in his wake.

Amberley grinned at Nicholas. 'Still hoping to be supplanted, Nick?'

'*Praying* for it, more like. Do you suppose he's going to put me out of my misery?'

'Right now, that is the last thing on his mind – but someone should be able to tell us. Ah.' This as the butler re-appeared. 'Well, Symonds?'

'His Grace begs you to forgive him and asks you to raise a toast in his absence, my lord.'

'And?' demanded Nicholas.

'Her Grace has been safely delivered of a daughter,' announced Symonds with all due ceremony. And added, 'I believe the name Vanessa Jane has been mentioned.'

Nicholas dropped inelegantly on to a sofa.

'Oh bloody hell,' he muttered.

* * *

In Mount Street, after the afternoon's callers had departed, Philip Vernon went looking for his wife and finally ran her to earth in the spare bed-chamber with the little girl on her lap. Looking at the child for the first time in daylight, Philip saw that her hair was a perfectly ordinary red, nothing at all like the distinctive shade possessed by Mr Audley; she was also a very pretty child ... gazing at him, thumb in mouth, out of big blue eyes.

Isabel looked across at him smiling.

'Her name is Alice and she doesn't speak of parents – only of a Mrs Dane. So it would seem she was taken from an orphanage, not stolen from her mother.'

This was when Philip got the first inkling of trouble. 'Maybe so – but we still need to find out where she belongs. I'll send a note to Bow Street asking them to look into it.'

'Must we?'

226

'Yes, Isabel – of course we must. If that wretched Silvarez woman stole the child, someone will be hunting high and low for her. And in any case … what else are we going to do with her?'

Isabel looked away, saying softly, 'Keep her?'

'What? No. We can't.'

'Why not? If she has no family, why can't *we* give her one?' Suddenly the brown eyes were swimming in tears. 'She's so *little*, Philip. She won't be any trouble. Why can't I keep her?'

Because the whole of society knows some female tried to pass her off as Sebastian Audley's bastard, thought Philip. But he said, 'Isabel … sweetheart, I know how badly you want a child. So do I. But this isn't the way. Surely you can see that?'

'No. I can't.' She brushed a hand impatiently across her eyes and looked back at him stubbornly. 'Make enquiries, if you must. But don't ask me to give her up unless it's to her rightful parents – because I won't.'

* * *

Although he wanted nothing more than to see Cassandra, Sebastian knew better than to broach the subject with her father. Sir Charles had made it clear that he wouldn't be welcome in Conduit Street until there was evidence that the intended scandal had been averted. Also, he'd promised he would keep his distance and doing so was the best way of convincing Cassandra's father that he had a care for her reputation. On the other hand, it couldn't do any harm to send a note, unsealed and enclosed in one for Sir Charles.

Deciding what to write, however, proved extraordinarily difficult and after he'd screwed up five attempts and was still dissatisfied with a sixth, he gave up in despair. Instead, he decided to dine at Sinclairs and discover what was being said of him.

Crossing the main gaming floor, the signs were mainly good. Three gentlemen stopped to commiserate with him on being the victim of such a God-awful hoax and a fourth asked how often his sisters told him that hair like his was wasted on a mere man. The weight that had been pressing down on Sebastian's shoulders began to lift.

On the way up to the private dining rooms, he met Aristide Delacroix who said, 'It appears you are once more the talk of the town – though this time through no fault of your own. Unless the female who approached you last night belongs in Bedlam, someone must have a serious grudge against you.'

'Someone does,' agreed Sebastian. 'Fortunately, she miscalculated.'

'I'm glad to hear it. You will find Lord Nicholas upstairs, by the way – already half-way through a bottle of Chambertin.' And in answer to Sebastian's look of enquiry, 'The Duchess of Rockliffe has given birth to a daughter.'

Sebastian continued on his way, grinning ... only to stop outside a partly open door when he heard Nicholas say, '*Why* may I not call on you?'

'You know why,' replied Madeleine Delacroix. 'You are not just a duke's brother. You are a duke's *heir*.'

'I'm tolerably aware of that fact,' his lordship grumbled, 'though I'd argue with the significance of it. You've become friendly enough with my sister.'

'That's different. And though I've called on Lady Elinor at her invitation, I haven't suggested that she visit me because it would be making too great an assumption.'

'Poppycock! Just because Nell collects people doesn't mean she doesn't do it with care. She likes you. And if you won't invite her to tea, I'll lay money that sooner or later she'll just turn up on your doorstep.' He stopped and then said, 'All right. If you won't let me call, come driving with me.'

'That's even worse! People will talk and heaven only knows what they'll say.'

'I don't give a tinker's curse *what* they say!'

'Then you should!' Her voice had grown suspiciously brittle. 'I don't understand you – or how you can persist in bothering with me. It – it's very unsettling.'

'That,' returned Nicholas more gently, 'is probably the nicest thing you've ever said to me. Come driving with me. Please?'

There was a long silence during which Sebastian edged quietly back along the corridor ... and collided with Philip Vernon.

'Audley? What the devil --?'

With a quick, warning shake of his head, Mr Audley said, 'Philip! What excellent timing! Aristide says Nick's here somewhere so I thought I'd join him for dinner unless he has any objection. Otherwise, perhaps you'll keep me company?'

'I'll be glad to,' muttered Philip. And with a morose glance into Sebastian's face, 'You're sounding particularly cheerful this evening.'

'Let's say I'm more optimistic than I was when I got out of bed this morning. You, however, look as if you've just dropped a few thousand at Hazard.'

'That would be better than what's brewing at home.' Philip stopped as Madeleine glided towards them. 'Good evening, Mademoiselle. Lord Nicholas already here, is he?'

'Yes. He was just expressing a desire for turbot which, unfortunately, we do not have this evening. Perhaps your company will make up for the lack. Please go and make yourselves comfortable. I will send Guillaume to take your orders.' And she moved on.

'Turbot?' asked Philip blankly. 'Nick usually eats virtually raw beefsteak.'

'I know. But she had to make some excuse didn't she? Come on.'

Nicholas gave his friends and would-be dinner companions an old-fashioned stare.

'Were you out there listening?' he demanded.

'I may have caught a few words,' replied Sebastian, 'Just out of interest ... did she say yes?'

'None of your business.'

'Say yes to what?' asked Philip, reaching for the bottle and pouring two more glasses.

'Letting Nick drive her in the park.'

Lord Nicholas groaned. 'All right. If it will shut the two of you up, she said she'll consider it. But if she thinks it's going to become a topic of general conversation before it's even become a *fact* --'

'Not another word,' said Sebastian. 'I hear Rock has a daughter. Is he disappointed?'

'*Disappointed?* God, no. He's bloody delighted,' said Nicholas. 'You'd think nobody ever had a baby before. According to him, Lady Vanessa Jane is the prettiest baby in all creation – an assertion I had trouble agreeing with considering the little scrap is all red and wrinkled. On the other hand, I suspect she'll improve since she's had the sense to inherit the Wynstanton hair and her mother's eyes. But all that matters to *me* is that she ain't a boy.'

'You'll get over it – and there's always next time. What do you say, Philip?'

'What?' Philip looked up abstractedly. 'Sorry. I wasn't listening.'

'I thought not. Do you want to tell us what's wrong? You and the others have all rallied around me today – so if there's anything I can do in return, you need only ask. I've sent a note to Bow Street about the child but --'

'So did I,' said Philip flatly. 'But Isabel wants to keep her.'

'Ah. That could be ... difficult.'

'Difficult doesn't begin to cover it. She's desperate for a child and so far ... well, so far we've been disappointed. *Now* she's refusing to part with Alice unless Bow Streets finds her parents.' He lifted his glass and half-drained it. 'Either way, she's going to break her heart over this. The only question is whether Fielding's fellows do it ... or *I* do.'

'Let me take the blame,' volunteered Sebastian slowly. 'If the child needs a home, I'll find her one on the family estate.'

'I can do that myself if Isabel will let me. And if it wasn't for the way it came about, I probably wouldn't stand in her way. As it is, though ... I just don't know.'

'It seems to me that babies are the very devil,' observed Nicholas. 'Isabel wants one; the pair of you have been accidentally stuck with one; and I'm left praying that Rock and

Adeline do better next time.' He raised his glass and added darkly, 'There's a motto in this somewhere, mark my words.'

'Motto?' queried Philip.

'I think he means a moral,' grinned Sebastian. 'Though what it may be is beyond me.'

* * *

Cassie looked in vain for Mr Audley, first at Lady Hervey's musicale and then at the Faulkner rout. Obeying her father's ban on calling in Conduit Street was one thing, she thought crossly; avoiding social engagements where they might ordinarily have met was quite another. He was resourceful, wasn't he? Not averse to taking the odd risk? So why hadn't he at least sent her a note? It had been three whole days. It didn't sound much unless one was plagued by a restlessness that never, ever went away and a feeling that one was slowly starving. The Valkyrie stirred again and decided to take matters into her own hands.

* * *

Sebastian looked at the note and groaned. He shouldn't go. That was clear enough. But he couldn't simply stay away, leaving her waiting and wondering why he hadn't come; equally, writing to her without her parents' knowledge would be tricky – if not impossible. All of which left only one alternative.

As before, he waited just inside the Duke Gate and watched her ride up, trailed by the same groom who'd accompanied her previously. He'd intended to be stern and sensible and tell her she shouldn't be here and neither should he and that he ought to turn around and go home. Instead, her smile had him saying weakly, 'This isn't wise.'

'I know. But just a few minutes can't hurt ... and I haven't seen you *anywhere* since that awful night.'

'I know. But I must avoid embarrassing hostesses with my presence until I'm quite sure that they all know there's no truth in what happened. I tried to write to you but couldn't find the right words when I realised I'd have to leave my letter unsealed for Sir Charles to read. I can't afford any more risks, you see. Your father has been a good deal more forbearing than I've any right to expect – particularly about Miranda's latest trick. One more cataclysm and he'd be right to wash his hands of me.'

'He can't. I won't let him.' She held his gaze with her own. 'Did he tell you what I said to him about how – how I feel?'

'Yes.' Sebastian bathed her in a slow, very sweet smile. 'He did. But do you think you might tell me yourself?'

'Yes.' Her colour rose a little but she didn't look away. 'I daresay there's a better way of saying this but I don't know what it is. I love you – and love you and *love* you. So much that there aren't enough words to describe it.'

Something shifted inside Sebastian's chest and, not for the first time, he damned the fact that he couldn't put his arms around her. So he said gently, 'I love you in exactly the same way. Always and forever.'

'I could have told you before. I wish I had. But ... somehow I couldn't quite believe that you meant it. It was only later that I realised you'd never say something like that if you didn't.' She shrugged faintly. 'Truthfully, the possibility that you might actually love me was too immense for me to grasp.'

'You think I don't feel the same? *I'm* the one whose doings have been laid out for public consumption in the scandal-sheets. It doesn't matter that most of it is fiction; that I haven't fought umpteen duels and bedded every woman from here to Constantinople. What matters is that people *think* I have – and it doesn't make me look very promising husband material.' He stopped, drawing an uneven breath. 'I never understood why you didn't read Olivia's scandal sheets. You should have.'

'No. That is the very last thing I should have done ... which is why I burned them.'

'You *what?*'

'After that night at the theatre, the mere thought of them made me feel sick. So I burned them. All of them.'

For several seconds, words failed him but finally he said, 'I wish we weren't on horseback in a public park. This is one of those times when only actions will do. And I have an overwhelming urge to show you *exactly* how I feel about you.'

'Oh.' A single pulse throbbed deep inside her and she said softly, 'I wish you could.'

'So do I.' He grinned at her. 'Your father swears I've turned you into a Valkyrie, you know.' And when she looked blank, 'An avenging shield-maiden, love – with a sword.'

'Oh dear.' She laughed. 'I wanted to make myself quite clear. But perhaps I overdid it.'

'You certainly left no room for doubt. Did you *really* say that if I asked you to marry me, you'd do it even it meant we had to elope?'

'Yes. At the time, I was ... well, I wasn't thinking very clearly. I was furious about what had happened and that we were being kept apart when I knew you must have been feeling wretched.' She looked down, fiddling with her reins. 'I probably let my tongue run away with me. And since you hadn't asked, I *definitely* took too much for granted when I told my parents what I'd say if you did.'

'No, love. You didn't. I'd have asked before if I'd thought there was the slightest chance you might say yes – and I'd ask right now if we weren't in a wholly unconducive location.' He smiled at her. 'I'd like to do it properly, Cassandra. A girl deserves to see the man who loves her on his knees at least *once* in her life.' A movement away to his left caught the tail of his eye but vanished before he could be sure he'd seen anything. It was enough, however, to make him say, 'Much as I deplore the necessity, we shouldn't linger and chance being seen by someone who might recognise either one of us. I believe I've made Miranda aware that any further attempts to ruin me will rebound on her and I think the damage from that scene outside the theatre has been averted. But I promised your father I'd have a care for your name ... and this isn't the way to do it.' He hesitated. 'Sir Charles *did* tell you that child was quite definitely *not* mine, didn't he?'

'Yes – but I knew that anyway.'

'You did? How, exactly?'

'Because if it had been yours, you would have taken care of it.'

Sebastian drew a long breath. He said, 'Yes. Yes, I would. And thank you.'

'For what?'

'For honouring me with the sort of trust I've done nothing to earn.'

She shook her head. 'Do you think I don't know you at all?'

'I think you had reason to wonder.' He leaned over to place his hand over hers. 'Try to be patient, sweetheart. This hiatus will soon be over and when it is ... when it is, I'll ask the question I haven't the right to ask now. Everything will work out. I promise.'

* * *

Sebastian arrived back in Cork Street to find two letters waiting for him.

Sir John Fielding of Bow Street informed Mr Audley that Alice Moore had been taken from an orphanage in Foster Lane, ostensibly by a female wishing to adopt her. The orphanage was willing to resume its responsibility for the child, if required and Lord Philip Vernon had been apprised of the situation.

Philip's note said, *Isabel won't see you. I told her you'd come – but she says Alice will leave this house over her dead body. Nothing is going to persuade her otherwise – and I can't bear to try. She and the little mite adore each other.*

* * *

That evening, just as Sebastian was debating the wisdom of attending Lady Moreton's soirée, an imperious tattoo at the front door heralded the arrival of a visitor. Two minutes later, the Earl of Sarre strode into the parlour and said crisply, 'What the devil's going on between you and Cassie Delahaye? Didn't I make myself clear on that subject?'

'Yes. And if you'll take off your hat and sit down --'

Adrian dropped his hat on the nearest table but remained standing.

'Tell me you're not using that girl to win our wager.'

'I'm not. And you should know better than to ask.'

'Then what *are* you doing?'

'Getting married, I hope.'

The earl's silver-grey eyes pinned him with an acute stare. 'Are you serious?'

'Very. Adrian – will you please sit down, take a glass of wine and let me explain? I've no idea what you've heard but --'

Tossing his gloves after his hat, Adrian finally sat down saying irritably, 'What I've *heard* is the gist of a virtually incomprehensible letter from Cassie which alarmed Caroline sufficiently to insist I ride eighty miles to get to the bottom of it.'

'Oh. My apologies for that. What did Cassandra say?'

'Far too much, in my opinion. It began with a lot of nauseating stuff about how handsome you are – and honourable and kind and utterly irresistible – but I mostly skipped over that part.'

'That's a pity. It sounds like the best bit.'

'Then came something about a play and a by-blow of yours being produced in front of a crowd of folk in Drury Lane – except that the child was absolutely *not* yours and Cassie would have been quite *certain* of that even if it *hadn't* had the wrong colour hair. No – please don't interrupt. I might lose the thread completely – not to mention the plethora of under-scorings. Next, as I recall, were more besotted ramblings about you and how, if and when you ask, she'll marry you no matter what anyone says – the point there, to my mind, being the fact that you *hadn't* asked. And finally, just when I thought it couldn't get any worse, an evil witch whom Cassie wanted to kill with her bare hands came into it.' Sarre surveyed Mr Audley with mocking invitation. 'I'll take that glass of wine now while you explain. But if you've any care at all for my sanity, you'll stick to the facts.'

'I'll try – though it's a tall order.'

Sebastian poured wine, handed Adrian a glass and began, for what felt like the hundredth time, to explain the recent machinations of Miranda. Then, when he got to the end, he said, 'The only thing that matters is this. I never intended to fall in love

235

with Cassandra but I could no more stop it happening than I can stop breathing. So rid your mind that it has anything to do with our wager. It hasn't. I love her and can't contemplate my life without her – and I fully intend to marry her as soon it's possible. She knows that and so do her parents. Unfortunately, there's another hurdle to cross – for which I'll need the help of my father. And there's no guarantee that I'll get it.'

CHAPTER SEVENTEEN

Her parents having been invited to dine with the Marquis and Marchioness of Amberley, Cassie attended Lady Linton's assembly with Jack and Althea Ingram. Since Mr Audley was unlikely to be present, she didn't expect to enjoy it very much … but nothing could have prepared her for what the evening had in store.

The assembly was the same as any other party hosted by Viscountess Linton – which was to say, less formal than most other functions and, like its hostess, vaguely haphazard. Cassie danced with some of her usual partners and chatted with various acquaintances. Several of the latter asked if she'd heard that the child the foreign female had tried to lay at Mr Audley's door was absolutely *not* his. Cassie expressed suitable shock, agreed that the whole episode had been quite dreadful and went on her way inwardly smiling. She was disappointed not to find Nell and Harry in attendance and surprised that Philip and Isabel were not there either – Lady Linton being Isabel's mother. Sighing, she wondered how soon Althea would be ready to leave.

She was about to adjourn to the ladies' retiring room when a footman appeared at her elbow and said, 'Beg pardon, Miss – but a note's just been left for you. Fellow as brought it said it was urgent.'

Startled, Cassie took the paper he was holding out as if he thought he might catch something. The reason for this, she realised, was that the note was scrawled on the back of a *School for Scandal* playbill. Frowning and finding an empty chair, she sat down to read it. Half a minute later, she was on her feet again, her brain in a whirl.

I'm in trouble, Cassie. I wanted to see the play but someone's picked my pocket and I haven't the money to get home. Please help me – and please, please don't tell Mama! I'm in Covent Garden by the theatre. Come quickly. I'm scared.
Olivia

Several thoughts jostled for position inside Cassie's head.
First came the realisation that she couldn't recall the last time
she'd seen her sister's handwriting so had no way of knowing if
this was it. Then she wondered if Livy really *was* stupid enough to
sneak out of the house alone to watch a play from the public pit
and expect to get away with it. Finally, with a groan, Cassie
realised that of course she could. There were times when Olivia
didn't have the sense of a flea. If she had, she'd have summoned
a hackney to take her back to Conduit Street where Bradshaw, the
butler, would pay the driver. It was what Cassie was going to
have to do since she had no money either. Consequently, there
was no possibility that this could be kept from Mama and Papa.
The best that could be hoped for was that no one else found out
about it. But right now, if Livy was alone at night in Covent Garden
of all places, something had to be done quickly.

Slipping from the ballroom, Cassie sent one footman to find
her cloak and another to inform Mistress Ingram that she'd been
unexpectedly called away and would explain everything
tomorrow. She hoped that by tomorrow she'd have come up with
a convincing lie. She also wished there was someone she could
ask to accompany her. Travelling alone at night in a hired vehicle
wasn't something she had ever done before and it suddenly felt a
little frightening. If Sebastian had been there, or even Nicholas ...
but neither were. In fact, the only gentleman present who she'd
trust to keep Olivia's indiscretion to himself was Jack Ingram; but
Jack wouldn't leave Althea alone at a ball – which meant she'd
have to come with them and thus making the whole mess even
more complicated than it already was.

It was whilst tying the strings of her cloak and noting with
some relief that a hackney coach stood idle across the street that
a measure of logic replaced her initial panic.

What am I doing? she thought. *I can't manage this on my
own and I'd be stupid to try. If something goes wrong, I'll be in as
much trouble as Livy – more, probably. And since Papa is going to
know about it anyway, what is the point of racing off to Covent*

Garden alone? I must have been as mad as Olivia to even think *of it.*

Reaching the coach and suddenly knowing exactly what she should do, she said crisply, 'Amberley House in Hanover Square, if you please. And quickly.'

* * *

Mr Audley and Lord Sarre returned to Cork Street from Sinclairs at a little after eleven. Agreeing that the evening was still young, they settled down with a glass of port and – since his lordship was averse to playing cards and flatly refused to make an idiot of himself over the chessboard – contented themselves with conversation.

'Is Mr Maitland still at Sarre Park?' asked Sebastian.

'No. He went back to Halifax a week ago. Meanwhile, the renovation of the north wing has taken place at unprecedented speed thanks to a regiment of workmen. God alone knows what it has cost. But we now have a new roof, new floorboards and no rot of any kind anywhere. Caroline is delighted and currently knee-deep in redecoration. She's even started talking of a small house-party in August if the house is ready by then. Just friends – of which she's hoping you will --'

The remainder of his sentence was cut off by a furious pealing of the doorbell. Having given his few servants leave to retire, Sebastian strode into the hall, opened the door and was promptly pushed aside by Sir Charles Delahaye who stormed past him, snapping, 'Where is she?'

Sebastian was suddenly very cold. He said, 'Not here. Why -- ?'

'*Not?*'

'No. What --?'

'Oh God.' A white shade bracketed Charles's mouth and he looked as if he'd aged ten years in a single moment. 'It was my only hope.'

Sebastian's hands were shaking and a rock had wedged itself in his throat, making speech impossible. Adrian gripped his shoulder briefly and said, 'Sir Charles ... sit down and tell us what has happened. It's Cassie, I take it?'

'Of course it's Cassie!' Charles allowed himself to be led into the parlour but remained on his feet. 'If she's not here, I don't know where to look. She was at the Linton assembly, then she left in a hackney. She told the driver to take her to Amberley House but she never got there.' He tugged at his already loosened cravat and added, 'It's been almost two hours, for God's sake! She could be anywhere by now.'

Sebastian finally managed to lock away the fear that had been paralysing every part of him. 'Have you questioned Lord Linton's servants?'

'What do *you* think?'

'Then you must have some idea of what would make Cassandra leave a ball, alone and in a hired carriage.'

'There was a note. Something scribbled on the back of a theatre playbill, apparently. The footman who gave it to Cassie didn't read it because he couldn't. But whatever it said caused her to ask for her cloak and send Althea Ingram word that she'd had to leave.'

'Without saying why?'

'Yes. But if she was going to Amberley House, it was to find me. Serena and I were dining there.'

'So the note said something she felt should be kept in the family.'

'I – yes. I suppose that must be true. But she didn't get to Amberley House and she isn't at home either. I thought – I *prayed* that she'd changed her mind and come to you instead.'

'Two hours ago, I wasn't here. Cassandra wouldn't have known that – or where she might find me.' The suspicion he was too frightened to contemplate swelled like a rising tide inside his head and set up a chant of, *No, no, no. This can't be happening –* except that he knew it could and that what he needed now was clear thought and immediate action. Wheeling back towards the hall, he mumbled, 'Excuse me. I need boots.'

Watching him take the stairs two at a time, Charles shouted, 'Wait! If you know something --'

'I don't,' called Sebastian from half-way up. 'I can only guess.'

Sir Charles was left staring helplessly at Lord Sarre. 'What does he mean?'

'I imagine,' replied Adrian, his tone very grim, 'he thinks that, like the baby at Drury Lane, this may be the work of Miranda Silvarez.'

'But – but *why*? How can that woman even *know* Cassie?'

'I've no idea and doubt if Sebastian has either. But he has to start somewhere. And given recent events, if you were him, what would *you* think?'

Sebastian came back, having changed his footwear. Crossing to the bureau, he took the jewelled Russian knife he'd worn to Bedford House from a drawer and slipped it into his right boot.

'That is a bad idea,' said Adrian flatly. 'Put it away.'

'It's a precaution. Would you prefer I took a loaded pistol?'

'I'd prefer you didn't go armed at all. And it's nearly midnight. If you're thinking of descending on your former mistress, her servants aren't going to let you in.'

'I don't plan on giving them a choice and will wake the whole damned street if I have to,' came the clipped reply. 'Go home, Charles. Her ladyship must be distraught. You should also send word to Bow Street in the hope they can find the driver of that hackney. One of the street urchins they pay for information might have seen something. And if they want to prevent a potential murder, they might also like to send an officer to number eleven, Half Moon Street.' He glanced around, his expression iron-hard. 'I don't know why or how Miranda would take Cassandra but I can't think of anyone else who'd do it either. If I learn anything, I'll send word.'

He turned on his heel and swung away to the door. With a brief muffled curse, Adrian strode after him, saying, 'Don't be an ass, Sebastian. How the hell do you think you'll manage this on your own? I'm coming with you.'

En route for Half Moon Street, Adrian said, 'Would she know you want to marry Cassie?'

'No. Aside from yourself and Cassandra's parents, no one does. But Miranda's devious, vindictive and capable of anything. She's also apparently obsessed – not just with making my life a misery but with bringing me down to her own level. She learned Cassandra's name a couple of weeks ago at Vauxhall. If she's been having me followed – which isn't impossible – she may know we went riding together. I don't know, Adrian. *I don't bloody know!* But I've got to do something and this is all I can think of.'

Like its neighbours, the house in Half Moon Street was in darkness. With unrestrained violence, Sebastian plied the knocker and then hammered the door with his fist until it shuddered. Eventually, a light showed. Sebastian continued his assault and shouted, 'Open up! *Now*, curse you – before I summon the Watch!'

Lights were also appearing at the houses on either side. A window was thrown open, through which a night-capped head emerged, demanding to know what the *devil* was going on. Ignoring it, Sebastian shouted again and kicked the door. And finally there were sounds of bolts being withdrawn and the door opened a crack.

'Sir, I must protest --' began a querulous voice.

Sebastian shouldered the door wide and stepped inside. 'Where's your mistress?'

'N-Not at home, sir.' Clad in his nightshirt, the butler who had admitted Sebastian on his one and only previous visit shivered and wrung his hands.

'No?' Sebastian surged past him and headed for the stairs. 'You'll forgive me if I don't believe you. Which is her room?'

'No – really, sir. She isn't here. And I can't permit you to --'

'I didn't ask for permission. Adrian – check downstairs. I'll take the bedchambers.'

'You bloody well won't.' A muscular fellow roughly the size of a barn door walked out to plant himself at the foot of the staircase. 'You'll turn around and sod off, if you know what's good for you.'

'Likewise, if *you* know what's good for you, you'll get out of my way,' snapped Sebastian, not pausing in his advance.

'Madam's not 'ere and you ain't going rampaging about through 'er 'ouse.'

'Yes,' said Sebastian, 'I am.'

And without further hesitation, he drove his elbow under the man's jaw. The bruiser staggered but regained his balance and charged at Sebastian, roaring. Sebastian spun sideways delivered one hard kick to the kneecap, a second to a place even more painful and was off up the stairs before his adversary hit the marble floor, clutching his groin.

'If he gets up, keep him busy,' he shouted, before disappearing round the turn of the stairs.

Lord Sarre grunted something incomprehensible and prepared to do his best.

It did not take Sebastian long to find Miranda's bedchamber. It was in darkness, the fire almost burned out and the bed empty. He lit a couple of candles and started a rapid search, hoping to find a letter or note – anything that might give him some clue about Miranda's current activities. There was nothing. Sebastian swore viciously and flew back downstairs.

He found Adrian on the floor, holding the hulk by the ears while the rotund, night-shirted butler sat on his chest. At some other time, it might have been funny. Right now, the black hole in Sebastian's chest was swallowing up every thought save one.

'I had to hit him again but he'll be coming round soon enough,' said Adrian. 'Meanwhile, we've established that Andrews here knows nothing at all but that the girl hiding over there in the stair-well might.'

Sebastian peered into the shadows. 'And you are?'

'Polly.' A scowling, angular young woman advanced into the light. 'In another house, I'd be a ladies' maid. In this one, I'm a bloody dogsbody. As for Madam with her nasty temper – she never says where she's going or when she'll be back. Like as not, she's spending the night in some fellow's bed but I couldn't tell you whose.'

'Have there been any visitors today?'

Polly shook her head. 'The only visitor she ever has is that Mr Penhaligon and *he* hasn't been near for days.' She pointed at the recumbent figure on the floor which was now just starting to stir. 'Randall's the one to ask about what Madam might be getting up to. He comes and goes at all hours and never lifts a finger in the house – so I reckon she's paying him to do some dirty work for her. Common as muck and poisonous as a snake, she is.'

'You have that right.'

A jerk of Sebastian's head told Adrian and the butler to move aside; and when they did so, he put one foot in a strategic location with just enough pressure to cause discomfort. Randall's eyes flew open in time to see a long, wicked-looking blade being slid from one highly-polished boot. He said hurriedly, 'Now look, mister – there ain't no need for that.'

'Whether there is or not will depend on how fast you answer my questions. A lady was abducted tonight. A *lady* – do you understand? If you had anything to do with that and harm comes to her, I'll see you hanged. So tell me what you know and make it quick.'

'I don't know nothing about no abduction, mister. Honest, I don't. I bin following you a bit like Madam asked – don't mind admitting that. But --'

'And seen me doing what?'

'Coming and going from your ken in Cork Street and that fancy gaming club off St. James'.'

'What else?' Seeing in Randall's face that there *was* something else but that he was reluctant to reveal it, Sebastian leaned a little more heavily on the man's marital equipment and simultaneously brought the knife-point to within an inch of his throat. '*What else?*'

'Couple of times I seen you riding in the park with a young gentry-mort. And – and after that, Madam set me to watching *her* instead. Then tonight I took a note to a ken in Clarges Street.

There was an old rattler waiting and Madam said I was to stay till I seen the gentry-mort get in, then come away. So I did.' He hesitated again until the knife pricked his skin. 'The rattler was on the dark side of the street so I could be mistook but I thought – I thought the jarvey might have been Long Jake as sometimes drives Mrs Grendel. And that's everything – so move your boot, will you?'

'Presently. Who is Mrs Grendel?

'Abbess of the nunnery on Mercer Street, near the Garden.'

Bile rose in Sebastian's throat and for a moment he thought he might actually throw up. Taking an iron grip on every nerve and sinew, he withdrew both the blade and his foot and in a voice like cracking ice, said, 'Finally. Let's go.'

Having seen the moment of weakness but knowing better than to remark on it, Adrian suggested that it might perhaps be sensible to wait for the Runners.

'While Cassandra may be in a bloody brothel? No.'

His lordship sighed. 'You just want to break heads personally.'

'Wouldn't you?' Striding towards the door, Sebastian said, 'Andrews – if and when the Runners turn up, insist one of them waits here. It's clear that Lady Silvarez is involved in tonight's abduction – probably solely responsible for it – and if his lordship and I don't catch up with her, she's got to come home some time.'

And then he was gone, Lord Sarre hard on his heels.

* * *

An hour or so earlier, Cassie had awoken feeling sick and groggy, in a room she didn't recognise and with no recollection of how she'd got there. Eventually, as her mind became clearer, she remembered the note from Olivia and an ancient hackney carriage ... and finally, the large rough hand that had pressed a damp, pungent cloth over her nose and mouth. Her breathing began to accelerate as she absorbed three crucial facts. This wasn't Amberley House; there was no sign of Olivia; and she herself had walked straight into somebody's trap. As to who that somebody was ... well, there was really only one possible answer.

She swung her feet to the floor and had to grab the bedpost for balance as a wave of dizziness washed over her; then she ploughed an erratic course to the door. It was locked. Something at the back of her brain had told her it would be but still she couldn't help tugging at it. Panic crept several steps closer, urging her to beat her hands against the panels and shout for help; she took a moment to push it back, leaning her brow against the wood. Panic wasn't going to help and it would be stupid to summon someone from the other side of that door when she had no idea who that someone might be. Better to let them believe she was still unconscious and give herself time to think.

From somewhere below, she could hear raucous male voices and screeches of female laughter. What on earth *was* this place?

Turning, she examined the room. There was a lot of balding red velvet and far too many mirrors. Her reflection looked back at her from all directions; small, pale and very frightened. Aside from the fact that they existed, Cassie knew nothing about bawdy-houses but instinct told her that she was in one now.

On the opposite wall, curtains were closed over a small window. She lurched towards it, knowing it was probably useless to hope but unable not to. Dragging the curtains back, she looked out into blackness from what seemed to be the third floor. The window itself proved to be jammed shut but she fought with it for a time anyway before coming to the conclusion that, if there was help to be had from outside, she'd wouldn't get it without first smashing the glass ... and letting her captors know that she was awake.

Defeated, she sat down on the edge of the bed and forced her brain to work logically. The note had not been from Olivia. Her sister had never been in any trouble and was, presumably, safe in bed at home. And the hired carriage she'd stepped into had been waiting for her. No matter what destination she'd given the driver she would still have ended up here – wherever here was.

All right, she thought, forcing herself to breathe evenly. *No one knows where I am except the woman who arranged for me to be abducted. That's not good. I don't know how long I've been here so I've no idea how soon I'll be missed. If I'm lucky, Althea and Jack became concerned when I just vanished. Perhaps Papa is already looking for me. But where will he start? With the servants at Linton House? Yes. They must have heard me direct the jarvey to Hanover Square – only of course I never got there.* She stopped, squeezing her eyes shut. Crying wasn't going to help. *Please, please God – let Papa have gone to Sebastian. He'll know where to find the Silvarez woman and she's the best chance they've got of rescuing me before things get any worse.* Something half-way between a laugh and a sob shook her. *Can things get any worse? Locked up somewhere I don't know and probably at the mercy of the Evil Witch who I'm beginning to think is actually quite mad? But I can't just sit here like a lamb awaiting slaughter. Papa told Sebastian I was a Valkyrie so I ought to try thinking like one.*

It had taken some searching to find a book in the library that explained about Valkyries collecting fallen heroes from the battle-field and carrying them off to Valhalla – which was apparently the Viking equivalent of heaven but was less about harps and angels and more like Roman orgies. Still, Cassie had liked the sound of the fearless shield-maidens. She just didn't feel very much like one at the moment.

Sooner or later, someone is going to come through that door. And when they do, I'll need a weapon. She looked around without much hope until finally the chipped ewer on the wash-stand caught her eye. *I suppose that will have to do. It won't kill anybody but it might serve to discourage them. Oh Sebastian. Please come and find me. This is ... well, it's really quite frightening not knowing what will happen next.*

What happened next was that she heard a key being inserted into the lock. Flying across the room, she seized the water jug to stand poised and ready. The door opened, a woman came in and, without waiting to find out who it was, Cassie smashed the ewer hard against a white-blonde head. The woman dropped to her knees, howling and Cassie wasted no time in making a dash for freedom. Unfortunately, she collided in the doorway with an extremely fat woman who simply used her bulk to push her gently back inside the room.

'The little bitch *hit* me!' Clutching her head, Miranda hauled herself up into a chair. Then, looking down at her fingers, 'I'm bleeding!'

'So you are.' The newcomer shut the door and leaned against it. 'Can't blame the girl for that. I reckon if somebody had snatched *you* away, you'd have done worse.' And to Cassie, 'Sit down, dearie. I'm sorry about the oil of vitriol. Jake did it for the best but he knows better now. Meantime, you won't be here long and nobody's going to hurt you.'

Hoping beyond hope that, if she wasn't actually an ally, the fat lady might at least be sympathetic, Cassie said unevenly, 'If that's so, why am I here at all?'

'That's for *her* to explain. I've just been paid for the room and the use of my driver.'

'And privacy, Mrs Grendel.' Holding a lace-edged handkerchief to her temple, Miranda suddenly seemed strangely calm. 'I paid for *privacy*. So go away.'

'I'm going. But you remember my terms. The young lady's to be returned home, safe and sound. If you hurt her, don't count on me keeping quiet when folks come asking. And don't even *think* of letting any of my customers get a glimpse of her. There's not one of 'em would believe she's here willingly – and I'm not having Runners at the door on account of you.' Mrs Grendel turned towards the door and then, looking back at Cassie, said bluntly, 'This ain't a place you want to be seen, Miss – so stay here till somebody comes to show you the way out.'

Watching hope disappear and hearing the key turn in the lock, Cassie sat down on the edge of the bed and folded her hands in her lap to hide the fact that they weren't steady. Then she looked Miranda in the eye and said, 'I've no idea who you are, Madam but --'

'Liar. We met at Vauxhall. But you knew who I was before that.'

'I *do* recall you attempting to foist your acquaintance on Lady Elinor and myself at Vauxhall – but why you should think I already knew you --'

'It was written all over your face, silly girl. And you were the woman with Sebastian Audley at Bedford House, weren't you?'

'*Me?*' Cassie's nerves snarled but she managed a tiny, incredulous laugh. 'Hardly.'

'Oh, I've been told no one would believe it of a milk-and-water Miss like you – that you've got them all nicely fooled. But I know the truth.' Miranda's teeth gleamed in a savage smile. 'I know you were in the library that night at Cavendish House, as well. I heard what you said about it.'

Cassie couldn't remember what she'd said; neither could she spare the additional concentration it would take to try. She said, 'I don't know what you're talking about – and suspect that you don't, either.'

'Keep pretending if it makes you feel better. It won't help.' Miranda paused and then, her tone gathering a note of jeering spite, 'Where were you hiding? Did you watch him kissing me and wish it was you? Yes. Of course you did. He makes you hot for him, doesn't he?'

Oh God, thought Cassie despairingly. *She thinks there's something between Sebastian and me ... but I can't let her know she's right or this will get much, much worse.*

Hoping that, for once in her life, she could lie convincingly, she said, 'This is all nonsense. Unless you have anything sensible to say, I'd like to leave.'

'I daresay. But I'm not finished with you yet. Indeed, I've barely started.'

'Then perhaps you could get on with it. So far as I can see, you've had me drugged and dragged here against my will purely to talk about Sebastian Audley. Why?'

'I wanted to find out what he sees in an ordinary little thing like you.'

'What makes you think he sees anything?'

'I know him. I know him very, *very* well. And early morning meetings in the park?' Miranda shook her head. 'You should have been more careful.'

It gave Cassie a jolt to realise what she should have known from the start. The witch had been having Sebastian watched; and her, too it would seem – for how else could she have known Olivia even existed? It posed the question of how much *more* she knew.

Managing a suitably careless tone, she said, 'Since I had a groom with me, it was scarcely clandestine. And why should I not ride out with my own cousin?'

'What?' Shock drew a line between Miranda's brows. 'He's your *cousin*?'

'Didn't you know? Sebastian is my cousin and a close friend of my brother. Now, for heaven's sake come to the point!'

'Very well.' The blue gaze passed disparagingly over Cassie from head to toe. 'My name, in case you've forgotten, is Lady Silvarez. And I'm Sebastian Audley's lover.'

Returning look for look, Cassie raised what she hoped were supercilious brows.

'I might congratulate you except that what you mean is you *were* his lover.'

'Was – and will be again. This confusion of his is only temporary. He's mine. He's been mine for a very long time. Sooner or later, he'll realise it.'

The utter confidence with which she spoke sent a shiver down Cassie's back. When she'd wondered if Miranda was mad, she hadn't actually considered that it might be the literal truth. Now she was beginning to. She said, 'I'd be surprised if he agreed with you. In fact, it sounds highly unlikely. Oh – don't mistake me. I daresay you and Sebastian had an *affaire*. But it must have been some time ago.'

For the first time, Miranda looked less than certain. 'He's *discussed* this with you?'

'Naturally not. Even as cousins, that would be highly improper. But we milk-and-water Misses aren't entirely naïve, you know. We're aware that gentlemen have these little …

250

arrangements. But they don't mean anything and they don't last. Also, a gentleman doesn't marry a woman he can have for the price of a few coins and a trinket or two.'

'Watch your mouth.' In two strides, Miranda was looming over her. 'If you're wise, you won't make me angry. I can hurt you without leaving a mark.'

'And I can scream the house down.' Managing not to flinch, Cassie shrugged and tried to sound faintly bored. 'I don't know what you expect to gain by abducting me but do you honestly imagine you'll get away with it? It's a serious crime and my father will see you behind bars for it.'

'By the time I'm done, your father will have more important things to worry about.'

Cassie didn't like the sound of that. 'Meaning what?'

'You'll find out.' With a careless shrug, Miranda turned away to the small, heavily spotted mirror above the empty fireplace and inspected the damage to her temple. The cut was just on her hairline and seemed to have stopped bleeding so she deftly re-arranged her curls to cover it. 'So ... Sebastian is your cousin. Do you think he'll marry you?'

'What makes you suppose I want him to? But I certainly don't think he'll marry *you*. Even if your goose hadn't already been cooked on that score, I imagine the nasty scene you engineered outside the Theatre Royal would have done the trick. And yes, I *do* know that was your doing. But what I *don't* understand is why you're so determined to chase after a man who plainly doesn't want you. It's rather pathetic. Don't you have *any* pride?'

There was a brief unpleasant pause. Then, 'Clever little bitch, aren't you?'

'Clever enough to recognise desperation when I see it.'

'*Desperation?*' Miranda whirled away from her reflection, her face contorting with fury. '*Look* at me, you stupid child! I can have any man I choose!'

'Not quite *any* man, apparently.' Cassie decided that, since the gloves were off, she might as well continue fighting back. 'I don't dispute that you're beautiful – but what's inside your head isn't. Sebastian has presumably made it clear that he doesn't want you and for some reason, you're afraid he might want me instead. That's why I'm here, isn't it? Because you are jealous? And probably because you've decided that if *you* can't have him, no one else should.' Something changed in Miranda's expression, causing Cassie to press home her advantage. 'That's it, isn't it? After all, even *you* can't be idiotic enough to imagine that putting him in the public pillory would make him like you any better. You did it to make him unacceptable to any other lady of his own class. How disappointed you must be that it didn't work.'

The azure gaze narrowed and became suddenly extremely astute.

'Oh dear. *Now* who's pathetic?'

'I beg your pardon?'

'You're in love with him. Aren't you?'

Cassie's pulse thudded a warning to be careful.

'Oh – for heaven's sake! Where on earth did you get that idea?'

'You're not hard to read. You've fallen in love with the pretty face and the charm and that spectacular body – just like all the others.'

'Just like you, you mean?' asked Cassie sweetly. 'But you're letting your imagination run away with you again when what you *ought* to be doing is sticking to the point. Do you think I'm going to keep quiet about tonight? I'm not. Sebastian will know you did this. He will *know* … and between them, he and my father will make sure you face the consequences.'

An odd expression crossed Miranda's face and then she walked to the door and knocked on it. As the key was turned from the outside, she said, 'Perhaps. Perhaps not. We'll see. Meanwhile, you can go.'

'At last.' Taken aback and suddenly suspicious but wanting only to escape while she could, Cassie rose to shake out her hopelessly crumpled petticoats. Then, 'Was there any point at *all* to this ridiculous game of yours?'

'It wasn't pointless and it wasn't a game.' Miranda gestured to the man standing motionless outside the door. 'Jake will show you the way out. Goodbye.'

With a jerk of his head, the coachman invited Cassie to follow him down the stairs.

She hesitated, naturally wary of putting herself in the power of the fellow who'd brought her here in the first place. Had it not been turned midnight and pitch dark, she'd have insisted on finding another conveyance. As it was, in addition to feeling deathly tired, she suspected she wouldn't necessarily be any safer with anyone else – let alone wandering unfamiliar streets on her own. Since there seemed no sensible alternative, she turned her back on Miranda and followed.

'Beg pardon about the oil of vitriol, Miss,' murmured Jake, when they emerged in the deserted alleyway. 'Couldn't risk you squawking while I was taking you into Ma Grendel's. Somebody might've seen you.'

'How thoughtful.' Wrinkling her nose, Cassie stepped into the hackney. 'Now take me to Conduit Street.'

He said nothing, merely slamming the door shut and taking his place on the box. Cassie kept her eyes open, staring through the window until she was sure the carriage was heading in the right direction. Then, finally giving way to the fear she had been fighting off for the last hour, she dropped her head into her hands and let herself shake.

When the carriage came to a halt and Jake opened the door, she was half-way through it before she recognised that this was not Conduit Street.

'Oh – for heaven's sake! What *now*?' she demanded, looking about her and swiftly coming to the conclusion that the coach had halted somewhere in the vicinity of St James – a respectable enough area but one where many young men had lodgings 'You were supposed to take me home. This isn't it.'

'Can't take you the whole way, Miss – sorry.' Taking a firm hold on her arm, he marched her briskly to a nearby door and pulled the bell. 'Not leaving you alone in the street, neither. But the gentleman as lives here'll see you safe home.'

'Is that what *she* told you? ' Cassie slammed her elbow into his stomach and felt as if she'd driven it into a brick wall. 'It could be anyone in there. Let go of me! I'll walk the rest of the way. Let me *go!*'

Jake simply pulled the bell again and light showed in the glass arch above the door.

'It'll be all right,' he insisted. 'Honest, it will.'

She made another violent attempt to wrench free but merely succeeded in tearing the sleeve of her gown. Then the door opened, a sleepily surly voice demanded to know what the hell was going on ... and Cassie found herself face to face with a gentleman wrapped in a scarlet brocade chamber-robe.

It was Richard Penhaligon.

CHAPTER EIGHTEEN

At around the time Mistress Delahaye and Mr Penhaligon were staring speechlessly at each other across his doorstep, Mr Audley and Lord Sarre arrived in Mercer Street. Having taken a slight detour to check that Cassie was still missing, the two men had run virtually the entire distance.

'What now?' gasped Adrian. 'You can't go storming in, kicking down doors and shouting. If Cassie's here – and we don't know for sure that she is – we need to get her out without making it public knowledge.'

'I know that. But I can walk in through the front door like any other customer.'

'And then what?'

'Find the Madam and ask.' Sebastian took a moment to steady his breathing. 'It's been a few years since I visited this sort of establishment but I expect money still works.'

Despite the inevitable dishevelment resulting from their race through the streets, the brothel's burly doorman recognised the pair as gentlemen even before one of them slid a coin into his palm saying, 'Is Mrs Grendel about tonight?'

'And every night, m'lord. Just go on in. She always finds new faces.'

Inside the air was stale and overladen with the smell of tobacco, cheap perfume and sweat. Adrian grimaced.

'God. Do these places always stink?'

Sebastian didn't answer. Through an open doorway to their right, he saw a very large woman robed in purple silk rise from her chair and glide towards them with surprising grace. He said, 'Mrs Grendel, I presume?'

'You presume right, sir. Welcome to my establishment.' She encompassed them both in a warm smile. This wasn't difficult. She'd always appreciated handsome, well-built young men and these two, though very different, were equally easy on the eye. 'What would be your pleasure this evening?'

Knowing that Sebastian was incapable of maintaining even the façade of courtesy, Adrian said, 'I wonder if we might speak privately?'

Her smile faded but she stood aside and gestured for them to enter her office.

'Well, sirs?'

Sebastian opened his mouth, then snapped it shut when Adrian dropped a warning hand on his shoulder and said smoothly, 'Unless we have been misinformed, a young lady was brought here this evening against her will. We are here to retrieve her. So long as she is unharmed and allowed to leave with us immediately, this unfortunate episode need cause you no trouble.'

The threat was subtle but Mrs Grendel wasn't a stupid woman. With an irritable sigh, she said, 'That'll teach me to ignore my better judgement, won't it?'

'What do you mean?' demanded Sebastian. And unable to stand it any longer, 'Where *is* she?'

'The lady your sweetheart, is she?' Mrs Grendel gave his arm a sympathetic pat. 'I'm sorry. I daresay you've been off your head with worry, haven't you?'

'That's one way of putting it. Where is she? And don't try saying she's not here --'

'Well, that's the thing, dear. She's not.'

'*What?*'

'She *was*. No point in denying that. But she should've been safe home some time ago.' She stopped, when she saw the blood drain from Sebastian's skin. Then, drawing a long breath, she said flatly, 'But she's not, is she?'

'No,' said Adrian. 'She's not.'

'Oh bloody hell.' Mrs Grendel shut her eyes for a moment and then said, 'In that case, do what you must. But first, let's be clear. This wasn't my idea and I set rules to protect the young lady. If she's not where she should be, it's because the bitch changed Jake's orders and he hadn't the wit to tell me. So go on upstairs and shake the truth out of her. Third floor, second door on the right. You won't be disturbed.'

Sebastian was already heading for the stairs. Adrian murmured a swift, 'Thank you,' and wasted no time in following.

Aware that returning to Half Moon Street before the final part of her plan had reached fruition wasn't a good idea, Miranda had decided to stay where she was. Kicking off her shoes and pulling the pins from her hair, she ordered supper and settled down to make herself comfortable.

When she heard feet pounding up the stairs, she was reclining on the scarlet covered bed with a glass of brandy, smiling maliciously and wishing she could see Richard's face when he realised what she'd done. Then the door burst open and Sebastian was staring down at her with murder in his eyes.

The brandy slopped over her hand as she struggled to get off the bed but he was quicker. In two strides, he was hauling her to her feet in an iron grip.

'Where is she?' he demanded, his voice low and raw. 'Tell me now and make it the truth – otherwise I'll hurt you.'

Her eyes slid to where Adrian stood leaning against the closed door, then returned to his face. She said, 'You won't. You've never hurt a woman in your life.'

'I don't mind making you the first. *Where is she?*'

'I sent her home.'

'Liar.' The brandy glass fell to the carpet as he closed his fingers around her wrist and dragged her across the room to shove her down in a chair. 'I've neither the time nor the inclination to be polite, Miranda – so don't depend on it. I'll ask you one more time. Where did you send her?'

'Home. If she's not there, that isn't my fault.' She tried to twist away only to be forced back into her seat.

'There's no part of this that *isn't* your fault. But I've no interest in excuses and no time even to care why you took her. Adrian – I need a hand. And your cravat.'

'My cravat?' His lordship watched Sebastian pull off his own and use it, despite Miranda's nails clawing at him, to tie one of her wrists to the arm of the chair. 'Oh well. I suppose I can't look much more disreputable than I already do.'

'Stop this!' she shouted. 'I haven't hurt the stupid girl. All I did was talk to her and --'

She stopped speaking when, with ruthless efficiency, she found herself securely tied to the chair. But when Sebastian pulled the knife from his boot, her eyes widened and she said a trifle breathlessly, 'That's a pretty toy but it doesn't frighten me. I know you won't use it. And no matter what you say, I know you'll never hurt me.'

From his place by the door, Adrian wished he was as sure. After what Sebastian had gone through in the last couple of hours, the veneer of civilised behaviour had worn very thin and this was one of those times when life had no room for gentlemanly scruples. Certainly, if it had been Caroline who'd fallen into this woman's clutches, he himself would have done whatever it took.

'You have no idea what I would and would not do. You don't know me at all. If you did, you'd have taken no for an answer and stayed well away from me.' He twisted a long, curling lock of her hair around his fist. 'Last chance. Tell me where to find her.'

'How should I know? I've told you. I sent her --' She stopped again, this time with an outraged screech as the Russian knife sliced through her hair. 'What the hell are you doing?'

'Getting answers.' He dropped the hair in her lap and reached for another ringlet, this time, cutting it off without waiting for her to speak. As that, too, landed in her lap, he said, 'You could always have it made into a wig. But if you want to keep it on your head, I suggest you start talking. Well?'

In the brief time she hesitated, a third coil fell on top of the other two. Tears of fury gathered on her lashes and she tried appealing to Adrian.

'Sir – make him stop. Please! Surely you can see that he's quite mad?'

'Not mad. Inspired.' Adrian watched critically over folded arms as yet more hair fell. 'I'd answer Mr Audley's question now, if I were you. Barbering is not one of his skills. And you'll get no sympathy from me, Madam. My wife would be very displeased if she thought I'd been too feeble to help her closest friend.'

Still wielding the knife, Sebastian stepped back to assess his handiwork before lifting up a section of hair from the crown of her head. He said, 'Still undecided, Miranda? Perhaps a glance in the mirror will help you decide. Adrian?'

Nodding, his lordship unhooked the smallest mirror he could see and strolled over to hold it in front of Miranda. She howled with rage, cursed and tried to spit in Sebastian's face.

His answer was to pull hard on the hair he held and say softly, 'So far I've restrained myself from doing irreparable damage. You now have five seconds to persuade me not to cut it half an inch from your scalp. One ... two ... three ...'

'All right – all right!' she screamed. 'Fourteen, Park Place – off St James' Street. There! Now let go of me and get out, you bastard.'

Sebastian remained perfectly still, frowning.

'Why? Why send her there? Whose address is it?'

'Go and find out for yourself.'

'I don't think so.' He tugged at the lock of hair he still held. 'This will be quicker and I'm nearly out of patience. Who lives in Park Place?'

Miranda held out until the mirror showed her what the knife was doing. Then, her voice thick with spite, she spat the name he wanted and added, 'We planned it together, he and I. Every tiny bit – together!'

* * *

While Richard Penhaligon and Cassie stared at each other in mutual disbelief, Jake said happily, 'See, Miss? I told you it'd be all right. I asked Suzie. She used to be his particular when he come to Ma Grendel's regular and she said he always treated her nice.'

During the course of this speech, Mr Penhaligon's face gradually turned nearly as crimson as his dressing-robe but,

STELLA RILEY

striving to ignore Jake, he said chokingly, 'I don't understand what's happening, Mistress Delahaye – but you can't be here!'

'And I wish I wasn't. But I am, aren't I?' For some reason she hadn't quite worked out yet, Cassie was suddenly neither frightened nor furious. Instead, Mr Penhaligon's appalled expression wrapped a mantle of calm about her. 'Jake says you'll take me home.'

'What? No! You!' he snapped, as Jake started ambling back to his carriage. 'Take the lady to Conduit Street at once.'

'Can't.' Jake shook his head and continued walking. 'Her ladyship said they'll be on the look-out and I'll be arrested. She said to bring Miss here to you – so I have.'

'But you can't leave her here!'

'Don't see why not.' He heaved himself up on to the box and gathered the reins. 'It's only a step to Conduit Street, ain't it? And anyway, I got a note to deliver afore I'm done for the night.' And he set his horse in motion.

'No – stop, damn you!'

'He won't,' Cassie informed him. 'He isn't very intelligent and he thinks he's done the right thing. Meanwhile, I'd stop shouting, if I were you. If you wake the neighbours and they look out to see me standing on your doorstep --'

'Yes. All right. I take the point.' Richard swung back into the narrow hallway, muttering, 'This is a bloody nightmare! What the devil are you doing here?'

'That,' said Cassie, following him and deliberately leaving the front door ajar behind her, 'is a very good question – and the second time I've asked it this evening. But what surprises me most right now is that you don't seem to have been expecting me.'

'Expecting you?' He wheeled round to face her. 'Of course I wasn't expecting you. What on earth made you think that? Oh – never mind. Give me a few minutes to dress and I'll escort you home.'

She waited until they were inside the parlour and then said, 'Miranda Silvarez had me abducted this evening.'

Richard stopped dead and then turned very slowly to face her.

'What?'

'You heard. She had me drugged and taken to a brothel so she could interrogate me about Sebastian Audley. Then instead of sending me home, she arranged to have me deposited here with you.' Cassie sat down, folded her hands in her lap and eyed him meditatively. 'It appears you knew none of this. But --'

'Of course I didn't! What do you take me for?'

'But your name and address can't have been a random choice ... so I'm wondering how well you and Miranda know each other,' she finished as if he hadn't spoken. '*You*, I imagine, are wondering why she's implicating you in my abduction ... and leaving you to answer a lot of very angry questions from men like my father.'

Mr Penhaligon raked a hand through his hair and looked back at her a little wildly. He said, 'As you've just observed yourself, I had nothing to do with any of it. If it becomes necessary, you'll say as much, won't you?'

Cassie took her time about answering while she considered the possibilities.

'Eventually, I expect.'

'*Eventually?*' He nearly yelled the word and then, recalling that the rooms above his own belonged to the busiest tongue in London, abruptly lowered his voice. 'What the hell does that mean?'

'Well ... after such a horrible experience, I'll probably be too upset and confused to think coherently.'

Richard stared her, wondering if Cassie Delahaye's body had been taken over by a complete stranger. He said grimly, 'I never saw anyone less upset and confused in my life.'

'No. Not now,' she agreed. 'You're not going to hurt me or take ungentlemanly advantage. And in a little while you're going to take me home – after which it will probably be best to pretend I was never here. But first I want answers. I believe I've already asked the questions.'

He continued to stare, still unable to equate this girl with the one he'd thought he knew. But finally, he drew a ragged breath and said, 'All right. I know Lady Silvarez better than I want to. She's involving me in this because I told her she'd have to stop persecuting Audley and would get no further help from me. But I'd no more idea about tonight than I had about that business in Drury Lane – though as soon as it happened, I knew it was her handiwork.' He paused, his mouth twisting wryly. 'I don't pretend to be the perfect gentleman ... but I do have a *few* principles. And now, if you wouldn't mind, I'd like to put some clothes on and get you away from here before --'

'Richard? Rich, dear boy ... if you're holding a party, why were Dudley and I not invited? It ith motht unthivil.'

'Oh Lord' groaned Richard, pushing open the door behind him. '*Ansford!* Cassie – in there! Now!'

Cassie didn't need to be told. Viscount Ansford's whole *raison d'être* was the collection and dissemination of gossip. She shot towards the bedchamber door while Mr Penhaligon flew in the opposite direction to trap his unwanted visitors in the hall. Unfortunately, both of them were too late.

'Pengalion!' slurred Mr Dudley, lurching into the parlour two steps ahead of the decorative viscount. 'Good to shee you. Got any port?' Then, peering at Cassie and attempting an unsteady bow, 'Ah. Apol-pologies, ma'am. Didn't know Pengolagin had company.'

Richard swore under his breath. Dudley was blind drunk. Ansford, unfortunately, wasn't; and he was advancing on Cassie with a sly smile as he took in her tumbled hair and crumpled gown.

'Why Mithtreth Delahaye! Whatever can you be doing here tho late at night? Or perhapth,' he finished coyly, 'I shouldn't athk?'

'No,' said Cassie flatly. 'You shouldn't. I've had a very trying evening and am indebted to Mr Penhaligon for his help. But it's no concern of yours, sir – and you'd be wise not to make it so.'

'Dear me! Ath if I would *dream* of thuch a thing!'

262

'Quite,' said Richard dryly. 'So perhaps you'll excuse us? I was just about to escort Mistress Delahaye home.'

'Like *that*?' asked Viscount Ansford, indicating Richard's state of undress with a wave of one lily-white hand. 'My dear fellow – you are in complete *déthabillé*! Your valet will thimply die of shame!' He glanced about. 'Where ith he, by the way?'

Mr Dudley, still apparently hunting for the port, spared Richard the need to admit that his man was away visiting his sick sister by choosing this moment to trip over a footstool, fall flat in the middle of the room and remain there, apparently unconscious.

'Oh – for God's sake,' said Richard disgustedly. 'He can't stay there. You brought him here, Ansford – so take him up to your own rooms.'

'How? I can hardly *carry* him, can I? It will *ruin* my coat.'

'Oh well done, Lord Ansford!' Cassie stepped over Dudley's recumbent form to reach the jug on the table. 'A whole sentence without a single lisp.'

Beneath the cosmetics, his lordship's face turned puce. 'Madam – I protetht!'

'Oh dear. That was abominably rude, wasn't it? I fear I'm becoming a trifle hysterical,' she replied. And emptied the jug of water over Dudley's head.

He twitched, choked and spat. 'Wha -- ?'

'There, sir. Get him on his feet while you have the chance. Mr Penhaligon will help, I'm sure.' She turned a severe gaze on Richard who had put his head in his hands and given way to weak laughter. 'Or perhaps not. It seems that *he* is a trifle hysterical as well.'

'What,' snapped a new and extremely cold voice, 'is going on here? Richard! An explanation, if you please.'

Mr Penhaligon's laughter stopped as if cut by a knife. His hands fell to his sides and, every vestige of expression draining from his face, he said, 'Good evening, Clarence. Perfect timing, as always. But dare I ask what brings you here at this time of night?'

'That,' snapped Lord Keswick, slapping a piece of paper down upon the table. 'A note informing me that you were entertaining a virtuous young lady alone in your rooms. A note, I might add, that I had fully expected to be a lie.'

'A note,' echoed Richard with a fleeting glance at Cassie. 'Of course. But as you can doubtless see … we are not alone. Unfortunately.'

'I shall remove mythelf directly,' volunteered Lord Ansford. 'Indeed, Lord Kethick, I would have done tho immediately I realithed that we were *de trop* had not Mr Dudley been overcome by – by --'

'Don't trouble searching your vocabulary, sir. It is perfectly plain what ails Mr Dudley. But I believe we may dispense with both his presence and your own. *Now*, if you would be so good. And you, Richard, can do Mistress Delahaye and myself the courtesy of retiring to your chamber to make yourself presentable. I will wait.'

'Oh good,' muttered Mr Penhaligon, stooping to help Viscount Ansford haul Mr Dudley upright. And under his breath to Cassie, 'I'm going to *murder* Miranda.'

'There's likely to be a queue,' she replied, watching the viscount struggle to keep his burden upright as far as the door. 'And my father will be at the head of it. Or perhaps --'

The door burst open, slamming into Lord Ansford's back and causing him to drop Mr Dudley again. And just on the other side of it, with the Earl of Sarre at his shoulder and looking exceedingly dangerous, was Mr Audley.

'*Sebastian!*' Cassie's voice broke on his name but her smile was utterly radiant.

Sebastian wasn't sure he dared trust his voice at all so he merely bore down on the light of his life, neither aware nor indeed caring, that he trod on Mr Dudley's fingers and had to shove Viscount Ansford into a corner to do it. Then his arms were tight about Cassie and he was breathing in the familiar scent of her hair and finally he managed to say, 'Cassandra, love … are you all right? Has anyone hurt you?'

She shook her head. 'No. I'm fine. Better than fine, now you're here.'

'Are you sure? *God!* I've never been so frightened in my life. What did that bitch do to you?' Over the top of her head, his eyes found Mr Penhaligon. 'And him. Has *he* laid a hand on you? If he has, I swear I'll carve him into little pieces.'

'He hasn't.' She could feel the hard, too-fast thud of Sebastian's heart and see the wild pulse beating in his throat. 'None of this is his fault.'

'He would say that,' growled Sebastian. And then, as if finally noticing, 'The blackguard's half naked!'

'Mind your language, sir,' snapped Keswick. 'And unhand that lady.'

'No,' said Sebastian, holding Cassie even closer. 'And who the hell are you anyway?'

'Allow me to introduce my brother, the Earl of Keswick,' offered Mr Penhaligon weakly. 'Clarence ... Mr Sebastian Audley.'

Neither man acknowledged the introduction. Deciding it was time to take matters in hand, Lord Sarre said, 'Sebastian ... I'm going to get rid of the two idiots you most assuredly *don't* need. And then --'

'You are inthulting, my lord,' interrupted Ansford. 'I do not care for your tone.'

'I don't give a damn whether you do or not.' Adrian heaved Mr Dudley upright again and draped him over the viscount. 'Now take him away – before I kick the pair of you down the steps.' He turned back to Sebastian. 'I'm going to tell Cassie's parents that we have her safe. Please *try* not to hit anyone before Charles and I get back. Or if you must, at least make sure there's a good reason for it.'

Then he was gone.

Continuing to behave as if Keswick didn't exist, Sebastian glared at Mr Penhaligon over Cassie's head and said, 'She said you planned it together. The abduction – this – all of it.'

'She lied,' replied Richard wearily. 'I knew nothing of any of it until Cas-- Mistress Delahaye was deposited here a little while ago. Barring interruptions, I'd have dressed and escorted her home. But I can't prove it, so you'll have to think what you like.'

'It's true, Sebastian.' Cassie tilted her head until she could look up at him. 'If he and Miranda had planned it together, Mr Penhaligon would have been expecting me – fully-clothed, I imagine. As it is, he was completely shocked and did his best to make Jake drive me home. Only Jake wouldn't because he thought he'd be arrested … and also of course, he had to deliver Miranda's note to Lord Keswick so that his lordship would arrive here in time to find me with his brother. I imagine Miranda's plan was that he'd have to marry me.'

Sebastian's jaw set hard. 'Over my dead body.'

'Will one of you please explain?' demanded Lord Keswick, tired of being ignored. 'What is this talk of abduction? Who are Jake and Miranda? And why should anyone suppose that my brother was involved in some plot? I'm beginning to feel that I've strayed into a theatrical production.'

'You have. Miranda Silvarez's Marionette Extravaganza,' said Sebastian. 'Sir, the details don't matter. Suffice it to say that Cassandra was abducted, then brought here to either implicate your brother in the abduction or to force him to do the honourable thing because she appeared compromised.'

Lord Keswick stared at his brother. 'Is this true?'

'Yes. Why *else* do you think you received a note? You've made no secret of the fact that you want me to marry. And if we're to be honest, had Audley not been here you'd already be marching me round to Conduit Street. As it is, even *you* must be able to see that I'm superfluous to requirements. And now, if no one minds, I'm going to dress.'

Deciding, with some reluctance, that it was safe to let Sebastian go, Cassie stood on tiptoe to place a kiss on his jaw and then gently disengaged herself. She said, 'How did you find me?'

'With difficulty and a lot of running.' Still needing the contact, he laced his fingers through hers. 'Are you *sure* Miranda didn't hurt you?'

'Perfectly. In fact, it was the other way about. I smashed a ewer on her head.'

He gave a crack of startled laughter. 'Cassandra the Valkyrie?'

'Something like that.' She fell silent, suddenly realising how tired she was. 'I suppose she told you I was here?'

'Eventually, after I'd sliced off some of her hair.' Sebastian turned his head. 'Good. Sir Charles is here – hopefully with a carriage. You look exhausted, love.'

'You're the one who's been doing all the running,' she objected, then left Sebastian's side as her father strode in, white with strain.

'Cassie.' Charles caught her in a hard hug. 'Thank God. Are you all right?'

'Yes, Papa. I'm safe. I wasn't hurt. And I'm so sorry you've been worried.'

'*Worried*?' Charles's embrace tightened. 'My dear child, you have no idea!' Over the top of her head, his eyes met Sebastian's and he said, 'Thank you. Words can't express my gratitude ... but right now I'm taking my girl home.'

'Just one moment,' said Lord Keswick. 'How do you intend to resolve the matter of your daughter being found in my brother's lodgings? Thanks to Ansford and Dudley, it can't be kept quiet.'

'Yes it can,' remarked Lord Sarre from the doorway. 'If Penhaligon and I get Dudley back to his rooms, he won't even remember *being* here; and you may safely leave Ansford to me. As to you, Lord Keswick ... I presume we may count on your discretion?'

'Certainly,' snapped the earl stiffly. 'Though I still don't see --'

'I told Mr Penhaligon that it would be best if I was never here,' said Cassie. 'He's as much a victim in this as I am – and the truth won't help anyone, will it?' She stifled a yawn. 'So if we're all agreed on that, can I *please* go home?'

'Immediately,' agreed Sir Charles. 'Sebastian ... you'd better come too. We need to decide what to do about that blasted madwoman.'

* * *

Once home in Conduit Street, Cassie was whisked away by her mother for hot milk and other much-needed comforts while Sir Charles ordered food and wine to be brought to the drawing-room for Mr Audley.

'Now,' he said when they were finally alone. 'Tell me everything.'

So between mouthfuls of ham, Sebastian did. And at the end said, 'We left Miranda tied to a chair in the brothel and asked the Mrs Grendel to keep her there till morning. The question you and I need to address is whether or not we want her answering questions in Bow Street. Personally, I'd be happy to see her thrown in a dungeon. But a charge of abduction is going to make the whole thing public and drag Cassandra's name into court.'

Sir Charles nodded. 'The alternative, however, is to take the law into our own hands – because I'm damned if I'm going to let her get away with this or leave her free to try anything else.'

'That can't happen. We need a permanent solution.' Sebastian shoved back a lock of hair and said wearily, 'I don't know where this fixation with me has come from or how to put an end to it. But targeting me is one thing. Hurting Cassandra is quite another.' He paused, trying to think. 'Do you recall the threat I made to Richard Penhaligon at Angelo's?'

'Social ruin through the scandal sheets?'

'Yes. Leaving Penhaligon out of it, I could focus on Miranda's dubious background and morals, her determination to foist herself on polite society and her plot involving the baby. What do you think?'

'It might serve.'

'It doesn't seem enough though, does it? Damn. I'd like her dragged kicking and screaming to Bow Street and frightened out of her wits at the prospect of prison ... but it can't happen, can it? I'm going to have to go back to Half Moon Street now and tell the officers to go home.'

'No. You've done enough for one night and there's a way to make use of Bow Street. I'll ask Sir John to detain and question her – but discreetly since, at the end of the day, I won't be pressing charges.' Charles smiled faintly. 'We're old friends so I can rely on John to put the fear of God into her. And that leaves you free to set the gossip mill turning. Indeed, you might even hint that she's of interest to the authorities.'

'Now that *is* a good idea. It would make a nice finishing touch.' Sebastian stood up. 'I ought to go. I'll send word once I've spoken to Adrian about Ansford and --'

'You will *not* send word – you'll come yourself. I will tell Cassie she may expect you.'

'You will? Oh. That's – thank you, sir.'

'There's no need to look so surprised, Sebastian. What else would I do?'

The door opened upon Lady Delahaye. Her hair not quite tidy and her eyes suspiciously bright, she walked quickly across to put her arms about Sebastian and kiss his cheek.

'Thank you,' she whispered. '*Thank* you. And don't say there's no need for thanks or any other such nonsense because there is. Without you, this whole ordeal might have lasted a lot longer and have ended very badly. Of course, Cassie wanted to come down and thank you herself but she's exhausted, so I forbade it.' Releasing him, she turned to her husband and said, 'She left the Lintons' in response to a plea from Olivia who was supposedly stranded alone outside the Theatre Royal.'

'*What?*' snapped Charles.

'Quite. It wasn't true, of course – but it might have been. Olivia and Margot Claydon had been hatching a scheme to see *The School for Scandal* and the pair of them had been planning it in any number of places where they might easily have been overheard.'

'And with that mystery explained,' remarked Sebastian, 'I'll take my leave.'

Serena patted his arm and looked expectantly at her husband.

'Have you told him what we discussed?'

'I have told him to *call*,' Charles replied firmly. 'And that will do for tonight. Go home, Sebastian. We'll see you tomorrow at whatever hour is convenient to you.' He held out his hand. 'And I echo Serena's sentiment. We are in your debt.'

CHAPTER NINETEEN

Over a very late breakfast, Adrian told Sebastian that he and Richard Penhaligon had frightened Viscount Ansford into silence merely by pointing out that he *really* didn't want to make Mr Audley any angrier than he already was.

'The fellow has three yards of tongue and a spine made of jelly,' he added trenchantly. 'As for Dudley, he was still out cold when we dumped him in his own hallway. Neither of them need concern you.'

'Thank you.'

'Don't thank me. Just stop pushing food around your plate and go and ask Cassie to marry you.'

'It's not that simple.'

'Yes, it is. After last night, Charles isn't going to stand in your way, is he?'

'He's relieved and grateful. What he *isn't* is either stupid or careless of his daughter's future.' Sebastian pushed back his chair and stood up. 'He hasn't mentioned hearing from my father, so presumably he hasn't – which means the problem is the same as it's always been. But he invited me to call and said Cassandra would expect me ... so that's better than nothing.'

'And the thorny question of Miranda?'

'She should be under arrest by now,' replied Sebastian and briefly explained what he and Sir Charles had decided. Then, 'I imagine you're eager to go home.'

'Always,' agreed Adrian, smiling. 'But in fact, I was considering suggesting that Caroline join me. She probably needs a new hat. What do you think?'

'By all means. And if she'd prefer I lodged elsewhere --'

'Don't be a bigger idiot than you can help, Sebastian. Just take yourself off to Conduit Street. And only think! If Charles lets you pay your addresses to Cassie, you'll have won our wager.' He grinned. 'Yes. I can see that's been foremost in your mind all along.'

* * *

On Mama's instructions, Cassie had tried to take her breakfast in bed but was far too restless to do more than drink a cup of chocolate before summoning her maid and embarking on the all-important task of choosing a gown. This took some time but she eventually settled on a simple dress of leaf-green tiffany, trimmed with narrow blonde lace; then she told Susan to dress her hair equally simply. If Sebastian wanted to kiss her – and she hoped very much that he would – she didn't want either of them to have to be careful.

She was just dabbing a hint of bergamot scent here and there when Olivia knocked, put her head round the door and, for the first time ever, said, 'May I come in?'

'So long as you don't ask endless questions – yes.'

Olivia slid inside but remained standing by the door, looking subdued. She said, 'I came to say I was sorry. Last night was my fault, wasn't it?'

Cassie swivelled round and looked at her sister.

'No. If the woman hadn't used *you* to lure me out of Linton House, she'd have found some other way.'

'Perhaps. But Mama said it wasn't so much the note itself as the fact that you believed I might actually *do* something as silly as that.'

Turning back to the mirror, Cassie picked up a single strand of pearls to match the ones already in her ears. She said, 'That's an entirely different matter, isn't it? But I shan't echo what I imagine Mama has already said.'

Olivia toyed with the ribbons on her bodice. 'She's angry with me.'

'Then, it's fortunate that I'm not, isn't it?'

'You're not? Really? I – I thought you'd be furious.'

'No.' Cassie smiled to herself, knowing better than to tell her sister that she was too happy to be furious. 'Though it was frightening at the time, no real harm has been done.'

'Mama said Mr Audley and Lord Sarre rescued you. That must have been quite exciting and – and romantic, I should think.'

Olivia waited and when no reply was forthcoming, said carefully, 'Can I ask just one *tiny* question?'

Cassie sighed, met her sister's eyes in the mirror and said, 'No.'

'But you don't know what --'

'I do. And I'm not answering it. Yet.'

* * *

Having sent a note asking the Duke of Rockliffe to receive him later in the day, Sebastian dressed even more carefully than usual before driving to Conduit Street. He could have walked ... but the sun was shining and even if Sir Charles didn't allow him to propose to Cassandra, he might at least permit him to take her for a drive. And that was more than he could have hoped for this time yesterday – which only went to show that there was always a silver lining somewhere.

With an oddly benevolent smile, the butler showed him immediately to Sir Charles's study despite the fact that Mr Audley could now walk there blindfold. Then Charles was holding out his hand, saying, 'You look better than you did last night. But then, I suppose I do, too.'

'Yes.' Sebastian took the chair he was offered. 'It's odd, isn't it? I've risked my neck a number of times with little more than a qualm. But I've only experienced true fear twice; those last days while Theo was ill ... and last night while I didn't know where Cassandra was or what might be happening to her.'

'It's always harder when the thing you're facing is outside your control. If you marry and have children, you'll know that feeling on a regular basis.'

Sebastian coloured a little, wondering if there might be an underlying meaning in that remark but knowing better than to ask. Instead he said, 'I've drafted a piece for *The Whisperer* and am hoping Rockliffe's man-of-law will put an official gloss on it. Adrian says Ansford will keep his mouth shut and Dudley won't remember anything.'

'Good. You are very fortunate in your friends.'

'Yes. I am. Have you heard from Sir John Fielding?'

Charles nodded. 'Lady Silvarez was arrested when she returned to Half Moon Street this morning and has been lodged in prison. John felt a day or two of incarceration prior to being questioned wouldn't do any harm. Eventually he'll make it plain to her that Bow Street will be keeping an eye on her and that if her name comes to his attention again, she'll face the full weight of the law for the crime of abduction. So I think we may regard the matter as closed ... unless you feel the need to confront her personally.'

'I don't. When I terminated our affair in Lisbon, she refused to accept it. I couldn't stir a step without finding her there. So I moved on – but her letters still found me and I began to realise she had someone tracking me. It was impossible to vanish without trace because I had to make sure the family could find me if necessary – but God knows I tried. I'd got as far as Prague when I first hoped I'd shaken her off and moved on to Buda to make sure of it.' He paused frowning down at his hands and then said bluntly, 'You might say I learned some sort of lesson or was merely frightened. It could be either. But since then and despite my blasted reputation, there hasn't been ... I haven't indulged in any similar liaisons.'

There was a long silence. Finally, Sir Charles said, 'If you're telling me you are capable of fidelity, it's unnecessary. Neither, after last night, do you need to prove yourself.'

'Last night?' Sebastian shrugged. 'As it turned out, I didn't do very much at all. If I'd caught up with Cassandra while Miranda had her, that would have been different. But she was in no danger from Penhaligon.'

'No. As we are all well aware, the danger at that point was his brother's desire to see the two of them at the altar.' Raising one quizzical brow, Charles said, 'I'm surprised you haven't asked me how I'd have dealt with that eventuality.'

Sebastian hadn't asked because he wasn't sure he'd like the answer.

'And how would you?'

'I'd have told him that my consent wouldn't be of the least use – since Cassie was never going to give hers. And I might have mentioned that I'd already given tacit approval to a previous applicant.'

This was not merely better than he'd dared hope. It was astonishing. On the other hand, it didn't fundamentally change anything so Sebastian said flatly, 'That is very generous of you, sir – considering that my financial position remains unchanged. At least, I assume it does, having heard nothing to the contrary.'

'Ah – did I not say? No. I probably didn't. It was the day after the Drury Lane debacle. Lord Wingham acknowledged my letter and said he would look into the situation.'

'But nothing since then?'

'No. So Serena and I have decided not to wait upon his lordship's pleasure.'

Something lurched inside Sebastian's chest.

'I'm not sure I understand you, sir.'

'It's very simple. When you are married, your father will have no option but to fulfil his responsibilities towards you; but if interim measures are required, I will take care of them. In short, I see no reason to allow this stalemate to continue.' Charles stood up. 'You'll find Cassie in the drawing-room, Sebastian. Go and say whatever you wish to her and take as long to do it as is necessary.'

Finding himself on his feet without knowing how he got there, Sebastian said, 'Forgive me if I seem a trifle slow ... but you are saying that if Cassandra accepts me, you will permit a betrothal?'

'*If* she accepts you?' Charles laughed. 'Oh – for the Lord's sake, just go and *ask* her!'

Alone in the drawing-room since being told of Mr Audley's arrival, Cassie had checked her appearance in the mirror five times and begun to wear a trail in the carpet. Then the door opened and he was there ... standing just inside the room, looking at her.

Her immediate impulse was to behave exactly as he had last night and run straight into his arms. But sudden ridiculous shyness caused by a renewed awareness of all that extraordinary male beauty rooted her feet to the floor and made it hard to breathe.

He always dressed well and he was never less than handsome ... but today everything about him seemed enhanced. He wore a brocade coat of the very darkest shade of green over a pale grey embroidered silk vest and the burgundy hair had been brushed till it shone and was tied with long sable ribbons. But it was the bone-melting smile lurking in those twilight eyes that stopped her breath and made her realise more clearly than she had ever done before just how much she wanted this man; and just how miraculous it was that he wanted her in return.

Finally, when the thread between them had tightened to an excruciating degree, Sebastian walked towards her saying softly, 'I would have asked if you have recovered from last night's ordeal ... but you look so beautiful I can see there is no need.'

Smiling, Cassie shook her head slightly. 'I don't believe I thanked you --'

'Don't.' He stopped a mere two steps away. 'You have nothing to thank me for – neither should there be any question of gratitude. You must know there is nothing I wouldn't gladly do for you.' He paused, uneasily aware that the moment had caught him unprepared; that he had no words ready. But perhaps it was always this difficult; perhaps every fellow who'd ever proposed marriage felt as clumsy and unsure as he did right now. He said slowly, 'I've just had a rather unexpected interview with your father and am still a little unbalanced. I don't suppose he gave you any clue about what he intended to say to me?'

'Papa doesn't deal in clues. He says things straight out or not at all.'

'Ah. So *that's* where you get it from.' Her laughter made him feel better; as if the ground had regained some of its customary solidity. Reaching out, he took her hands in his and dropped smoothly to one knee. He saw her lips part, heard her breath catch and all but drowned in the look that glowed in her eyes.

Suddenly it wasn't difficult at all. He said, 'I love you, Cassandra. So much and for so many reasons I can't begin to put it into words. All I can say is that you fill my heart and I can't imagine a life without you. Will you --?'

'Yes.' Laughing and crying at the same time, Cassie tugged at his hands. 'Yes and yes and *yes*!'

Answering laughter lit Sebastian's eyes but he continued to kneel and said reprovingly, 'If you knew how much courage it takes to do this, you'd let me struggle on to the end.'

Distantly, she wondered if there was another man in the entire world who could melt a girl's heart in one breath and tease her with the next. She said demurely, 'I beg your pardon, sir. Please go on.'

'Cassandra Delahaye ... will you do me the very great honour of accepting my hand in marriage? On the clear understanding,' he continued firmly, as she opened her mouth to speak, 'that agreeing to be my wife is likely to entail putting up with me for a very long time.' Then, rising and pulling her into his arms, he murmured wickedly, '*Now* you can say it.'

'*Now* I wonder if I ought not to reconsider. However ...' Her hands slid about his neck and she smiled tremulously back at him. 'I think I might *just* manage to put up with you – even for a very long time. So yes, Mr Audley. Yes and yes and --'

'Good,' said Mr Audley. And captured her mouth with his.

He had hungered for this moment but the gift was too precious and too new to be squandered in haste. From her mouth, his lips made a lazy voyage of discovery along her cheekbone and jaw to the tender skin beneath her ear and then on down her creamy column of her throat. Pressing closer, Cassie threaded her fingers into his hair. Taking this as both invitation and encouragement, he possessed her mouth again, teasing and caressing until she offered what he wanted. Then he took the kiss deeper and deeper until his blood was on fire and his body was getting the kind of ideas his brain was struggling to veto.

Time to pull back, he told himself. But she tasted of strawberries and her hair smelled of summer flowers ... and if he gave that ribbon just one tiny tug ...

The ribbon floated to the carpet and Cassie's hair fell in a soft torrent over his hands and down her back. Sebastian groaned and buried his face in it for a second. Then, with a huge effort, he allowed himself one last lingering kiss of incredible sweetness before creating a small, very necessary space between them. It was ironic, he reflected vaguely, that you wanted a woman to know you desired her but instinctively hid the evidence of it.

He said huskily, 'It shall be as you want, of course ... but it's only fair to warn you that a long betrothal may well kill me.'

Her breathing as disrupted as his, Cassie let her hands slip from his shoulders to his chest. Colour blossomed in her cheeks as she said shyly, 'As soon as we can, then.'

'You're sure?'

'Yes. I don't want to wait either.' She cupped his cheek with tender fingers and said, 'I love you, Sebastian. One look at you and nothing else exists because there is no room for it – nor need either. You are everything.'

'Oh God, sweetheart. I'm not worth that much ... but I'll try to be. I promise I'll try.'

Later, when she was sitting curled up at his side and toying contentedly with his hair, she said, 'Is making an offer of marriage really so very difficult?'

'Difficult? Have you ever thought what we poor fellows have to go through? After assiduously courting the lady, we have to jump through hoops for her father, all the time hoping that he'll either overlook or be unaware of the many times we made asses of ourselves. Then we have to rescue the lady from a fate worse than death – or in your case, marriage to Richard Penhaligon – and --'

'That wouldn't ever have happened,' she said, teasing the edge of his jaw with kisses.

'I know that but it sounds more heroic than the reality.' The kisses were becoming a serious distraction. 'Where was I? Ah yes.

Then, once we have Papa's permission, we have to pray that we've somehow managed to charm the lady into liking us enough to say yes when we're on our knees and laying our heart at her feet. The possibility that she might say no is sufficient to send strong men gibbering in a coal cellar.'

'You are so absurd,' she laughed. 'You knew I wouldn't say no.'

'I *hoped* you wouldn't say no.' Sebastian kissed the top of her head. 'Only a conceited idiot would take something like that for granted.'

Silence fell for a time as they both enjoyed the luxury in simply being together like this, able to touch and talk ... or not. Presently, however, Sebastian said, 'Lovely as this is, I suppose we should seek out your parents. I wouldn't want them to think I've been taking unseemly advantage – particularly when I've crucified myself being good.'

Smiling, Cassie let him pull her to her feet.

'I wouldn't have minded if – if you'd lapsed a little.'

He groaned again. 'That is just cruel. Come along, you wicked hussy.'

Since it had been expected, the only surprise their announcement caused was the warmth and pleasure of its reception. Charles shook Sebastian's hand and welcomed him to the family while Serena hugged Cassie very hard, her eyes glistening with tears and said, 'Oh my darling, I am so *very* happy for you. He is everything I hoped for – and everything you deserve. I don't think I ever saw a man quite so hopelessly in love. It is most touching.'

When wine had been called for and toasts drunk, Charles said, 'I shall send the appropriate notice to the *Morning Chronicle* immediately. Meanwhile, we should plan a betrothal celebration. What do you think, Serena?'

'A ball,' she replied promptly. 'The ballroom in this house is only of moderate proportions but will hold forty or fifty couples comfortably. However, if you want a crush, Cassie --'

'I don't. Here, with family and our closest friends would be perfect.' Tucking her hand into Sebastian's, Cassie said, 'Do you think we can persuade your father to come?'

'He'll come.' It was Sir Charles who answered, his tone edged with implacability. 'Lord Wingham and I have matters to discuss. So he'll come if I have to go and fetch him myself. Now ... how long will it take to arrange this ball?'

'Could we do it within the week, Mama?' begged Cassie.

'A *week*?' echoed Serena faintly. 'Well ... perhaps.'

'Let me guess.' Charles eyed Sebastian with sardonic resignation. 'Banns on the next three Sundays and the wedding the week after, I suppose?'

Sebastian felt Cassie's grip tighten. 'Yes, sir. That was what we'd hoped.'

'Wait!' Serena stared at them. 'A betrothal ball next week and the wedding in a *month*? Are the two of you *completely* addled?'

'One of us is,' agreed Sebastian, lifting Cassie's hand to his lips. 'The other is just grateful.'

Charles laughed. 'You may as well give in, Rena. I daresay we'll manage it somehow.'

'Thank you.' Sebastian stood up, looking down into his love's flushed, excited face. 'It's a lovely day. Would you like to drive with me in the park?'

'I am sure,' said Serena before her daughter could answer, 'that Cassie would *love* to drive with you, Sebastian. But since we have a betrothal ball and a wedding to organise in less than a month, we need to begin planning immediately.' She smiled suddenly. 'Don't look so downcast. You will see each other this evening at the Ainsley assembly. But before you leave, we had better break the news to Olivia that Wicked Cousin Sebastian is about to become her brother. If we're lucky, her guilty conscience over last night may prevent her saying anything untoward – but I wouldn't like to count on it.'

* * *

Having survived his first encounter with his soon-to-be new sister, Mr Audley handed his card to the Duke of Rockliffe's butler and after a short wait, was shown into the drawing-room where his Grace was walking back and forth by the windows holding a small bundle wrapped in a lacy white shawl while the duchess was engaged in pouring tea. Startled by the surprisingly domestic scene, Sebastian paused just inside the door and then, recollecting himself, said, 'Forgive me. I'm intruding and some other time will do just as well.'

'If you'd been intruding, Symonds would have told you we were not at home,' murmured Rockliffe. The baby made a small gurgling sound which turned into a sort of hiccup so he offered her one of his fingers and smiled when her tiny fist closed around it. 'Sit down and have some tea.'

Adeline sighed, shook her head and rose to greet their guest.

'You'll have to forgive Tracy,' she said. 'In due course, he'll remember that you and I have never met but for now we'll have to shift for ourselves. It's Mr Audley, yes?'

'Yes, your Grace.' Sebastian smiled and bowed over her hand. 'It's a great pleasure to meet you at last. May I congratulate you on the birth of your daughter?'

'By all means. It's nice to have it acknowledged that I played some small part.'

Rockliffe glanced across at her. 'That is unfair. I kiss your feet in gratitude daily ... metaphorically speaking.'

'Metaphorically? Is that what you call it?' Then, catching Sebastian's startled expression, 'I'm sorry, Mr Audley. Am I embarrassing you?'

'Not at all. I think any gentleman would count himself fortunate to be permitted to kiss your feet – metaphorically or in any other way.'

His words and the peal of laughter that followed them successfully commanded Rockliffe's attention.

'If you're here to beg a favour, Audley, flirting with my wife under my nose is not a good start. Unless, of course, you are eager to test your sword against mine in earnest?'

Catching the gleam of mocking laughter, Sebastian grinned back and shook his head. 'I'll happily fence with you at Angelo's. But if you were to call me out, I'd have the choice of weapons – and it wouldn't be swords.'

'Pistols? Really?' Rockliffe heaved a pained sigh. 'How disappointing.'

'No, your Grace. Not pistols.' Sebastian reached into his pocket, brought out an object some four inches high and held it out on the palm of his hand. 'This.'

The Duke stretched out his arm to take the piece and look closely at it.

'Dear me,' he said softly. 'That would certainly be novel.'

'What is it?' asked Adeline.

'The Black King ... from, if I am not mistaken, a particularly fine and very valuable Russian chess set.' Sitting down, his baby daughter dozing contentedly in the crook of his arm, Rockliffe placed the piece on the table so that she could see it. Carved from dark, sullenly-gleaming obsidian, the King wore a gold crown and exquisitely detailed robes, encrusted with tiny, blood-red rubies. 'Do you have the rest of the set?'

'Yes. I ... won it.'

His Grace's brows rose. 'And were allowed to leave Russia with it?'

'Yes.'

'Ah.' There was a long, meditative pause while Rockliffe studied the Black King. 'Are you, by any chance, the current owner of the Casparov set?'

Sebastian smiled but said nothing.

'Extraordinary,' breathed Rockliffe.

Looking from one to the other of them, Adeline said, 'Would either of you care to explain?'

'May I?' asked the Duke. And when Sebastian nodded, 'It's named after the man who made it – and allegedly gave it a life of its own. The Casparov supposedly chooses its owner – the last person who won a game whilst playing with it. Selling it, gifting it or, perish the thought, stealing it, calls down dire retribution. In recent years, it has reputedly been passed back and forth between just two people. And I would give a great deal to know which of them succeeded in losing it.'

'So would quite a few other people,' grinned Sebastian.

'Is it true?' asked Adeline. 'About the curse, I mean?'

'I doubt if anyone knows. But the Russians are a superstitious lot – even the most forward-looking of them. So having won it, I had to be allowed to keep it.'

'Forgive my asking,' murmured Rockliffe, 'but do you *always* carry such a valuable piece around in your pocket?'

'No. Only on days when I need some additional luck.' Sebastian shrugged and said, 'As for making the Game my weapon of choice ... I've been challenged four times. The first time, I opted for pistols. I deloped and the other fellow shot me. So on the three subsequent occasions, I chose chess. Two of those three gentlemen sneered and invited their friends to watch but both stopped laughing when I wiped them off the board in eight straight moves. The third took one look at that,' he pointed to the King, 'and withdrew his cartel. No one has challenged me since.'

Adeline eyed him thoughtfully. 'Just how well do you play, Mr Audley?'

He smiled, looking faintly embarrassed. '*Very* well, your Grace. Were that not the case, the Casparov would still be in St Petersburg.' And then, to Rockliffe, 'You are welcome to see it at any time. But now I should come to the point and leave you to enjoy your tea. It was merely that I wanted your permission to consult Mr Osborne again.'

Rockliffe made a dismissive gesture.

'By all means. But surely the editor of *The Whisperer* has not been stupid enough to repeat the offence?'

'No. This is different. Miranda Silvarez has been arrested for abduction. And though her victim is safe and no harm was done, it might have been. But Miranda can't be brought to court without her victim's name being dragged in there with her. I believe Bow Street will dissuade her from further villainy but want to prepare additional measures in case they're needed. An article in *The*

Whisperer should be sufficient to leave her with little alternative but to quit London and I'd like Mr Osborne's advice on suitable wording.'

Rockliffe nodded, frowning slightly. 'Who did she abduct?'

'Cassandra Delahaye.'

'*What?*' The duke and the duchess spoke more or less in unison.

'As I said, no harm was done.' And because he wanted so badly to shout it from the rooftops ... because pride, wonder and sheer euphoria was still exploding inside his chest ... Sebastian lifted his chin and said, 'If you are wondering about my own involvement, I should perhaps mention that earlier this afternoon Cassandra did me the immense honour of accepting my hand in marriage.'

Inevitably, Rockliffe showed no surprise. He merely smiled slightly and said, 'My congratulations.'

Adeline, on the other hand, clapped her hands and said, 'Cassie? You're going to marry *Cassie?*' And when he nodded, grinning helplessly, 'Oh, well *done*, Mr Audley. Well done indeed! At last – a gentleman with the wit to appreciate that lovely girl for what she is.'

'Rest assured that I'm wholly aware of my good fortune, your Grace.'

'That,' she replied, laughing a little, 'is completely apparent.'

Rockliffe rose and held out his hand. 'We will send Cassandra our felicitations ... and if you plan a bachelor party, I shall be pleased to attend. Meanwhile, since she is now safely asleep, you may wish to admire Lady Vanessa Jane.'

Still grinning, Sebastian gripped the offered hand and said, 'Certainly. I thought you'd never ask.'

* * *

Back in Cork Street, Lord Sarre took one look at his friend's face and also held out his hand. 'Far be it from me to say I told you so ...'

'But you told me so.' Sebastian dropped into a chair. 'I don't know whether I'm on my head or my heels – or that it was

284

possible to be as happy as this. Did you write asking Caroline to come? I hope you did. Sir Charles and Lady Delahaye are to hold a ball next week to celebrate our betrothal and --' He stood up again. 'Oh God. I need a ring. How does one *do* that?'

'One walks into a jeweller's shop.'

'I know that. But do I go and buy it myself or do I take Cassandra with me so that she can choose? What is the proper form?'

'You're asking the wrong person. I had the sense to elope with a wedding ring in my pocket but Caroline didn't get a betrothal ring until we'd been married nearly a month. However, for what it's worth, I chose a ring I felt suited her and it worked out well enough.'

'Right. I'll do it tomorrow. And flowers. I should have taken her flowers this afternoon, shouldn't I? Damn. She's going to the Ainsley party this evening. I could send a corsage. Where's the nearest flower shop?'

'Two streets away. Sebastian – just stop for a moment and calm down.'

'I can't. The reality of it is just beginning to hit me. The banns will be called for the first time on Sunday and in a month, we'll be married but I don't have a home to offer her. Charles said he'd help but that's just bloody humiliating. Christ, Adrian – aside from writing to my father, what the *hell* am I going to do?'

'You are going to buy some flowers; you and I are going to take an early dinner at Sinclairs while we talk; and then you are going to Ainsley House where you will stop worrying and dance with Cassie. Everything will work out all right. It generally does, you'll find.'

CHAPTER TWENTY

Before leaving for Sinclairs, Sebastian sent an impassioned appeal to his father and, over dinner, Adrian offered financial assistance if all else failed. Later still, at the Ainsley ball, Sir Charles said that he had also written to Lord Wingham – threatening to descend on him in person if there was no response within the next three days. Since, for the time being at least, the matter was out of his hands, Sebastian danced twice with Cassie, took her in to supper ... and spent the rest of the evening in the card room, thus creating a buzz of speculation which the gentlemen found amusing and many of the ladies, a potentially crushing disappointment.

On the following morning, notice of the Honourable Sebastian Audley's betrothal to Mistress Cassandra Delahaye appeared in the *Morning Chronicle* and the Honourable Sebastian set off for Ludgate Hill to buy a betrothal ring for the light of his life. This proved to be a lot more difficult than he had anticipated. After spending the best part of two hours at Theed & Pickett with nearly every ring in the shop laid out before him, he had made up his mind six times, changed it just as often and had the sanity of young Mr Rundell, the junior partner, hanging by a thread. And then, just when he was beginning to despair he saw it. A beautifully faceted diamond solitaire set in twisted rose gold; understated, elegant and perfect. Sebastian left the shop with a sense of achievement and a spring in his step. Mr Rundell saw him off the premises with a sigh of relief.

Once again, Sebastian took his carriage to Conduit Street – this time determined not to take no for an answer. With their betrothal now both official and public, he couldn't wait to put the ring on Cassandra's finger and he wanted to do it away from the house and her family. Ideally, he'd have liked to have the day with her – at Richmond, perhaps, or Kew; but since the afternoon was likely to bring an avalanche of visitors, wishing to offer their felicitations, this clearly wasn't an option. So he settled for Hyde

Park – both glad and sorry that it was too early yet for the fashionable crush; glad because he wanted to be alone with her ... and sorry because few people would see her sitting beside him looking utterly ravishing.

In a dusky pink carriage-dress and twirling a lacy parasol, Cassie positively glowed.

She said, 'You've rescued me. Again.'

He glanced at her, smiling. 'From what?'

'From spending virtually the entire day writing invitations. The list of guests has got to seventy-four so far and is still growing. Meanwhile, Mama is busy organising flowers, an orchestra, the supper menu and probably a dozen other things as well.' She tucked a hand through his arm and laughed up at him. 'In short, she's having a thoroughly *splendid* time.'

'What about Olivia? Is she helping?'

'Don't be silly. In between getting in the way and badgering Mama about a new gown for the wedding, she's penning gleeful letters to her friends in the happy expectation of making them green with envy.'

'And you, Cassandra? Are *you* happy?'

'Do you really need to ask? I feel as if I'm floating on air.'

'I'd better keep a firm hold, then – so that you don't float away entirely.'

'Yes.' Her colour rose a little but she said earnestly, 'You should *definitely* do that – if it's not too much trouble.'

'Minx.' Sebastian turned the horses into the park and set them on the main carriage-way. Away towards the Serpentine, nursemaids watched small children playing with balls and spinning tops. 'Am I rushing you, love? If I am ... if you'd like time to enjoy our betrothal and shop for your bride-clothes, you must tell me. I'll wait if it's what you'd prefer. And I won't mind.'

'Not at all?'

'Well, perhaps a bit. But not enough to spoil this for you. If you want our betrothal ball next week and a wedding in three months' time --'

'I don't. I want to marry you and I don't want to waste three months waiting to do it. And before you ask – yes. I'm quite sure.'

Her words and the way her fingers tightened possessively on his arm had the curious effect of making him feel ten feet tall whilst simultaneously turning his brain soft. He said, 'I love you, you know. And I want very much to make you happy.'

'You make me happy by just walking into the same room and even happier when you smile or take my hand. I have no doubts, Sebastian. None.'

That brought an ache to his chest.

'Has your father said anything about the situation with mine?'

'No. I presume they have to discuss money and settlements – things I don't care about at all and that I am quite sure they'll resolve.' She paused. 'But I do hope your father will come to the ball. He *must* want to meet me, mustn't he?'

'He'll love you. How could he not?'

She didn't observe, as she might have done, that this wasn't an answer. Instead, she noticed that they had left the main thoroughfare for a narrower track amongst the trees and was happily aware that Sebastian was seeking privacy.

He drew the carriage to a halt, twisted the reins about the bar and, despite the sudden churning of his nerves, turned to smile at her, saying, 'I have something for you.'

'You do?'

'Mm.' Pulling off his gloves and relieving her of the parasol, he began slowly unbuttoning the glove on her left hand. 'There will be callers later today, I imagine. Should I be in attendance?'

'I – yes.' The lazy trail of his fingers along the bare skin of her forearm on their way to her wrist was making her pulse beat faster and depriving her of breath. 'Yes.'

His head was bent over his task. Glinting through the trees, the sun turned his hair to liquid fire, while Cassie's bones became water. He murmured, 'How many gentlemen will be wishing me at the devil this morning?'

'Less than the number of ladies who'll be wishing *me* there,' she managed, as he drew the glove unhurriedly from her hand and then lifted it to place a warm kiss in her palm.

'I find that hard to believe. Impossible, in fact. Close your eyes.'

'Sebastian --'

'Humour me. Please.'

Cassie closed her eyes. She doubted there was anything she *wouldn't* do for him when he looked at her like that and asked in that slightly roughened voice. She felt him move beside her, before taking her hand in his. And then something cool and smooth slid on to the third finger of her left hand.

'You can look now,' he said, thinking, *Let her like it. Please, please let her like it.*

Cassie opened her eyes and stared, her lips parting on a tiny exhalation of breath.

Sebastian waited for her to say something – anything; and when she did nothing but gaze speechlessly at the ring, he said, 'It can be changed. If you don't like it, that is.'

'Not *like* it?' Brilliant with unshed tears, the storm-cloud eyes rose to meet his. 'I – I *love* it. It's perfect. It's the most beautiful ring I've ever seen. I just didn't expect ...' She stopped, swallowing hard. 'It's exactly right, Sebastian. Thank you.'

'Don't thank me. I'm glad – no, *relieved* that you like it. I was afraid you might not. But it somehow seemed important for you to be wearing my ring when the congratulations start pouring in.' He put his arm about her and drew her close, his eyes teasing her. 'Does getting it right merit a small reward?'

She nodded. 'I don't understand why you're asking. I've been waiting for you to --'

Her words were swallowed up by his kiss ... long, sweet and dangerously enticing. Cassie sighed into his mouth and laid her palm against his cheek. It was a long moment before Sebastian reluctantly drew away saying, 'I should take you back, shouldn't I?'

'I suppose so. But Mama said I could invite you to dine this evening.'

'I accept.' He handed over her parasol, pulled his gloves on and set the carriage in motion. 'I called on the Duke and Duchess of Rockliffe yesterday, by the way. Rock didn't seem unduly surprised at our news – but his wife was delighted and congratulated me very enthusiastically on my intelligence and foresight.'

'Did you see the baby?' she asked.

'I did indeed. But please don't ask me to supply details. Like most men, I can't tell one infant from another.' Sebastian glanced sideways at her, watching in some amusement as she turned her hand this way and that to watch the diamond catch the light. 'Clearly, that changes when the infant in question is one's own. Certainly, Rock is besotted and so unlike his usual self I had trouble not laughing. Needless to say, his duchess was showing no such restraint.'

Cassie laughed but said, 'They are devoted to each other.'

'Yes. I noticed.' *And finally understood.*

* * *

Handing Cassie down from the carriage, Sebastian escorted her to the door and was about to take his leave when Lady Delahaye appeared looking fraught.

'You'd better come in, Sebastian. I'll have your carriage taken round to the mews.'

'Is something amiss?'

'You might say so. Lord Wingham is here.'

'Here?' echoed Sebastian blankly. *'Now?'*

'Yes. He's in the library with Charles – and he is *fuming* because he has had to read about his son's betrothal in the *newspaper.*'

'Oh dear,' said Cassie anxiously. 'Perhaps we ought to have waited.'

'We *did* wait. Your father wrote to him before the Drury Lane fiasco but he failed to respond in any remotely useful fashion,' replied Sebastian grimly. Then, to Serena, 'I'm sorry. I'll go and see what I can do to make things better.'

Cassie took his arm. 'I'll come with you.'

'No. You won't. I'll not have you anywhere near him until he stops blustering and can be relied upon to treat you with proper courtesy and respect.'

Her ladyship nodded in agreement. 'Come along, Cassie. The afternoon's callers will start arriving any minute and you should at least tidy your hair. Also, Sebastian is quite right. You don't want to meet your future father-in-law while he's feeling aggrieved – because afterwards he would regret it a great deal more than you would.'

Outside the library door, Sebastian shut his eyes for a moment and drew a long, steadying breath. Then he set his hand to the latch and went in.

Sir Charles was sitting in an armchair looking resigned rather than annoyed, while Lord Wingham, leaning upon his walking stick, paused mid-rant to cast an aggravated glance over his shoulder. Then, aggravation turning abruptly to a full-scale glower, he said, 'Well! And about time, too. What have you got to say for yourself?'

'Several things,' returned Sebastian coolly, 'provided you're going to listen while I say them.'

'Good luck with that,' murmured Charles. 'I gave up ten minutes ago. For a man reputedly on his death-bed just a couple of months ago, Lord Wingham is to be commended on his remarkable recovery.'

Sebastian gave an involuntary choke of laughter.

'You think this is *funny*?' snapped his father. 'Do you think it is appropriate that the first I hear about my heir's intention to wed is a notice in the damned *Chronicle*? It is not! It is totally unacceptable – a complete disregard for both my feelings and my opinions! And you – you have the effrontery to *laugh*?'

'Sit down, Father.'

'I'll sit down when I choose to do so. I --'

'Sit *down*. And take a breath before you have another apoplexy and I have to send you back to Blanche in a box. She already dislikes me quite enough, thank you – and that would be the final nail the coffin, if you'll forgive the expression.'

This time it was Charles who had to hide a smile.

Lord Wingham finally decided to sit down. Resting both hands on the knob of his cane, he scowled over the top of it and chose to be diverted.

'What nonsense is this? Of course Blanche doesn't dislike you. You're her brother!'

'So was Theo,' returned Sebastian as evenly as he could. 'And she's made it clear often enough that it would have been better if God had taken me instead.'

This produced a sudden silence which Charles saw the wisdom of not breaking, much though he'd have liked to. Eventually his lordship said, 'Is that true?'

'Do you think I'd say it if it wasn't?'

'No. But ... has she actually *said* that?'

'Frequently. I believe the first time was immediately after we buried Theo – though on that particular day, I didn't find it such a terrible idea.' Sebastian stopped, feeling his throat grow tight and aware that both Sir Charles and his father looked horrified. 'Why are we discussing this? It's old history and nothing to do with what brought you here.'

Lord Wingham opened his mouth as if to disagree and then thought better of it, saying instead, 'Exactly when was I going to be informed of this betrothal of yours?'

'Both Sir Charles and I wrote to you yesterday. The letters are probably awaiting you at Audley Court.'

'Well, I'm not *at* the Court, am I? I'm here – and have been for three days.'

Three days? thought Sebastian incredulously. *What have you been doing for three days?* He said, 'And how, exactly, were we supposed to know that?'

'You didn't need to know it.'

'Pardon me for contradicting you – but it appears that we did. It was only yesterday that Sir Charles gave me leave to pay my addresses to Cassandra. Had you bothered to let me know that you were in Town, you would have been informed immediately afterwards. Not,' he continued coolly, 'that you weren't already aware of my intentions. Sir Charles wrote to you two weeks ago, did he not? Reminding you – since you appeared to have forgotten – that you haven't supported me since I left Cambridge. Oh – don't mistake me, Father. Up till now, it hasn't mattered. Aunt Flora's legacy was sufficient for my needs. But it won't enable me to make adequate provision for my wife.'

Lord Wingham suddenly looked both uncomfortable and miserable. And old.

'You could have written to me yourself,' he muttered. 'And you *should* have done.'

'That may be true – in which case I apologise. However, the reason I didn't was because you'd dictated my life once before by financial means. I thought – *hoped* – that my future father-in-law might have better success than I in preventing the same thing happening again.'

'That is enough, Sebastian! I am aware that you are a grown man. I'm aware of my responsibilities and what's due to you as my heir. I've no intention of – of dictating to you, damn it! Why the *hell* do you think I'm in London?'

'I've no idea, sir – just as I've no idea why no whisper of your presence in Town has reached me.'

'I've been staying in Chiswick with my old friend Emberton. He's as big a recluse as I've turned into. But if he hadn't thrown the *Morning Chronicle* at me over breakfast, I'd be no wiser about what's going on, would I?' His lordship frowned at his clasped hands, still resting atop his walking stick. 'So where is she?'

'Cassandra is in the drawing-room – hopefully showing her mother and sister her betrothal ring rather than fretting about what's going on in here. I refused to let her meet you until I could be sure you'd be civil.'

'*Civil?* Why, you insolent young jackanapes – who do you think you're talking to?'

'You, sir ... in a blinding temper,' said Sebastian, dryly. 'Cassandra is a lady. More to the point – forgive me, Sir Charles – she will soon be *my* lady. And I will permit no one to bark at her or show her disrespect.' He smiled a little. 'She's kind ... so she'd let you bark and not mind. But *I'd* mind.'

'What he said about Cassie is only true up to a point,' remarked Sir Charles. Deciding that the worst was now over, he rose and crossed to the decanter on the sideboard. 'She would let you rant. As long as you sat there looking hurt and upset, she'd smile and pat your hand and sympathise. She'd probably even apologise for having caused you any distress.' Having poured three glasses of Madeira, he handed one to each of his guests. 'But the instant you said something unkind to Sebastian or – God forbid! – objected to them marrying, she'd turn into something else. Something you wouldn't like, Wingham. Trust me. I've seen it. Yes – laugh by all means, Sebastian. I'll be laughing myself when *you're* on the receiving end.'

Sebastian shook his head. 'It won't happen – but if it did, I daresay I'd deserve it. And on the couple of occasions she's ripped up at me, I rather enjoyed it.'

'You don't know anything, do you?' said Sir Charles pityingly. Then, to the viscount, 'But perhaps we may get to the point, Robert? Why *are* you in London? And what have you been doing these last three days?'

'Making things right,' mumbled his lordship. 'I didn't want to write saying I *would* do it; I wanted to have *done* it – and that meant coming up to London. But what with Blanche and the doctor and even my blasted *valet* all convinced I was going to turn my toes up at any minute, getting away took a while. However, once here I spent a good deal of time with Hopkins, my lawyer fellow in the City. An allowance in accordance with your position as my heir and adequate for a married man will be paid, starting immediately, Sebastian.' He drank some wine and named a figure which made his son feel faintly dizzy. 'I also had Hopkins look about for a house for you – but at present, there only two suitable properties for sale.' He dug into the pocket of his coat and produced a pair of keys with address labels tied to them and slapped them on the table at his side. 'Take the young lady to look at them, choose whichever you like best, then notify Hopkins and he'll complete the purchase.'

The dizziness became a slight buzzing in Sebastian's ears. *An allowance? A house? And all in the space of five minutes?* It was almost too much to comprehend. He said, 'It would seem you've been extremely busy, sir. I – well, I *thank* you. I won't pretend I haven't been worried. But this ... this is generosity beyond anything I might have hoped for.'

'And not before time, you're thinking?'

'No. I was actually wondering if you'd care to remove from Chiswick and come to stay in Cork Street. Lord Sarre is also there at present and the countess will arrive in a few days – but I doubt if that will be a problem. And --'

'If you'll forgive me, Sebastian,' said Charles, 'I believe a better solution might be for Lord Wingham to stay with Serena and me. You'd be most welcome, Robert. Aside from the betrothal ball in five days' time, you'd be able to become better acquainted with Cassie.'

'*Better* acquainted? I've not so much as clapped eyes on her yet,' grumbled the viscount. And catching his son's eye, 'But yes. Thank you, Charles. I'd be pleased to accept your hospitality for a few days. Daresay Emberton will be glad to see the back of me anyway. And now ... when am I going meet my new daughter?'

Sebastian grinned and turned towards the door only to be halted by Charles, saying, '*I'll* fetch her. I'm sure you and your father would appreciate a moment or two of privacy.'

And he was gone.

Left looking at his father, Sebastian said, 'I *am* grateful, you know. You can talk all you like about your obligations towards me and what I'm entitled to ... but a *house*? With the allowance you're giving me, I could afford to lease one.'

'Leasing is a waste of money. And if I hadn't disposed of the house on Berkeley Square after Lizzie was settled, I wouldn't have needed to replace it, would I? But that's not what I wanted to say. I've something else for you.' He reached into the inside pocket of his coat and withdrew a folded parchment. 'When Audley men fall, they fall hard and fast. That's how it was with me and your grandfather before me. If it's the same with you and Delahaye's daughter --'

'Her name is Cassandra, Father,' interposed Sebastian gently.

'I know that! If it's the same with you, I thought you might not want to wait for banns and all the other claptrap.' He pushed the paper into Sebastian's hand. 'It's a special licence. Use it or not – it's up to you and Cassandra. I just thought you might like to have the choice.'

Just for a second, Sebastian felt as if the ground had shifted beneath his feet. Of all the things in the world that his father might have done or even *thought* of – this was without doubt the most unexpected. He said weakly, 'A special licence? I'm sorry. I'm having difficulty believing this.'

'Try harder,' advised his lordship, holding out his glass. 'Now put the paper away till you decide what you're going to do about it – and pour me some more Madeira. I'll say one thing for Charles Delahaye. He keeps a damned fine cellar.' Then, while Sebastian poured the wine, 'I'm sorry about Blanche. You should have told me.'

'To what end? It wouldn't have stopped her. And compared to the pain of losing Theo, it was of no consequence.'

'Was it not?' A truly unpleasant thought occurred to the viscount. 'You never ... for God's sake, Sebastian – please tell me you never thought that Blanche wasn't only speaking for herself? That perhaps your mother and I also ...' He stopped, unable to say it.

It *had* occurred to Sebastian because his sister had told him it was so. Handing his father the glass he said, smoothly, 'Theo and I were equally precious. I know that.'

The door opened again and Cassie stepped into the room, her expression a little anxious until Sebastian smiled and crossed to take her hand. Then she beamed up at him and let him draw her forward to where Lord Wingham was heaving himself to his feet.

'Sir, allow me to present my bride-to-be,' said Sebastian, with unmistakeable pride. 'Cassandra – my father, Viscount Wingham.'

Sinking into a curtsy, she said warmly, 'I'm happy to make your acquaintance, my lord ... and so *very* glad for Sebastian's sake that you have come. We both hoped you would.'

'Well, now.' His lordship possessed himself of one of her hands. 'So you are the young lady who's brought my idiot son to his knees, are you?'

Cassie coloured, laughing a little. 'Well, it's true that he proposed to me in time-honoured fashion ... but he can't maintain that position, can he?'

'He will if you ask it,' murmured Sebastian wickedly in her ear. And in his usual tone, 'Just reminding you both that I'm standing right here and haven't gone deaf.'

'You'd do better to ask your Papa if we have his blessing,' reproved Cassie. 'We have rather presented him with a *fait accompli* – which he might quite understandably resent.'

'My dear, Sebastian's made his choice. And a very charming choice it is, too.'

'Thank you.' Cassie reached up to kiss his lordship's cheek. 'Papa says you are to stay with us at least until after the ball which means we'll have plenty of time to talk properly later. But just now, visitors are beginning to arrive and Mama says that Sebastian and I must go back to the drawing-room to receive their congratulations. I believe that you may know some of our friends, my lord – so perhaps you will join us?'

'I'd be delighted,' he said, waving Sebastian away and offering Cassie his arm. 'And on the way, you can tell me what you see in this rascal of mine and what he did to deserve a lovely girl like you ... and how you plan to keep him in line once you have him. Go on ... I'm listening.'

* * *

On the following afternoon, Sebastian took Cassie to view the houses to which his father had provided keys. Since both were in easy walking distance, they set off through the bright May sunshine with Cassie clinging to his arm, pink with anticipation.

'Your father said he was sorry he sold the house on Berkeley Square – but I'm not,' she confided. 'The houses there are such huge, intimidating places and I'd much rather we lived somewhere more intimate.'

'Intimate?' Sebastian slanted a smile at her. 'Yes. I like the sound of intimate.'

Cassie was learning to ignore his innuendos when it suited her. She did so now. She said, 'Replies are already coming in to the invitations. No one has declined yet.'

'The Vernons will. Philip called in Cork Street yesterday to deliver his congratulations and regrets in person. He and Isabel are leaving for Hertfordshire tomorrow.'

'Are they? Why?'

Sebastian sighed and then said simply, 'You remember the child at Drury Lane?'

'Of course. I'm not likely to forget that night, ever.'

'Isabel wants to keep her.'

'Keep her? Adopt her, do you mean?'

'Perhaps. All that's clear at present is that Isabel won't give her up. But --'

'Well done, Isabel!' said Cassie. 'If the poor child ends up with a loving home, at least *one* good thing will have come out of that horrible business.'

Sebastian shook his head, grinning at her.

'And well done Cassandra for looking at it like that.' He glanced at the tag on the key he was holding and stopped walking. 'This is it.'

Cassie turned to look at the house. 'Oh,' was all she said.

'Oh,' agreed Sebastian.

It was a double-fronted edifice built of stark grey stone, with a pair of vicious looking griffins glaring at each other from either side of the stairs to the door.

'Perhaps it's nicer inside,' suggested Cassie. 'It's certainly very imposing, isn't it?'

'That's one word for it,' muttered Sebastian. 'But you're right. It may be better than it looks.'

The key squealed in the lock and, as the front door swung open, one elsewhere swung shut with an echoing clang that made Cassie jump. Panelled in dark oak, the hall yawned before them like a vast, gloomy cavern; a pair of rusting suits of armour guarded the broad, staircase and overhead, festooned in cobwebs, was a massive and very ugly chandelier.

Sebastian groaned. 'We can't live here.'

'No,' agreed Cassie, her voice oddly strained. 'Have you read *The Castle of Otranto*?'

'No. Why?'

'B-Because I think we're in it,' she said, dissolving into laughter. 'Come on.'

They toured the reception rooms hand in hand – in case, as Sebastian said, one of them got lost in the dark. Virtually all of the shutters had been left fastened and many appeared to have been nailed shut. They were in what they thought might be the formal dining room when Cassie said, 'Sebastian?'

'What?' he grunted, heaving fruitlessly at a catch in an attempt to shed a bit more light.

'Look up.' She was no longer laughing.

He did – and promptly wished he hadn't. *'Hell!'*

At just below ceiling height, the entire circumference of the room was decorated with hunting trophies. There were stags and foxes; tigers and wild boar; even a snarling wolf. In the half-light, the whole display was a mass of glassy eyes, teeth, tusks and dusty, moth-eaten fur.

'That,' said Sebastian, 'is just obscene. Let's go.'

She nodded. 'Yes, please.'

Outside on the pavement, they spent a few moments silently picking cobwebs off each other. But eventually Cassie said, 'Your father can't have seen it.'

'He hasn't seen Bruton Place either. But it can't be worse than this one. Can it?'

'*Nothing* could be worse than this one,' she agreed cheerfully, slipping her hand through his arm as they began walking again. 'It was lovely of Adeline to insist on Rock bringing her yesterday.'

'She's fond of you – as, I believe, is the duke.'

'He likes you, too, I think. He told me to ask you about something called the Casparov but I couldn't tell if he was serious. What *is* the Casparov?'

'A chess set I acquired in Russia. Basically, I won a game I wasn't expected to win and got the board on which it had been played.' Sebastian grinned. 'What Rock wants is to know is who I won it *from*. I daresay he already has some theories.'

'It sounds very mysterious.'

'It's not. But it will make more sense when you see the set,' he shrugged. And considered promising to show it to her on their wedding day.

He had said nothing about the special licence. He couldn't deny that it tempted him ... but he was already rushing Cassandra to the altar and a month wasn't long to wait. One part of him said he ought to tell her about it; another said that, if he did that, she might think it was what he wanted and say they should use it, regardless of her own feelings. All in all, he decided, it would be best to keep the matter to himself.

The property on Bruton Place was an elegant pale stone town-house with pillars flanking the door and generous windows. Cassie's hand gripped Sebastian's sleeve and she said, 'Oh – it's lovely!'

'It's certainly an improvement on the other,' he agreed, setting the key to the lock. 'Let us hope there are no dead animals glaring down on us in this one.'

There weren't. The hall was light, its black-and-while tiled floor spotless and its staircase rising upwards in a graceful curve. There were three spacious reception rooms, as well as a dining room and a cosy library; the master-suite comprised two elegant bedchambers, each with their own dressing-room and a large shared sitting-room; and there was even a little furniture – a table here or a chair there – all swathed in dust-sheets.

Cassie ran from room to room, exclaiming and laughing. Sebastian followed more slowly, enjoying her delight.

'I love it!' Twirling around in the middle of what, judging by the dainty floral décor was the mistress of the house's bedchamber, she threw her arms wide and said, 'It's perfect. Don't you think?'

What Sebastian thought was that there was actually a bed in the room; a bed he was trying not to look at. So, distracting himself by teasing her a little, he said, 'I don't know. The dining room is perhaps a little small. And do you think we can manage with only five spare bedchambers?'

'*Manage*? Don't be absurd. It's just right.' She stopped, eyeing him uncertainly. 'Do you really not like it?'

And that was where teasing had to stop. The very last thing he wanted was to spoil her pleasure. He said, 'Of course I like it, sweetheart. And you're right. It's --'

Hurling herself against his chest and nearly knocking him off his feet, Cassie twined her arms about his neck and gazed into his eyes. 'So please may we have it?'

'If you want it, my darling, it's yours.' And wrapping her close, he sought her mouth with his own.

Her response was immediate and purely instinctive. Her lips parted beneath his and Sebastian promptly stopped thinking. He took what she offered, deepening the kiss further and much faster than he'd done before while his hands took a path of their own. For the first time, he discovered the curve of her spine, her waist, her hips, a low sound of satisfaction escaping him when she pressed so close that they were joined from breast to knee. His mouth swept along her jaw; his teeth closed lightly over her ear-lobe; his tongue found the hollow at the base of her throat. With a sobbing moan, she released her hold on his hair in favour of pushing her hands under his coat to explore the muscles of his chest and back. Heat eddied and flowed between them; desire, untrammelled for the first time, soared up and up; the kiss and their hands on each other became a dangerous conflagration.

It was when his back collided with something that turned out to be the bed-post that Sebastian came to some vague awareness of what he was doing ... and that he was perhaps a minute away from pulling Cassandra down with him upon that oh-so-tempting mattress. Her hair was falling down her back, her fingers had somehow unbuttoned enough of his vest to enable her to slide her hands beneath it ... while he, having been defeated by the neckline of her gown, had actually begun unlacing it.

Sebastian froze, his heartbeat and pulse hopelessly erratic. He forced his hands back to the safety of her shoulders and gently set her away from him. Flushed and exquisitely dishevelled, Cassandra stared back out of dazed eyes, her breathing as uneven as his own.

For a moment, they merely looked at each other, neither of them quite knowing what to say. Then, turning away a little while he waited for the turmoil in his body to subside, Sebastian said huskily, 'I'm sorry.'

'Are you?'

'No. But I should be. I'm the one who knows what he's doing and I'm supposed to be a gentleman. I should have more control.'

'You'd have stopped if I'd asked, wouldn't you?'

'Yes! God, Cassandra of – of *course* I would!'

'That's what I thought. But I didn't ask, did I?' Sitting on the edge of the bed and letting her lashes veil her eyes, she said softly, 'I – I liked what you did. What *we* did. I *especially* liked knowing that you wanted to do it. How exactly does that make it your fault?'

The air evaporated from his lungs and he dragged his hand through his already untidy hair. The ribbon came loose and floated to the floor. Sebastian looked down, still helplessly adrift and saw the scattering of hairpins littering the floor around it.

He dropped on one knee and started gathering them up.

How on earth had they got there? What else *– while he'd been drunk on the taste and scent and feel of her – had he done* *that he didn't remember? And what else* might *he have done if he* *hadn't come to his senses in time.*

Without looking up, he said, 'You have my heart, Cassandra. Unfortunately, all the baser parts of me come with it.'

There was a long silence. And then, 'I don't know much about these things … but I suspect it might be a bit disappointing if they didn't.'

His eyes flew to her face and he made a surprising discovery. 'Are you *laughing* at me?' he asked.

'Not at all. But it's supposed to be me having the vapours.'

Just for a second, words failed him. 'I am *not* having the vapours.'

'Are you sure? Aunt Almeria has them sometimes and it looks just the same.'

Sebastian stood up and loomed over her.

'One more word, you atrocious girl – and I swear I'll shake you.'

Cassie smiled up at him. '*Now* who's laughing?'

He stretched out his fingers and traced the line of her cheek. Her face was incandescent with joy and love … an expression so bright it nearly blinded him. He said stupidly, 'You look so happy.'

'I *am* happy.' She captured his hand and held it. 'I love you. And in a month, we'll be married.'

A month. It was nothing, really. He could wait one month. Hell, *he'd wait for* twelve *or even longer if he had to. The trouble was that he'd been given something that meant he* didn't *have to.*

His brain was at war with itself.

Tell her.

Don't tell her.

Tell her and let her choose.

Don't. She might make a decision she'll regret.

Trust her – or start your marriage with a secret.

It was the last thought that did it. Sighing, he sat down beside her, pulled the licence from his pocket and handed it to her.

'My father gave me that. In many ways, I wish he hadn't ... and I'd half decided not to tell you about it. But I won't begin our life together by keeping things from you.'

Cassie unfolded the paper and read enough of what was written on it to understand what it was. Looking up into Sebastian's eyes, she said, 'A special marriage licence? Why?'

'When he applied for it, he wouldn't have known I'm already dragging you to the altar with indecent haste. And --'

'You are doing no such thing.'

'And he's got some notion about Audley men falling 'hard and fast', as he puts it – as if the ridiculous red hair wasn't enough of a curse. Anyway --'

'Your hair isn't ridiculous. It's beautiful. It's like --'

'Stop. If you love me, please stop. I've heard more adjectives applied to it than any self-respecting man should ever have to bear.' He took the paper back and replaced it in his pocket. 'At any rate, Father seems to have got the idea that we might not want to wait. But we can ignore it. In fact, I think we should. He won't mind. And I only told you because it didn't seem right not to.'

Cassie was silent for a very long time. Finally she said, 'Don't you want to even *think* about it?'

'Do you? And even if we both did – your parents would have a fit at the very idea.'

'Not necessarily,' she said slowly.

And for the second time in the last ten minutes, she deprived him of breath by making an utterly astonishing suggestion.

CHAPTER TWENTY-ONE

After another lightning tour of the house which this time included the servants' quarters and kitchens, they walked back to Conduit Street, discussing Cassie's idea as they went. At least, it *began* as a discussion; but very soon Sebastian was marshalling every counter-argument he could think of in order to find out, beyond any shadow of a doubt, whether this was what she wanted. Unaware of his motives, Cassie eventually began to lose patience. And finally, when he made the same point for the third time – albeit in different terms – she came to an abrupt stop in the middle of the pavement, causing other pedestrians to swerve around them.

'If you don't like the idea ... if the truth is that you really don't want to even consider it, let alone *do* it ... for heaven's sake just *say* so.'

'I thought we *were* considering it.'

'No. We're not. You are *arguing*. And it – it's boring.'

Sebastian folded his arms. He wondered how it was possible to fall more deeply in love with each day that passed.

'I,' he said flatly, 'am not boring. In fact, I am probably the least boring man in London.'

'You *were*. Right now, you sound like my Great-Aunt Maude with all this talk of What People Will Think and things that are Just Not Done.'

How Sebastian kept his face straight, he didn't know. But somehow he managed a mournful sigh and shook his head. 'Your father said this would happen.'

'He said *what* would happen?'

'That I'd end up henpecked and wholly downtrodden.'

'He did not!' gasped Cassie, outraged. 'He'd *never* say such a thing.'

'Not in those exact words perhaps ... but it's what he meant.'

Something must have given him away because her eyes suddenly narrowed and she said, 'You – you're being deliberately provoking.'

'And enjoying it immensely,' he agreed. Then, seeing that he'd finally rendered her speechless, he set her hand on his arm, held it firmly in place and led her onwards. 'Now, sweetheart ... think very carefully. If this is *truly* what you want, we'll lay the idea before your parents. If is isn't, we forget it right now – the same being true if, as I believe they will, your parents won't hear of it. And that, my love, is quite final.'

Cassie walked beside him in silence for a moment.

'You haven't said whether or not it's what *you* want,' she remarked.

'No. I didn't think I needed to.' Looking down at her he gave a sudden choke of laughter. 'Great-Aunt Maude, indeed!'

She smiled back. 'Should I apologise?'

'By no means. If you want to put a fellow on his backside, likening him to somebody's great-aunt will do it every time.'

* * *

They arrived in Conduit Street to find Lord Wingham taking tea with Charles, Serena and Olivia. Forgetting to curtsy or even take off her hat, Cassie sank down on a footstool beside the viscount's chair and said, 'Bruton Place, if you please, sir. We love it.'

'Not Mount Street?'

'*Definitely* not Mount Street,' pronounced Sebastian. 'Cassandra felt she'd stepped into Gothic horror story and I expected to find a corpse.'

Olivia giggled. 'How marvellous. Can *I* go and see it?'

'No. But you can come to Bruton Place with Mama and me tomorrow,' said Cassie. 'And I hope, my lord, that you will accompany us as well. You can't possibly give Sebastian and me such a generous wedding gift without seeing it!'

Lord Wingham shook his head at her and flicked her cheek with one finger.

'Well, puss ... if it would make you happy --'

'It would make me *very* happy, sir. Thank you.'

'I notice,' remarked Sir Charles, with a hint of amusement, 'that I am not invited.'

'Nor I, it would appear,' said Sebastian.

'Gentlemen are of little use in such matters,' remarked Serena, rising to pour tea for the late-comers. 'And the two of you have more mundane things to settle. You may do so tomorrow morning whilst the rest of us enjoy ourselves.'

Sebastian strolled over to draw Cassie first to her feet and then into the curve of his arm. He said, 'Cassandra and I have a suggestion we would like you to consider. A betrothal ball in four days' time and a wedding three weeks later is a lot to ask. So we wondered if the betrothal ball might not be transformed into a ... wedding party.'

There were perhaps three seconds of stunned silence before Olivia clapped her hands and said, 'Oh – yes. That's famous!'

'*What?*' gasped Serena. 'No. What on earth can you be thinking? It's quite impossible.'

'Technically, it isn't,' said Charles slowly. 'It merely requires a special licence.'

Sebastian withdrew the document from his pocket. Holding it up, his expression rueful, he said, 'Time for you to take the blame, Father.'

'*You* got them a special licence?' demanded Serena. 'What on earth for?'

'Thought they might like it,' mumbled his lordship. 'I *did* tell Sebastian he didn't have to use it.'

'And I hadn't intended to,' said Sebastian. 'But I couldn't *not* tell Cassandra about it.'

'A convenient scruple,' remarked Charles sardonically.

'No – it's true,' said Cassie. 'Holding our wedding on the day of the ball was *my* idea, not Sebastian's. He's spent the last half-hour trying to talk me out of it because he thinks I'll regret not having a fashionable wedding.'

'And won't you?' asked her mother.

'No. *Everyone* gets married at St George's in Hanover Square. But a private ceremony here with our family and closest friends … and then an announcement at the ball? I think it would be romantic.'

'Romantic,' muttered her mother. 'That's all we need.'

'Is this what *you* want, Cassie?' asked her father. 'Not just what Sebastian wants?'

'Yes. I'm absolutely certain. So may we?'

'Do not say a word, Charles,' snapped Serena.

'I wouldn't dream of it, my love.'

'Yes, you would. She'll twist you around her little finger. She's been doing it since she was two. And now it appears she's having the same effect on Sebastian.' She swung round to Cassie. 'Tell me. Have you given any consideration at *all* to what people will think?'

'Yes. Sebastian insisted on it. In fact, he became positively boring.'

'Just like Great-Aunt Maude,' murmured Sebastian. And reproachfully when Olivia giggled, 'It isn't funny. I was mortally wounded.'

'May we please stick to the point?' demanded Serena. 'The notice of your betrothal was in the newspaper yesterday and roughly a hundred people have received invitations to a celebration of it. *Nobody* gets married inside a week, Cassie – not unless there's some strong and usually unfortunate reason for it. And *we* don't have any excuse at all.'

Feeling that he had given the Delahayes sufficient time to have their say, Lord Wingham decided to play his ace. He said, 'Yes, we do. It's an Audley tradition.'

There was another stunned silence. Finally Sebastian said, 'A tradition? Really?'

'Yes. I married your mother by special licence ten days after we met and your grandparents ran off and got married over the anvil,' said the viscount calmly. 'I can't speak for earlier generations. But those I've mentioned both had exceptionally happy marriages … so I got the licence in case you and Cassandra wanted to carry on the custom. However, it's not my decision to make. It's yours.'

* * *

The following days passed in a blur during which Sebastian and Cassandra scarcely saw one another. *She* was caught up in fittings for a new gown, yet more lists for necessary re-arrangements and a host of other details; *he* had taken on the responsibility of making at least part of the house in Bruton Place habitable – a task which lack of time was turning into a nightmare. Fortunately, before he reached the point of tearing his hair out, Lady Sarre arrived and took control.

Smiling serenely at Sebastian, Caroline told her husband to take him away.

'Take him where?' asked Adrian.

'Anywhere. You'll be standing up for him at his wedding, so I'm sure you'll think of something. And I need to make the best use of the time we have left. I'll visit Bruton Place with Cassie to learn her preferences, see what needs to be done and then take care of it – making the bedchambers, dressing-rooms and sitting-room a priority. As for the furniture you were told couldn't be delivered until next week, Sebastian ... the shop will *not* say that to me.'

'They won't?' he asked, baffled but hopeful.

'No.' Adrian grinned. 'Five minutes and they'll either be grovelling at her feet or eating out of her hand. Now ... Sinclairs or White's?'

'Angelo's,' said Sebastian. 'And send a note asking Rockliffe to join us. Tell him that if he can disarm me in less than twelve minutes, I'll tell him who owned the Casparov before me. That ought to get his attention.'

* * *

Sebastian kept hold of his foil for a record *thirteen* minutes, for which he earned a round of applause and the right to leave his Grace in suspense. Cassie, meanwhile, spent two hours in Bruton Place with Caroline discussing everything from candlesticks to chamber pots and then left her ladyship with a list several pages long and three days in which to accomplish it.

On the following morning, Cassandra had a final fitting for the gown of pearl-coloured silk, exquisitely embroidered with delphinium thread that had unexpectedly become her wedding dress. So far, despite a clutch of new invitations summoning a select group to Conduit Street an hour before the start of the ball, no one seemed to suspect that plans had changed. With the exception of Lord and Lady Sarre who, of necessity, had been let in on the secret, everyone else continued to believe in the betrothal. Cassie wondered if that would last as long as was necessary.

Two evenings before the ball while the gentlemen gathered at Sinclairs, Caroline dined with the Delahaye ladies and reported that good progress was being made in Bruton Place.

'Everything should be ready in time,' she said. 'Sebastian's things have been transferred from Cork Street and your maid can bring yours tomorrow – though you won't need *everything* since you're unlikely to be receiving visitors or attending parties for a few days.'

This hadn't previously occurred to Cassie and she said, 'We won't?'

'No.' Caroline laughed a little. 'Sebastian will want you to himself for a time. And unless I completely mistake the matter, you'll want the same.'

Later that night after Caroline had gone home, Cassie considered what had been said and realised that the whirlwind of wedding preparations had temporarily caused her to lose sight of what they were all *for*. Now, curled upon the window-seat after her maid had prepared her for bed, she found herself contemplating the longed-for moment when she and Sebastian would be married; the moment when he would kiss her and touch her … and she might perhaps fall asleep in his arms and awake the same way; of not just hours but *days* alone with him. It was a possibility that made her body sizzle with an anticipation that, as yet, was beyond her comprehension.

Mama hadn't told her very much. She'd merely said that describing the marital act didn't do it any favours; that the first time – and *only* the first time – might hurt a little; and that she was fairly sure Sebastian could be trusted to make the experience pleasurable. Cassie had no trouble believing the last bit. Putting Sebastian's name and the word 'pleasure' into the same sentence made bits of her melt.

* * *

At Sinclairs, the exclusively male pre-celebration of Mr Audley's betrothal had grown increasingly convivial. Sebastian was surprised to find that, with the exception of Philip Vernon, everyone was there – even his father. Having wined and dined, nine gentlemen settled down to a little gaming. Lord Nicholas, as the only other unmarried man present, twitted Sebastian cheerfully on falling so rapidly into the parson's mouse-trap before eventually admitting that if a fellow *had* to dive into matrimony he could do a lot worse than Cassie.

'You had your chance,' replied Sebastian easily.

Nicholas shook his head. 'No. She doesn't take me seriously. Girls rarely do.'

Not for the first time in the last twenty minutes, his glance strayed to the door. It was a warm night and the room had become stuffy; windows had been opened and then, in the hope of catching a draught, the door to the corridor; and through it, Nicholas had gradually become aware of something unusual.

Madeleine, who normally remained largely invisible on evenings like this, had glided across his field of vision at least four times in the last hour. Admittedly, there was another, smaller party in the room next to their own ... but even so, it didn't account for Madeleine tripping back and forth or, more interestingly, letting him see her do it. It was tempting to wonder if she was hoping to lure him out in order to speak with him; but Nicholas was reluctant to make himself the butt of another round of teasing by obliging her – not to mention the fact that his brother was sitting on the far side of the table.

He might have remained firmly in his seat had he not seen her make another pass – this time with some fellow he didn't know lurching in her wake. Nicholas tensed, listening. He heard a slurred voice mumble something, immediately followed by what sounded like a slap.

Damn, he thought. And quitting his chair, strolled with apparent laziness into the hall.

A few feet away, the extremely inebriated gentleman had almost succeeded in pinning Madeleine to the wall and was trying to kiss her. Ramming both hands into his chest and simultaneously stamping on his foot, she said furiously, 'Get *off* me, you oaf!'

The man huffed a breath but was either too stupid or too drunk to relinquish his hold. Madeleine slapped him again and tried to twist herself free. He giggled.

'Oh for God's sake,' she muttered. And catching sight of Nicholas watching from just a few feet away, 'Are you just going to stand there?'

Grinning, he wandered over and hooked his fingers into the fellow's collar.

'He's on the point of passing out and you seemed to be doing well enough on your own. Also,' he said, 'I didn't want to get my head bitten off for interfering. But since you ask ...' And pulling the man away from her, Nicholas slammed him with moderate force into the wall and let him slide to the floor, unconscious. Then, dusting off his hands, he said, 'There's no need to thank me – which is just as well since I doubt you were going to. And here come your guard dogs.'

'About time.' Madeleine tried to straighten her hair whilst scowling at the pair of oversize footmen whose primary job was to protect her from annoyance. 'Dick; take *that* downstairs and tell Mr Jenkins to put him on the Black List. John; go to the blue salon and tell Lord Ansford that he and his party are to leave immediately or forfeit their membership.' She waited while the orders slowly sank in. 'Do it now.'

'Yes, Mamzelle,' they mumbled. 'Right away, Mamzelle. Sorry.'

Nicholas watched them depart in opposite directions, the unfortunate drunk slung over Dick's brawny shoulder. Then, folding his arms, he said, 'All right. You have my attention. What did you want?'

Madeleine lifted her chin and stared back defiantly.

'Why should you suppose I want anything?' And when he merely raised one brow and said nothing, 'Oh – very well. Your sister is taking tea with me tomorrow. I thought – it occurred to me that you – that you might care to accompany her.'

'To sit drinking tea with you and Nell?' He gave an incredulous laugh. 'Hardly! Or not without some damned good incentive.'

'Such as what?'

'Such as being allowed to take you driving.'

'You know my answer to that.'

'Yes. Here are two reasons to change it.' Nicholas's voice became unusually crisp. 'Firstly, I've just stopped that drunken sot mauling you. And secondly, this is the last time I'll ask. I've made a cake of myself over you for long enough. If you don't want to know me, say so and I'll walk away.'

Colour bloomed along her cheekbones. 'That sounds like an ultimatum.'

'It *is* an ultimatum. Choose.'

* * *

When the footman arrived with the note, Lord Sarre was watching the game of basset over Rockliffe's shoulder and Mr Audley had also quit the table on the grounds that he'd lost quite enough money for one night. This, as it turned out, was fortunate.

Come home, Caroline had written. *Sebastian has an uninvited guest. You may guess who it is. I'll keep her here – but hurry.*

Wasting no time, Adrian caught Sebastian's eye and summoned him with a slight jerk of his head. Then, handing him

---

Caroline's note, he said tersely, 'Leave the excuses to me – and let's go.'

Five minutes later they were outside and pelting along St James Street in the direction of Piccadilly.

'How the hell did she get in?' snapped Sebastian.

'No idea. More to the point, why haven't Sir John's fellows put the fear of God into her?' They swung into Old Bond Street. 'And why does being a friend of yours have to involve so much bloody running?'

Caroline was waiting for them in the hall. Holding up a hand to prevent questions, she said rapidly, 'She was here when I got home. If I hadn't seen a light under your door, Sebastian, and thought someone had left candles burning, I'd probably still be none the wiser. As far as I can make out, a disturbance lured the footman into the street and he left the front door open behind him – which is presumably when she slipped inside.'

'Hell,' muttered Adrian. 'Didn't anybody see her?'

'Such as who? This is a bachelor establishment with scarcely any staff. The cook and the maid had gone home; when Sebastian's out for the evening, he gives Hobson the night off; and my own maid is fast asleep in the attic. That leaves one footman. And he was distracted.' Caroline paused briefly and looked at Sebastian. 'It's possible that, between us, Thomas and I could have got rid of her. But I decided that, if this is ever to stop, it's up to you to stop it. So I locked her in.'

'Does she know that?'

'Yes. I found her ensconced in your bed as near to naked as makes no difference. I don't know which of us was more shocked. However ... I recovered first and told her that you'd be home presently, meanwhile I'd prefer her not to wander about the house looking like a trollop. Then, while she was still trying to close her mouth, I took the key and used it – leaving Thomas on guard in case she somehow manages to get out.' She glanced from him to Adrian and back again. 'What are you going to do with her?'

'I don't know,' groaned Sebastian. 'God knows, I've made it clear over and over again that there's nothing to be gained by pursuing me. And Charles says Bow Street released her on the understanding that further incursions would put her behind bars. But none of it seems to get through.' He shoved a hand through his hair and headed towards the stairs. 'If it was a man, the solution would be easy. As it is, I'm a hairsbreadth away from strangling her.'

'You might even get away with it,' said Adrian. Then, realising that his wife was following them, 'You should stay here, Caroline. This is likely to get ugly.'

'Good.' She sent him a grim smile. 'She's going to try dazzling the pair of you with her attributes. Let's see if she still tries it with another woman in the room.'

Upstairs, Thomas struggled to his feet and said miserably, 'I'm sorry, Mr Audley, sir. I didn't know as she was here and --'

'It's not your fault,' returned Sebastian, turning the key. 'Just stay within call.' Then, opening the door and striding through it, 'I won't ask what the hell you're doing here, Miranda. Just get your clothes on and leave.'

Completely ignoring the fact that Adrian and Caroline were two steps behind him, Lady Silvarez propped herself on one elbow and sent Sebastian a sultry smile. As Caroline had said, she was clad in a diaphanous pink thing which left nothing to the imagination and her partly-shorn hair had been artfully re-styled so that it clustered around her head in a halo of curls.

'You don't really want me to go,' she said huskily. 'Send them away ... and I'll remind you why.'

He didn't bother to answer. He simply crossed the room, grabbed hold of her wrist and started dragging from the bed only to have her lock her free arm about his neck and pull him off-balance so that he half-collapsed against her. The heavy scent of her perfume clogged his throat and her attempt to glue her mouth to his made him want to vomit.

Pushing roughly away from her, he said, 'For Christ's sake, what is the *matter* with you? I know you're vain, self-centred and

315

stupid – but are you completely insane as well? I do not want you. I will *never* want you – and planting yourself in my bed won't change that.'

She laughed. 'It would if you'd let it. Why do you insist on lying to yourself?'

'That's your province, not mine.' He paused, trying to hold on to the shreds of his temper and regulate his breathing. 'You've got to let go of this ridiculous obsession before it destroys your life. Is that what you want?'

'I want you. I've always wanted you and --'

'Want away, then – because it will be a cold day in hell before you have me.' Seeing her clothes laid over a chair, he picked them up and hurled them on top of her. 'This is my last warning, Miranda. Get dressed and go while you still have the chance.'

'You don't mean it. Why don't you stop fighting and admit that you love me.'

'*Love* you?' It was Sebastian's turn to laugh. 'Not only do I not love you, I've actually started to learn what hate feels like. Merely *looking* at you turns my stomach. All I want is for you to get the bloody hell out of my life and stay there.'

'Why are you being so cruel?' She shook her head, as if confused. 'It's not meant to be like this. You're mine. You'll *always* be mine. I love you.'

'Oh don't be so ridiculous!' snapped Caroline, moving several steps closer around the bed. 'Of course you don't love him. You don't even know the meaning of the word. If you *loved* him, you'd leave him alone.'

'And what would *you* know about it?' Miranda's tone switched abruptly from sadness to spite. 'A plain, dull woman like you? What man has ever wanted you so badly he'd sooner *die* than live without you?'

'This one,' said Adrian laconically, picking up a pair of scissors from the wash-stand. 'And if you don't want me to finish what Sebastian started, you'll keep your filthy tongue off my wife.'

Miranda's jaw dropped. Beaming, Caroline said softly, 'Thank you, Adrian.'

'Well it's true,' he replied. And to Miranda, 'Face it. You are a whore – and Sebastian is done with you. If he wasn't, do you honestly think he'd be standing there looking ready to throw up?'

She gave a shrill laugh. 'And just who might you be?'

'The Earl of Sarre, Madam – and absolutely *not* at your service.'

Miranda shrugged and her gaze returned to Sebastian. She said again, 'Send them away. If you do that, we'll talk.'

'If I do that, I'll probably resort to violence,' came the swift, hard retort. 'I'll give you five minutes to dress and leave – otherwise Lord Sarre and I will take you back to Bow Street exactly as you are. You were released on condition you left me alone. Since you haven't, this time I'll press charges and make sure they throw away the key.'

'You won't. You didn't want your name in the newspapers before and you won't feel any differently now.'

'*Before*, it wasn't my name that bothered me. Hasn't anyone told you that your scheme to tie Richard Penhaligon to – to my cousin didn't work?'

Her mouth set in an ugly line. 'That doesn't make any difference.'

'Actually, it makes all the difference in the world,' corrected Adrian, 'Tell her Sebastian. It's the only thing that might cure this mad delusion – so just *tell* her.'

Sebastian hesitated. He didn't want Cassandra's name brought into this unholy mess but it was possible that Adrian was right.

'Tell me what?' demanded Miranda.

He hauled in a breath and then loosed it.

'I'm getting married the day after tomorrow.'

'*Married?*' She gave a jeering laugh. 'To that whey-faced so-called cousin?'

He wondered if she knew how very close he was to hitting her.

'To a lady who is everything you are not,' he snapped.

'You're a fool! You'll be bored within a week – and wishing you had me back within two.'

'No. You just can't see it, can you?' Sebastian folded his arms and summoned the most insulting tone he could find. 'I don't know how much plainer I can make it – but let's try this. There isn't a woman in the world who wouldn't be preferable to you, Miranda; to put it bluntly, I'd rather lie down with a doxy from the gutter. So stay away from me. If you don't ... if you ever come near either me or my wife again, I'll probably kill you.'

Very slowly, she sat up to stare at him for countless seconds out of eyes grown utterly blank. Then, from beneath the pillow, she produced a pistol and, holding it steady in both hands, aimed it at his chest. She said calmly, 'Say goodbye to your wedding, darling. If I can't have you, no one will.'

Sebastian froze; Adrian swore, his gaze riveted upon the pistol; and Caroline said, 'Stop! Think! You won't get away with this. They'll hang you.'

'Perhaps,' said Miranda, her eyes still locked with Sebastian's. 'Perhaps. But that won't help you, will it?'

And she pulled the trigger.

In the instant he saw her grip shift, Adrian used the full weight of his body to send Sebastian crashing sideways into the wall; the bullet tore through Adrian's own sleeve just above the elbow before burying itself in the door; and Caroline cut off Miranda's howl of frustration by grabbing the nearest object and, with a furious scream of her own, slamming it against the other woman's head.

Miranda keeled over, semi-conscious. Caroline stood beside her, breathing hard and still holding the leather-bound tome she'd used as a weapon. Then the footman rushed through the door and she snapped, 'Thomas – get the pistol and find something to tie her hands with.' And flying to her husband's side, 'How bad is it?'

'A flesh-wound,' grunted Adrian disgustedly, clutching his arm and peering down at the blood seeping through his fingers. 'Hell. I was quite fond of this coat.'

'Damn the coat,' said his wife, deftly removing it.

'You *idiot*!' Sebastian's face was bone white. 'The bitch could have *killed* you!'

'But she didn't – whereas she *would* have killed you, since you were behaving as if your feet had been nailed to the floor. Ouch! Caroline – that hurts!'

'Well you shouldn't go round getting shot,' she said crossly whilst blinking tears aside. 'Twice in six months, for heaven's sake!'

'Sorry.' He gathered her into his sound arm and kissed the top of her head. 'I'll try not to make a habit of it. Meanwhile, I'll get over the destruction of my coat ... but can you please help me *not* to bleed all over my vest? It's new.'

* * *

Tied, gagged and half-naked beneath an enveloping blanket, Sebastian and Thomas delivered Miranda back to Bow Street. Since it was turned midnight it was a surprise to find Sir John's secretary in the hall.

He eyed the wriggling, squealing bundle with resignation and said, 'Oh dear. We were hoping we'd seen the last of her. What has she done now? Or no. Don't tell me. Just bring her in. Sir John was about to leave but I'm sure he'll make time for you.'

Sebastian remained silent until he and Thomas had hauled Miranda before the magistrate known to most of London as the Blind Beak and dumped her unceremoniously in a corner.

Then, his voice cold and hard, he said, 'Earlier this evening Lady Silvarez broke into my home where she attempted to kill me. Clearly, she failed in that. Instead, she managed to put a bullet in the Earl of Sarre – as I and the Countess can testify. Both the earl and I want her charged and sent for trial. I don't know if she belongs behind bars, on the gallows or in Bedlam. But I've reached the point of not caring which it is – so long as the only time I ever see her again is in court.'

CHAPTER TWENTY-TWO

'How is your arm?' muttered Mr Audley, resisting the urge to tug at his cravat.

'Sore but functional, thank you,' replied Lord Sarre.

There was a pause. Then, 'I'm going to be sick.'

'No, you're not.' His lordship's amusement wasn't without sympathy. He remembered how he'd felt in the last hour before his own wedding – his main fear being that, at the crucial moment, Caroline would say *I don't* instead of *I do*. 'Take a few deep breaths.'

'I can't. My cravat is strangling me.'

Adrian grinned. 'It's not. But you wouldn't be normal if you didn't think so.'

Around them, the room was filling up with guests.

Sebastian knew about half of them; Rockliffe, Amberley, Jack Ingram and Harry Caversham, all with their wives ... Dolly Cavendish, Charles Fox and Nicholas Wynstanton. Caroline, of course, was somewhere above stairs with Cassandra.

Then there were a clutch of Delahaye relatives of whom, despite having been introduced to all of them, he could name but two. One was Aunt Almeria who didn't look at all the sort of female prone to the vapours; and the other was his one-time partner in reckless folly, Cassandra's brother, who eyed him quizzically and said, 'It's been a while, hasn't it? But you and Cassie? That's not something I'd ever have expected.'

'No. I didn't exactly expect it myself.'

'I don't imagine one ever does.' Gerald paused. 'Father says you've given up hell-raising. I hope it's true for your sake – or I'll be putting your head through a wall.'

Sebastian nodded. 'If I deserve it, I'll let you.'

'Yes? Well, in that case – welcome to the family.' And he held out his hand.

Sebastian had known that his own family would be represented only by his father. He'd assumed that no one would be stupid enough to invite Blanche. And of his other sisters, Jennifer, Charlotte and Elizabeth all lived at some considerable distance and Beatrice was expecting again. If, as originally planned, the wedding had been in three weeks' time, he supposed that one of them *might* have come … or then again, not. And then the door opened again and a dark-haired lady in blue launched herself at his chest saying, 'I could murder you, Sebastian! And if I wasn't so very happy for you, I *would*!'

'Lizzie?' Stunned, his arms closed round her while, over her head, his eyes met those of his brother-in-law. 'How on earth --? No. This is … I didn't dare hope.'

Jonathan prised his wife away from her brother before she could completely ruin his coat and, gripping Sebastian's hand, said, 'You didn't think we'd miss it, did you?'

'I never dreamed you could get here in time. Thank you!'

'Don't be idiotic,' said Elizabeth, brushing away a stray tear and looking around. 'Where is Cassandra? I want to meet her.'

Realising that even *they* didn't know what was about to happen, Sebastian grinned and said, 'She'll be here soon. Meanwhile … I don't believe you are acquainted with, Lord Sarre. Adrian – Lord and Lady Holdenby.'

Greetings were still being exchanged when the butler caught Lord Sarre's eye across the room. Nodding in response, Adrian said quietly, 'Sebastian – it's time.' And with a brief word of excuse for Elizabeth and Jonathan, he bore Mr Audley unobtrusively away while the butler successfully reduced the company to silence.

Stepping forward, Lord Wingham said, 'Ladies and gentlemen, you may think it odd that it is I who am addressing you now rather than Sir Charles – but the fact is that you have all been brought here under false pretences. In short, we will *not* be celebrating a betrothal this evening.' He paused to absorb the startled expressions around him and then went on. 'It is my especial pleasure to announce that Sebastian and Cassandra have chosen to uphold the Audley tradition of the last two generations

– and dispense with a betrothal. Instead, Sir Charles, Lady Delahaye and I invite you to witness their wedding.'

There was an instant of acute silence and then, not bothering to lower his voice, Nicholas said, 'Sebastian still can't quite resist setting the world by its ears, can he?' And the hush dissolved into a buzz of shocked chatter and a scattering of laughter.

Precisely on cue, footmen opened the double doors to the next room where chairs were set out amidst huge vases of white roses while a pair of violinists burst jubilantly into the *Vivace* of the Bach double concerto and the Reverend Sir Henry Brockhurst awaited them, smiling.

'I suppose,' said Serena resignedly to Rockliffe, as everyone took their seats, 'that you'd guessed?'

'Let us merely say that I had … wondered,' came the suave reply. 'After all, if Mr Audley became *completely* conventional one might be a trifle disappointed, don't you think?'

Standing ramrod straight beside Adrian and refusing to look behind him, Sebastian hissed, 'Did Lizzie knock my cravat askew or crease my coat?'

'No.'

'Are you sure?'

'Yes. For God's sake - if you looked any prettier, you'd outshine the bride.'

Sebastian managed something that was almost a smile. 'Not possible.'

'I know. Now relax, will you? Trust me. This will be over before you know it.'

The music transitioned smoothly into the haunting *Largo* and, behind him, Sebastian heard a rustle of movement as the guests rose. She was coming. Drawing a very deep breath, he turned slowly and found Cassandra's eyes. She smiled at him – so radiantly that everyone else in the room ceased to exist. If he'd been asked, in that moment, what she was wearing he couldn't have answered. He only saw the joy and love in her face … and his heart swelled up until it seemed to be filling his entire chest.

Walking slowly on her father's arm between the smiling faces of their friends and relations, Cassie's gaze never strayed from the man waiting for her before the cleric. His coat was of dull gold brocade, worn over an extravagantly embroidered vest; the twilight eyes called to her and, in the candlelight, the dark wine-red hair glowed like embers of fire. He was so utterly beautiful that, for one fleeting moment, it seemed impossible that he was waiting for *her*. Then she was at his side, his fingers closing warm and firm about hers; and she knew she was home.

The guests sat down, the music stopped and, waiting until he had the attention of the bridal pair, the Reverend Brockhurst embarked on the solemnisation of marriage.

'Dearly beloved, we are gathered together in the sight of God ...'

Gradually, thanks to the familiar ritual and the feel of Cassandra's fingers in his, Sebastian's nerves began to relax. Then came, 'If either of you know of any impediment why you may not be joined together,' and all his muscles went into spasm again.

He told himself he was being stupid. *Miranda isn't here. She can't be. But if she could find a way into* my *house ...*

He held himself motionless through the silence; those seemingly endless seconds when someone could stop the wedding. Then the vicar said, 'Sebastian. Wilt thou have this woman to thy wedded wife ...?'

And after that, it was easy. He smiled down into Cassandra's eyes and said, 'I will.'

His voice was perfectly-pitched and steady. Cassie's was less so but her gaze didn't stray from Sebastian's and she managed his full name without stumbling.

'I take thee, Sebastian Gervase Montfleur Audley ... to have and to hold from this day forward ... and thereto I give thee my troth.'

And in no time at all it seemed, the ring was on her finger, the reverend was pronouncing them man and wife and without waiting for permission, Sebastian scooped her into his arms and kissed her, long and hard.

'Behave, Sebastian,' called Nicholas, over a scattering of male applause.

And, 'Save it till later,' advised Harry. 'Let Sir Henry finish.'

Reluctantly releasing her mouth, Sebastian whispered, 'I love you, I love you, I love you. Thank you for loving me too.' And wanted to shout out in sheer exultation when, with tears of happiness sparkling on her lashes, Cassandra whispered back, 'How could I not?'

They knelt for the blessing and signed the register. Then, walking from the room between the smiles of their friends, Cassie looked up at him and said, 'Montfleur? Really?'

'Thanks to one of the Conqueror's hangers-on, all the Audley men get that. But Gervase isn't too bad. Poor Theo got stuck with Augustine. When I was being particularly repellent, I used to call him Gussie.'

He realised with a jolt that it was the first time he'd been able to speak of his dead twin without pain. He thought, *I wish you were here now, Theo. I'd have liked for you and Cassandra to know each other.*

And then they were in the antechamber where refreshments had been laid out for the wedding guests and Cassandra was wrested from him by the ladies, while the gentlemen shook his hand or clapped him on the back – or, in the case of Nicholas, both.

Nell eyed Cassie unsmilingly. She said, 'You might have told me.'

'I know – and I'm sorry. But it was all decided very suddenly and Mama insisted it should be kept secret if the whole of London wasn't to know before it even happened.'

'You told Lady Sarre.'

'Since Lord Sarre was to be Sebastian's groomsman, that was unavoidable.' Cassie sighed. 'Don't be cross, Nell. If you recall, the first I knew of your betrothal to Harry was when it appeared in the *Morning Chronicle*. So --'

Nell's face broke into a smile. 'I know. And I'm happy for you. I just couldn't resist teasing a little. But honestly, Cassie –

engaged and married inside a *week*? How on earth did Mr Audley manage to persuade you?'

'He didn't. *I* persuaded *him*,' confessed Cassie. And turned away to accept the good wishes of Althea Ingram and the Duchess of Rockliffe.

Adeline kissed her cheek and said, 'Well, you had us all nicely bamboozled – and I don't blame you in the least. It was a lovely wedding, my dear. And aside from clearly being head over heels in love with you, Mr Audley is an extremely remarkable man – and exactly the sort of husband you deserve.'

'Thank you,' replied Cassie. 'I am ... I know how very lucky I am.'

'And so does he, I should hope,' remarked a vivacious lady in blue, smiling and holding out her hand. 'I'm Lizzie Holdenby. Sebastian's sister – and now yours.'

Cassie clasped the outstretched hand, saying, 'Oh! We so hoped one of you would come but Lord Wingham wasn't sure it would be possible. Does Sebastian know you're here?'

'He does. He also knows I've been waiting for him to introduce us – but the other gentlemen have him surrounded so I decided to do it myself.' Elizabeth's grin bore a striking resemblance to that of her brother. 'Trixie, Lottie and Jenny are sorry they couldn't attend but have asked me to represent them and furnish them with *every* detail. As for Blanche, she's always so horrible to Sebastian that he wouldn't want her here.'

'Horrible?' Cassie frowned. 'Why?'

'It's just her nature,' shrugged Elizabeth, clearly unwilling to elaborate. 'This is *so* like Sebastian. The only *real* surprise is that he didn't carry you off over his saddle-bow. But from what I've seen so far, I don't think you'd have minded, would you?'

'No,' agreed Cassie simply. 'I wouldn't have minded at all.'

Sebastian waited until he thought that both he and Cassandra had spoken to most people and then, unable to wait any longer, he drew her away, murmuring, 'Father says that he and your parents have gone to receive the other guests – but we are to stay here with those who attended the wedding, thus guarding the secret until Sir Charles is ready.'

'Yes. That's what was arranged.' She looked up at him, wondering but not really caring where they were going. 'I like your sister. But why did she say that Blanche is horrible to you?'

'Because she is.' Sebastian whisked her inside Sir Charles's study and closed the door behind her. 'I've better uses for our moment alone than talking about Blanche.'

'Oh?' She linked her arms about his neck. 'Such as what?'

'Such as telling you how beautiful you look.' His lips cruised across her cheek to her ear. 'And how much I love you.' He feathered kisses along her jaw. 'And how happy you've made me. And ... kissing you.'

Finally, his mouth found hers and Cassie leaned closer, absorbing the scent and taste of him ... and more than that, the promise of what she hoped would come later. Sensing that she was in no greater hurry to re-join their friends than he was, Sebastian took his time, moulding the line of her spine with his hands and looking forward to doing the same thing in a few hours' time without the impediment of a corset.

Someone knocked at the door. He held Cassandra tighter and ignored it.

'Sebastian?' Adrian's voice contained a note of laughter. 'Stop what you're doing and come out. It's time to go up to the ballroom.'

Sebastian lifted his head and looked into Cassandra's eyes.

'Damn,' he growled. 'It's a dastardly plot.'

Laughing up at him, she placed one last kiss against his throat and said, 'No. It's my moment of glory. So let's go – before Papa starts without us.'

At first largely unnoticed, they halted at the top of the shallow flight of stairs which led into the ballroom. Then the orchestra played a brief fanfare and Sir Charles said, 'Serena and I crave your forgiveness, ladies and gentlemen. A little over an hour ago – and at Lord Wingham's suggestion, I might add – this evening's betrothal celebration became a wedding.' He held out his hand towards the newly-wedded pair. 'I have enormous pleasure in presenting my new son-in-law and his bride; Sebastian and Cassandra Audley.'

But for the Duke of Rockliffe, there might have been a yawning silence. As it was, while footmen circulated with trays of champagne and before anyone else could react at all, his Grace said, 'If Charles and Serena will forgive my presumption ... on behalf of those of us fortunate enough to have witnessed the ceremony, I would like to propose a toast to the health and happiness of bridal pair.' He raised his glass. 'Sebastian and Cassandra.'

'Sebastian and Cassandra!' came the obedient response.

'Clever Rock,' remarked Caroline approvingly to Adrian. 'No one will *dare* make any sly innuendos about indecent haste now.'

The orchestra launched into a gavotte. Sebastian led his wife down the steps, bowed and kissed each of her hands, murmuring, 'My dance I think, Mistress Audley. As, indeed, are all the others.'

'We can't!' she objected – though not, he noted with any great conviction.

'On the contrary. This is the one and only time we *can*. Tonight, Madam, you dance with no one but your husband – whom, in case you've forgotten, you just promised to obey.'

In fact, though Sebastian was adamant about claiming every dance, good manners meant that they trod every other measure and spent the ones in between accepting the good wishes of those who hadn't already offered them. But when the supper dance loomed, Sebastian said softly, 'Do you think we might slip away? We could have supper in our new home ... and you can take off your shoes.'

Cassie's breath stalled and her pulse rate increased but his remark about the shoes made it easy to smile and nod. Ten minutes later, thanks to Adrian's forethought in ordering a carriage, they were on their way to Bruton Place.

* * *

The main reception rooms were no more furnished than they had been a week ago but Caroline had wrought miracles in the master suite. Followed more slowly by Sebastian, Cassie flew from room to room admiring everything as she went. Beds, hangings and curtains; rugs, mirrors and wash-stands; vases of fragrant roses and a tray with wine and glasses; and in the sitting-room, a sofa and comfortable chairs by the hearth, a breakfast-table near the window and even a small, elegant escritoire complete with pens, ink and paper.

'Caroline has thought of everything!' said Cassie, running her fingers over the glossy surface of her dressing-table. 'Goodness only knows how she's done it in the time – or how she's managed to choose exactly what I'd have chosen myself.'

With due solemnity, Sebastian agreed that Caroline was *indeed* a genius; that yes, he *loved* the Nile blue hangings in his bedchamber; and his dressing-room had been fitted with *just* the right amount of drawers, shelves and closets.

Cassie laughed at him and put her arms about his waist.

'Don't tease. You like it, don't you?'

He rested his cheek on her hair. 'Yes. But mostly I like that you are here.'

There was little point in mentioning that the presence of Cassandra's maid was a very large fly in his ointment and that he was having a hard time not wishing her at the devil. It wasn't the girl's fault. She was unobtrusive, efficient and plainly devoted to Cassandra. The problem was that she was there at all. If he'd wanted servants hovering about them, he'd have brought Hobson with him; but what he'd *wanted* was to have his wife completely to himself just for a few days; and tonight especially he'd looked forward to disrobing her with his own hands ... very, very slowly.

Well, that wasn't going to happen. He'd have to put up with the convention of kicking his heels elsewhere while Cassandra's maid prepared her for bed ... and praying the bloody girl didn't trip into the bedroom tomorrow morning with a cup of chocolate or some such.

'Come and take a glass of wine with me while we wait for supper,' he said. And in her ear, 'I seem to recall promising to take off your shoes.'

Flushing a little, she nodded and let him draw her into the sitting-room. Choosing the sofa so that he could sit beside her, she watched him remove his coat and pour wine. Then, setting both glasses on the table, he knelt at her feet and slid warm hands about her ankles, whilst his eyes held hers. Cassandra's mouth felt suddenly dry and though she had no idea what she wanted to say, she tried to moisten it. Sebastian's gaze dropped to her lips. Finally, he said huskily, 'What was I supposed to be doing?'

'R-Removing my shoes.'

'Ah. Right.' He drew off the left one and then the right, on each occasion taking the time to trace her ankle-bones and the arch of her instep. Presently, he said, 'Is there anything else I can help you with? Hairpins, perhaps? Jewellery?' A long pause, during which she could see a pulse beating in his throat, 'Your stockings?'

Heat flared low in Cassie's belly. She wanted to say yes. Even more disconcertingly, she realised that she wouldn't have minded him removing every stitch she was wearing. But before she could say anything at all, a tap at the door heralded their supper.

'Damn.'

Sebastian rose smoothly to his feet and told the footman to enter. The possibility of dragging Cassandra into his bedchamber and barricading the door occurred to him. He decided that might merit serious consideration later.

Although neither of them ate very much, food and talking about the wedding had the effect of lessening the tension that had begun vibrating the air between them. Sebastian said nothing about the dramatic events of two nights ago. He would tell her, of course – but it wasn't something he wanted intruding on their wedding day. However, Cassandra made it impossible for him to completely avoid the subject of Blanche, so he said negligently, 'She doesn't like me. She never has. And she makes no secret of it.'

'But *why*?'

'I'm a blot on the family escutcheon.'

329

'No you're not.'

'*Now* I'm not,' he agreed. 'Now I'm a respectable married man. And if I misbehave, Gerry has threatened to put my head through a wall.'

'He *what?*' demanded Cassie, sitting very straight. 'He'd better not try!'

'That's my girl!' laughed Sebastian, rising and offering his hand. 'No need to tell him he'll be putting his hand in a wasps' nest, though. If the occasion arises, I'll enjoy seeing you reduce him to pulp.'

Returning to the sofa, he sat down and pulled her into his lap. For a time, he just held her, his cheek against her hair before tilting her head up for a long, inviting kiss. Then he said, 'Are you tired?'

'No. I probably should be, but I'm not. This – us being together like this – is all too new and precious.' She traced his cheek with her fingers. 'I know we have the rest of our lives. But I can't bear to say goodbye to today. Is that silly?'

'No. And you don't have to say goodbye to it.' His voice took on a darker, slightly roughened note. 'We have tonight.'

Once again, the curl of heat in her belly caught her unawares. Not knowing how best to phrase it, she said awkwardly, 'Perhaps I might m-make myself more comfortable?'

'You're not comfortable here?'

'Yes but that's not --' She stopped, catching his expression. 'I didn't mean that.'

'I know.' He stood up, taking her with him. 'Go and rid yourself of the demon corset, by all means – though I should perhaps mention that we bridegrooms aren't averse to helping with that kind of thing.' He saw her eyes widen but prevented her from speaking with another brief kiss. 'Off you go. I'll have the dishes removed … and shed my cravat, if you've no objection.'

'No. *Only* your cravat?' And fled to her bedchamber before he could answer.

While the footman cleared the remains of their supper, Sebastian made his own preparations. Smiling a little, he discarded rather more than his cravat, washed, freed his hair from the jewelled clasp he'd worn for the wedding and brushed it out. Then, having donned a resplendent bronze-green dressing-robe, he returned to the parlour, bearing a large brass-bound box and proceeded to set out its contents on the low table by the sofa.

This was more than a means of passing the time while he waited. It stopped him dwelling on the artificiality and ritualism of a bride being readied for her husband and also helped silence his niggling anxiety about making love to a virgin. Although he knew the theory, it wasn't something he'd done before – and the idea of hurting Cassandra twisted something inside him. He was also only too aware that no matter how slowly he intended to take things, his body would soon have ideas of its own. And so, since worrying wasn't going to help, he concentrated on a task his hands could have performed in the dark.

Hesitating self-consciously in the doorway behind him, Cassie watched for a moment and then said, 'I'm sorry. Have you been waiting long?'

'All my life, darling,' he began, rising and turning so quickly that the robe swirled about him. Then he stopped, barely able to breathe as he took in the loosened hair tumbling down her back and the trailing white robe, worn open over a nightgown of the finest silk which outlined the curve of her breasts, and was caught up here and there in strategically-placed pink bows. Both garments were cut to invite, rather than conceal; and beneath the hem, her bare toes peeped out ... dainty and perfect with small pearly nails. Desire ripped through him like a tidal-wave, forcing him to clench his hands on the sash of his robe rather than reach for her.

Hell, he thought despairingly. *If I can't calm down, this is going to kill me.*

On a slow exhalation, he said, 'But it would be *worth* a lifetime to see you as you look right now.'

'That is ... a particularly lovely thing to say.' Uncertainly, Cassie advanced a couple of steps, taking in the glories of his dressing-robe and shocking herself slightly by wondering what, if anything, he was wearing underneath it. 'What were you doing?'

Taking care not to go any closer to her until he had himself under control, he stepped to one side and gestured to the table. 'It's the Casparov chess set I told you about.'

She moved to his side, staring down at the pieces on the board. The black ones were ruby-studded obsidian; the white, pale emerald-encrusted jade; and the kings and queens were crowned in gold.

'It's beautiful.' Cassie perched on the arm of the sofa, studying the board. 'But also a bit ... I don't know ... sinister?'

'I agree.' Putting the White Queen in her hand, Sebastian sat down and toyed idly with its black counterpart. 'There's a legend attached to it which says it must always belong to the last person who won a game whilst playing with it.'

Cassie watched the drift of his hair against his cheek and the way his fingers touched the finely-carved piece. Both called to her body. 'You.'

'Yes. I wasn't expected to win but I did. And now I intend to keep it.' Setting down the Queen, he took her hand and teased the inside of her wrist and her palm with his thumb. 'On our eighth birthday, Great-Aunt Flora gave Theo and me a chess set. Theo took to it straight away. I had less patience.' He smiled crookedly down at their joined hands. 'After Theo died, I couldn't bear to look at a chessboard. It wasn't until Cambridge that I began playing again and discovered I had an aptitude for it.' He hesitated and finally looked into her face. 'The Casparov is always set up and apparently in play. It's not unusual to practice by playing against oneself. But I ... insane as it sounds, *I* imagine I'm playing against Theo.'

'Oh.' Cassie slid off the arm of the sofa and into his lap. Brushing back his hair and kissing his brow, she said, 'It's not insane if it brings Theo close for you. Put it wherever you wish and I'll make sure no one but you ever touches it.'

'Thank you.' Breathing in the scent of her hair, he allowed his hand to trail lightly over her hip and thigh, then back again. He said, 'It's our wedding-night and I've been talking about chess. If you name a forfeit, I'll pay it.'

You weren't talking about chess. You were talking about your brother, thought Cassie. *And I'm glad that at last you're able to.* But she said, 'Anything?' Beneath the opulent brocade robe was the warm skin of a firmly muscled chest. For a few seconds, the discovery made her dizzy.

'Yes.' His tongue found a sensitive spot beneath her ear and he concentrated on her quiver of response rather than the drift of that small, soft hand. 'Anything.'

'Well, I've been wondering ...' Finding that his shoulders were no less splendid than his chest made it impossible to think so she tangled her fingers in his hair instead.

Sebastian set his jaw. 'Yes?'

'I was wondering,' she whispered, 'if you are wearing anything at all under your robe.'

The air evaporated in his lungs and he had to force himself to breathe.

'Wouldn't you like to find out for yourself?' he managed to ask.

She buried her face against his neck. 'Yes. I think ... Sebastian, I think it's time you took me to bed. If that would be all right?'

He stood up, taking her with him and said, 'It would be very much all right, darling. To be truthful, I don't think I could have held out much longer.'

As he carried her towards his bedchamber, Cassie said, 'Why hold out at all?'

'Because it's your first time, love.' He smiled at her. 'I want you so very badly, you see ... but even more than that, I want to make it good for you. So I need some self-control.' He pushed the door shut with his foot. 'Lock it. I'm not risking further interruptions.'

She did so and he carried her over to the bed to set her on her feet and gently nudge the flimsy chamber-robe from her shoulders. His senses were full of her and his hands were no longer quite steady so he folded his arms about her and kissed

STELLA RILEY

her. A tiny sound escaped her and he felt her melting even closer, her hands clinging to his shoulders. Finally, he lifted his head and, creating a little distance between them, said, 'All these pretty bows ... do any of them do anything?'

Cassie swallowed hard. 'Wh-Why don't you find out?'

His heart missed its usual beat, then resumed with a thud.

'I'd like that.' He appeared to contemplate the various choices and eventually tugged lightly at one of the ribbons at her shoulder. It slithered free and the silk fell away, exposing one breast. With a groan of mingled torment and appreciation, Sebastian stroked the lovely curve with his palm and marvelled at her immediate response.

Sucking in a breath, she reached for the sash of his robe and then hesitated.

'May I?' she asked, meeting his eyes uncertainly.

He laid his hands over hers but said, 'Yes. You don't need to ask. You may do anything you wish and be sure I'll enjoy it.' And with a smile as he freed her hands, 'Men are simple creatures, sweetheart. And I love you.'

Cassie untied the sash, pulled the two sides of the robe slowly away from each other ... and was suddenly very still. With the merest hint of a shrug, Sebastian sent the robe to the floor and stood equally still, watching her. Somewhat belatedly, it occurred to him that letting his innocent bride look at a fully aroused naked male wasn't perhaps the best idea he'd ever had. But mercifully Cassandra hadn't got to the aroused bit yet. Her eyes were too busy devouring his upper torso.

She said, 'Simple? You – you're beautiful. I had no idea. That is ... I *had* but I didn't realise ...' She stopped abruptly, her eyes widening and her breath escaping in a sort of whoosh. '*Oh!*'

Sebastian felt fairly sure he was blushing but had the faintly hysterical thought that Cassandra wouldn't know because her gaze was riveted elsewhere. Oddly enough, she didn't look alarmed or even shocked. She looked ... intrigued. No. She looked curious.

And he'd just told her she needn't ask.

He caught the thought the instant it was born and managed to check her hand's descent. Then, answering the question she hadn't asked and in the most matter-of-fact tone he could manage, he said, 'By all means – but not just now, if you don't mind. In fact, I think we'll ignore that for a while.'

'Ignore it?' she echoed incredulously. '*How?*'

He shouldn't have laughed. Given that his arousal was heading towards discomfort and he'd just been embarrassed by her perusal of a currently ungovernable part of his anatomy, he shouldn't even have *wanted* to ... but somehow he couldn't help it. He said unsteadily, 'You may leave that to me – though I thank you for the unintentional compliment. For now, however, it doesn't seem fair that I'm the only one of us standing here without a stitch on.' And making swift work of two more bows, he watched the nightgown slide slowly, almost reluctantly to the floor, revealing slender curves and pink-tinged alabaster skin, inch by glorious inch. Desire was thundering through him with an insistent beat and he skimmed the line of waist and hip with his fingertips; he wanted to lick every bit of her. He said unevenly, 'Did you know I fell in love with your back at Bedford House?'

Distantly, Cassie wondered why she wasn't embarrassed ... why the way the heat in his eyes as they feasted on her only sent yet more sparks rushing through her blood and why answering heat was pooling low in her belly. 'My back?'

'Yes.' He turned her slightly. 'The most sinuous, desirable back I've ever seen.'

She felt him press a kiss to her shoulder while his curved knuckles followed the line of her spine and his other hand reached around to scorch a maddeningly slow path over breast, ribs and stomach to come to rest on the place where an increasingly impatient pulse throbbed. An involuntary and incoherent sound escaped her and she put her hand over his. Then he drew her closer so that the part of him he'd said could be ignored, pressed demandingly against her. Cassie trembled and said, 'Sebastian?'

'Yes, love. Come to bed with me.'

Down on to the soft velvet of the counterpane; down into a sea of delight as his mouth was finally able to follow the trail of his hands; down into a whirlpool of pleasure so exquisite that it was almost pain. Sebastian stretched his control to breaking point and beyond, determined to bring her to the ultimate fulfilment before he had to hurt her; and when she broke, shuddering and sobbing his name, still he managed to wait until he believed she was ready before finally – slowly and very gratefully – joining his body with hers. Cassie tensed, gazing up into his eyes and he waited again. Then a warm, loving smile lit her face and she pulled him even closer, saying, 'Yes. Oh ... *yes*.' And somewhere in the distant reaches where thought still existed, it seemed the most beautiful thing that had ever happened to him.

They fell asleep wrapped in each other's arms and in the morning it was Sebastian who woke first and therefore had the pleasure of watching his love sleep, one of her hands tangled with his. Not for the first time, he wondered what he had done to deserve her and why he'd never suspected that this was what he had always wanted.

She woke slowly, stretching languorously against him in a way that had him sternly reminding his body to behave. Instead, he propped himself on one elbow and waited for her eyes to open.

Finally, she blinked up at him and smiled; it was the same smile she'd given him last night and it brought a wave of emotion so strong that for a moment he thought he might weep. In an effort to avert that particular catastrophe, he smiled back at her and said, 'Good morning, Mistress Audley. How does it feel to be thoroughly married?'

'Nice,' she yawned.

'Nice?' he echoed. '*Nice?* That's just insulting.'

'Is it?' Cassie smoothed her hands over his chest. 'Well ... now you mention it, it's *very* nice. Quite lovely, in fact. Can I do this every morning?'

'Darling, you can do it whenever you like,' he promised. Then, thoughtfully, 'Of course, there's a price.'

'A price?' Having apparently tired of his chest, she began twining a lock of his hair around one finger for the fun of watching it spring free.

'Mm. Or perhaps a reciprocal agreement might be a better term.'

'Oh?'

She'd moved on again, this time to the morning stubble darkening his jaw. Sebastian had the feeling she wasn't really listening. He found it hard to concentrate himself when he could see her taking ridiculous delight in each new and apparently fascinating discovery. Deciding that two could play at that game, he let his fingers drift back and forth over the smooth thigh lying invitingly across his own and said, 'Do you still have the red dress?'

'What?'

'The dress you wore to Bedford House. Do you still have it?'

This finally got her attention. She said, 'You didn't like it.'

'I never said that.'

'You said it was a torment.'

'And it is.' He grinned and kissed her nose. 'But it doesn't mean I didn't like it. Quite the reverse, in fact. And I've no objection at all to being tormented in private.'

Pursing her lips to hide a smile, Cassie considered this. Finally she said, 'That sounds a trifle ... naughty.'

'*Naughty?*' Sebastian tutted reprovingly, laughter dancing in his eyes. 'My darling, the word you're looking for is *wicked*. And I've a suspicion we might both enjoy it very much indeed.'

If you have enjoyed *The Wicked Cousin*, you may also enjoy other books by Stella Riley.

Roundheads & Cavaliers series
The Black Madonna
Garland of Straw
The King's Falcon
Lords of Misrule

Stand-alone titles
A Splendid Defiance
The Marigold Chain

Rockliffe Books 1 - 3
The Parfit Knight
The Mésalliance
The Player

The Rockliffe Series and *A Splendid Defiance* are also available in audio, narrated by Alex Wyndham.

For the latest news and a chance to chat with Stella, look her up on **Wordpress.**

Printed in Great Britain
by Amazon